# THE ANGE⌷

## Michael I. Farrar

Earl F. Pedersen
20 Academy Ln Apt 135
Mystic CT 06355

Many, many thanks for taking such good care of my mother, Rose, at Academy Point. We all appreciate your efforts.

Michael J Farrar

iUniverse, Inc.
New York Lincoln Shanghai

# The Angel Falls Option

All Rights Reserved © 2004 by Michael J. Farrar

No part of this book may be reproduced or transmitted in any form or by any means, graphic, electronic, or mechanical, including photocopying, recording, taping, or by any information storage retrieval system, without the written permission of the publisher.

iUniverse, Inc.

For information address:
iUniverse, Inc.
2021 Pine Lake Road, Suite 100
Lincoln, NE 68512
www.iuniverse.com

ISBN: 0-595-32010-4 (pbk)
ISBN: 0-595-66461-X (cloth)

Printed in the United States of America

"This novel is dedicated to those who never lost faith in me, long after I lost faith in myself. They know who they are."

# Contents

# Prologue

It was early evening in Caracas when he heard the knock on his hotel room door. Steve Giles did not want to answer. It had been a long, hot day and all he wanted was a shower, a hot meal and a cold beer. Nothing more. Instinct was telling him to leave the door unanswered. The knocking persisted. Reluctantly, he opened the door.

"Buenos Noches, Senor Giles." It was Christina, the translator from the Ministry of Energy who had been assigned to Steve whenever he met to discuss official business.

"Buenos Noches, Christina. What a nice surprise," he lied. She was dressed for stepping out, a black slinky dress that clung to every curve. Her long black hair and perfect makeup produced a stunning effect, a far cry from the Plain Jane look she wears at The Ministry.

"The Director wants me to take you out tonight to show you a little bit of Caracas nightlife. It will be very entertaining. I know you will enjoy it."

"Thank you very much, Christina, but I was hoping to turn in early and get a good night's sleep. I hope you will understand."

"Please Senor Giles, my boss told me not to take "no" for an answer. I am afraid I will lose my job if you do not come."

He now understood the situation. It would indeed be an insult if he were to refuse, and her position would be jeopardized. There was too much at stake with the project to run the risk of upsetting the sole government entity that grants the exploration licenses in Venezuela. He was no longer hesitant.

"Please wait in the lobby. I'll be down right after I shower."

Fifteen minutes later the taxi pulled away from the hotel and was winding its way through the teeming streets of Caracas. Darkness had descended upon the city and the streets were bathed in a blaze of colors and sounds. After about forty five minutes of winding their way to the outskirts of the city, the upscale hotels and restaurants had long receded in the taxi's rearview mirror. The streets became narrower, and were lined with bars, brothels and dingy hotels. They had entered the infamous Red Zone, where just about anything can be obtained for a price. So long as the activities are contained here, the police turn a blind eye.

"So this is the Red Zone," Steve exclaimed. "I had heard stories but have never been here."

"It's not as bad as the stories," Christina said. "This is the real Caracas, not the fancy restaurants and clubs that most foreigners visit downtown. My uncle owns a bar just up ahead. I come here often. It is safe if you are not looking for trouble. But if you look, it will find you."

"I'm not looking."

"We are here." She tapped the driver on the shoulder and beckoned him to pull over.

The taxi came to a halt in front of a small bar, one of dozens that lined the street. Over his protests, Christina insisted on paying. Steve had wondered why they were not using a Ministry car and driver, but reasoned that an official government car might not be well received in this seemingly lawless part of town.

With Christina leading the way, they made their way into the dimly lit bar and found an empty table. The place was crowded, and loud. Latin music pounded from an aging jukebox. A disco globe, minus several mirrored tiles, rotated erratically above the crowded patch of dance floor. Christina disappeared briefly, then returned with two beers. They sat in silence, sipping their drinks and taking in the sights. She had grown quiet, almost sullen, occasionally glancing at her watch.

A fight erupted just a few feet away. Two drunken men appeared to be brawling over a woman. She stood back, holding their drinks, while the two went at it. The dance floor had cleared but the music still pounded and the lights flashed as if in sync with the fighting. The two wrestled to the floor and rolled over to Steve's table at the edge of the dance floor. He grabbed Christina and pulled her back as the table collapsed around them, beer bottles crashing to the floor. The fight began to spread as onlookers became embroiled. Bottles and chairs were being thrown about the room. Women were screaming.

Christina took Steve by the hand and yelled.

"Let's get out of here. Come with me. I know another way out."

She deftly led him along the wall to a back office and out through a rear door. They stepped out into a dimly lit alley. It stank of stale beer and rotting garbage. Steve stopped to brush the dust off his shirt, the sounds of the brawl quickly receding behind him.

"I'll say this for you, Christina, you sure know how to show a guy a good time. Wait til they hear about this back in Plano."

He turned to face Christina, only to see her fading back through the door to the bar, her eyes a clouded mix of sadness and fear. He found her actions puzzling. He didn't have long to wonder.

He never heard them coming. The knife was thrust deeply into his lower back, severing vital organs. As he began to scream, a calloused hand clamped tightly over his mouth. With head pulled back, the blade quickly slit his throat. A fountain of blood erupted. Steve managed a few gurgling sounds, choking on his own blood. The attackers let his body slump to the ground.

He should have gone with his instincts.

# CHAPTER 1

# *Return To Plano*

## *DAY ONE*

As the American Airlines flight from Miami touched down at the Dallas/Fort Worth Airport, David Hastings grimaced at the cruel twist his life had taken in a little over a week. Last week a chauffeur driven limo had met him at the very same airport. His career was in full throttle and a highly visible and lucrative future with OilQuest International was assured.

Now he was expecting to be greeted by the Dallas police and arrested for murder. His family was in hiding and his company was actively engaged in discrediting him and, if necessary, eliminating him for good. They had tried to kill him and his family, leaving no loose ends. With the fate of Venezuela at stake and billions of dollars involved, his life was a mere annoyance to those who stood to profit.

He somberly recalled the events of the past week, commencing with his return to Dallas the week before.

"Welcome back, Mr. Hastings," the chauffeur greeted David as he departed the plane at Dallas/Fort Worth Airport, taking David's garment bag and briefcase from him.

"Good evening Ian. Good to finally be home."

"Any checked luggage, sir?"

"None, just carryon and one fatigued passenger."

Those would be the only words to pass between the two for the duration of the forty minute drive to Plano, the sprawling affluent suburb just north of Dallas where David lived with his wife and two young boys.

As the Cadillac left the airport and made its way toward Interstate 635, David sank deeper into the car's leather upholstery, relieved to be heading home after three grueling weeks on the road. It had been exhilarating: the high level corporate meetings, press conferences, receptions and the occasional television or radio appearance, but it was time to get back to the office and back to Angel Falls. It was the possibility of a supergiant oil discovery at Angel Falls in the Venezuelan jungle that had given rise to David's fame, and he wanted to make sure that trend continued.

David Hastings worked for OilQuest International, a division of OilQuest Ltd. The corporate headquarters were in New Orleans, but the international division, where David worked, was based in Plano, Texas, just outside of Dallas. At thirty-eight years old, he was one of a multitude of mid-level managers in the oil patch that was caught in the dual crossfire of continued downsizing of the oil industry coupled with the general corporate trend toward management reductions. Although he was well respected at OilQuest International and while he genuinely enjoyed his work as a regional exploration geologist, there was little hope of upward mobility. He had to satisfy himself with his work, which was prospecting for oil and gas in the South American Region.

David was loyal to a fault. He joined OilQuest fresh out of graduate school, at the age of twenty-five. His undergraduate degree in geology was from Wesleyan University in Connecticut and his master's degree in structural geology was from Stanford University. He had been urged to go on for a doctorate by his advisors at Stanford, but was lured away by the oil industry with promises of big salaries and limitless opportunities. In actuality, the salaries were quite generous and David had no complaints. He had also grown weary of academia and was anxious to seek his fortune as an explorationist.

The whole idea of being an explorationist had a romantic appeal to David. There was travel in the form of geologic field expeditions to exotic places far from the time worn paths of the common tourist. There would be the occasional overseas assignment for two to three years and the chance to truly steep oneself in the culture of a different people. And there was the work itself, the chance to make a significant discovery. He felt like a modern day adventurer on a noble quest to secure the energy needs for his country.

Of course, not everyone felt the same as David regarding the nobility of the search for hydrocarbons and his longtime college friend, Helene Langtree, was one of those persons. She was an environmental activist of the highest order, being an active member of numerous environmental organizations and on the board of a few. Whenever she and David would get together, it was like the apocalyptic collision of two worlds. Fortunately, there was always a common respect that sanctified their relationship and allowed them to remain such good friends. Those spirited debates with Helene helped prepare him for the public relations effort he was now undertaking.

David and his family would often visit Helene and her husband, Tom, at their house on the pond in Weekapaug, Rhode Island. Even though Weekapaug was basically a summer beach community on the shores of the Atlantic, David's favorite time of year was the Fall. That was when most people left and when Weekapaug was at its best. It had been a year since he had taken the family to Weekapaug, and David felt the inner tug of the crisp days and cool, silent nights beckoning him once again. But Weekapaug and charged debates with Helene would have to wait. The Angel Falls Project was his first priority.

It was nearly three years ago when David first glanced at the aeromagnetic and gravity data as part of a regional geophysical and geological study over southern Venezuela. This part of Venezuela was relatively uncharted from an exploration standpoint. It was primitive in all aspects, as both jungle and mountainous terrain had successfully hampered the encroachment of civilization. Dirt roads were few and local tribes lived in relative obscurity.

The original purpose of the study was to delineate the southernmost extent of the Orinoco heavy oil belt as it thinned out when it ramped up against the Guyana Shield.

The Orinoco crude, a thick, low quality oil, was both difficult and costly to extract and process. It had to be blended with higher quality crudes in order to be marketable, which of course reduced the value of the better crude. While numerous oil companies were constantly clamoring to explore in Venezuela, the Orinoco belt was not high on anyone's list.

The Venezuelan government, through its Ministry of Energy, however, had linked the award of exploration licenses in the more prospective Venezuelan basins to investment in the Orinoco belt.

OilQuest, anxious to acquire exploration rights in the prolific Maracaibo basin in the Gulf of Maracaibo in northwestern Venezuela, had committed to the Ministry to undertake a study of the Orinoco belt to determine its southernmost limit and to ascertain if there might be a sweet spot where the quality of the crude might be better. No one at OilQuest was betting any money on this possibility. Not even David, who regarded himself as positive and open to even the wildest of geological concepts. If anything, the quality of the crude was expected to worsen as it shallowed on the Guyana Shield, and the oil reservoir would certainly thin and eventually pinch out altogether against the Shield.

The Guyana Shield is that stable part of the South American continental plate that consists of a thick section of igneous and metamorphic rocks, totally non-prospective from a hydrocarbon exploration perspective. It extends over a large area of southern Venezuela and Brazil, including most of the Amazon rain forest. Since the Shield lacks any sedimentary rocks from which oil and gas could be generated and reservoired, all past exploration work had stopped at its outer edges.

The northern perimeter of the Shield, however, was poorly defined since it was overlain by the rain forest and was nearly impenetrable from the ground. Geologic field expeditions, of which there had been several in the past, were both costly and time consuming, and could only cover a very limited area.

Besides, the Brazilian government had grown increasingly sensitive to these relatively minor scientific incursions across their northern borders, especially when accompanied by the Venezuelan army.

In addition, worldwide environmental organizations were putting pressure on both governments to refrain from any activities, no matter how slight or ephemeral, which would impact one of the world's last remaining rain forests.

Hence, the decision was made to conduct a non-destructive geophysical study by a specially equipped airplane carrying magnetic and gravity instrumentation. It was unlikely to reveal any surprises, but at least it would provide for a much needed regional overview, and would certainly demonstrate a good faith attempt by OilQuest to comply with the wishes of the Ministry of Energy.

Hastings and his geophysicist partner, Steve Giles, had been assigned to the study since South America was their geographic area of responsibility. Orders from senior exploration management were to rapidly evaluate the project and bring it to a quick conclusion so we could move onto something meaningful and press the Ministry for the Maracaibo area license. At least that was the initial intent.

As the gravity and magnetic data poured into the office over a several week period, David and Steve had worked efficiently to quality check the data and get it plotted and contour mapped, all pretty much routine procedures. Initial results were predictable and the mapping was well along when David had noticed a linear pattern developing in the gravity data which was trending in a north-south direction and extended from the northern part of the Shield, where the Orinoco belt thinned to zero, across southern Venezuela and deep into Brazil.

The linear pattern was of a second order and not seen on any of the previous maps that had been computer contoured. This particular map was based on reprocessing the raw data to remove the effects of surface terrain. Since the study area had a significant amount of topographic relief, this map had an entirely different appearance. The presence of the lineament on this map was unmistakable, and it ran contrary to the general outline of the Shield.

David and Steve decided to rework the data and map it by hand in order to see if an alternate interpretation could be made. This approach, which would delay putting the project to bed for several more weeks, did not endear the two scientists to an impatient management. Daily visits from the VP of Exploration, who scorned this seemingly low-tech approach, only heightened their concerns about the political damage they might sustain.

Nonetheless, the pressure also served to spur on the efforts as quickly as possible. Within ten days after first detecting the lineament pattern, the new hand contoured maps were completed. While not as fast or as smooth as a computer, the data had been honored and the results were astounding. While the first order features conformed to the general shape of the Guyana Shield, there was clearly a second order lineament cutting north to south through the Shield in the form of a gravity and magnetic low. The Shield normally had high gravity and magnetic readings due to it being near surface basement igneous and metamorphic rock. The significance of the low gravity and magnetic readings were not lost on the two scientists. There was clearly an uncharted sedimentary basin that extended into the Shield. The existence of intra-cratonic basins was well documented in other parts of the world, but none had ever been detected in South America. The fact that it was linear was further proof that this feature was a rift basin, and that the Shield had been tectonically pulled apart, possibly during the Jurassic period, and had at one time been the site of an ancient sea. Sediments accumulating in this rifted basin could, under the right circumstances, be hydrocarbon bearing. The search for oil was afoot.

The rift was forty miles wide and at least one hundred and eighty miles long, probably longer since the lineament continued to the very end of the data into Brazil. It was not huge by world standards, which had helped conceal it from notice until now. As David and Steve overlaid the rift on a topographic map, the surface terrain was remote, dense rain forest with no major roads and sparsely populated by a few local tribes. The rift also cut directly across one of Venezuela's most beautiful natural wonders, Angel Falls.

From that day forward, the study was referred to as the Angel Falls Project. That was two years ago.

OilQuest executive management was still skeptical when shown the map results, but knowing the Ministry of Energy would now press for further study of the area, consented to a limited seismic survey and geologic field work over a selected portion of the rift on the Venezuelan side. While limited in scope, the project was costly since there were no nearby airstrips or access roads and none could be constructed due to environmental concerns. The fieldwork was therefore limited to four men using helicopter support.

The seismic instrumentation was portable and eight traverses were made, with each traverse being ten miles in length. Rock samples were also collected for detailed analysis back in headquarters. A small base camp was made near a stream which not only provided a source of fresh water and fish, but also allowed the supply helicopter to land on a natural gravel bar alongside the stream. Thus, clearing a landing pad was avoided. Daily excursions were made from the camp, which was intentionally situated in the very center of the survey area. David and Steve, while usually confined to the office, were given leave to oversee the survey and managed to spend a third of their time there.

During the course of the fieldwork, there were brief encounters with the local Yanomama tribesmen. Never hostile. Mostly curious. Occasionally some would come to the fringe of the base camp and just watch for hours. Some attempts were made to communicate, but they did not speak Spanish and sign language had its limitations. A few trades were made as a gesture of friendship, but handouts were discouraged and fraternization kept to a minimum. They were excellent fishermen, however, and since money was of no use to them, extra cooking gear and clothing such as T-shirts proved an acceptable barter medium.

David had been taken by the simple beauty of their natural lifestyle, and their gentle, graceful manner. They moved quietly and effortlessly through the forest, and, aside from their tiny village and modest plantings, left no trace of where they had been. Civilization had made some encroachments, as their traditional, primitive garb was slowly giving way to trousers and T-shirts, albeit tattered and not always worn correctly. Many of the women were still bare breasted, and their jewelry consisted mostly of artifacts from their native surroundings. A thin, beaded necklace hung about their necks and between their breasts. Tattoos from natural pigments adorned their bodies and small, thin, rattan like reeds sometimes protruded from their lower lips like porcupine quills. David attributed this modest self-mutilation to ceremonial rites. It was either that or it was just the fashionable thing to do in the Venezuelan jungle. He had seen far worse from the skinheads and punks in London's Leicester Square only last year.

There was one native girl in particular that had taken an interest in David. She had followed him at a safe distance for an entire day during one of his traverses. She looked fifteen and her wide, brown eyes possessed a look of serenity that far surpassed her youth. They had exchanged smiles and, at the end of the day, David gave her his Texas Rangers baseball cap. She was thrilled and returned the gesture with a bone from her lower lip. David tried to get her to pronounce his name, repeating it over and over, but she would just smile silently. He called her Lolita, although he had no idea why this seemed so appropriate.

The last time David saw her was when he was boarding the chopper for the final time as the camp was being cleared. She was partially hidden by the vegetation at the edge of the camp, but stepped into the clearing when David looked back. He waved. Still wearing the Rangers cap, she waved back.

The field survey results were highly encouraging. The rock samples included a selection of sandstones and shales, thereby verifying that a sedimentary basin did exist. Age dating, coupled with paleontological analysis, placed the rocks in the Jurassic to Cretaceous time period, or roughly sixty to one hundred seventy five million years ago. Just as important, the shales were rich in organic material and therefore suggestive of an oil prone source rock.

Most telling of all, though, was the discovery of a small oil seep along a rock cut stream bank on one of the traverses. The oil, which was little more than a faint trickle from a fracture in the rock, meant that at least part of the organic matter trapped in the buried shales had been buried deeply enough and had been sufficiently heated to have generated oil. Just how much oil could not be ascertained, but the basic elements of an oil play were beginning to come together.

Now what was needed would be to identify a subsurface structure that would trap any oil that would have been generated by the shales and would have migrated upwards into a porous and permeable reservoir rock within the structure. That is where the seismic data came in. From the raw field data, the seismic recordings had been computer processed to remove any spurious readings and Steve had set to work on interpreting and mapping the seismic reflections. The end result was a series of subsurface structure maps that resembled an ordinary surface topographic map, only these maps were of horizons ranging from eight thousand to fourteen thousand feet below the earth's surface.

Steve had worked for two solid months on the maps back in Plano, and when the final pictures emerged, a series of structures had been identified, running the length of the basin. One structure in particular stood out as being significantly larger than the others. It was an oblong shaped domal anticline whose crest was at a depth of about eleven thousand feet. The rough dimensions of this buried hill were four miles long by two miles wide with over two thousand feet of vertical relief. The total area of the structure encompassed over five thousand acres.

Even in the middle of nowhere, it was big enough to drill.

David and Steve wasted no time in presenting the study results to management. There were far fewer skeptics this time around, as the potential for a major discovery would do wonders for the company. It had been three years since the last discovery of any merit, and the Board of Directors was making some noise about having to make some dramatic changes from the top down. Hence, while diligent economic evaluations were performed on the Angel Falls Project, all knew at the onset that this prospect would fly.

It had the potential for being a true company maker, and suddenly all internal resistance vanished. Now everyone wanted to be a part of the team. David would spend half his day actually working on the project, and the other half briefing superiors and members of other departments as to what was being done. Nonetheless, he was too excited about the project to let the usual office annoyances bring him down.

David was appointed Project Leader with clearance to tap other disciplines to accelerate the drilling of the structure. The first well would, appropriately enough, be called Angel Falls #1. Its location, while not far from the Falls, was in dense rainforest. There were no roads, and this time not even a convenient stream or clearing in site.

The idea of cutting a temporary road through the rain forest to the drill site in order to bring in conventional heavy drilling equipment was dismissed as far too costly. The nearest road access point was one hundred and eighty miles away. David had also argued that a road would pose potentially harmful and lasting environmental concerns. And since this well was a true wildcat with only a ten-percent chance of making a commercial discovery, it was likely the road would not be needed by OilQuest again in the event of a dry hole. Management agreed, although David was certain that economics had been the governing factor.

The decision was made to use a helirig, or a portable rig whose components could be transported by workhorse helicopters. It was an expensive option, since the cost of transporting an entire rig along with all other ancillary equipment necessary to sustain a drilling operation by chopper was staggering.

Nevertheless, it was still far cheaper than a road, and the Public Affairs Department saw this as a golden opportunity to tout OilQuest's concern for the environment. This latter endeavor yielded mixed results since some of the hard line environmental groups reacted negatively to the press release on the project, protesting that no exploration activity whatsoever should take place in the rain forest.

Extreme care was taken to mitigate an environmental backlash. Only four acres of land was cleared, an absolute minimum for a drilling venture of this magnitude. It took three months of twice daily chopper runs to bring in all the equipment and men. A totally self-contained water, power and waste system was constructed. Before the drill bit even started turning, the operation had already expended over eight million dollars.

Finally, eighteen months from when David had first laid eyes on the aeromagnetic and gravity data, the Angel Falls #1 wildcat well spudded in and drilling commenced. The well was targeted to drill to a depth of fourteen thousand feet, but the zone of interest started as shallow as eleven thousand feet.

After forty-five days of drilling, the well was below eleven thousand, six hundred feet and there had not been even a trace of oil. The last six hundred feet of rock cuttings contained black shale and brown claystone, but no reservoir quality sandstone. David, who was monitoring the progress from Plano, was becoming increasingly apprehensive, and the daily barrages from his superiors only aggravated matters. Total cost to date was twelve million. This well was not only costly, but it was now being viewed as critical to the long term profitability of OilQuest, and it seemed as though the eyes of the entire company were riveted on David.

On day fifty-six of drilling operations, the well penetrated a porous sandstone layer and oil began flowing into the circulating mud pits. The seasoned drill crew quickly brought the well under control and a core barrel was lowered into the hole to core a section of the rock. It confirmed a sandstone of excellent porosity (thirty two percent), and high permeability (eight hundred to twelve hundred millidarcies). The analysis of an oil sample indicated a high quality, low sulfur, crude oil of thirty-nine degree gravity. It was an exceptionally good reservoir rock.

The well was then drilled down to fourteen thousand feet and a variety of instruments called logging tools were run down the hole on a wireline to record selected petrophysical measurements. The logs confirmed the presence of over eight hundred feet of oil saturated sandstone.

On day eighty-six, the first drill stem flow test of the oil zone was conducted. The well flowed at a rate of eight thousand, three hundred barrels of oil per day, confirming the existence of a major, and potentially world class, oil discovery.

Executive management at OilQuest was exuberant!

David and Steve immediately set to work revising the maps based on the drilling results in order to arrive at a preliminary estimate of reserves. By David's estimate, there were nearly four billion barrels of oil in place, of which one billion three hundred million barrels could be conventionally recovered. However, these reserves could only be classified as "possible" since at least a second well would be needed to confirm the extent of the oil over the entire structure. This appraisal, or confirmation well, would essentially prove up the reserves for commercial purposes.

Since the first well was on the very crest of the structure, the second well was designed to drill down the flank of the structure in order to determine the lowermost limit of the oil reservoir. This lower limit was still unknown and had to be determined before the true size and extent of the field could be established with any degree of certainty.

Within a month after completion of Angel Falls #1, a second well location was selected. In typical fashion, the next well was to be called Angel Falls #2. Rather than clear another site in the forest and move the rig, it was decided to leave the rig at the original location but directionally drill the well at an angle such that it would reach the target reservoir approximately 5,000 feet away from the #1 well.

The Angel Falls #2 well "spudded" (commenced drilling) three months ago and was just days away from reaching the objective. In those three months, David's life had moved at the speed of light. Both he and Steve had been promoted and he had worked feverishly with the Reservoir Engineering and

Project Facilities people to lay out a scenario for field development in the event that the #2 well was successful.

From an environmental impact standpoint, field development produced the gravest concern. Traditional field development would call for roads, multiple drill sites, oil tank storage batteries, operations buildings, crew quarters, pipelines and probably an airstrip. The impact on the Amazonian rain forest and its inhabitants would be potentially devastating. David and a few others lobbied long and hard to devise an alternate scenario which ultimately won the day. It would be much more costly, but the executives felt it would be worth the PR value.

Essentially, the existing site would be slightly expanded to six acres from which twelve development wells would be directionally drilled. A second site of similar size would be cleared three miles away and the drilling program would be repeated. Thus, the entire structure could be tapped from just two locations with a total of twenty-four wells. A one-lane gravel road for conveying personnel would connect the two sites. Power would be supplied from diesel generators fueled by some of the produced oil.

The big stumbling block was getting the oil out of the rain forest. Laying a twenty-four inch diameter pipeline a distance of one hundred eighty miles was no small engineering feat even under the best of circumstances. It required large, heavy equipment that needed to move by roads, big roads at that.

When David suggested laying three, eight-inch diameter pipelines by hand as a substitute for the twenty-four inch line, bedlam ensued. When he further recommended that each pipe segment be air dropped by helicopter and trenches dug, by hand, so as to bury the pipeline, the engineers went berserk. The cost differential would be astronomical and the construction time tripled.

When the costs were tallied, David's proposal exceeded eight hundred million dollars versus three hundred fifty million for the more conventional approach. This half billion dollar variance was not lost on David. While the project would still be highly profitable to the company, the net income impact was substantial.

Needless to say, a decision of this magnitude had to go to Executive Management, who then presented it to the Board of Directors.

News of the oil strike had circulated widely and already various environmental groups were firing salvos at the company. Wall Street reacted favorably, however, and OilQuest's stock had climbed six percent since the first press release on the test results of the Angel Falls #1. Still, the Board was cognizant of the impact the environmental movement could have on their retail business, particularly the service stations and petrochemical products.

With the picture of an organized protest movement picketing every OilQuest service station from Boston to Los Angeles, the Board opted for David's plan.

Not missing an opportunity to capitalize on a potential disaster, the Public Affairs department touted the plan as if the thought of taking the easy and more profitable road never even entered their collective corporate minds.

The project was turned into a media extravaganza rivaling that of Hollywood. Press conferences were called on an almost daily basis and full-page ads were taken out in every major publication, including a few environmental monthlies.

David had been selected as the lead spokesman for the project and had spent the past few months on the road presenting the details of the project to universities, professional organizations, and even the many environmental groups whose primary mission was preservation of the rain forest. Steve maintained project momentum from Plano with an occasional site visit to Venezuela.

Although David was met with skeptical and sometimes hostile audiences on more than one occasion, he had managed to win over the majority of the public. This acceptance he had attributed to his deep belief in the project as a viable compromise between the preservation of the rain forest and the energy needs of the world. He had come across as sincere, credible, straightforward and balanced. By the end of the campaign, the initial public outcry had subsided to a few isolated letters of protest from hard line conservation groups who were small in number and had drifted far from the mainstream of the environmental movement.

Now it was time to go home and get back to the business of exploration. As the limo turned off Interstate 635 and headed north on the Tollway toward Plano, David allowed himself to finally turn his thoughts toward home. It had been weeks since he had slept in his own bed and he painfully missed his wife and two young boys. The frequent phone calls from his hotel room were no substitute for being there and all he wanted was to spend some time together, to catch up on lost moments, and to root for his kids at their soccer games.

The limo left the Tollway and began to cruise past the vaguely familiar sights of suburban Plano, eventually turning into his subdivision, charmingly but misleadingly entitled Willow Forest.

Plano was just what the name conjured up. Once a flat and nearly treeless spread of farms and ranches, it was now one suburb after another, distinguished from each other only by the price of the houses. Though land was readily abundant, the houses were tightly packed, and they stretched in a seemingly endless sprawl toward Oklahoma, punctuated only by a strip mall or a corner service station.

But the schools were good, especially for Texas, the crime rate was low with the exception of garage bandits, and the city was well planned. Too well planned, according to David's wife, Mallory. She had often called this lifestyle the Texas version of the Stepford Wives. Chevy Suburbans, also known as the Texas station wagon, blended easily with the abundant Mercedes, Volvos and BMWs that signified the affluence of this Dallas suburb of one hundred eighty thousand people. Although there was a certain sterility to the Plano environs, David and his family were quite happy to be living there, for now. Transfers were inevitable in the oil patch, and even desirable as far as David was concerned, so Plano was just fine, for now.

The limo turned onto David's street. It was getting late, about ten, and warm lights glowed invitingly from the windows. The homes on his street were all custom built, two story brick, on a postage stamp lot. David could never understand why, with all this land, the developers intentionally made the building lots so small. His simple conclusion was greed, but reasoned there had to be more to it than that. Houses were no more than fifteen feet apart. The homes were large by most standards, more than four thousand square feet, and would appear quite stately when situated on a few acres. Yet, in this setting they appeared ostentatious and misplaced. His was a red brick colonial with four imposing white columns and double front doors flanked by palladium windows. Nearly all houses came with swimming pools and his was no exception. The first floor contained a sumptuous master suite with two living areas, a formal living room with marble fireplace, and an oak paneled family room that the boys trashed on a routine basis. The kitchen was expansive, with state-of-the-art appliances and abundant marble counters and teak cabinets. It was designed to Mallory's exacting standards in order to accommodate her passion for cooking.

A circular staircase led from the front hall up to a large, open landing where three bedrooms and two baths branched in every direction from the open space. The boys each had their own rooms, separated by one of the baths, and furnished in western motifs. A tastefully decorated guest bedroom with private bath awaited those who could tolerate the noisy, mischievous juvenile delinquents in the adjoining rooms. There was nothing that set it apart from every other house on the street, or in the entire subdivision for that matter. But it was home, and David never tired of returning to it after a long trip, or even a day at the office.

Ian pulled the car into his small circular drive that consumed nearly the entire front yard. The house was all-alight and David could see the drapes at the living room window pulled aside with two little heads peering out. When they saw the car, Eric, age seven, and Matt, nine, gave out a yell and bolted for the front door. David jumped out of the car just as the front door opened and was nearly bowled over by the kids as they leapt into his outstretched arms. They clung tightly to him, screaming one word over and over "Daddy! Daddy! Daddy!"

David felt his throat tighten as he knew they had missed him as much as he had missed them. He looked up to see Mallory standing silhouetted in the doorway, the lights from inside highlighting her blond hair and setting her entire body aglow. Her five-foot, five-inch slender frame was cloaked in a wispy green dress, barely masking her athletic build.

David walked up to her, a kid in each arm. For a brief moment neither spoke as they exchanged a flood of emotions in one longing glance.

"Do I know you?" she teased softly as David put the children down.

"I seem to recall attending your wedding. Lovely ceremony. Excellent caterers," smiled David as he reached out and pulled Mallory to him.

Still in the doorway, they kissed gently, followed by a long, tender embrace. The boys rolled their eyes.

Although way past their bedtime, Eric and Matt stayed up just long enough to rummage through David's luggage to find the treasures he always brought home for them. Their favorite was the mounted piranha fish, mouth agape with tiny, sharp protruding teeth. With the hunt successfully concluded, David carried each of them upstairs and put them in their beds. He kissed them both on the forehead, told them he loved them, and gave them one last hug before encircling them with their menagerie of favorite stuffed animals. In minutes, they were both asleep.

When David came downstairs, Mallory had a brandy snifter of his favorite single malt whiskey, Bushmills, waiting for him. He would never drink it on the road because almost no bar carried it, and besides, it made him homesick.

David showered quickly and wrapped himself in his floor length, terry cloth monk's robe. When he came out of the master bath into the bedroom, Mallory stood before him wearing only a white lace body suit. The sight took his breath away. He stood there, unable to speak at first, and marveled at how beautiful she was. Regaining some composure, he drew close to her and softly whispered.

"You look stunning."

"I bet you say that to all the women you meet."

"Only the stunning ones in white lace."

They kissed, this time much longer and far more passionately than the tender embrace at the door. David dropped his robe as they climbed into bed.

The passion, pent up for weeks, finally found release.

# CHAPTER 2

# *The Office*

## *DAY TWO*

David awoke at the early hour of five the next morning. Jet lag was his nemesis and would continue to plague him for several more days, and nights. To make the most of it, he decided to get up and go to the office early. There would certainly be plenty of catching up to do. Besides, he was extremely anxious to get an update on the Angel Falls #2 well which would be nearing the target depth any day now.

As he looked in the mirror while he prepared to trim his beard, he felt as though he could see himself aging. His once full, dark beard had given way to a salt and pepper appearance. His brown hair was just starting to gray at the edges. He was grateful for that. At thirty-eight, many of his colleagues were already bald.

He stepped on the scales and was relieved to see that he was maintaining a respectable one hundred sixty five pounds for his five foot, ten inch frame. Not bad for three weeks on the road, he thought to himself. Still, he made a mental note to hit the bike path with his kids on a more frequent basis.

By the time he had showered and dressed, Mallory was up and had the coffee on and his favorite cereals lined up for selection. She could be extremely efficient in the morning. David looked lovingly at her. There was a time when she had beaten him out the door in the morning. A time when her career as a financial analyst was in full swing. With an MBA from Wharton and a mind like a supercomputer, she was a powerhouse.

Yet when the boys came along, everything seemed to change. At first David and Mallory tried the dual career path with a hard-to-find nanny looking after Matt at first, and then Eric. The daily routine had become exhausting, with little time or energy left for the children at night. And with David being away for weeks at a time, it created an even greater strain on the increasingly fragile situation. Mallory, like most working moms, carried more than her share of domestic responsibilities, which she harbored with a growing resentment. Arguments over who does what were increasingly commonplace. And although their combined income was spectacular, the quality of life had deteriorated to the point where the family had become totally dysfunctional and in serious danger of breaking apart.

Mallory was the first to visualize the danger. But the dramatic change in their lives would turn on a simple incident. She returned from work one night, late as usual. David was somewhere in South America, again. The nanny had just finished bathing Eric and put him down to sleep when Mallory came in to kiss him goodnight. Eric looked at Mallory and the nanny standing over his bed, then reached up and pulled the nanny toward him. With a kiss to the nanny's cheek, he simply said, "Good night, Mommy." Ignoring Mallory, he lay back down and turned his head away from her. She was devastated.

Mallory turned in her resignation the next day. And although Eric was only two at the time, Mallory still feels he knew exactly what he was doing.

Yet, despite the sacrificed career and the impact on their income, she never looked back. That was five years ago. The kids were now happier, the warmth and passion returned to her relationship with David, and the nanny was gone.

"By the way," said Mallory. "I forgot to mention to you last night that Steve called about three days ago. He wanted to get in touch with you but you were between cities. He was calling from Caracas."

"Did he say what he wanted?"

"Not really. Oh wait. He did mention something about an Angel Falls option or something."

"What option?"

"I don't know. He didn't elaborate. He seemed in a big hurry."

"I'll check with him this morning at the office."

David always left the house before the kids would wake. It made for a less frenetic start to the day. He would usually arrive at the office by seven, a full hour before the official start, just to get a jump on the day. Today was no exception as he navigated his Ford Explorer along the easy five miles of lightly trafficked roads to the office.

The drive to the office was short, taking only about fifteen minutes from door to door. As David drove past one subdivision after another, he was relieved that his constant travels broke the monotony of life in Plano. Pulling into the gated parking lot, he fumbled around in his briefcase for the keycard that gave him access to nearly every nook and cranny of OilQuest. David regarded the security as more of a nuisance, often stating that the company gave more secrets away at every shareholder's meeting.

OilQuest was housed in a sprawling six story office complex that was typical of those constructed in the eighties, lots of tinted glass with a dark granite facade and neogothic arches and angles just to make it look interesting. David found its familiar appearance comforting after being away. He made his way up the five flights of stairs, his only form of exercise over the last six months, and strolled down the map-adorned corridor toward his office.

He passed by Steve Billing's office with barely a glance since Steve never came in until eight, but out of the corner of his eye he noticed that Steve's nameplate was missing. David paused for a moment and returned to Steve's door. He turned the handle, not expecting it to open because all doors were kept locked as a security precaution. Since the Angel Falls Project both of them had been extra careful to lock up all data each night. The door opened. David turned on the light and was startled to find the office empty with the exception of a desk, drafting table, file cabinet and a few chairs. The desk drawers were empty and the same for the file cabinet. Steve's map rack, which contained copies of all the maps on the project, was gone. There wasn't even a phone in the office.

David felt his stomach tighten in panic as he turned and quickly continued down the hall to his office. He was mildly relieved to find his door still locked and his nameplate intact. Upon opening his door and taking a quick glance around, however, he realized that something was wrong. He immediately picked up his phone and called Security.

"Security. Johnson speaking."

"This is David Hastings in room 525. I've been away for several weeks and have just returned to my office and there are some important documents missing. Also, Steve Giles' office, room 541, is completely empty."

"Mr. Hastings, there have been no thefts. The contents of Mr. Giles' office were relocated only yesterday to another office area under our supervision, along with some of your data."

"Under whose authority?"

"The orders came directly from the president, Mr. Keith. He had Rick Watson and his people actually oversee the move."

Rick Watson. The sound of his name made the hairs on David's neck stand on end. The two had worked together in Indonesia during the mid-eighties where Rick was a drilling supervisor. They were constantly at odds over the drilling of exploration wells. Rick was abrasive, as most drillers tend to be, but was also known for his sometimes ruthless tactics in order to get a well drilled under budget. His shortcuts were inevitably at the expense of necessary exploration data. Oddly enough though, his cost cutting efforts earned him a promotion back in Corporate and the title of Manager of Special Projects. This galled David but he was relieved to be rid of him.

"Johnson, do you know where Steve Giles' new office is located?"

"New office? Sir, there isn't another office for Mr. Giles."

"I'm afraid that I don't understand. Then where have they relocated Steve?" David felt the panic rising in his voice.

"Sir, Steve Giles is dead. He died a couple of days ago. I'm sorry. I thought you knew."

David was stunned. His hands began to tremble. He struggled to compose himself for the next question.

"How did he die?"

"I understand that it happened in Caracas."

"What happened?"

"All I heard was that he was killed, Mr. Hastings. I really don't know anymore. You'll have to talk to Employee Relations or a relative or something."

"He didn't have any relatives." David responded as he slowly put down the phone.

David sat in his chair and just stared out the window. Cars were slowly starting to pull into the office parking lot. David didn't notice. A tear fell, followed by many.

It was nearly eight a.m. when David was shaken from his grief by a gritty, cackling voice from the doorway.

"So, looks like we get to tango once again."

David turned toward the direction of the voice, although it was recognizable and brought back a stream of bad memories. Rick Watson fit the typical profile of a vintage driller. He was short, stout and barrel chested. A belly that protruded far over his silver belt buckle overshadowed his five foot five inch muscular frame. Even at headquarters he wore cowboy boots. His hands and face were leathered and dark, testimony to his early years on the rigs.

Rick was cunning, and his "good ol' boy" demeanor belied a dark side. He was prone to fights in the field, using any weapon at hand to gain an advantage. In the office, his tactics were usually more subtle. But Management kept him because he could get the job done. No one dared ask how.

"Hello Rick. I see you've been busy." David scowled.

"Extremely. Thanks to you geologists we're already behind. Not to worry though, I'll soon have us humming along."

"A bit premature, don't you think? After all, we're still drilling the appraisal well. We don't even know if we have a commercial accumulation."

"Maybe you don't know," gloated Rick, "but the rest of the company thinks that this is the big one, and all the resources have been put at my disposal to work up a plan to rapidly develop the Angel Falls discovery. I've already assembled a team of engineers, hand picked of course, and we've taken over a wing on the fourth floor. It is dedicated strictly to the project. We even have our own secured access. If you're nice to me, I'll let you visit.

Oh by the way, we borrowed a few things from your office, maps and stuff. We also moved your partner's office contents into our area. Guess he won't be needing them anymore. Too bad about him. Guess you and he must have been pretty good friends?"

David could barely control his anger as he gripped the sides of his desk.

"His name was Steve Giles. And he was a very good friend, you tactless bastard. Now get the hell out of my office!" shouted David as his anger finally gave vent.

"Welcome back." snickered Rick, as he slipped out the doorway and swaggered down the hall, content in having pushed all the right buttons to get David so riled.

In the office for less than an hour, my best friend is dead and my project is in the hands of a madman, thought David as he pondered how the rest of the day might go.

He didn't have to wait very long to find out.

The phone rang. David thought twice before picking it up. It was Lisa Voorhees, vice president of Employee Relations.

"Hello David, this is Lisa Voorhees. Welcome back. How did the trip go?"

Small talk, thought David. Definitely not Lisa's style. She was direct, brutally frank, quick witted and took no prisoners. David knew she wasn't calling just to chat, so he decided to go on the offensive.

"Hello Lisa. I'm glad you called. I just heard about Steve Giles. Can you tell me what happened?"

"Actually, that's why I'm calling. Can you come up to my office now so that we can discuss it?"

She wasn't asking. She never asked.

"I'll be right up."

David arrived at Lisa's office a few moments later. Lisa's secretary, Martha, had David wait just outside the open door while she announced his presence. David found this little routine to be somewhat annoying, as if Lisa was holding court, but he didn't let it show.

As Martha escorted David into her office, Lisa offered an outstretched hand. David shook it as he noticed a man standing by the window just a few feet away.

"Thanks for coming, David. You know Peter Bealls, Chief of Security from our corporate headquarters in New Orleans?"

"I've heard the name but we haven't met before. Nice to meet you." said David as they shook hands.

Peter smiled, nodded, but did not speak.

"Gentlemen, please have a seat." remarked Lisa as she pointed to the two wing back chairs facing her kidney shaped cherry wood desk.

"Would either of you care for some coffee? I can have some brought in? It won't be any trouble."

"None for me." commented David.

Bealls just shook his head.

There was a civility in her tone that immediately put David on alert. Lisa Voorhees was a lot of things, but hospitable wasn't one of them. He wondered if she had always been so ruthless or whether having to cut her way through a very traditional male bastion in the oil industry hierarchy had reduced her to this. She was brilliant and had keen instincts, but lacked compassion and ruled by fear. It was ironical that she headed up Employee Relations. Under her reign, the department earned the nickname "Employee Devastations".

Yet she wasn't unattractive, thought David. She was slender, graceful and a classy dresser. In her early forties, Lisa had moved quickly through the ranks and was clearly targeted for higher positions in the company. She was married with one young pre-schooler at home with a nanny. Her husband also worked for OilQuest in the Finance Department. He was reputed to be a wimp, but David figured the guy never had a chance to develop his own career and reputation in the company.

"David," began Lisa, "Peter has already told me what happened to Steve, but I wanted you to hear it from him. In addition, we were hoping that, since you and he were good friends, you might be able to shed some light on the incident."

"I'll do what I can." stated David somberly.

For the first time since David entered the office, Bealls spoke.

"Steve Giles was killed in Caracas three days ago. We were informed by the American Embassy in Caracas shortly after the local police notified them.

He apparently died of multiple stab wounds. His body was found outside a shady establishment in a rough part of the city in the early morning hours by a routine police patrol."

David sat stunned. Bealls continued, occasionally referring to a small notebook for details.

"Steve Giles was returning from the well site and was overnighting in Caracas before catching the morning flight back to the States. He checked into the Hotel Tamanaco that afternoon.

The local police, with the assistance of a U.S. Embassy staffer, investigated the incident. He was robbed but the hotel key was found on his body, so the police were able to trace him back to the hotel where they made a positive ID by locating his passport in the room. When the police realized he was an American, they called the U.S. Embassy. It's routine procedure."

Bealls paused to let the details sink in, before continuing.

"However, the joint investigation turned up some rather disturbing information."

David stomach was already churning.

"According to the police," Bealls continued, "Giles took a taxi from the hotel to the red light district. He went into one of the bars frequented by prostitutes, drank for several hours and left with a prostitute. The police figure he was robbed by her accomplices. When he put up a fight, they knifed him, took his money and then dumped him in a convenient spot. It happens all the time."

"I just can't believe it!" exclaimed David.

"It's a very common occurrence. Giles was just unlucky." responded Bealls matter-of-factly.

"Needless to say, this raises several rather sensitive issues." commented Lisa with blandness in her voice. "OilQuest doesn't need this kind of publicity. We would prefer to handle this quietly and efficiently."

That's more like the Lisa we've all come to know and despise, thought David, wondering when she was going to get around to it.

"We tried contacting his mother without any luck. She is the only emergency contact he has listed in his personnel file. She is also listed as the only beneficiary of his life insurance and saving's plans. We understand you were close friends and that, aside from you, he rarely associated with anyone else at the office. Is that true?" inquired Lisa.

"Pretty much," David responded. "Steve was an only child and both of his parents have since passed away. His mother died a little less than a year ago. Steve probably forgot to change the beneficiary designation and emergency contact number. He'd socialize a little with the people in Exploration, but I was probably his best friend at work."

"At work? Does that mean he had other friends outside the office?" Bealls inquired.

David cast him a quick stare and responded "Why does it matter who his friends were? He's dead."

Lisa interceded. "If they were close friends we may want to notify them of the funeral arrangements. Otherwise, we will probably have a very private service."

David took a few seconds to digest Lisa's comment before replying "Of course. I'm sorry. This is all just too horrible to believe."

"Now tell us. Did he have any other friends?" Bealls asked with icy intent.

There was something about this line of questioning and its tone that alarmed David. He could accept that Lisa and Bealls lacked compassion for the situation, but this went beyond that. There was more to it than insensitive corporate efficiency at work. They were far too intense. David decided to lie, although he couldn't explain his motives.

"He had no other friends. At least none that I know of, and I probably would have known."

The lie had its desired effect. David could see the quick glance exchanged between Lisa and Bealls, followed by a visible sense of relief.

Bealls eased back in his chair and, in a transparently nonchalant manner, asked "Did Giles talk to you at all when he was in Venezuela this last time?"

David thought back to this morning when Mallory remarked that Steve had called.

"No. I was on the road all the time. We never talked."

Another glance exchanged between Lisa and Bealls.

"Strange", Bealls said, "Giles' hotel bill shows a call to your house."

David looked from Lisa to Bealls. This was no casual conversation. He was being interrogated. The shock of it ran through him. He had to think fast.

"He may have called but I wasn't home. Come to think of it, my wife did mention he had called, but he didn't leave a message."

This time it was Lisa who spoke. "He didn't say anything to your wife?"

"No. Only that he was looking for me. Nothing other than that. As I was between cities at the time, we never did connect. I didn't think anything of it when my wife told me. I knew we'd see each other back at the office."

David didn't like where the conversation was going and decided to short-circuit the process.

"Do you suppose Steve knew he was in danger and was trying to contact me?"

The question had its desired effect.

"Probably not." Bealls responded unhesitatingly. "After all, how could he have known anything in advance? This was obviously a random act of violence."

"Of course, you're quite right," said David. A brief pause before David broke the agonizing silence.

"Will there be anything else?"

Lisa ended the discussion. "That's all David. Thanks for your help."

Once outside Lisa's office, David ducked into the men's room to regain his composure. At least, he thought to himself, this is one place where Lisa can't harass me. He hoped he had been convincing in the meeting, but he wasn't sure. He had never been interrogated like that before. He was sick at the thought that his best friend was dead. Something was terribly wrong. Steve Giles was dead and David knew that it wasn't due to a seedy involvement with a prostitute in the Caracas red-light district. He and Mallory were the only ones who knew that Steve was gay.

More so, Steve was faithful to his companion who lived and worked out of state, which was why OilQuest did not discover the secret. The company took a dim view of these kinds of alternative relationships, and Steve was very careful in keeping this quiet. It would have cost him his job, thought David, but not his life. That was why David had lied to Lisa and Bealls. To volunteer that Steve was gay would poke some serious holes in their story about his death. And to identify Steve's partner might put him in danger, although why and from what David couldn't fathom.

It then dawned on David what had to be done next. To safeguard Steve's secret for now, David had to get to Steve's apartment and remove all trace of his lover. For if he was discovered, then Lisa would know that David had lied. Suddenly, he thought of Mallory and the kids and fear began to tug at his insides. Don't get carried away with this, he thought to himself. There may be a very reasonable and non-threatening explanation for all of this, and I shouldn't expect the worst. Or should I?

As he calmed himself, David decided that he should go to Steve's apartment, for which he had the key, and at least remove the articles, letters and photos relating to Steve's lover and ship them to him. That would be the respectable thing to do, and would also keep them from being discovered. Later today, David would call Steve's friend in Ohio and try to explain the situation.

At noon, David left the office and drove over to Steve's apartment complex. It was one of the newer complexes just a few miles from the office. Like most single people in Plano, Steve had elected to take an apartment to avoid the more mundane chores associated with home ownership. In addition, it was a good way to avoid paying Plano property taxes that were substantial.

As David approached Steve's apartment, he immediately saw that the living room window, which faced the front, was broken. The break was small, but just enough to access the window lock. The drapes were still drawn so he could not peer inside. Steve did not have an alarm system, feeling he never had anything worth stealing.

David carefully unlocked the door and pushed it open. He stood at the doorway a moment and glanced inside before stepping across the threshold and closing the door. The place had been thoroughly trashed. The sofas and pillows had been torn open with a knife, the dishes broken, and the walls spray painted with four letter words. As David made his way from one room to another, the story was the same. Closing his eyes, David tried to picture each room before the break-in, and he then made a mental inventory of what was missing. In the living room, the TV set, answering machine and sound system were gone. The kitchen and bathroom were both devastated but nothing significant seemed to be gone. The medicine cabinet had been dumped in an apparent search for drugs, but Steve took no medications.

His bedroom was also a shambles. The closet was ransacked and clothing was strewn about the room. Wall hangings were slashed. Steve had converted the second bedroom into a study and it was hit hardest of all. The computer,

Steve's favorite toy, was missing. The contents of the file cabinet had been unceremoniously dumped on the floor and strewn about.

David went back into the bedroom, righted a chair and sat down. It certainly looked like the work of druggies. That which was stolen, mostly electrical items, could be sold on the black market. Steve had no jewelry to speak of. The vandalism could be attributed to being on drugs at the time of the break-in. It fit a familiar pattern that seemed to be plaguing Plano in recent months.

With a reluctant sigh, David scanned the room for the phone to call the police. It normally sat on the night table next to the picture of him with his gay friend, Mark. No phone and no photo. David suddenly jerked upright. Something else was missing. He hadn't noticed it before with all the debris strewn about. No pictures anywhere. He distinctly remembered that Steve kept pictures of Mark on his night table and dresser. He rummaged about the debris on the bedroom floor and found nothing. They were gone.

He rushed to the living room where Steve had kept a few pictures of his departed family members, as well as a picture taken of himself with David and Mallory at the last company picnic. Steve had jokingly referred to these as his respectability pictures. These were also missing.

What would druggies want with family pictures, thought David? Druggies wouldn't, but somebody else might. But who, and why? If this was only meant to look like the work of druggies, then what were they looking for? David had no answers, only more questions.

Assuming the perpetrators were not looking for fast money, but information instead, what else would they want? David put himself in their place for a moment. Letters? No, Steve didn't write, and hence probably did not receive, letters. Bills, especially phone statements? No, Steve prided himself on being a paperless person. He paid his bills by computer and tossed the invoices. He kept no paper records whatsoever. Address books? No use looking for them since Steve put all of that also on computer files. Computer files! Of course, the computer files. David could have kicked himself for being so dense. His excitement, however, quickly gave way to despair. His startling revelation was another dead end since the computer had also been taken. No way to prove anything other than that a few pictures are gone. The police would probably chalk it up to druggies with a strange perversion to other people's photos.

David was about to give up when it hit him. The computer may be gone, but what about backup disks? Steve would definitely have backed up his data. This was like a religion to him and he would not violate one of the prime commandments. David went back into the study and began the search at the computer table. Nothing. He waded through the debris on the floor and also came up empty. All he could find was one pack of new, unopened diskettes, some computer manuals and power cords.

The backup disks had been taken. For money? Doubtful, thought David, since used diskettes don't sell on the black market. They could be damaged or contain a virus. However, new diskettes might bring a few dollars, as well as the computer manuals. David checked to see if the manuals still contained the original diskettes. They did.

"Bingo", whispered David to himself.

Confident that this was no ordinary break-in, and that it may be in some way related to Steve's death. David decided to forgo calling the police for the time being. He would let the break-in be discovered in due time by a neighbor or the apartment staff.

What about my fingerprints, he thought. Then he dismissed the notion. Shouldn't be a problem. No reason why my fingerprints shouldn't be in Steve's apartment. After all, we're best friends. At that thought, David grew sad and slowly left the apartment of his best friend for the final time.

As he walked through the apartment parking lot, David looked over and saw that Steve's beat up Taurus was sitting in its usual spot. He just used it for commuting and around town, but he never took care of it. How it still ran was always a mystery to David. Steve never seemed to mind how it looked, so long as it ran.

Upon returning to the office, David busied himself sorting through his mail while also trying to sort out the situation in his mind. Nothing made sense, which is what really bothered him.

By the time David had arrived home, he had made up his mind to call Steve's gay friend, Mark, and tell him what had happened. Not the full story, of course, but he needed to know about Steve's death. Upon seeing Mallory when he came through the door from the garage, he only now realized that he hadn't even told her.

"Hello my man." she cooed as she slinked up to him, put her arms around his neck and gave him a long, deep kiss. "You're home early. I thought for sure you'd be very late given it's your first day back. I'm not complaining, mind you."

For a moment, David nearly forgot the traumas of the day. "Where are the boys?"

"Soccer practice. They have a ride home and won't be here for another hour. Why? Want to fool around?"

"Tempting, but I need to tell you something. Actually, I need to tell you a lot."

The serious tone instantly told Mallory that playtime was over. She strolled over to the nearest chair and sat down, looking both curious and scared at the same time. "Go ahead." she said softly.

"I was told that Steve was killed in Caracas."

"Oh David, no!" she gasped. "How did it happen?"

"The police said he was robbed and stabbed in the red-light district, apparently after drinking and being with a prostitute."

"But—"

Before Mallory could utter another word, David responded "I know. It couldn't have happened that way. I do believe he is dead, however, since they will be flying his body up here for the funeral shortly. Sad part is that we will probably never know what really happened to Steve, since the Venezuelan police aren't likely to pursue what looks like a routine crime to them. And the American Embassy is worthless on these kinds of matters unless it happens to someone very, very important."

"Does Mark know?" Mallory inquired.

"No. I planned on calling him tonight. It's not an easy phone call to make, and I didn't want to call from the office because I needed to discuss something with him."

"Discuss what?"

"Here's where it gets complicated." David replied.

But before he could elaborate, Mallory interrupted. "Funny, there was a call for Steve just today."

"Who was it?"

"Just some car repair shop telling me that Steve's car was ready. The guy said that Steve left our number as a contact point."

David's eyes grew wide.

"What's wrong?"

"I don't know. Possibly nothing. But tell me. Did this person leave a name or number?"

"Actually, he gave his first name in the beginning but I forgot it. I didn't take a phone number or the name of the shop because I thought Steve would know where he took his car. I was just going to leave a message for Steve that his car was ready when he got back in town."

"What did you tell this guy?" David continued the interrogation.

"Only that I would relay the message to Steve. That was it."

"That was it?" David asked.

"That was it." she repeated. "Now tell me why you are making such a big deal over this."

"Because, Steve's car is right where it always is, in the apartment parking lot."

Mallory grew edgy. "David, tell me what is going on."

"I wish to God I knew. But let's stick with the phone call for the time being. Why would someone do this?"

"I don't have a clue."

David continued. "The caller may have been trying to see if you were home." He paused to consider this for a few seconds while Mallory eyed him carefully. "No. If that were the case, there would be no need to cook up an elaborate story about Steve's car."

"Maybe we should focus on who, instead of why." commented Mallory.

David, annoyed at first with the distraction, slowly began to see the logic in this approach. For an instant, he allowed himself the luxury of contemplating how much he loved her.

She brought him back to reality. "Whoever it is must know us as well as Steve. This was no random phone call."

"That's a scary thought. Mallory, did you recognize the voice?"

"No, but he was very polite, almost too polite."

"We're not getting very far." snapped David.

"Well, someone we know is trying to find Steve."

"Or, David paused, someone who knows us is trying to find out something. Tell me. When you picked up the phone, who did the guy ask for? Did he ask for you, me, Steve or just anybody?"

"Let me think. He asked for me. He specifically asked for Mrs. Hastings."

"When did he call?"

"About an hour ago."

"Then if he knew Steve was dead, he now also knows that I didn't tell you about it."

"What? I'm afraid I didn't make that giant leap of logic." Mallory's voice contained the slightest twinge of sarcasm.

"They must think I have something to hide, but what?" David puzzled.

"Who are they?"

"I don't really know. But, you see, upon learning of Steve's death, the natural reaction would have been for me to call you this morning. I did not. Instead I went to Steve's apartment and discovered it had been burglarized. It looked like druggies, given the vandalism and missing electronic items. However, the pictures of Steve with us are missing, Mark's picture is missing, and his back-up computer disks are missing. I think it was meant to look like a burglary, but the real intent was to search the apartment for something specific, possibly information. That would explain the missing back-up computer disks. Perhaps Steve was hiding something and they think one of his close friends may have it. I can't think of any other reason to take our photos from Steve's apartment. I spent all afternoon going over and over this and it's the only thing that makes sense."

Mallory took a deep breath and calmly said "Are we in any danger?"

David saw the growing concern on her face and realized she was thinking about the children. He needed to defuse the situation quickly.

"I can't see why. We don't know anything. Steve was not into anything weird that I know of, and we knew him better than anyone, with the possible exception of Mark. He would also never put us in a compromising position. Still, it wouldn't hurt to be a little more careful the next few days." David could see that his remarks did little to reassure Mallory.

David continued. "Speaking of Mark, that's how we got started on this discussion. I'd better call him now and warn him."

David pulled the address book from the phone table in the living room and dialed Ohio while Mallory sat intently, not wanting to miss at least half of the conversation.

"Hello." answered Mark in a slow, flat tone.

"Mark, this is David Hastings calling. I'm afraid I've got some bad news. I only found out today that—"

"I know." interrupted Mark with a sob. "He's gone."

David felt his own throat tighten. "I am truly sorry. He was a good friend to our entire family." There was a long pause while both men tried to regain their composure.

Finally, it was Mallory who broke the silence. "David, did Mark already know?"

David nodded his head.

Mallory continued. "How did he know?" "Who told him?"

David grew quizzical. By this time, Mark was sobbing away on the other end of the line, stopping only to say how much he had loved Steve.

David finally spoke up. "We all loved Steve. Mark, how did you find out?"

"Someone from OilQuest called me when I got home from work today. She said he was killed in Venezuela. I asked her how it happened and all she could say was that it was an accident and still under investigation. Do you know anything more about his death?"

"I'm afraid not." David lied. No use putting Mark through the story he had been told, especially since it didn't ring true.

"Mark, do you remember who called you from OilQuest?"

"No. Only some woman from Employee Relations. She said her name but I forgot it when she told me about Steve." More sobbing. "I just can't believe this has happened. We were planning to go to Europe next month. I already have our tickets."

David persisted. "Mark, was the woman's name Lisa Voorhees?"

"I don't know. It was Lisa something but I just can't remember. It's not important anyway."

David shut his eyes as the impact of the last statement sunk in. Mallory saw his expression and rose from her chair. She went over to the kitchen and slowly picked up the phone without making a sound. In the meantime, David had resumed the questioning.

"Mark, this may be important. Please think. Did Lisa ask you anything else?"

"Why, was Steve in trouble? Did he do something wrong?"

"No, but I was curious as to how she got your phone number."

Mark was slowly regaining his composure and the responses became more coherent. "That's a good question, but she never mentioned it and I never asked."

"Do you recall what she did say or ask?"

"Well. Let's see. She first asked if I was a relative. I told her that I was a very close, longtime friend. That was before she told me what had happened. I came unglued when she told me."

"Then what happened." David prodded.

"She wanted to know if I had heard from Steve in the last week. She said it might help in their investigation. I told her I hadn't. He never calls when he is away on business trips. Steve was always careful about my phone number showing up on hotel statements that would be submitted with expense reports and his cell phone doesn't work overseas. That's how cautious he was about keeping our relationship a secret. You and Mallory are the only ones who knew. Steve was afraid OilQuest would find out and force him to quit some-how."

"What else?"

"Nothing else really. I asked about the funeral and she said she would get back to me with the details. She said she was sorry to call with the sad news and then said good-by. Wait a minute. She also asked if I knew anyone else she should call. When I mentioned your name as the only other person she said that you already knew. I didn't get you into trouble, did I?"

"No, Mark. You didn't get me into trouble. I'm just trying to sort out a few things. I'll call you as soon as I find out about the funeral arrangements. I assume you'll want to come."

"Of course."

"Mark, feel free to call if you need to talk to someone, either me or Mallory."

"Thanks. I may take you up on that."

"Good-by Mark."

"Thanks David, and good-by."

As he hung up the phone, David heard Mallory put down the receiver in the kitchen. Mallory came around the corner back into the living room.

"Did you get that?" David asked knowingly.

"Most of it. But I still don't know how OilQuest got Mark's number."

"Perhaps it was in Steve's belongings when he was found, although he would most likely know that number by heart. It would certainly have been at the apartment, but Steve kept his phone directory on his computer, which is gone."

"So where does that leave us?"

"It leaves Lisa Voorhees with the knowledge that I lied to her today when she asked me if Steve had any other friends or relatives."

"You lied? But why lie about something like that?" Mallory asked incredu-lously.

"It was not so much the question but the tone. I felt that Lisa and Peter Bealls, of Corporate Security, were actually interrogating me. I lied because I sensed they were lying to me about why they wanted the information. And most of all, I lied because I know Steve wasn't with a prostitute. And now, Lisa and Bealls know that I lied, because they found Mark and he said he knew us."

"OK. Let's assume that all this is true." responded Mallory. "So what! So what if you lied. So what if they find out that Steve and Mark were lovers. OilQuest can't hurt Steve now. And they're not going to fire you over lying about Mark. You could just claim a temporary memory lapse due to the shock from learning about Steve. What is the big deal here?"

"Precisely." said David. "Just what is the big deal? Even OilQuest wouldn't go to such lengths to ferret out a homosexual relationship of one of its employees. Especially a deceased employee. And Lisa lied to Mark. First, she lied about how he died, although that is understandable. But she also lied because she already knew the funeral arrangements for Steve, yet she deliberately didn't tell Mark. Instead, she said she would call back when she had the details."

David continued. "Lisa called Mark to find out who he was, how close he was to Steve, whether he had heard from Steve in the past week, and if Steve had any other friends. It's a very similar line of questioning that I went through this morning. Bealls even had a copy of Steve's hotel phone bill showing he placed a call to us, but we know he didn't call Mark. They must have gotten Mark's number from Steve's apartment. They broke into his apartment. Lisa or Bealls or someone hired by them."

Mallory was following closely now and spoke up. "If that were true, then they must have been looking for something, possibly on the computer. And assuming they found nothing, then they might think Steve told someone instead. But it would have to be someone he trusted. That's why they questioned you and called Mark."

David came back. "And when Mark said he hadn't spoken to Steve in over a week, then Lisa ended the conversation. She found out what she needed to know. It also explains why they asked me about the call Steve made to our house when I was away. The phone call. Mallory, what was it Steve said when he called? Did he sound nervous or scared or different in any way?"

Mallory thought pensively for a few seconds. Then she walked over to the kitchen phone, picked it up and started a conversation with herself.

"Hello Steve. Where are you calling from? This is a lousy connection.

Caracas! Not again. You ought to take up residence there. I hope your Spanish has improved.

I'm fine and the boys are doing great, thanks. But I'm afraid that David is on the road again. He'll be back in a few days.

I'm afraid he's leaving LA for San Francisco today, so you won't be able to reach him until he gets into San Francisco later tonight. Would you like his phone number in San Francisco? He's staying at the Hilton on the Bay.

You have it already? Good, since I'm not sure where I left it.

In case you two don't connect, any message you want me to pass on when he calls in?

You want to talk about the Angel Falls Option? Is that it? No details?

OK Steve, good luck with the rest of your trip. We'll have you over for a barbecue when you get back into town.

Take care. Bye."

With that, Mallory put the phone down and turned to David. "Well, how did I do?"

"I'll never understand how you can do that, but I love it." said David. Now, do you remember exactly when he called and his state of mind?

"He called about three days ago in the late afternoon. He sounded rushed, but nothing out of the ordinary."

"I think he may have made that call just before he was killed. He never contacted me in San Francisco."

"What is the Angel Falls Option?" asked Mallory. "Is it important?"

"I don't know the answer to either of those questions, but I may be able to find out tomorrow."

With that having been said, Eric and Matt bounded through the front door, dirty and sweaty from a hard afternoon at soccer practice.

"I'm hungry," blurted Matt.

"You're always hungry," said David as he grabbed the two of them and wrestled them to the floor.

"Enough of that." scolded Mallory. "Now put away your gear, get washed up and come to the table. By then your favorite, most disgusting food will be ready."

"All right! Hot dogs and beans." exclaimed Eric.

Mallory turned to David. "We will be having veal picata in a white wine sauce."

"The kids get all the good stuff." mused David.

The concerns of the day were put aside, at least for the moment. It was time to be a family for now. David would take up the quest again in the morning.

# CHAPTER 3

# *Confrontation and Confirmation*
## *DAY THREE*

David arrived at the office early the next morning. It had been a fitful night and rather than bother Mallory, who could sleep through a bomb blast, he had his usual cold cereal and headed into the office. Much of what transpired the day before did not make much sense, other than it all seemed related. He knew this might be a difficult day for him since there was a reasonable expectation of another meeting with Lisa, something he was not looking forward to. Lisa would want to know why David had lied about Mark. He needed a plausible excuse. Yet more than that, he needed to find out what would compel Lisa, and presumably Bealls, to go to such lengths to find out who Steve had spoken with shortly before his death.

Rather than wait for things to happen before reacting, David had decided to test the waters a bit on his own. He grabbed a cup of coffee, trying to make today look like any other, ordinary day, and strolled up to the new work area assigned to the Angel Falls Project Team.

He was surprised to find the corridor doors leading to the work area locked. These were usually intended to be fire doors only, and were open in all other areas of the building. Next to the door was a small sign that read "Authorized Personnel Only. Contact Rick Watson for entry." Next to the sign was a card key box. David pulled his magnetized badge from his shirt pocket and inserted it into the slot. Nothing happened. He tried several more times. Still nothing. Apparently he was not cleared for entry.

Undaunted, he took a few steps off to the side and waited for someone to walk through the door, then he quickly grabbed the closing door and walked through with a polite "Thank you. Saves me the bother of searching for my badge." It worked like a charm. The other person didn't give it a second thought.

Once inside, David walked deliberately down the hall, quickly glancing inside the offices from the corners of his eyes. He also made a mental note of the nameplates alongside each door. None were familiar to him. How could that be, thought David. Surely some of the former team would be assigned to the project. Yet he recognized no one. He passed one workroom with maps and blueprints on walls and tables, with several men pouring over the maps spread out on the table. He nearly stopped and peered in, but thought better of it and kept slowly walking.

"Can I help you?" came a woman's voice from a desk at the intersection of the two corridors.

"Wouldn't you know it," mumbled David under his breath, "caught by a nosy secretary." Thinking quickly, he casually responded.

"Why thank you. You certainly can. I'm looking for Rick Watson. Can you please tell me where his office is?"

"He's just down the hall. Last room on the left. Listen for the shouting."

They exchanged a quick laugh and David thanked her and headed toward Rick's office. As he approached the office, he understood what she meant. He could hear Rick's voice booming through the walls. When David reached the door to Rick's office, he stood outside for a moment while the shouting continued. It was soon apparent that he was on the phone. David peered in to see him standing by the window with his back to the door, phone in hand.

"I don't pay you to give me excuses. I pay you to get the job done no matter what. Every day this operation slips costs us $120,000. If you need more men and equipment, then we'll get them, but don't tell me we can't make it in time. I don't care how much it rains. Just keep drilling!" With that final statement, Rick slammed the phone down and turned back to his desk. His eyes grew wide as he saw David standing at the doorway.

"Hello Rick? Having a good day?" David asked with a big smile on his face.

Watson went ashen, then bright red, and then came the rapid-fire questions.

"How the hell did you get in here?

Who let you in?

You're not authorized to be here unless I say so.

What do you want, anyway?"

David couldn't resist yanking his chain a little tighter. "The door was wide open so I just walked in. Yep, real tight security you've got here, Watson. Do you run all your projects this way?"

Watson came unglued and exploded into a non-stop string of expletives that seemed to go on forever. David just smiled. More cursing ensued. For a moment, David wondered if Rick might get physically violent, but dismissed the idea. Watson was crude but smart. He would never jeopardize his career over something this petty.

Finally David interrupted. "When you have a minute, I'd like to discuss work. That is, if your not too busy."

Rick finally regained control of himself, stopped cursing and sat down in his chair. He did not sit fully back, but rather on the edge of his chair as if to pounce should David make another sarcastic remark. David knew he could easily set him off again, but he had had his fun and now it was time to get serious.

"I came to get caught up on the well," said David in a serious tone.

"And what well might that be?" This time it was Watson's turn to play games.

David remained calm, but persisted. "I believe we are only drilling one well at the moment, the Angel Falls #2. I just want to know what the latest developments are. We should be getting pretty close to final depth. Have we seen anything yet?"

"As much as it pains me," Watson said with a smirk, "I can't tell you."

"Could it be because you don't know yourself?" David tried to goad Rick into a response but it was even too obvious for him.

"Nice try, but it won't work. Angel Falls #2 is a tight hole. In case you forgot, tight hole means we are keeping it a <u>big</u> secret, especially from people like you."

David was growing weary of the simple minded word games, but needed to keep the conversation going if he was to find out anything.

"Look, Rick. Just tell me where we are on the well and I'll be out of your hair. Lest you forget, you wouldn't be here if it weren't for our discovery."

"It really is a tight hole and you really are an asshole." Watson's faced beamed with pride at the self-acknowledged witticism.

"Who declared the well tight?"

"The old man himself."

"Raymond Keith?" asked David incredulously.

"That's the one."

Raymond Keith, 53, was president of OilQuest. He had risen to power the old fashioned way, from the ground up. He was, in the oil field vernacular, a lifer. Keith started with OilQuest 37 years ago as a roustabout at age 16, working the rigs in west Texas. He took a leave of absence to go to Texas A&M University where he excelled in petroleum engineering. Upon graduation, OilQuest made him a reservoir engineer.

Keith then rose quickly through the ranks, making a name for himself in the Middle East and Indonesia with some very large oil field projects. His last eight years were spent with Corporate, learning the ins and outs of the other divisions at OilQuest.

He caught the eye of the longtime Chairman of OilQuest, who named Keith to be President of the company two years ago. Even this position was viewed as an interim measure until the Chairman retires. Keith was the hand picked successor to be Chairman.

As President, Raymond Keith had one driving ambition, to make a giant oil discovery, similar to those of decades past. Trouble was, giant oil discoveries were very rare these days, and many oil companies failed employing this strategy. Most companies were now focused on moderate to low risk exploration and development projects, which typically yield modest reserves. Not Keith. He wanted to make a name for himself by bringing in a big one. And Angel Falls was that big one in his mind. This was his ticket to the Chairmanship.

With this in mind, David understood why Keith was so closely involved with the project, even down to declaring the #2 well tight. David himself harbored aspirations of reward and recognition for the project and hoped it would be a giant oil discovery. Nor did he mind Keith's involvement because it had opened a lot of doors for him in recent months. Until now.

Prior to this project, David had minimal exposure to Raymond Keith. Since assuming the Presidency two years ago, Keith had subjected all projects and personnel to intensive reviews. The results were sometimes devastating, with projects being canceled and people either reassigned or terminated. The process went on for months and morale had plunged to lows David had not seen since the oil crash of the mid-eighties.

At the end of it though, OilQuest was viewed by the Securities Analysts as a tighter, leaner, and a better focused company. The stock price had stabilized and even rose slightly, leading all to conclude this was a healthy exercise.

Although David was far from complacent while the re-focusing effort was going on, he felt his work and his project were reasonably secure, and this was confirmed with the ultimate support for drilling the Angel Falls #1.

Yet despite the relative security of his own position, David privately questioned the value of the "right sizing" campaign. At the end of the day, if OilQuest didn't make a major discovery soon, the love affair with Wall Street would be short lived.

"Do you really believe Mr. Keith intended to exclude me from the Project?" snapped David.

"He personally approved the tight hole status." responded Watson. "I'm the one who decides who sees, knows, or does anything with respect to Angel Falls. And right now, you are not authorized. So get the hell out of here before I call Security and have you dragged out of here on your ass."

"Just tell me this and I'll leave," said David. "Why all new people? Not one person connected with the project is on this floor."

"That's easy. Orders. Now get the hell out of here" roared Watson.

As David left the office and headed down the corridor, he could hear Watson bellowing through the speakerphone to his secretary:

"Get me Bealls. I need to tighten up the security on this floor. It's practically non-existent. Worse than a goddamned shopping mall in here!"

David smiled as he walked out through the security doors.

Orders, thought David. Whose orders? And why? It didn't make any sense to replace an entire technical team at such a critical stage in the operations. Even Watson knew that, so it couldn't have been his idea. It had to be someone above Watson, whoever he was reporting to.

David returned to his office to see the message light flashing on his phone. He punched in the access code to hear Lisa Voorhees voice on the other end asking David to stop by as soon as possible to discuss the funeral arrangements for Steve.

David knew this was merely a subterfuge. Lisa wouldn't handle funeral arrangements personally and she certainly wouldn't bother to phone David about it. His first inclination was to ignore it and go on about his business. Trouble was, there was no more business. His project had been pulled out from under him and he had no new assignment. Why was he being excluded now, at such a crucial time? For an instant he considered requesting a new assignment but just as instantly dropped the idea. He was going to see this through no matter where it took him. And there wasn't much to be gained by avoiding Lisa Voorhees. So he decided to take her on.

"Hello Lisa. I got your message about the funeral arrangements."

Lisa, working with head bowed at her desk, was startled at first but quickly regained her composure. The secretary stood at the doorway with a helpless look on her face and shrugged her shoulders as if to ask for instructions.

"It's okay, Rita. You can go back to work," quipped Lisa abruptly, showing irritation at her failed attempt to block David.

Turning to David, Lisa changed her facial expression to a feigned smile which must have pained her and said

"Hello David. Thanks for coming. Please sit down."

David took a seat in the plush wingback and moved to the offensive.

"Lisa. I'm sure whatever arrangements you have made for Steve are fine. I'm here because I really want to talk to you about the Angel Falls Project. Why has Rick Watson been assigned to head up the project and why isn't anyone from the old team, including myself, allowed to work on it anymore?"

This shook Lisa more than a little, as the smile faded quickly and she stood up from her desk. She was about to lash back with a quick retort but caught herself and stopped. Instead she walked over to the credenza near the window and poured herself a coffee. She took a sip and stared briefly out the window before responding slowly.

"David. I must confess to being a bit surprised. I would have thought you'd be more concerned about the death of a close friend than a project."

She is really good at this, thought David. However, lest she take the upper hand so quickly, David continued relentlessly.

"Please don't misunderstand. I feel deep grief over Steve. He was a good friend. But I also know that, as VP of Employee Relations, you are very capable of handling the funeral arrangements yourself, and I thank you for not troubling me with the details at a time like this."

David continued

"But I also know that this project was very important to Steve, and to me, and to OilQuest. It just doesn't make sense to jeopardize the whole operation by changing out the entire project team. The loss of continuity could make for some major mistakes. And I'm sure no one wants this project to succeed more than Mr. Keith."

David felt he had pulled out all the stops, especially by invoking Raymond Keith. He paused to take delight in his tactics.

The delight was short lived.

"David. Who do you think conceived of this whole idea? Who do you think brought in Rick Watson? It was Keith."

David was dumbfounded. This time it was Lisa who was wearing a smug look of satisfaction.

"But why?" was all David could muster.

Lisa was back in control.

"I don't know but I'm sure he has his reasons. And I'm sure those reasons are very good, even if he neglected to check with you first."

She could still be very nasty when she wanted and David was starting to get a taste of it. He wanted to grab her by her long slender throat and choke the life out of her, but elected instead to dig his nails into the upholstery.

"Now it's my turn to ask the questions," she said as she came from behind the desk and lowered her head until her face was but a few inches from David's. Her eyes were steely blue. Her black hair was pulled tightly back. David drank in her perfume while he felt her warm breath on his cheek.

"Why didn't you tell me about Steve's friend Mark?"

David took a second longer to gaze upon her face, wondering whether there might be a soft side to this woman. He had been prepared for such a question and had no trouble in responding.

"Because Lisa, Mark and Steve were lovers. I thought it best that it not become common knowledge. Steve wanted it that way to protect his job, Mark's job and their relationship. It was a private matter and had no impact on his work."

There was no harm in this statement, as David knew that Lisa already was aware, having called Mark yesterday.

"Tell me Lisa, how did you find out about Mark?" inquired David, hoping to catch her in a lie.

"We found his name and phone number in Steve's desk when we cleaned it out yesterday."

Gotcha, thought David, knowing that Steve was too careful for that and that his desk had been cleared for several days. But he decided to play along.

"Did you call Mark?" asked David innocently.

"Yes, to invite him to the funeral," Lisa stated blandly. "But more importantly, is there anyone else you forgot to tell us about?"

"That's all. I'm sorry for the deception," said David, attempting to sound sincere.

"No harm done," said Lisa, walking back to her desk.

"Anything else?" asked David, rising from his chair.

"All for now."

"Didn't you want to discuss the funeral arrangements?" David inquired, calling her on her own pretext.

"I'll have my secretary send you the details. Nothing for you to worry about." Lisa sat back down and began pouring over the papers on her desk, in effect dismissing David.

David walked to the door just as Peter Bealls came rushing in, startled to see David in the office.

"Doesn't anyone knock anymore!" exclaimed Lisa in an exasperated tone.

"You!" shouted Bealls, poking his index finger repeatedly into David's shoulder. "You caused a helluva commotion in the secured area. Watson was having a fit because of your little performance this morning. That area is off limits to you. Next time you pull a stunt like that, I'll get you fired." Bealls was red faced and shaking as he ranted.

David calmly replied "Just trying to help by pointing out a few of the short-comings in the system. Glad it got your attention." With that, David left the room. Bealls was still fuming in disbelief.

David returned to his office. He needed some time to sort things out. First was the fact that Lisa now knows that he didn't believe the story as to how Steve was killed. Second was why Raymond Keith set up a whole new team for the Angel Falls Project, and why go tighthole on the project to such an extreme?

Going tighthole usually meant confining information on a well or project to those who were directly involved. It was designed to minimize the chance of a leak to the competition. Such an action was certainly understandable for the Angel Falls Project, given its magnitude. To cordon off an area of the building and to restrict access was a bit extreme. But to completely displace the entire project team was unheard of. And to cut David out was particularly painful. This was his baby and Steve's. Besides, David had just wrapped up a publicity tour touting the environmental precautions taken by OilQuest in the Venezuelan rain forest. Surely his exclusion from the Project was merely an oversight, an administrative blunder that would soon be rectified.

But there were other elements to consider. The interrogation yesterday by Bealls and Lisa. Steve's death under very mysterious circumstances. The break-in at Steve's apartment. The phone call to Mallory about Steve's car. And Lisa Voorhees relentless quest to find out about Steve's friends.

Wait. Was it Steve's friends she wanted to know, or was it what Steve may have told them? After all, upon learning that Mark had not spoken recently to

Steve, Lisa ended the phone conversation. What was it Steve knew? Was it enough to get him killed? Is that what Lisa and Bealls wanted to find out? Or did they already know?

"I'm getting nowhere." David said to himself as he peered out the window at the omnipresent water tower that dotted the Plano landscape.

"I need answers. Not more questions."

David spent the remainder of the workday engrossed in thought. He accomplished little, barely making his was through the pile of correspondence that had accumulated during his absence.

His office was in slight disarray, owing in part to his habit of filing items by topic in various stacks around the office. This was compounded by the fact that the contents of his office that related to Angel Falls had been confiscated by Rick Watson.

As he gazed about his office, David realized how very thorough Watson had been. There wasn't even a shred of paper remaining that related to Angel Falls. "Nothing left. Not a trace," he murmured as he glanced about.

As David twirled about in his desk chair, his eyes fell on his computer on the credenza that wrapped around behind his desk. He brought his chair to an abrupt halt, pulled it toward the keyboard and switched on the computer. Within seconds it was operational, asking for his password. David typed in "ERMA" for Eric and Matt. He figured first names were way too commonplace, so a combination would be somewhat obscure while still allowing him to remember his own password, especially as he was away for weeks at a time.

The screen came to life.

Avoiding the desire to check his e-mail for messages, David began to call forth his data files related to Angel Falls. As he listed one after another, the words "no file name exists" came across the screen.

David then listed his entire file directory. He was astounded. All files related to Angel Falls were missing. All other files were intact.

Incredible, thought David. Someone took the time to painstakingly go through every file on my computer to remove anything related to the Project. Got to hand it to Watson, he is thorough.

Hold on a minute, he suddenly realized. Watson couldn't do this. At least not on his own authority. Bealls! Who else but the Chief of Security could get access from Data Services to ferret out my password? Good Lord, they've gone through a massive effort to obliterate any prior efforts related to this project.

David was both furious and impressed at the same time.

"These guys are good!" he exclaimed aloud.

David decided he needed to know more, and the answers could possibly be found in the project offices. Trouble was, he had just made things tougher on himself by has arrogance this morning. Not only would they rectify the security shortfalls, but they would also be keeping a special eye out for David. He wouldn't be able to waltz in there like before.

David was able to confirm his thoughts by taking a casual stroll up to the fourth floor. In the corridor leading to the entrance to the Project Team offices, an unarmed security officer sat at a desk. As people came and went, the guard would check the badges and log them in.

That didn't take long, thought David. Primitive in this day and age of hi-tech, but effective nonetheless.

David contemplated a daring nighttime raid on the offices. Problem was, even if he managed to access the area, the individual offices and workrooms were likely to be locked.

Tapping into their computers via the company network would no doubt be discovered as this gets tracked by the Data Services Group.

He contemplated sifting through their daily trash. Even though this idea had some merit, he decided to hold off for now. The trash is generally shredded, especially maps and data. This was a routine procedure throughout the company, and would surely be enforced by the Project Team.

Perhaps he could learn something from a search of Lisa Voorhees' or Peter Bealls' offices. Voorhees office, however, was way too exposed. Being a large corner suite on the ground floor located near the main entrance to the building. Even though the large picture windows of her office were tinted to reflect the rays of a scorching Texas sun, activity could still be viewed from the outside. And at night it would be even more obvious.

Bealls had been assigned a temporary office down the hall from Voorhees, as he was normally officed at the corporate headquarters in New Orleans. Although less conspicuous, this office could still be observed from too many directions, both inside and out. Besides, as Chief of Security, he would most likely take maximum precautions to safeguard any sensitive documents.

David felt he was at a dead-end. He sighed, gave up the chase for the time being and decided to do something constructive yet mindless. He began work on his expense account from his recent and rather extensive trip. As he spread the various receipts across the desk in a first pass attempt at sorting, he cast his eyes over the numerous hotel bills he had to clear. And it suddenly hit him. He knew a way to at least find out a little more about Bealls.

Being from out of town, Bealls had to be staying at a hotel. And since Plano had a pathetic dearth of good hotels, it would take but a few phone calls to locate the one where Bealls was staying. Once located, it shouldn't be too difficult to gain access to his room for a few minutes. And maybe Bealls was less cautious in his hotel room where he would not suspect a work-related intrusion.

David picked up the phone and began dialing for directory assistance for the number of the first hotel. After the third digit he paused as if he's changed his mind. He stopped dialing and slowly hung up the receiver. It occurred to him that his phone and room might have been bugged. He was tempted to dismantle the phone and search the room but he realized he probably wouldn't know a bug even if he found one, especially if it was in the midst of other electronic gear such as a phone or computer. Besides, he thought, it might be more useful if they thought he didn't know it was bugged. But before he tested this out, he needed to find out where Bealls was staying.

David left his office and walked downstairs to the cafeteria. It was a little late in the day, 4:00 p.m., but he wasn't interested in food. There wouldn't be many people about, other than cafeteria workers, so this was a good way to be sure he wasn't being followed. To make it look legitimate, he purchased a candy bar from one of the vending machines in the cafeteria. Nothing suspicious and no one had followed him.

On the way back to his office, David ducked into an empty conference room, making sure that no one was watching. He closed the door behind him. Picking up the phone in the conference room he dialed for directory assistance and obtained the phone numbers of the three top hotels in Plano. He dialed the first hotel.

"Courtyard by Marriott." Came the voice on the other end.

"I'd like to speak with Mr. Peter Bealls, please."

"One moment, please."

About 30 seconds passed before the voice returned.

"Would you spell that please?"

"B-E-A-L-L-S" David spelled out.

About 10 seconds later

"I'm sorry, there's no one by that name registered here."

"Thanks. Goodbye." And David hung up. He quickly dialed the next hotel.

"Omni Hotel. How may I help you?"

"I'd like to speak with Mr. Peter Bealls. His last name is spelled B-E-A-L-L-S."

"Thank you. Please wait."

A few seconds later David heard the phone re-connect to a room and start ringing.

"Bingo!" he whispered to himself.

After about ten or twelve rings, the hotel operator came back on the line.

"I'm sorry sir. There is no answer. Do you wish to leave a message?"

"Not at this time, thanks. Can you tell me what room Mr. Bealls is in?" inquired David.

"I'm sorry sir. We are not allowed to give out room information." Came the standard reply.

David thought fast

"Of course. I understand. Can you please give me his extension number so I can save time when I call back?"

"It's 88714."

"Thank you very much. Goodbye."

"Have a good day, sir."

David hung up the phone and smiled.

Perfect, he thought. It won't be easy, but it's doable.

David was somewhat intimate with the Omni. He and his family had stayed there for six weeks when they had first moved to Plano. And more recently he spent a week there as he was hosting a Venezuelan delegation to OilQuest and it required he stay at the hotel with them to make sure there were no problems.

David knew that extension 88714 simply referred to room 1714 on the 17th floor. The double eights merely represented the 10th floor or above. David also knew that Bealls was on one of the "Executive Floors" which maintained restricted access to the floor. One needed to insert their room key into a special slot in the elevator in order to access these floors.

One of the things that particularly irked David about this hotel was the laundry service. The laundry/dry cleaning would usually arrive around 9:00 p.m., just when David was showering or changing for bed. Now he finally found a way to make this little nuisance work for him.

David left the conference room and returned to his office.

At the very least, I'm going to know if this place is bugged, he thought as he picked up his phone and punched the autodial number for his house.

"Hello." Mallory's voice was soft and uplifting. David nearly forgot why he called.

"Hi sweetheart. Having a good day so far?"

"I'm glad you called. Everything is fine here. How was your day? Did you manage to find out anything more?"

"Excellent, thought David. She couldn't have done better if he had written a script.

David responded, "Well, I think I may be onto something, but I'll need to come back later tonight. I believe I can get some answers from the Project Offices, but it's a little awkward right now. Best I come back around eight or so, when there will be fewer inquiring minds."

"David," Mallory said in a concerned tone. "you're not doing anything dangerous, are you?"

"Of course not," he lied. "I just need a little privacy."

"Will you be home for dinner?"

"I'll be leaving momentarily. What's for supper?"

"Fettuccine Natasha for us. Fish sticks for the boys."

"I'm one my way. Love you."

"Love you too. Goodbye."

"Bye."

David placed the receiver down. "That should do nicely," he said to himself as he prepared to leave the office.

Dinner passed quickly that night as David had many preparations to undertake. Mallory quickly lined up a sitter for the boys, not an easy feat on such short notice. However, at twice the going rate, one of the usual sitters was more than willing.

At 7:30 p.m., David left the house, still dressed in his suit. He carried his briefcase and a computer carry bag, which was larger than a briefcase and a very typical accessory for many businessmen.

He backed his car out of the garage and into the alley behind his house. Looking about casually, he saw no one, and continued on down the alley which entered his street about 6 houses down from his. There were a few cars parked on the street and along a few of the circular drives in front of many of the houses. Nothing looked out of the ordinary but David rarely took notice of his neighbor's cars, so it was difficult to tell if a stranger was parked on the street.

David slowly turned the corner, checking his rearview mirror for headlights. Nothing. David wasn't sure whether he should be relieved or disappointed.

He made his way to the office in ten minutes. Even though it was quite dark, traffic was light and the stoplights were in his favor tonight. Still nothing obvious behind him.

As he drove along the road in front of the office, he could see that most of the offices were dark with the exception of a few lights, either a few dedicated souls working late, or the cleaning crew. David took particular care to notice that Lisa Voorhees and Peter Bealls offices were dark. He couldn't tell if any lights were on in the Project offices as that wing faced the rear of the building.

David pulled his car up to the entrance gate for the employee parking lot. During the day the gate was manned by a security guard. But at night, it went into fully electronic mode.

David rolled down his car window and inserted his badge into the key slot outside the guardrail. The entire parking lot was surrounded by an 8-foot cyclone fence that connected to the employee entrance to the building. A few well-placed security cameras covered the gate and panned the parking lot.

David removed his badge from the slot. After a few seconds, the cyclone gate slowly swung open. This was followed by the raising of the guardrail. The rail was only designed to keep cars from getting too close to the gate as it swung open.

He drove through and looked over his shoulder to see the gate and guard rail easing back toward the closed position. Once in the parking lot, David parked close to the employee entrance, got out, carrying his two pieces of luggage, and locked his car. He then walked to the entrance and inserted his badge into the final door lock and walked into the building. David knew that, even if the cameras hadn't observed him, he would at least be registered every time he put his badge in one of the slots. He had seen a printout once. It listed the badge number, employee name, and exact time of entry.

David casually made his way toward his own office, not bothering to be quiet. Instead, he acted much the same as if he was arriving for work in the morning. The corridor to his office was dimly lit for nighttime mode. He unlocked the door to his office, turned on the lights and walked over to his desk. He spent about 20 seconds rustling papers and moving loudly about the office. Peering out into the hallway, David quietly picked up his two cases and moved down the other end of the hall from which he came. This led to a rear corridor that ran parallel to the larger, main corridor that ran the length of the building along the front.

David quickly and quietly moved unseen along the rear corridor and entered a stairwell. Taking the stairs down to the first floor, he then cut across an intersecting hallway until he came out at the Visitor's entrance to the building. Unmanned after 6:00 p.m., the Visitor's entrance had two sets of locking doors about 30 feet apart for security. "The irony", thought David, "is that this system was designed to keep people from getting in, not from getting out."

To get out, all David had to do was press a button to the right of the doors and the electronic locking mechanism released temporarily. You didn't even need a badge. Therefore, no one knows when or if you leave the building, only when you arrived.

For all they know, David mused, I'm still in there somewhere.

He walked out into the cool dark night and into the Visitor's parking lot. This lot was ungated and easily accessible from the street. No surveillance cameras. Mallory's car pulled up in front of David and he got in.

"Everything's okay so far. Are the boys okay?"

"Yes", said Mallory nervously. "I left ten minutes after you and dropped them off at the sitter's house."

"Followed?"

"I don't think so."

"Good," David remarked, reaching for the cell phone. "Now let's see if Peter Bealls is home."

David dialed the Omni and asked for Room 1714. No answer. He was then able to confirm it was Bealls' room. Everything was proceeding according to plan. If David was right, Bealls was back at the office preparing to catch David in the act of breaking into the Project Team offices. David smirked as he pictured Bealls with his Gestapo security men waiting to pounce.

Mallory drove to the Omni Hotel, which was only about a five-minute drive from the office. She pulled into the parking lot. David got out, still carrying his tow cases.

"This should take about thirty minutes," he called to Mallory as he stepped out.

"For God's sake, David. Please be careful. Don't forget you have a wife and two kids to support," Mallory said in a halfhearted manner.

"Is that supposed to put this in perspective?" inquired David as he looked through the still open passenger door.

"We gave up perspective a long time ago. I'm just going for survival now," smiled Mallory.

"It's never far from my mind."

With that parting comment David closed the door and headed toward the entrance to the hotel. Phase two was about to be but into effect.

David entered the very familiar lobby. He walked over to a house phone and dialed Bealls' room one more time to confirm his absence. Then he walked over to the concierge desk. True to form, the day's cleaned laundry was stacked in boxes or on hangers next to the desk.

David spoke to the paunchy, middle aged man in the tired and poorly fitting uniform.

"Good evening. Anything for room 1714?"

"Let's see." said the concierge as he began to check the laundry bedside the desk.

After a brief moment.

"Ah yes. We have some shirts and some folded items for you. Here you are," and the concierge began to hand them to David.

David quickly responded "I'm afraid I can't manage that with what I'm already carrying." He raised his arms to show the briefcase and computer case. Then David put down the briefcase and pulled out an already prepared five dollar bill and handed it to the concierge, saying

"Tell you what. How about bringing the clothes up to my room in about 15 minutes. I want to retire early tonight."

"Certainly, sir," and the man gratefully accepted the money. "I'll be there in fifteen minutes. Sooner if you like."

"Fifteen minutes will be just fine," responded David, and he turned and headed for the elevators.

"That was the easy part," thought David as he punched the elevator button. He figured the odds were in his favor that there would be laundry for Bealls. And if there wasn't, David had a backup plan to have the concierge come up and pick up dirty laundry from the room. With a big enough tip, it would have worked.

When he got on the elevator, David looked at the floor buttons and confirmed that floor 17 was an executive level and required a room key to activate the button for the 17th floor. So he punched the button for the 16th floor.

Once on the 16th floor David had two options. He took the easiest one first, the stairs. He quickly found the exit sign and opened the door to the stairwell. He made sure the door would open from both sides before allowing it to close completely, then opened it again just to be sure. Once satisfied that he could return to the 16th floor, David made his way up the stairs to the door marked 17. David tried the door. No luck. It was locked on his side so that people could leave the 17th floor but not re-enter.

"Damn," David swore under his breath. "Looks like they thought this one through."

Quickly he turned and retraced his steps to the 16th floor. Once on 16, he walked around the hall until he came to the service entrance to the floor which was easy enough to locate as it had a set of wide double doors at its entrance.

Making sure there was no one around, David cracked open the double doors, peeked in, and then ducked in. At the other end of the room was a service elevator. David walked over and pushed the "up" button.

The elevator was agonizingly slow, but it eventually arrived. David stepped in and looked at the floor panel. He punched "17" and it lit up, with the doors closing slowly. David sighed in relief "Looks like they didn't think of everything after all."

Once on 17, he was fine. He looked like a businessman that belonged on the executive floor. He walked around the hall until he located room 1714. He listened briefly at the door for any sounds. David turned and followed the signs for ice and drinks. It was a straight shot at the end of the hall. He walked down to the ice room and entered the alcove. Now it was going to get tricky.

There was some movement down the hall and David waited until the people passed by the ice room. He busied himself by purchasing a soft drink and chips from the vending machines located adjacent to the icemaker. It had been about 10 minutes since he spoke with the concierge.

Poking his head into the hall, David made sure no one was coming. He then began to quickly undress. In less than a minute he was down to his briefs. Opening the computer case, David extracted a lightweight bathrobe. He slipped it on and quickly stuffed his clothes into the empty cases. Lifting the lid to the large plastic trash bin beside the vending machines, David gently placed the cases inside and replaced the lid.

He glanced around the corner of the ice room in the direction of room 1714. No one yet. As he ducked back into the room, a woman in her early thirties came around the corner from the other direction. They startled each other. She let out a brief "Oh," and stopped in her tracks, dropping the ice bucket that was in her hands.

Recovering quickly, David responded "I'm sorry if I startled you. I was just getting myself some snacks. Please forgive my attire. I didn't expect to meet anyone on the way." He smiled.

Regaining her composure, she returned the smile, saying "That's okay, but you gave me a bit of a start."

"Here, let me help you with the ice," said David, stalling for time as he waited for the concierge.

She gave him the ice bucket. David quickly filled it from the dispenser and returned it.

"There you go. Service with a smile."

She laughed said thanks and turned to leave.

As she left, David heard a knock on the door at the other end of the hall. It was the concierge at Bealls' room.

"It's show time," he whispered.

Grabbing the soda and chips David exited the ice room and headed down the hall toward the concierge.

As David approached the concierge who was knocking for a second time he called out.

"Boy, am I glad to see you. I stepped out for a soda and chips, and I clean forgot to take my key with me."

Sizing up the situation the concierge cheerfully replied, "No problem, sir. Can I have your name again please?"

"It's Bealls. Peter Bealls."

The man looked at the name on the laundry tag and gave a confirming nod. He then pulled his master key card from his vest pocket, opened the door, flicked on the light switch and stepped aside to allow David to enter first.

"Thank you so much," said David. "Please put the laundry in the closet."

The concierge followed David into the room and obligingly placed the laundry in the closet. He then turned to David, saying "Have a goodnight, sir," and walked out the door.

"Thanks again," replied David, as he followed him to the door, turning the master lock once he had closed the door.

"I'm in," he said in a whisper.

David scanned the room. It was a mini-suite, a bedroom with an adjoining sitting area. Slowly and systematically he started the search. He began with the sitting room, moved to the bedroom, bathroom and finally the closet.

There was no briefcase. Bealls must have it with him. David rummaged through all the drawers and the clothes in the closet. Nothing that gave him any clues. The clothes were off the rack, standard gray and blue suits as befitting a security man who wanted to blend in with his environment. Even the ties were nondescript, except for one. It was brightly colored with yellow, green, and orange floral patterns. David turned it over. The label read "Hecho en Venezuela" for "Made in Venezuela.

Curious, thought David. I didn't realize Bealls had been to Venezuela.

Aside from that David found nothing. He was exasperated. He sat on the bed, frustrated, and scanned the room one more time. His eyes came to rest on the movie placard on top of the TV that listed the pay movies presently available. He wondered how many adult movies Bealls has watched, or for that matter, how long he's been here."

And then it hit him. Video checkout, where you could review your statement and have the bill directly charge to your credit card. David grabbed the remote and turned on the TV. He raced through the menu that appeared and made the selection for reviewing the statement. There was a pause as the record was being automatically called up, and then the first page of Bealls' hotel charges lit the screen.

David noted that Bealls had checked in ten days ago. David began to page through the statement using the TV remote. Meals and laundry seemed normal. Bealls had also had his share of late night movies, most likely from the adult entertainment selection.

There were a number of phone calls, many long distances. David pulled the phone pad and pen off the desk and began copying down the phone numbers in a systematic fashion. He froze when he saw his home phone number appear on the list. It was yesterday, the same day that Mallory got the call about Steve's car. He kept writing numbers.

In case he missed any numbers, David quickly scanned back through the pages of the statement. On page three David stopped.

How unusual, he thought. There are three days of room charges only. No meals. No laundry. No phone calls. Not even a dirty movie. What happened?

David looked at his watch. It had been thirty minutes since he entered the hotel. No time for contemplating mysteries. It was time to get out. He copied the dates of the 3 days of room charges only alongside the list of phone numbers and turned off the TV.

He tore off the list, including a few blank pages in case Bealls was astute enough to lift the numbers from the indentations on the blank pages underneath. David had seen enough Sherlock Holmes episodes to know that trick went way back.

One last look around to be sure nothing was amiss, and he quietly opened the door, looked out to make sure no one was in the hall, and stepped out. He returned to the ice room and retrieved his cases from the trash bin.

Two minutes later he had changed back into his suit, stuffed the robe back into the computer case, and walked to the elevators. Once on an executive floor he wouldn't need a card key for the elevator down to the lobby.

As David passed through the lobby, he walked by the concierge who looked up in surprise.

"I forgot something," remarked David as he kept walking.

The concierge merely nodded.

Once outside, Mallory had kept watch from a distance. She pulled up to David and they sped off.

"Did you find anything?" she asked.

"I think so, but it may take a little sorting out. In the meantime, let's head back to the office."

By 9:00 p.m. they reached the visitor's entrance to OilQuest. David jumped out, leaving his cases with Mallory, now that they were no longer needed.

"I won't be far behind. See you at home." he said.

"Don't forget I have to pick up the kids."

"Right."

Mallory drove off as David approached the visitor's door. He pulled out his badge and ran it through the slot. Seconds later the outer doors unlatched. He repeated this for the second set of doors to gain entrance to the building.

"If they bother to check the computer printout tomorrow for visitor access, they'll realize I reentered the building," David figured.

"However, it won't make any difference because I'll have achieved what I set out to do. It will make them mad as hell to have been so easily duped."

David made his way back to his office. Still no one to be seen. He turned off his office lights, locked the door, and headed for the exit leading to the employee parking lot. As he went through the doors he turned his head and peered back into the dimly lit building. At the far end of the main corridor David could see three figures standing, facing in his direction. He could tell by the hats that two were security guards. The third figure resembled Bealls.

A smile swept across David's face as he got into his car and exited the employee parking lot.

"Sorry to disappoint you," David said to himself as he sped away.

Once home, Mallory and David busied themselves with getting Matt and Eric to bed. It was nearly 11:00 p.m. before they sat down to discuss the evening's outing.

Mallory fixed some tall drinks, a Tanqueray and tonic for herself, and a single malt, neat, for David.

"Well, what have we got so far?" she inquired.

David was pleased she used the word "we" implying she had bought into this adventure. He smiled. Mallory knowingly returned the smile.

"A few scraps. Not sure if it will add up to anything, but let's see where it takes us."

First, I have a list of phone calls Bealls make from the room."

"How did you get that?" Mallory interrupted.

"From the video checkout on his TV."

"Aren't you a clever boy!" she mocked.

"One of the numbers is ours."

Mallory's playfulness disappeared as she strove to make the connection.

David closed the loop for her. "Bealls called here yesterday, the same day you got the call about Steve's car. It was probably Bealls."

"He also made a number of calls to Venezuela, mostly Caracas. And there are some local calls, numbers I don't recognize."

"The odd thing I noticed about his account was the low level of activity for three days. Other than a room charge, there were no other charges at all. It's as though he really wasn't there."

"When was that?" asked Mallory.

"Last week sometime."

"When was Steve killed?" she persisted.

David jerked his head back as the implication sunk in. Mallory had been ahead of him on this one.

"Same time frame. Bealls could have easily been in Venezuela. He could have grabbed a flight out of Houston or connected through Miami." David had done this many times himself. And then the next piece of the puzzle came together.

"The TIE!" he exclaimed.

"The what?" Now it was Mallory's turn to follow.

"In his closet. Bealls had a god-awful tie that was made in Venezuela. I remember it because it was so out of character with the rest of his wardrobe. It must have been a gift or souvenir or something. At any rate, this means that Bealls has probably been to Venezuela, and coincident with Steve's death."

"Maybe he went down right after Steve was killed, in order to investigate the circumstances," Mallory interjected, lest David get too carried away with his line of reasoning.

David thought back to the discussion with Bealls and Voorhees. At the time, the exact day of Steve's death was not critical. Now it was, but he couldn't remember. Finally he responded.

"You may be right. I can't pin it down exactly. Except Bealls never said anything about going down to investigate. He only mentioned the police report and the U.S. Embassy investigation. Why keep his involvement a secret?"

"Perhaps he kept a low profile so as to minimize exposure to OilQuest."

Mallory was now playing devil's advocate.

"I still think the timing doesn't fit."

They sat in silence, sipping their drinks, running through the few shreds of clues. Then David reached for the phone. He picked up the list of phone numbers from Bealls' room and ran his finger slowly down the list. He noted a 1-800 number and started to dial it when Mallory broke in.

"David, it's the middle of the night. Don't you think it would be better to do this during the day? It might arouse suspicion at this hour."

"I agree, but this is an 800 number which may be operational 24 hours or have a recording. Either way I'll find out who Bealls was calling."

He finished dialing. The phone rang twice, followed by a recorded message that stated "Thank you for calling American Airlines. All our reservation agents are currently busy. Please remain on the line and you call will be answered shortly."

David hung up.

"It was American Airlines, and the call was made the day before the hotel charges flat lined. Looks as though Bealls took a trip. And my guess is one of these calls will verify he was in Venezuela."

"I'll do the calling tomorrow," Mallory volunteered.

"Be discrete."

"I always am. Now let's go to bed, discretely."

# CHAPTER 4

# *Day of Discovery*

## *DAY FOUR*

Despite the late hours and excitement of the previous night, David slept fitfully, waking at five a.m. Rather than wait for Mallory and the kids to rise, he set off for work by six.

He was confident that Mallory would ferret out any clues from the phone list, so he decided to prepare himself for the events of the day. It was likely that Bealls would question him about being in the office last night. However, as nothing transpired David could just feign ignorance. There was nothing they could prove or do. Same for Lisa Voorhees and Rick Watson, although a confrontation from somewhere could be expected. But exactly where, David wasn't sure.

Besides, he had one more avenue he wanted to pursue. It had come to him during the very brief and restless night. David just couldn't accept that every shred of information related to the Angel Falls Project had been confiscated and removed to the secured area. He also couldn't accept that the new Project Team was totally self-sufficient. He knew they needed their computers, but had already decided he wasn't skilled enough to penetrate the obscure world of Data Services without being discovered. It was in contemplating the computer approach that David hit upon his next scheme. It occurred to him that most explorationists and some engineers relied heavily on what used to be called the Drafting Department. Now, however, since the adaptation of computer aided design (CAD), the drafting group was now referred to as the "Graphics Technology Department". It was here that geologic maps and engineering blueprints would be plotted, enhanced, and distributed to the authors.

Watson and his team would require extensive use of the Graphics department, but it was highly unlikely Watson would create an entirely new department for his support. There wasn't enough time for starters. Equally significant, however, was that it would never occur to them that this area also needed to be secured. Graphics was a service, like maintenance and the mailroom. It was a highly specialized service, but a service nonetheless.

David unlocked the door to his office, opened up his briefcase and set it on the side of the desk in order to give it that lived in look before heading over to the Graphics department. He noticed his message light blinking on the phone but decided to ignore it for the time being. He flicked on his computer and pulled up his electronic mail—No messages. It wasn't all that long ago when the screen would have filled with 25-30 messages a day. Now, it was as though he didn't exist within the company.

Upset that this was the status, he left, walking down the hall to the coffee room. Being the first to arrive, David made the first pot. He doubled the amount of coffee per pot, having developed a taste for stronger coffee while in Venezuela. Taking a few sips, he then made his way back to his office. Normally he would have finished the coffee in a few minutes, but he deliberately left the unfinished drink on his desk. He wanted it to be obvious that he was at work. He spread a few papers on the desk to help with the illusion.

Even though it was still quite early, David knew that a few of the people who worked in Graphics would arrive by seven. David often met with them at this hour because it gave him a leg up on their work schedule for the day. He would also bring them donuts from time to time.

Nice bunch of hard working folks, David thought. Hate to deceive them but can't risk telling them what's going on and can't do what I need to do without going through them.

It pained him to take this approach with people he knew and liked.

Before heading over to Graphics, David decided to clear his phone message, if for no other reason than to stop the annoying blinking red light. There was only one message, and it was Peter Bealls.

"No surprise," David said under his breath. Bealls had called at six thirty a.m. to ask David to come down to his office as soon as he arrived for work.

"Damn! Doesn't that guy ever sleep!" David was more angry with himself for having taken the message. Regaining his composure, however, he responded negatively when the phone recording asked in a stiff, mechanical, female voice if he wanted to clear the message. By retaining the message, the light would keep flashing, giving at least the appearance that he never took the message to begin with.

Rather than remain in his office any longer and risk running into Bealls, David made his way over to the next wing where the Graphics department was housed. Since other early birds were beginning to arrive for work, David took great pains to avoid any encounters on his way to Graphics.

He entered the Graphics department and was pleased to see just a few workers present that he recognized. No other employees, and none of Watson's team were there. Timing was perfect.

As David glanced about, he couldn't help but be amazed at the impact of computer technology on this part of the business. Where there once used to be a dozen or more drafting tables with skilled artisans meticulously hand drawing maps and geologic cross sections, now there were only 2 drafting tables. And these had been relegated to the back of the room to be used to update the older maps that were still in use. In their place was a half-dozen computer workstations. By corporate decree, all designs were now done on the computer. It was faster, and changes could be made almost instantaneously. David saw and appreciated the benefits brought by the computer, but he also missed the artistic abilities and the personal touch of the draftsman. His reminiscing came to an end as he saw Emilio Ortiz heading toward him.

"Hola David," smiled Emilio as he extended his hand. "You have been a stranger. It's good to see you again. I was very sad to hear about Steve."

"Hola, mi amigo and gracias," said David as he warmly shook Emilio's hand. It has been awhile, but it's good to be back. How is everything going?"

"Busy as usual. But that's the way we like it. Otherwise, we're out of a job."

"There will always be work for you and your people," David replied sincerely.

Emilio smiled "I hope you are right."

Emilio was the Drafting Supervisor, now called the Director of Graphic Technology. He was one of the few who successfully make the transition from draftsman to computer technician. Not everyone could. Not everyone wanted to. But Emilio saw the future and he knew what he needed to do. From time to time, both David and Emilio would commiserate on the direction drafting had taken, but both knew that change was inevitable. Emilio had at least maintained a balance between old and new, taking the best from each. It was quite an accomplishment and he was proud of it and of his department.

"Emilio," said David. "I need to revise some of my Angel Falls maps. Can you or one of your people help me?"

"Of course, but I thought access to that project was restricted to Rick Watson's team."

Got to hand it to Watson, thought David. The guy doesn't skip a beat.

David quickly responded "It is restricted, but I'm cleared." David hated to lie to Emilio, and he knew his voice had faltered as he spoke.

Emilio paused for a moment, looking David right in the eye. Then he slowly moved his eyes over to the wall and up towards the ceiling.

David followed Emilio's eyes. Neither person moving their heads at all. Both sets of eyes came to rest on the security camera positioned on the far wall. Its wide-angle lens could capture almost the entire room.

Emilio allowed his gaze to return to David. Then he spoke.

"Mr. Watson left me a list of people allowed to work on the Angel Falls Project." Then he smiled knowingly and said "I seem to have misplaced the list, but I am almost certain your name was on it."

David nodded in deep gratitude.

"Let me help you with what you need," said Emilio.

"Thank you, my friend."

"De nada. Steve was my friend too."

Emilio led David to a workstation and turned it on. In a moment it was up and running. Emilio sat, hands on the keyboards, dual screens lit up while David stood, hunched over him.

"Where do you want to start?" Emilio inquired.

"Let's go to my last set of structure maps and see if there were any revisions."

Emilio stroked the keyboard and within seconds had retrieved a listing of the structure maps. The list was several pages long, since it was policy to retain the original map each time a new revision was made. Even for a very slight modification, the policy was the same. As they scanned the listing, the date of each revision also appeared on the screen.

Emilio spoke first.

"No changes made for two months, and the last revision was yours."

David nodded. At least no one had tampered with the basic structure maps.

"Let's look at the well file for the Angel Falls #1 well."

"Coming right up."

Once again, the screen filled with a directory of files.

"This one has seen some recent action," said Emilio. "And not by you."

David grew tense and peered over Emilio's shoulder.

"Open up the last 3 files."

"As you speak," Emilio was starting to enjoy the sleuthing.

David quickly scanned the first file. It was a redisplay of the well logs from the first well. He saw no changes to his interpretation of the logs.

"Nothing. Try the next one."

The same as the first.

"Nothing. Try the third file."

Nothing again. Although David wasn't sure what he was looking for, he knew it wasn't in these files. They were merely redisplays of previous files.

"Nothing again." David pulled up a chair and sat down beside Emilio. Looking frustrated he just sat and stared at the screen.

Emilio sensed his frustration. He looked at his friend for a brief moment, then smiled as he spoke.

"There are other files, you know."

David perked up. "Other files?"

"Yes, engineering files."

David closed his eyes for a few seconds. How could I have been so stupid! Of course there would be engineering files. Files for drilling, for well testing, for completion facilities, for the pipeline, for God knows whatever else engineers do. David, a geologist, had neglected to account for the engineering role in the Project. Instead, he was myopically focused on the geology.

"Thank you once again Emilio. Can you please list the engineering files for me?"

"Already did it while you were daydreaming."

Both smiled and returned their eyes to the screen.

"David, there are 327 files here. It will take all day to look at them. In twenty to thirty minutes, this office will start to fill up. And sometimes one or two of Rick Watson's people come in."

"I understand," David replied. Thinking quickly, he asked Emilio,

"Can you please print out the list of the files, along with dates and author? That would be a great help."

"Okay. It will take about five to ten minutes. Then I think we better stop there."

"Agreed."

Emilio set the printer in motion and within seven minutes, they had about twenty pages of engineering file listings. Emilio pulled them off the printer and spoke as he handed them to David.

"Via con Dios."

"Gracias," said David as he took the pages and left the room. The workday was just beginning for the rest of the company.

As David returned to his office, he was stunned to find Watson and Bealls waiting for him.

"Well gentlemen, what a pleasant surprise," beamed David as he circled around to his desk to face the two seated before him. As David sat in his desk chair he casually dropped the computer file printout into his open briefcase. As he closed the briefcase and moved it to the floor beside his desk, he said,

"Here, let me get this out of the way so we can have an unobstructed view of each other."

Bealls spoke first,

"I left you a phone message that I wanted to see you first thing this morning. Didn't you get it?"

David pivoted his chair so as to look at his phone, where the red light was still flashing.

"Guess not. At any rate, it's only eight o'clock so no harm done. Now, what can I do for you gentlemen?"

Watson was remarkably calm, given his highly volatile temperament, but Bealls was barely containing his rage.

Gripping his chair till his knuckles turned white Bealls glared and blurted out "We know you were here last night. Late last night. What were you doing?"

David feigned an innocent, injured look.

"Why, I was working of course. What else would I be doing?"

"That late?"

"I wouldn't call 8:00 p.m. late. And besides, I often work late, especially after a long business trip."

"What were you working on, specifically?"

Bealls inquired persistently.

"Mostly just getting caught up, going through my correspondence and e-mail, working on my expense account. The usual stuff."

Now it was time for David to go on the offensive.

"Why? Is something wrong? Did something happen while I was here last night?"

Watson smirked. He appeared to be enjoying this. Bealls, however, was not a happy camper. Neither spoke, so David persisted.

"Did something happen?"

Finally Bealls responded. "No. Nothing happened."

"Oh, thank God," David exclaimed as he put his hands to his heart in mock relief. "Since Rick is here I thought something might have happened to the Angel Falls Project."

Watson sneered. "No, nothing happened to the Project. And nothing will, at least not on my watch."

"Glad to hear that Rick," responded David. "I'm sure all of America can rest easy now."

Watson glared at David before leaning over the desk so that both were eyeball to eyeball and said, "Nothing will happen because I'd kill anyone who tried. Got my drift?"

"I'd say you've already drifted a little too far. Don't you think so, Bealls?"

Bealls got up and motioned to Watson.

"Let's go."

Then turning back to David he said "I'll be watching you very, very carefully."

"I feel safer already," quipped David as the two stormed out of his office.

Alone at last, David took a moment to reflect on the altercation.

I've got them rattled, but I still don't know why, he pondered. What could possibly be worth all this intrigue?

Unable to answer his own questions, David picked up the briefcase and extracted the computer printout from within. He ran his fingers down the list slowly trying to absorb the title of each file as well as each author and the date of entry. The titles sounded very appropriate for an engineering related project. There were files on development well patterns, facilities designs, processing plants, living quarters, power supply, pipelines, infrastructure, and communications. The authors were all from Watson's team.

And then his eyes fell upon a file listed only as "Option." It was authored by Watson himself.

There's that word again, thought David. I've got to find out what's on that file. But how?

The phone rang. At first David resisted picking up the receiver, but then realized by the ring that it was an outside call. Relieved that it wasn't an internal call, he finally answered.

"Hello."

"Hi Love, How's it going so far?" Mallory's soothing voice brought a sense of calm over David.

"Not too badly, seeing as how the day has only just begun. Had a nice chat with Rick Watson and Peter Bealls. Delightful chaps. Spirited conversationalists."

"I can imagine. Listen, the reason I called was to tell you that I've checked on a few of the phone numbers from the list. I think you'd be interested to know that Bealls…"

"Honey, I can't talk now. I have to go." David quickly interrupted. "I'll call you later."

Mallory was so startled the most she could muster was an "Oh, okay."

"Love you. Goodbye." Said David

"Love you too."

David put down the receiver and wondered if the conversation had been monitored. It was easily within Bealls' capabilities. And if that was the case, how much could he have gleaned from the few comments made by Mallory?

David walked out of his office and down the hall to an empty conference room. Closing the door behind him he walked to the phone that was sitting on a corner table and dialed his house. Mallory picked up quickly.

"Hello?"

"It's me, sweetheart; I didn't want to discuss this over my phone or in my office. I'm probably overreacting a bit, but why take chances?"

"I thought as much," said Mallory "which was why I was waiting by the phone for you to call back."

"What did you find out?" David asked impatiently.

"Well, began Mallory "Do you remember the 1-800 number call he made to American Airlines?"

"Yes, of course I remember."

"The very next number was a call to Caracas, specifically the Hilton Hotel. So I called the Hilton and pretended to be Peter Bealls' wife and that I needed to contact him immediately because of an illness in the family. The hotel informed me that he had already checked out on the 17th."

"You sure you haven't done this stuff before?" queried David.

"Positive. But I am kind of good at it."

David's jaw tightened. "The 17th was the day after Steve was killed."

"There's more," said Mallory.

"Go on."

"Bealls wasn't alone. The hotel volunteered that he was traveling with Rick Watson. And, one of the local numbers from the phone list is Watson's home phone. I called and got his answering machine. Bealls had called Watson several times earlier that week."

"Can't say that I'm surprised. Anything else?"

"A few other calls to Caracas, but when I called all I got was an 'Hola'. I then asked to speak with Peter Bealls in my pathetic Spanish. When I did that, the man at the other end demanded to know who I was, so I just hung up. On another number, the person hung up when I asked for Bealls."

"Good work. Still don't know why all of this is happening, but good work anyway."

Mallory sensed David's frustration on the other end.

"David, we may not have much, but the pieces do seem to be coming together."

"I know. But it's like putting together a jigsaw puzzle without first being able to look at the picture on the box."

"There's one more piece," Mallory continued the analogy.

"What's that?"

"Bealls called another local number several times, twice before he went to Caracas, and once the day he returned."

"Let me guess. Voorhees."

"You got it."

"Whatever is going on, it looks as though the three of them are in it together. Dangerous combination."

"David," Mallory spoke softly.

"Yes?"

"Be careful."

"I love you too. See you tonight."

"Don't forget I have soccer practice for both boys, so we don't get home till around 6:30, as I'll be taking them to McDonald's again."

"I'm afraid I've been away so much that I've forgotten your routine. See you when you get home. Bye."

"Bye."

David stood for a moment in the silence of the conference room, absorbing the finer details of the conversation with Mallory. As he went for the door he saw that it was slightly ajar, ever so slightly. He poked his head out the door but there was no one in sight.

"I'm sure I closed it." he grimaced to himself as he walked back to his office.

He entered his office and sat in his swivel chair, back to his desk, and stared out the window. A few minutes passed in deep reflection before he turned around to face his desk. His mouth gaped open and his eyes bulged in disbelief. They were gone! The list of computer files was gone. In the ten minutes he was in the conference room, someone had stolen the list. Possibly the same person who followed him to the conference room and listened in on his call to Mallory.

"This is terrible," David groaned to himself. "Not only do they have the list, but they can nail me for having possessed it. And they can crucify Emilio for helping me out."

David started to call Emilio's extension to warn him but checked himself before picking up the phone. Instead, he headed out the door back towards the Graphics Department. As he rounded the final corner to enter Graphics, he saw that he was already too late. He stepped back around the corner and peered back into the office. From this limited vantage point David could only view a narrow slice of the room, but it was enough. One of the security officers was talking to Emilio. David could see Emilio shrug his shoulders from time to time while shaking his head from left to right. Even from where David was standing, he could see that Emilio was playing dumb.

Finally the security guard beckoned for Emilio to follow him. Together they headed out of the room. David quickly jumped into the nearby men's room to avoid being seen Poor Emilio, he thought. I got him into this mess and there's nothing I can do for him. But, he's fast on his feet so I hope he can talk his way out of this. After all, I was a big part of the project so maybe he can just feign ignorance or forgetfulness.

David returned to his office, still in anguish over Emilio's situation. Even through the tint of his window, the grayness of the day pervaded the room. The familiarity of his office with his belongings brought him no solace. For the first time since this whole ordeal had started, David felt alone. In despair, he collapsed into his chair and slowly pivoted it in half circles. While he had learned a great deal in the last two days, he was still looking for a reason, a purpose to all the suspicious activity. Yet ha saw none, and the moments turned to hours in the impenetrable haze that enveloped him.

At lunch, David headed for the employee cafeteria to get a sandwich. After selecting his favorite turkey and Swiss on whole wheat, and a diet cola, he paid the cashier and started to leave. Normally he would have taken his lunch back to his office, as he preferred to eat in solitude. However, he noticed Watson sitting at a table with Bealls. The two of them were alone, in a corner. The very manner of their discussions, seemingly intent, acted to ward off uninvited guests. David stared at them for a moment, contemplating his next move. He really wanted to just go back to his office and quietly eat his turkey sandwich. But he also realized he was quickly approaching a dead end. He was running out of options.

Options, thought David.

Then he walked slowly and deliberately across the cafeteria, past the tables where people were happily engaged in lively conversations with their fellow colleagues, oblivious to the drama that was unfolding. Out of the corner of his eye, David caught a glimpse of Lisa Voorhees sitting at another table with members of her own department. She had stopped talking, her eyes fixed on David and they followed him as he made his way over to the table in the corner.

Watson and Bealls were so engrossed in conversation that they didn't even notice David until he was right on top of them. They looked up just as David arrived and placed his drink and sandwich on their table. Then he drew up a chair and sat down.

Watson and Bealls stared in disbelief. David began first. "Afternoon gentlemen." Then he slowly unfolded the sandwich wrapping, making himself comfortable at the table.

"I'll say one thing for you, Hastings," Watson said with teeth clinched. "You've got balls, steel ones at that."

"I know. Raises hell with metal detectors at the airport," replied David in continuing with the theme.

Bealls finally broke in. "I'm surprised you still have balls with the stunts you've pulled lately."

Ignoring the last remark, David took a bite of his sandwich and leaned back in his chair. From there he noticed that Voorhees was still watching from her table, although she would engage her table mates from time to time so as not to appear obvious. David swallowed his food and took a long drink before firing the next salvo, this one directed squarely at Watson.

"You know Rick, I've been wondering. The last few days I keep running across reference after reference. While some of the information has been highly revealing," David lied, "I was hoping you might be able to fill in the gaps."

"What in god's name are you rambling on about." Rick was starting to get irritated. Bealls looked on with concern.

David finally dropped the bombshell.

"Why, the Angel Falls Option, of course. What else would I be talking about?"

Watson was stunned. Bealls' eyes bulged. They looked around to see if anyone was within earshot. David noticed that Lisa Voorhees had sensed the heightened intensity and was watching closely.

Watson was the first to react. He pointed his table knife at David in a threatening gesture, leaning forward, voice raised.

"Listen, you asshole, I'm tired of playing word games with you. You stay out of my business or I'll make it my business to get you out, permanently. Do you understand or do I have to carve it into your forehead with this knife?"

"No need to twist off, Rick. Just wanted to discuss this in a professional manner, but I can see that's out of the question with you. Probably because you're not a professional."

Watson was out of his chair on that last remark, knife still in his hand. Heads were beginning to turn in the cafeteria. Bealls held up his hand to Watson, motioning for him to sit down. Watson stood his ground for awhile longer before complying. Bealls turned toward David with a cold look and inquired,

"What do you know about the Option? I want you to tell me everything. And just to add a little incentive, we just fired Emilio for that little episode this morning—you could be next."

David's heart sunk. Emilio was over fifty. It would be close to impossible for him to find work. Plus, he had a large family to support.

All this happened because he helped me, thought David. Then he pondered his own fate, wishing he had gone with his initial desire to eat lunch in his office. Still, he had obviously struck a nerve. His anguish for Emilio gave way to anger, and his concern over his own career vanished. Turning to face Bealls, he leaned toward him and went for the jugular.

"Tell you what I think, Bealls. I think Steve Giles knew something. And that knowledge cost him his life."

Bealls froze, eyes wide, speechless. David continued.

"And, I think you and Watson had something to do with it. Steve's dead because of the two of you."

Although Bealls was frozen to the spot, Watson exploded. He jumped up and grabbed David by the throat, pulling him down onto the table. Watson was a powerful man and he pinned David face down against the table, gradually squeezing the life out of him. Although quite athletic himself, David was no match for Watson. His face turned red and he could feel himself on the verge of losing consciousness. He flailed about with his hands but, being pinned face down, his wild punches fell far short of their mark.

Bealls had completely backed away from the table and was staring in disbelief, as were most of the people in the cafeteria. Except for Lisa Voorhees. She had been watching the incident with great intent, and at the first sign of violence, she commandeered the people at her table and made straight for the two combatants. Pushing Bealls out of the way, she ran up to Watson and grabbed him by the tie, yanking him down to her face and shouted.

"Rick, let him go. Now!"

As she shouted, several of her colleagues had grabbed Watson and began pulling him off David. Even with all this, it was another few seconds, a lifetime to David, before Watson released his grip on David's throat.

David slid off the table and slumped to the floor. It took him a moment to get his breath back and regain his composure. A few onlookers helped him to his feet.

As he rose, Lisa was barking out orders like a marine drill sergeant.

"Rick, I want you in my office in ten minutes. Peter, you'd better come too."

Then she turned to David in disgust.

"Mr. Hastings, you go down to the nurse's office and get checked out."

"I'm okay," David responded hoarsely.

Lisa glared, "I wasn't asking."

"Okay."

As David turned and started to walk away, he heard Bealls say to Lisa,

"He knows."

"Shut-up," she snapped.

David visited the nurse, who released him after casting a dubious glance at his story of the re-enactment of a hockey game with his office pals. David felt it best not to report the incident as it actually happened. It would be his word against Bealls and Watson. The outcome was predictable.

He spent the remainder of the afternoon in his office, fully expecting to be called on the carpet by Voorhees. Yet no call came. By quitting time, David had surmised that they couldn't nail David without implicating Watson. After all, the cafeteria was loaded with witnesses. Watson was clearly the heavy in the picture. They would probably let the incident itself go unpunished, but there was no question in David's mind that there would be some indirect form of retribution. He had definitely and intentionally pried open the lid on something highly sensitive, and there would be no putting the lid back on as if nothing had happened.

He had succeeded in planting the notion that he knew more than he actually did. If they would fire Emilio just for helping him with the computer search, he figured they would have something far more elaborate planned for him. After all, they could have fired him already if they wanted to. OilQuest was terminating people all the time, weeding out the politically incorrect by means of "right sizing" the company. David speculated that, because of his recent high profile both within the company and, perhaps more importantly, with the public, that a termination might raise some very pointed questions.

At any rate, David had pretty much played his last card. The next move was up to the triumvirate from hell.

He left the office exactly at 5:00 p.m., not wanting to spend another minute more than he absolutely had to. This was unusual for David, as he had a reputation for putting in long hours. At this point, however, he had no reason for the long hours since he was off the project. And he had yet to be assigned to another project. This left him with little more than the public relations work he was doing with regard to the Angel Falls project. Apart from his last lengthy trip, all that there was for now was some correspondence from environmental groups, other public interest organizations, and some industry related engagements. David knew that even this aspect of the job would eventually be transferred to someone else. It would only be a matter of time. Then, he figured, when he was no longer in the limelight, he would either be pushed out or aside. No one would notice, and no one would care.

This last thought saddened him as he drove the monotonous route home from the office. Coupled with the fact that Mallory and the boys would not be home for another hour, David was in no particular hurry. He thought about linking up with them at soccer practice but couldn't remember which field they were at. It had been that long. Instead, he drove the speed limit in a trance like state, to the irritation of other drivers more anxious to arrive home for the day.

Although nightfall was not for another hour, the gray, autumn sky cast a dusky pall as David turned into his neighborhood. He was contemplating a healthy glass of Bushmills Single Malt before Mallory and the boys returned from soccer practice. It was cool enough for a fire, so David could already envision the fire, the scotch, and the stillness. A chance to reflect on the events of the day.

David pulled into the narrow, one lane, alley behind his street in order to access the garage. His house, with garage facing the alley, was nearly halfway down. Wooden stockade fences, eight feet high, broken only by garage driveways, formed the walls to the alley. The stockade, or "privacy" fences, as people liked to call them, had the notable affect of making the postage stamp lots seem even smaller. And yet, without them, there would be no privacy whatsoever. In this way, people could come and go without ever being seen by one's neighbor. In fact, most neighbors only see each other if they happened to be mowing their respective front lawns at the same time, and that was only if they didn't subscribe to a lawn service.

As David slowly made his way down the alley, he noticed a dark sedan at the other end. Despite the tinted glass, David could see a man in the driver's seat. He didn't recognize the car or the driver, but he didn't give it much thought. He only knew half his neighbors. Besides, it was common courtesy for a car in the alley to stop in order to allow an oncoming car to access their garage. David had done this himself countless times.

Upon reaching his driveway, which was only about twenty feet in length, David turned in and pressed the automatic garage door opener. It responded, albeit slowly. He reminded himself, as he had numerous times before, to grease the door tracks. While waiting for the door to fully open, for what seemed like an eternity, he casually glanced around. The driveway, like all others, was also bordered by a high privacy fence. A wooden gate on the right side provided access from the backyard to the driveway. David noticed the gate was slightly ajar, just a few inches. This was unusual since he and Mallory made it a point to keep the gate locked from the inside for security reasons.

Plano had, in recent times, experienced a rash of robberies where the criminal would lie in wait for a victim to drive into their garage. The perpetrator would hide behind landscaping or a fence until the victim, returning home, opened the garage door and drove inside. Before the garage door would close, the thief would rush in and confront the victim, who was usually a housewife, very often with children. Threatened with bodily harm by knife or at gunpoint, the victim was then robbed. The robber easily escaped down the alley, unseen by any neighbor with the aid of the privacy fences.

In many cases, the victim was stabbed or shot if they offered any resistance whatsoever. In some instances, the robber had killed simply to avoid detection. It was particularly tragic where children were involved. The frequency of such incidents had subsided in recent months, due largely to increased awareness and stepped up neighborhood crime watch groups. The Plano police had beefed up patrols in the targeted, more affluent, neighborhoods. But as most of Plano was affluent, the police could not monitor every single alley.

David's gaze on the open gate was broken by the loud click as the garage door fully opened and the drive mechanism came to an abrupt halt. He slowly began to pull into the garage. The car was fully in the garage and David was shifting into park when he detected a movement in his rearview mirror. He turned to his left and looked over his shoulders in time to see a short, Latino looking man bearing down on him. The man was pulling a handgun out of his jacket as he approached the driver's side of the car.

David let out a panicked cry as he immediately understood the peril he was in. For a brief second his body nearly went limp as fear began to paralyze him from the legs up. The car was still running as the man reached the driver's door. He grasped the handle but the door was still locked. For an instant, David stared into the man's eyes. They were the lifeless eyes of a killer. The man dropped his hold on the door with one hand and slowly raised his gun outside David's window until it was level with David's face. David saw the menacing black barrel with a silencer just a few feet from his face.

As he stared, his hands and feet reacted instantly. He shifted into reverse while flooring the accelerator. The car leapt to attention and shot out the garage. At the same time David dropped his head and jerked the steering wheel to the right. The man with the gun squeezed off two rounds through the driver's window where David's head had been a split second before.

As the killer lowered his sights to fire again, David put the car in drive and the car jerked to the left, slamming the man into the wall of the garage. The gun dropped from his hand as he slumped across the hood of the car. David lifted his head above the level of the dashboard to survey the carnage. The man was not moving, and David wondered if he was dead, having been crushed between the car and the wall.

He didn't have long to assess the situation when he heard a car break to a squealing halt in the alley at the end of the driveway. David glanced over the seat to see the same dark gray sedan that was parked at the end of the alley. The danger was far from over. Oh god! The killer had a partner. David gathered his wits and quickly considered his options. The sedan, a Lincoln Town Car, was big and blocked off the driveway's entrance to the alley. David knew he could not get by it with his car. He contemplated ramming it in reverse, but his Taurus would probably come up the loser. And to what end? He would only hit the passenger side.

His thoughts then turned to the house. He could seek refuge there. He could even activate the alarm. Hell, he could even run out through the front door if he was still being pursued.

There was no time to consider any other options, as the driver of the sedan got out and walked around the car and faced the garage. He was a tall, slightly built, white man in his mid forties. Impeccably dressed in a custom fitted navy blue suit. David thought he could fit in any boardroom in corporate America. That is, with the exception of the Uzi he was pointing in David's direction. This got David's immediate attention.

"It's now or never," David gritted his teeth and kicked open the driver's side door in preparation for his leap to the door from the garage into the house. When the door flung open, the man opened up with his Uzi. The door was peppered with 9mm bullets as he continued his assault on the car. The rear window shattered, showering glass over David as he crouched low in the front seat. Bullets whizzed everywhere as the assassin swept up and down the Taurus. Even the first killer was hit by the strafing, but the second man didn't give it a passing thought. As there was no silencer on this gun, the shots echoed up and down the alley. David hoped this would arouse the neighbors. But knew he couldn't rely on them. Not when seconds counted.

The shooting came to an abrupt halt as the killer emptied the gun. An eerie silence hung in the air. Then David could hear him pulling the empty clip from the gun.

"Oh my God! He's reloading."

Without another thought David slid out through the open, bullet-ridden door and climbed over the first man and onto the hood. He had been shot several times but had hardly bled. Obviously, he was already dead from the car crushing.

David slid off the hood of the car and began to race the few feet to the door of the house. As he reached the door he could hear the second killer ram the new ammo clip into the Uzi and slide the first 9mm round into the chamber. David grabbed the doorknob, all the time saying to himself "I can make it," and he turned the knob. But the knob wouldn't turn. It was locked. In fact, it was always locked. David just happened to forget this little item in all the excitement. Worse yet, the keys were in the car.

David turned to see the assassin raise the Uzi to chest level in preparation for firing. He was about 40 feet from David, who was exposed from the chest up. The man began to walk towards David as he opened up. David dove to the garage floor in front of his car. The shooting continued for a few more seconds and then stopped. Judging from how long it took to fire off the first clip David knew the killer was not out of ammo yet. From his position on the garage floor, he could look out under his car to the driveway. The killer was slowly, cautiously approaching the garage. Rather than walking directly up to the garage, he moved from side to side to check if David was on either side of the car. As David followed this with his eyes, barely breathing, his heart was pounding madly. He felt his heart alone would give him away. When the killer shifted to David's left to check down the passenger side of the car, David's eyes caught sight of the handgun from the first assassin. It lay a few feet from the car on the passenger side, about six feet from David.

The man with the Uzi was now only 25 feet away. He had stopped moving. Then David saw him bend down to look under the car. Their eyes met for an instant. Then David rolled to his left toward the gun. The killer tried to fire under the Taurus, but the angle of the driveway and the wheels of the car kept him from getting a clean shot at David.

David reached the gun just as the killer stood back up. The man realized what David was doing and stood up to move in for a clear shot. David also saw him coming and rolled back behind the front of the car as the man reached the right rear of the Taurus.

Hoping there was still plenty of bullets left in the handgun, David rose to his knees, steadied the gun on the hood of the car, and shot through the rear window. He squeezed off 3 rounds in rapid fashion. The first two hit their mark, spinning the killer around and dropping him to his knees with a loud, pained grunt. The Uzi discharged as he was hit, firing wildly around the garage. And then all was quiet.

David could hear a police siren in the distance. He wanted to just jump up and run out of the garage. But he didn't know if the attacker was alive. The rear wheel partially obscured his view as he peered under the car. He could tell, however, that the man was still on his knees. The Uzi was nowhere in sight, and David had to presume it was still in his hands.

Should he expose himself or wait? David opted to wait for the police as the sirens grew louder. He settled himself on the floor, with gun aimed under the car in the direction of the killer, just in case he made a move.

Then he heard a familiar sound that brought terror to every fiber of his being. It was Mallory's Volvo, in the alley. She had stopped in front of the killer's Lincoln, unable to get past. He heard the familiar honk of her horn. Then to his utmost despair, he heard a car door open. Someone began to run up the alley towards the driveway. From the steps, David knew it was one of the boys. Then he heard "Daddy, Daddy." And David knew it was Eric, the youngest. From under the car, David could now see Eric's small feet as he appeared at the foot of the driveway and approached the garage. A grunt emanated from the other side of the car.

Without another thought, David rolled to his left, out from the protective cover of the car. As he pitched to a stop, he was in clear view of the killer whose back was turned. The man had turned his gun sights on Eric.

David screamed "No" as he unloaded the gun into the back of the assassin. The first few shots sent the killer sprawling back out into the driveway, coming to rest at Eric's feet

Eric stood motionless, paralyzed from fear. Mallory was out of the car, racing up the driveway to Eric as David slowly emerged from the garage. Matt was still in the car, at Mallory's command.

Mallory scooped up Eric in her arms, both sobbing, Eric hysterically. David walked up to them, gun still in hand but lowered now. He was speechless. All he could do was hold them both. Tears welled up in his eyes as he squeezed them tightly, eyes shut. Matt finally emerged from the car and joined in, even though he didn't know what was going on. Just the sight of everyone hugging and crying made him want to join in.

The sirens grew louder as the Plano Police converged on the alley. Neighbors followed. It was going to be a long night.

The first police officers on the scene had their guns drawn, on David. After all, he did have a gun in his hand. Despite pleas from Mallory, kids, and neighbors, David was still handcuffed until a senior officer arrived on the scene. After taking some preliminary statements, David was finally uncuffed and treated for the multiple cuts he received from rolling around in the broken glass.

The bodies were photographed and eventually removed. David also went to the police station to provide a more detailed statement. At the station, David spoke once again with senior officer who had him uncuffed at the scene, Lieutenant Jacobson.

"Lieutenant, I've never had anything like this happen to me before. Is this how these usually go?"

"How do you mean?" The lieutenant looked puzzled.

"Well, has this been happening a lot lately?"

"Not as much as last year. It's trailed off quite a bit."

David persisted, unsatisfied with the response.

"Was this typical of how these assaults or robberies usually occur?"

The Lieutenant threw back his head so as to indicate he finally caught the gist of the conversation.

"Oh. I see where you're heading. Well, to tell you the truth, this one was a little unusual...."

Then he checked himself and said "No, it was more than a little unusual. It was a lot unusual."

"How so?" David felt he was finally making progress.

"For starters," Jacobson began, "these guys were well equipped. The average garage bandit doesn't get Uzis and silencers off the back of a truck. And these guys! They were definitely in a class of their own. The tall one with the Uzi was wearing a $1200 suit and about $2000 worth of jewelry."

"So, you're telling me these guys are not your run of the mill crooks?"

"You have definitely been assaulted by the cream of the crop," mused Jacobson. "But there's more."

"Please go on."

"These boys aren't from around here. Most of these assaults are local boys, usually carrying knives."

"What do you mean? Where are they from?"

"Don't know. They had forged driver's licenses, and no other IDs. They were also carrying a wad of cash with them, over $20,000. The car was a rental. And the guns had their serial numbers filed off."

David grew concerned. Although he was already overly exhausted from the ordeal, his apprehension over what he was hearing was giving him an adrenaline surge.

"Lieutenant, are you telling me that this was a professional job? That their intent was not to rob, but to kill?"

"Looks that way. Any reason someone might want to do you or your family in?"

"My family?" David was aghast.

"Yes, Your wife and kids could have arrived home first, couldn't they?"

"Oh my God." David fell back into his chair, overwhelmed by the complexity and occurrences of the past few days.

"What?" Is there someone who would want you or your wife dead?"

David paused for a brief moment. He could see the Lieutenant eyeing him suspiciously. Although David wanted to tell him about Steve Giles and what had transpired at the office, it was impossible to connect it with the shootings. It seemed far fetched, or just too complicated. Right now all David wanted to do was to go home and check on Mallory, Matt and Eric.

Finally he responded "Can't think of anyone offhand."

Upon seeing that this did not seem to satisfy the Lieutenant, David continued.

"If I can think of someone or something I'll let you know. I'm kind of tired. Is it okay for me to go now?"

The Lieutenant sighed and said "Sure. We'll have one of our officers take you home. But if you think of something, please give me a call."

"Thanks, I will."

"One more thing."

"What's that?"

"This may not be over. They may try again. So be careful. Especially with your kids."

"I understand."

"I certainly hope so. Your lives may depend on it. Goodbye Mr. Hastings."

"Thanks again," said David, shaking hands.

David arrived home around 11:00 p.m. Mallory was waiting as he walked in the door. Without saying a word, they held each other in a tight embrace for a prolonged moment. Finally David spoke.

"Boys asleep?"

"Yes, they went to bed late though. They just had to call their friends and tell them about all the excitement."

"Are they okay?"

"Eric had a real scare. It might give him nightmares. Not sure about Matt. David, they're only seven and nine years old. Who knows if this will leave scars?"

"I understand. We'll need to be extra sensitive to them over the next few days. Help them work through this.

"I'm going to meet with the principal and their teachers tomorrow. Just to put them on the alert to any abnormal behavior."

"Good thinking sweetheart. Might have known you'd be on top of this already."

"Not entirely, David."

They were still embraced, only David now pulled his head back to look Mallory in the eyes.

"What do you mean?" he inquired.

"David, I'm scared. I almost lost you and Eric tonight. You killed two people. How would you expect me to feel?"

"I know. It scared me too. But, we're okay and its over." David tried to soothe her.

"But it's not over, is it?" Mallory demanded.

"Of course it's over, honey. Those guys are both dead. They are never going to harm us again. And I doubt if anyone else would try to rob this house after tonight."

Mallory grew stern. Her eyes turned a steely gray. David could see the storm clouds rising.

"Don't patronize me, David. Those guys weren't here to rob. They wanted you dead. Didn't the police tell you that?"

David was on the defensive. "Well, not in so many words. By the way, why did you get home so early? I didn't expect you for another hour."

The diversion didn't work.

"Soccer practice let out a little early, so we decided to skip McDonalds and come home so we could all have dinner together. Now, what did the police tell you?"

"They told me to be careful," David said in an exasperated tone. Then he continued. "Honey, I'm awfully tired. I'd really like to take a hot shower and go to bed. Can we continue this tomorrow? Please?"

Mallory looked at her husband, tired and dirty, dried blood on his face and arms, And she softened. Poor David, she thought to herself. He must be exhausted. Two people are dead. He was shot at, cut up, hand cuffed and interrogated. Maybe he needs a little attention.

"Pour yourself a drink. I'll start your shower while you undress," she said softly.

"Sounds wonderful. Only thing missing is you" he smiled warmly and kissed her gently on the lips. "Come shower with me. I need you close."

"Are you sure you're up to this?" she returned the kiss. Only more passionately.

"Be gentle with me. I've had a tough day."

"Maybe." And she reached to unbuckle his belt.

# CHAPTER 5

# *A Plan Evolves*

## *DAY FIVE*

Morning came quickly for the Hastings. Despite, or perhaps because of the trauma of the night before the entire family slept soundly, with one exception. David relived the scene with Eric running up the driveway and the killer turning his sights on him. Just as he was emptying the handgun into the killer's back, David bolted upright in bed Catching his breath, he looked over at Mallory. She stirred briefly in her sleep. He looked lovingly at her, knowing that it was no longer safe for them in Plano. But where would they be safe? He got up and walked upstairs to the boys' bedrooms. They were both fast asleep, clutching their favorite stuffed animal. While conducting another perimeter check on the house, he glanced out the front through the leaded glass panels on the side of the front doors and saw a Plano police cruiser parked across the street.

"Thanks, Lieutenant," David whispered, and he went back to bed.

At breakfast the boys peppered David with questions about the incident as well as what transpired at the police station. David tried to keep it vague and non-threatening but the boys persisted in wanting to know every detail. This was interrupted repeatedly by phone calls from the local media, wanting the inside scoop on the matter. Mallory finally took the phone off the hook. Reporters were beginning to camp out in the front yard.

As the boys got ready for school. Mallory and David sat on the family room sofa to enjoy a cup of coffee. This was a habit, or tradition, they had started quite by happenstance. Yet they both so enjoyed the few moments together at the start of the day that it just continued. In fact, both missed it when David was on the road.

Sipping their coffee, sitting beside each other, Mallory was the first to speak. "We need a plan."

David cast a puzzled glance at her and replied "What do you mean?"

"We can't just pretend nothing happened. Nor can we assume it was an isolated, one time incident. I believe it is connected to Steve's death. Don't you?"

David wondered if her last question was rhetorical, but decided to respond to it anyway.

"I know it is terribly coincidental, but I can't make the connection. However, I do agree that we shouldn't take any chances. That police car can't say out there forever. And they can't protect all four of us all of the time."

"I think we should go away for awhile," said Mallory.

David took a long, slow sip from his coffee mug, absorbing the impact of Mallory's last comment. He could tell from her tone that she had already made up her mind. Changing it was no simple feat.

"I agree," said David.

Mallory was stunned. She didn't expect to win this one without a struggle. David continued.

"I agree that you and the boys should go. But I should remain. Otherwise, the problem could follow us."

Mallory was torn. Privately, she felt he was right. Yet she didn't want to split up. They were a team, and a good one at that. She felt he needed her, and he did. But so did the boys.

"David," she protested, "we are a family and we need to stay together."

"Honey, I feel the same way. But it's the family I'm thinking of. You saw what might have happened to Eric yesterday. I could never have forgiven myself. We need to get the boys to safety and you're the best person to do it."

She said nothing but looked away, and then slowly nodded her head in agreement. Just as the boys came bounding in, ready for the ride to school.

David accompanied Mallory and the boys to school, since his car was all shot up and had been confiscated for evidence. The meeting with the principal went well. Since the story had already been broadcast on the late night news, the Hastings were instant celebrities. Matt and Eric were immediately surrounded by a horde of students who eagerly listened as the boys recanted yesterday's harrowing experience. As David and Mallory spoke with the principal Mallory would often cast a concerned glance at her boys in the playground.

Assured that the boys would be looked after while at school, Mallory and David left.

While driving David to a car rental in Plano, Mallory spoke, worry lines still etched on her forehead.

"David, do you think they'll be okay?"

"For today, yes, but you may want to be there early in the afternoon to pick them up. Now we need to make arrangements to get you and the boys somewhere safe. I think we should leave the relatives out of this. It seems too obvious and too easy to track."

"I'm with you so far. No relatives. Then who?"

"I think Helene would help."

"Helene!" Mallory exclaimed. "You mean you want me to take the kids to Weekapaug now?"

"Yes," said David matter-of-factly.

And then there was silence.

David took this as a good sign. It meant that Mallory was already working out the details in her head. He had thought of Helene a few hours ago, and then put her aside as he considered other options. But in the end he came back to her. No relation, so there would be no record of her at my office. And Weekapaug would be quiet this time of year. Not much activity out of season, so it would be relatively easy to keep an eye on the boys and be alert to anything out of the ordinary. Besides, Rhode Island is beautiful in the Autumn. It would be a holiday for the boys.

Finally Mallory spoke up.

"There's a lot to do. First, we have to see if Helene will agree to this."

"Let's find out. Pull over at that gas station and we'll give her a call. I don't want to use our home phone for this anyway."

Mallory pulled in and parked. She thumbed through her purse and quickly located her address book.

"Who wants to talk?" asked Mallory.

"I'll leave this to you, but we may need a few weeks to sort this out. Make sure she understands there's an element of danger here."

"If I tell her that she won't be able to resist."

"I'm counting on that."

While Mallory went to use the phone David pulled up to the self serve pumps and gassed up the Volvo, all the while keeping an eye on Mallory and movements around him. He was now on high alert and would be until his family was safe.

When David was finished he pulled the car up to the store next to Mallory. She had made contact with Helene and was still in explanation mode. This could take some time, thought David.

Finally Mallory hung up and returned to the car, this time as a passenger. "It's done," she said. "Helene will be expecting us at anytime. We'll stay with her and Tom for as long as is necessary. I told her I'd call after I make the plane reservations."

"I knew she'd come through," David sighed with relief. "Now, I'll keep driving the Volvo since it's already known. You take the rental and we can drop it off at the airport. Make the plane reservations for this afternoon if possible, but don't call from the house. Pick up a rental car, a big one, at the Providence airport."

"I'll need money," interrupted Mallory.

"Good thinking. Hit the Credit Union and withdraw several thousand in cash. Try not to use credit cards at all, even for the plane tickets."

"What are we going to tell our parents? They'd panic if we just disappear off the face of the earth."

"True. How about if we told them you were taking the kids to Florida or Hawaii, and that I will join you shortly?"

"I'll tell them Hawaii. And I'll use our home phone in the hope that someone is listening in."

"Excellent. Now, let's get you a rental and I'll get to the office."

"What are you going to do at the office?" Mallory inquired.

"I'm not really sure," he said.

It was late morning before David arrived at the office. There was a flurry of notes on his desk and his phone was blinking, no doubt because of the news reports of the incident in his garage. He didn't even bother with the e-mail on his computer. Before he could even begin, the departmental secretary popped in to inform David that he was summoned to the President's office—immediately.

Good, thought David. He had some questions for him as well.

He made his way to Raymond Keith's office area, which was distinguished from the rest of the office building by its plush carpet, upgraded furniture, high priced artwork, and the hushed tones of the clerical staff. It was surreal compared to where the real work was done.

David positioned himself squarely in front of the desk of the executive secretary, the gatekeeper to the President's office. Before David could say more than a "Hello" she held up her hand to silence him and pointed to a chair in the small waiting area. David dutifully took his seat while she disappeared into Keith's office for several minutes. She then came out and returned to her desk without saying a word. David picked up a magazine and pretended to read. The secretary began making phone calls but her side of the conversation was unenlightening.

Less than ten minutes later, David understood what the phone calls were about as Lisa Voorhees and Peter Bealls showed up within minutes of each other. David was alarmed but tried not to give himself away. All exchanged glances and a brief hello, but the secretary gathered them all before they could say more and escorted them into Keith's office.

He was at the window, seemingly transfixed by the water tower across the road. The three were directed to chairs in front of his desk by the secretary who then quietly left the room, closing the door behind her.

Finally, Keith spoke.

"David, I heard about last night. We are all greatly relieved to hear that you and your family are unharmed. It must have been quite an ordeal."

"Thank you sir. It gave us a real scare."

"Everyone okay now? Family, I mean."

"Yes, we're just being a little more careful now."

"Good. I want you to know that OilQuest is here to assist. Lisa can arrange counseling for you or any member of your family, and Bealls here can look your house over for a security upgrade. I wish we could afford to hire body-guards for all of our staff, but, hell, they don't even do that for me!"

Bealls and Voorhees chuckled gratuitously.

David managed a polite smile before responding. "Thank you sir, but I don't think it will be necessary. Actually though, with all the travel and long hours I've been putting in, I would like to take a few weeks off. Maybe get away for awhile with the family."

The others exchanged glances. David could see the concern in Bealls' face. Voorhees was cool as a cucumber.

"Sounds like a splendid idea, son. You've certainly earned it. Get a good rest. Come back when you're ready and we'll have a new assignment for you to tackle."

"New assignment. But sir, I'd prefer to remain on the Angel Falls Project. I still have some unfinished busi…"

David stopped himself mid-sentence. He had already said too much. He had forgotten that Bealls and Voorhees were in the audience. They stared intently at him.

"What sort of unfinished business?" inquired the president.

David was in a quandary. He could tell all he knew, or at least suspected, but with Bealls and Voorhees sitting there, they would surely deny all. He had little evidence regarding Steve's death, and no connection whatsoever to the incident yesterday in the garage. This would probably be dismissed as the ramblings of a man under a lot of stress. There's no way he would be allowed to stay on the Project after that. He needed to think fast.

"It's just that I wanted to see this Project through. It's got a big piece of me and Steve in it and I'd like to see it succeed," David said, hoping to sound convincing.

As he could feel all three sets of eyes boring into him, Keith finally responded.

"I'll give it some thought. In the meantime, you get a good vacation with your family, and we'll talk when you get back."

With that the meeting was over. David stood up to shake Keith's extended hand, responded "Thank you, sir," and left.

Bealls and Voorhees remained behind. This alarmed David, who sensed he was growing more paranoid by the minute. The secretary barely looked up as David exited the plush executive office area.

Meanwhile, Mallory was busy making some rapid arrangements. After picking up the rental car, and withdrawing five thousand in cash from the Credit Union, she drove to the Clarion Hotel off the Central Expressway in Plano. There, American Airlines maintained a reservations and ticketing office. As Dallas was the home for American, these offices were scattered throughout the greater metropolitan area. She had no difficulty purchasing three tickets on a four p.m. flight to Providence. It would arrive around midnight but it would have to do. Following David's instructions she paid cash for the tickets. The agent looked at her a trifle suspiciously as Mallory peeled off a string of one hundred dollar bills. After confirming they were not counterfeit, the agent issued the three tickets.

Then Mallory used a pay phone in the hotel to reserve a rental car at Providence airport. Upon arriving back at the house, she parked in front, not being in possession of a garage door opener. The media was already gone.

That didn't take long, thought Mallory. Maybe we just had our fifteen minutes of fame.

Rather than walk in immediately, she scanned the outside perimeter for signs of intrusion. Satisfied that all was safe, she then peered down the street

*A Plan Evolves*    89

for unusual activity or strange vehicles. Nothing. She opened the door, walked in and disarmed the burglar alarm. She paused for a moment by the alarm, with its panic button inches from her hand, as she listened attentively while surveying all that was visible from her vantage point. Finally, she breathed a sigh of relief and closed the door behind her. "Wonder how long it will be before I stop doing this," she thought.

Wasting no time, in less than an hour she had called the relatives and told them that she and the boys were off to Hawaii for two weeks, with David to follow as soon as he could break away from work. Since none of them lived in the Dallas area, they would probably not learn of their near escape from death. And Mallory felt it best not to alarm them.

After the relatives, came the neighbors. Given the shootings, they certainly saw the logic in getting away for awhile. Mallory arranged for the mail to be picked up and the paper to be stopped. Then it was time to pack, for all three. Mallory was highly organized and extremely efficient. In fact, she was at her best in a crisis. David had long ago jokingly labeled Mallory and her sister "The Disaster Twins" after watching them swing into action during an approaching hurricane. They were relentlessly thorough in their preparations, anticipating every contingency. Now, the threat was even more real, and this time it was personal.

She was finished packing when she decided to call David with an update. It was nearly one p.m.

David answered after the second ring.

"Hastings."

Mallory was actually surprised that he answered.

"Hi David. It's me. I'm calling from the house."

David understood the warning.

"Hello, sweetheart. How are things going?"

"Quite well," responded Mallory. "I have the Hawaii tickets and we'll be out of here late this afternoon. I'm packed so I'll pick up the boys soon and go directly to the airport. How is your situation?"

"Well," said David "I've had an interesting session with our president. He said it would be okay to take a few weeks off."

"David, that's great. Can you come with us?"

Mallory's enthusiasm made it even harder for David to stay.

"I'm afraid not yet, Mallory. I've got a few items to wrap up here. Then I hope to join you."

"Oh," said Mallory softly, and with disappointment ringing in David's ear. She finally remembered that he had intentionally wanted to put some distance between himself and the rest of the family, just in case.

"You and the boys get started and I won't be far behind. Believe me. I'm looking forward to the break."

"I understand. Well, the mail and paper and school have all been taken care of. There's some frozen lasagna in the freezer, but I'm sure you'll use this opportunity to gorge on junk food."

"You know me too well."

"David?"

"What?"

"I love you. Please be careful."

"I love you too. You and the boys won't be out of my mind for a minute. Now go and have a good time."

"Okay. Bye."

"Bye sweetheart," as be blew a kiss over the phone and hung up.

David steeped in the loneliness of his office. Although relieved that Mallory and the boys would soon be safe with Tom and Helene Langtree in their reclusive retreat on the Rhode Island shores, he knew this was only a temporary solution. If nothing were done, then the problem would still be there upon their return, along with the danger.

David knew he couldn't afford to wait. He needed to act, to provoke. Yet his last provocation nearly got him and his family killed. Bealls, Voorhees and Watson were a formidable triumvirate. If he was going to take them on he would need some help. The problem with this approach was that anyone who got involved stood a good chance of getting hurt, or worse. Emilio was a case in point. And there was no sense in going to the police with fragments of facts laced with suppositions and innuendoes. While he was certain that Steve's death, the Venezuelan Project, and the attempts on his life were all connected there was nothing tangible to prove the connection.

At first David thought he would write all this down and leave a copy with a lawyer in case an unfortunate accident should befall him. How melodramatic, he thought. A lot of good this would do after I'm dead. And besides, it might place the family in jeopardy.

David continued to think through the various alternatives, of which there were few. It was as though he was in a chess game, but could not see all of the opponent's pieces. Any move on his part brought unforeseen consequences, and they were becoming increasingly more aggressive.

After more than an hour of contemplation in which plan after plan was conceived and rejected, David found himself returning to the simplest and most direct approach. He would take this to the president of OilQuest. He would have to go back to Keith, only alone this time. Although David recognized that his story was incomplete, and that it involved some of President Keith's most trusted people, at least he would be alerted to a possible conspiracy. And while David ran the risk of being officially pulled off the Angel Falls Project by this action, it should produce the desired effect of removing him and his family from danger. With the president being informed, it was less likely that the trio would make a move against David, even indirectly.

David spent a few more minutes composing his thoughts, then left his office for the conference room to use the phone, the safe phone.

He dialed the extension of the president.

"Mr. Keith's office," came the quick, crisp response from his secretary.

"Hi. This is David Hastings, and I would like to meet with Mr. Keith before the end of the day."

"About what?" she responded curtly. "You just met with him this morning."

David was taken aback by this query, but he checked himself before becoming defensive, realizing she probably did this to most everyone.

"It's related to the Angel Falls Project and it's quite important."

"Shouldn't you be talking to Mr. Watson instead? After all, he is the Project Manager," snapped the secretary.

David could see that she was going to be even more difficult than usual, so it was time to get tough. "Be polite but firm," his father had always told him.

"No. If I needed to speak with Mr. Watson, I would be talking to him now. I need to see Mr. Keith. It is important and I am certain he would want to hear this."

Silence on the other end of the phone. David could tell she was seething.

"I'm afraid Mr. Keith is all booked up for the rest of the day, and he will be away from the office tomorrow."

Damn she's good, thought David. I could use her to handle all those unwanted phone solicitations. He decided to soften his approach. Taking a deep breath he started back in.

"Please Barbara, I wouldn't be doing this if it weren't really important. And I know Mr. Keith would want to hear what I have to say. Can't I please get just a few minutes of his time, today?"

"Hold for a minute and I'll see what I can do."

"Thank you very, very much."

After a very long minute, the secretary came back on the line.

"Mr. Hastings?"

"Yes?"

"I'm putting you through now."

Before David had the chance to even say 'Thanks' and catch his breath Mr. Keith was on the line.

"Hello, David. I understand you have something very urgent to tell me. I only have a few minutes, so make it brief."

"Yes sir," David began, almost forgetting where to begin. "I have reason to believe that Rick Watson, Peter Bealls and Lisa Voorhees are involved in some sort of cover up of illicit activities related to the Angel Falls Project. Furthermore, I also believe that the death of my partner, Steve Giles, may be related to this in some way. And finally, I think the attack on me last night is also connected."

"Just a minute, son," said Keith. David could hear him on the intercom to his secretary, asking her to hold his next appointment and to close the door. More discussion between Keith and his secretary, but the words were muffled by a hand over the phone. Finally Keith came back on the line.

"That's a helluva story. Do you have anything to back it up?"

David was expecting that question and quite relieved to have gotten this far.

"Only fragments so far, but it is starting to connect up. I know Bealls was lying about where he was when my partner was killed because he was in Caracas the same time as Steve. And I know that Voorhees brought Bealls in on this and that he is taking his orders from her. And whenever I mention the phrase "Angel Falls Option" to Rick Watson, he goes ballistic. And those two guys who nearly killed me last night were hit men, not garage bandits."

David paused to give it time for his comments to sink in.

"Son, even if all this was somehow connected, and I still don't see how, why would three of our best employees be engaged in something like this? What in the hell would they stand to gain from killing people? The Employee of the Month Award?"

By that last comment David could see he had failed to convince.

"Sir. I don't really know what their motive would be. But as the Project in Venezuela seems to be involved, it is possible that some corrupt practices are in play, possibly kickbacks. This is a big project with a lot of money involved, a lot of contracts to be awarded. Millions of dollars could be siphoned off or padded on contracts. Watson would control that, while Voorhees and Bealls would ensure that no one from the company could interfere."

Brief pause.

"I see. Well, Hastings, even though this still strikes me as being far fetched, there may be something to it. At least you've suggested a plausible motive. Who else have you discussed this with?"

"Only my wife, sir. I didn't know who else to talk to. I don't have anything solid to give the police. Since the company appears to be involved I thought you should know. I realize it all sounds bizarre, but too many things have happened to be a coincidence."

"David, I'm glad you came to me. Let me think about this awhile. I have an independent way of checking on matters like this. Tell me, how did you find out that Bealls was in Caracas?"

"A little investigative research, sir. I have phone records, airline and hotel information."

"Very good. I may want to see that for myself, if that's okay with you?"

"Certainly. I have it in my briefcase. I'll bring it right up."

"That would be fine. Put it in an envelope and leave it with my secretary, along with any other information you've picked up on this matter."

"Be happy to sir."

"Now you take that vacation we were talking about and by the time you get back I'll have this thing all sorted out."

"Thank you, sir. I appreciate your hearing me out."

"Nonsense. You did the right thing. To think what we could accomplish if we had an army of men like you working for OilQuest! Goodbye and I'll see you in a few weeks."

"Goodbye Mr. Keith, and thanks."

David hung up and sighed with relief, comforted in the knowledge that he at least had an impartial and very powerful third party keeping an eye on this. He now felt he had done all he could for the time being and could join Mallory after all. This brought a smile to his face as he pictured the four of them walking the deserted, windswept beaches in Weekapaug by day, and cuddling around a blazing fire at night.

He hurried back to his office to perform the final tasks before leaving on vacation. He pulled the papers from his briefcase, put them in a confidential company envelope, which he then labeled for Mr. Keith.

David was about to seal the envelope but suddenly stopped. He thought for a moment, eyes gazing nowhere in particular, and then walked down the hall to the copy room.

Upon returning to the office he put the originals in the envelope for Mr. Keith. He placed a copy in his desk drawer and locked it.

"Won't take them long to find this one," he calculated. "Maybe it will throw them off for awhile."

He then put the final copy in a mailer, addressed it to Mark, Steve's companion in Ohio, and locked it in his briefcase. David then went up to the Executive area and delivered the president's envelope to his secretary. She knew it was coming.

"Thanks for putting me through to Mr. Keith. This is for him, personally," said David as he handed her the packet.

"Just doing my job," came the deadpan reply. "I'll see that he gets this, personally," she replied in a sarcastic tone.

David nodded and walked away.

One the way home he stopped by the Post Office and mailed the envelope from his briefcase. If something happens to me, thought David, maybe Mark can pick up where I left off. He may not do it for me, but I know he'd do it for Steve.

# CHAPTER 6

# *Weekapaug*

## *DAY FIVE*

The drive from the Providence T.F. Green airport to Weekapaug took a little over an hour at night. Both Matt and Eric fell asleep before they had even left the city limits. It was a quiet but familiar drive for Mallory. She had driven down old U.S. Route 1, referred to locally as the 'Boston Post Road' many times before. The lights of Providence and Warwick receded as she leisurely made her way past rural farm communities and coastal fishing villages. The hectic pace of life seemed to ratchet down a notch in this realm, affording rich and poor alike the opportunity to imbibe in the more natural course of time and events, rather than being overtaken by them.

As Mallory turned off the Post Road at Dunn's Corner, the boys instinctively awoke. It was uncanny how they could sense the proximity to Weekapaug and the Atlantic surf that alternatively caressed and crashed upon her shores.

"Are we almost there?" asked Matt, still half-asleep.

Mallory smiled. "You tell me."

Both boys peered out their respective windows. Even though the dark night was barely illuminated by their lone car and the occasional dim street lamps, recognition set in.

"I know where we are!" shouted Eric.

Matt chimed in. "Me too. It won't be long now."

The solitude that Mallory had enjoyed since Providence quickly dissolved as the boys rapidly called out every landmark they could recognize. Nonetheless, it gave her a warm feeling to know that Weekapaug was also a special place to them.

The rental car was now running on a narrow lane parallel to the Breachway, the inlet between the Atlantic Ocean and Winnapaug Pond, a large salt water lagoon behind a barrier beach. At a fork in the road Mallory turned left onto Neptune Lane.

The right hand fork crossed a small bridge over the Breachway to Misquamicut. The boys loved Misquamicut, the barrier beach with amusements and wild surf. Here is where the young people came, to surf by day and party by night. While the boys were still too young to partake of all that Misquamicut had to offer, they still enjoyed what they could, and dreamed with anticipation of future opportunities.

Mallory took Neptune Lane at a slow pace. Even though it was a cold October night, she lowered her window. The boys instinctively followed. The smell of salt air permeated the car. All breathed deeply in silence before Mallory broke in.

"Mmm. I missed the smell of the ocean."

"Me too," quipped Eric.

"I can hear the ocean," yelled Matt.

"I can't hear anything if you don't stop shouting," replied Eric.

A brief silence before Eric spoke again, this time in a low hushed tone.

"I miss Dad."

"Me too. I wish he was here, now," said Matt.

"So do I," whispered Mallory, and all fell silent again as each drifted with their thoughts out to the foamy, wind swept seas that unfolded before their eyes.

The road ran parallel to the shore, which was fortified in places by large granite blocks to defend against the ravages of winter storms and autumnal hurricanes. Pocket beaches nestled in the crevices between the headlands. Even in the darkness, Mallory could picture the clean, white, coarse sand beaches. Summer memories of the boys body surfing, boogie boarding, and building sandcastles flooded her mind, bringing a smile to her lips. She was tired but at peace.

Houses began to appear, set back off the road on the landward side. They were neatly spaced, each on their own acre, with wide sweeping lawns down to the road. Most of the houses were dark, being seasonal in nature. An occasional light and vehicles in the driveway indicated some had been converted for year round occupancy.

The road took a bend inland a few hundred yards and then once again ran along the shore. This allowed for houses to be erected between the road and the rocky sea wall that protected the spit of land jutting defiantly into the water. Here a handful of larger turn of the century homes, each occupying a few acres, stood majestically in the night. Unlike Plano, here there was no need for privacy fences. Space gave privacy. Each lawn folded into the other so that property lines became indistinguishable. The expanse of land gave all residents a panoramic view of open ocean and extensive coastline set against a backdrop of rolling green lawns and coastal dune grasses.

Mallory turned into the second gravel driveway and pulled into the turn-around area separating the garage from the house. The house was ablaze with lights and smoke curled from one of the several chimneys. It was such an inviting a sight. The car had barely stopped before the boys bounded out and made their way to the door.

Mallory yelled after them. "Hey, what about the luggage?"

But it was too late. Not that they were out of earshot. They just chose to ignore her and kept their steady lope to the house. Before they got to the door, however, they were intercepted by Samson and Delilah, two full-grown Great Danes belonging to Tom and Helene, who appeared out of the darkness. Samson emitted a deep bark that temporarily froze the boys in their place. All four, boys and dogs, stood still for barely an instant, and then recognition set in.

"Samson! Delilah!" shrieked the boys in unison.

The dogs leapt on the boys, nearly bowling them over. Together they wrestled in the cold, damp grass, long lost friends reunited at last.

Tom and Helene appeared at the door to investigate the commotion.

"I see you've already met our welcoming committee," said Tom as he came down the steps toward Mallory, who was still trying to unload the luggage from the car.

"Tom" said Mallory, dropping a suitcase and extending her arms. They embraced with a great hug.

"Welcome back, Mallory."

"I can't tell you how good it feels to be back, and to see you and Helene."

By then Helene had made her way toward them.

"All right, no fooling around in the driveway. The neighbors will think we're having a love fest." And with that the two women, friends since their first days in college, hugged each other tightly.

"Helene" was all Mallory could muster before tears welled in her eyes and a lump formed in her throat.

Helene, despite her lighthearted entrance, was also overcome with the power of the moment. Tom finally broke the silence.

"Well, shall we collect the boys and head in?"

The boys were still romping and rolling with the dogs. Even though fully grown Danes, they were playful as puppies and were especially fond of Matt and Eric as they played together last summer and the summer before that. Since Tom and Helene had no children of their own, the dogs spent their entire time with the boys whenever they were around.

Mallory managed to separate boys from dogs long enough for Matt and Eric to extend a proper greeting to Tom and Helene. With a loud whistle from Tom, the Danes obediently came to his side. Mallory greeted each dog with a hearty rub on the forehead.

At long last, men, women, boys, dogs and luggage made their way up the steps and went inside.

The cedar shingled "cottage" was a grand old house built at the turn of the century. Its last major renovation was after the 1938 hurricane that devastated most of the northeast coast. Three stories tall, it could sleep eighteen in a pinch, and sometimes did whenever Tom and Helene had the relatives in during the summer months. All nine bedrooms on the second and third floors had breathless views, whether out to sea or inland. Tom and Helene occupied a suite on the second floor overlooking the sea wall and the Atlantic. On a good day one could see Block Island, about 10 miles to the south.

The main floor of the house contained the kitchen, dining room and sitting rooms. Wide board floors gave it a country charm, while the numerous sailing and beach pictures and memorabilia on the walls gave a constant reminder of one's proximity to water.

The kitchen, the heart of the house, was huge and occupied a third of the floor. There seemed to be two of everything in it; sinks, ovens, dishwasher, even refrigerators. The planned redundancies would become necessities when the house was full. In the center of the kitchen was a large oak table. Designed as a worktable, long and narrow, it could seat twelve if there was overflow from the dining room. Yet inevitably, most would take their meals here, at the center of activities and where the atmosphere was more casual. Many an hour had passed at this table between the two sets of friends. Even the boys were fond of the kitchen, having conducted their own crab races one summer's eve. The dogs, having had their noses pinched as puppies, were terrified at the sight of a dozen blue shells scrambling across the kitchen floor. To this day, they give a wide berth whenever they spot a crab washed up on the beach, dead or alive.

The dining room gave the appearance of formality, with the long table adorned with candles and silk flowers. Yet when in use, with up to eighteen vacationing relatives feasting on the traditional New England fare, formality dissolved in an instant and the din of the dinner conversation would rise and fall in seeming unison with the waves on the rocks before the house. With none but the six of them here, however, most meals would be taken in the kitchen.

Each room opened to the next with a wide archway. Doors, at least in the common rooms, were nonexistent. The archway leading from the dining room and common room framed both rooms as a Norman Rockwell painting. The overly large common room was anything but common. The furniture was cozy and comfortable, with stuffed pillow sofas and high wing back chairs. While most of the furniture was gathered round either the massive beach stone fireplace or expansive ocean side picture window, little sitting areas occupied quiet corners. Bookcases, lining the inner walls, were crammed with books, puzzles and games that would captivate all ages on a rainy day.

It was in this room tonight that the fireplace was ablaze with seasoned birch logs. The fire cast dancing shadows across the room and the warmth permeated every corner. The boys were instantly drawn to the fire, and under Tom's watchful eyes, they poked and prodded until the blaze forced them back. The dogs settled on a hearthrug nearby, heaving a comfortable sigh as they dropped to the floor.

Mallory drank in the warmth of the room. "This is exactly what I had pictured. Thank you both so much."

"We aim to please" Tom said. "Especially when it involves the Hastings. I only wish David were here so he could take over the firewood duty."

"Believe me, Tom, there's nothing he would enjoy more than tending to that fire. He loves it."

"Looks like it's hereditary," quipped Helene, pointing to the boys who were still stoking the fire.

"Okay, boys, that's enough for now. The fire is just fine," Mallory chastened.

After a brief snack, which included homemade blueberry pie, the boys were whisked off to bed. They offered a mere token resistance as it had been a long and exciting day. Helene let them choose their room and they ran from one room to another, inspecting each as if they were prospective purchasers. They finally settled on their old favorite, which was the ocean facing room with twin beds on the top floor. Not wanting to be the only occupants of the third floor, both Matt and Eric begged Mallory to take an adjoining room. She quickly consented as this would also make it easier to keep an eye on them.

Once the boys were settled in bed, Mallory came in to kiss them goodnight. At first she was startled to see that Delilah had taken her position on the rug between the two beds, but she quickly recalled that she had always done this since the boys were infants. After kissing the boys, Mallory bade goodnight to Delilah who responded with a low "woof" upon hearing her name.

Coming downstairs she nearly tripped over Samson, who had nestled on the landing halfway up the stairs between the first and second floors. Samson was several years older than Delilah, and he was starting to show his age. He didn't care much for the varnished wood stairs as he tended to lose his footing too easily. So, each night he compromised by making his way up the half dozen stairs to a comfortable pad on the landing. From this vantage point, he could gaze upon the activities in the common room while simultaneously maintain vigilance to all traffic on the stairs.

How strategic, marveled Mallory.

Tom, Helene and Mallory occupied the sofa and chairs around the fire and sipped coffee while Mallory recounted in detail the events of the past week. It took over an hour, but despite the late hour, Tom and Helene were spellbound.

"My God. It must have been terrifying for you" gasped Helene. "Especially with the shooting."

"It was, and it still is, because it's not over."

"Well, you and the boys are safe here with us" Tom reassured her. "Are you positive you left no trail?"

"I think so. Even the relatives think we're in Hawaii for two weeks."

"Good. And don't worry. We'll take good care of you. Besides Samson and Delilah, we've taken a few more precautions. Since that break-in last year, we've made a few modifications to our alarm system. This house may look turn-of-the-century but our security system is state-of-the-art. And if all else fails, I keep Dad's old hunting rifle in the closet. It's only a 22 that he used on the woodchucks that were tearing up his lawn, but I keep it well oiled."

"Enough talk about guns" Helene interjected. She could sense that Mallory was still unnerved by the shooting. "Let's get some sleep. The boys will be up before you know it."

"I'd like that. And thank you both for letting us come stay."

"We love you. We want to help," responded Helene.

"We're glad you came to us", said Tom reassuringly. "That's what friends are for."

It was past two a.m. when the three said goodnight and climbed the stairs, being careful not to disturb Samson on the landing. He lifted one eye lazily and gave a snort as Mallory gave him a pat goodnight. She checked in on the boys before going to her room. Delilah picked up her head and acknowledged Mallory as she looked in on the boys. There was a bit of a chill on this floor, but with warm nightclothes and quilts piled high on the bed, the boys would be very cozy. Finally, alone in her room, she quickly undressed and slipped into a thick flannel nightgown. Without David to cuddle with, she slipped on a pair of socks for added warmth.

As her head hit the pillow she softly whispered "Goodnight, David. I love you," and then added "and please be careful." Sleep came quickly.

So did morning.

# CHAPTER 7

# *Plano to Caracas*

## *DAYS FIVE–SIX*

David spent the evening at home, a quiet dinner of leftovers and a glass of cabernet. All was still in the neighborhood as darkness fell. David kept the house well lit and curtains drawn. He conducted several perimeter checks during the course of the evening, and put in a call to the Plano police to request a little more attention on their part. They were accommodating.

He turned in around 9:30 and read for awhile before turning out the light. The house alarms were set. "Hope I wake up tomorrow," thought David in half amusement.

No sooner had his head hit the pillow when the phone rang. David was tempted to let it go to the recorder but then thought it might be Mallory so he reached for the receiver.

"Hello."

"Hastings, this is Watson. I hope I woke you."

"No, but you weren't far off."

"Maybe I'll have better luck next time."

"Look, Rick, I know you didn't call just to check up on my sleeping habits, so what's up?"

"You're up. You can forget about going back to sleep. I've got orders to get you down to Venezuela immediately."

"Me? Why?" David's apprehension was growing. He was now fully awake.

"Because our geologist got called away suddenly and we are nearly at the target depth. With him gone, you are the only other geologist who has worked this project and who knows enough to keep this moving. By the time you get to Angel Falls, we will be drilling through the pay zone and preparing to run wireline logs. We require a geologist for that operation and you're it."

"Tell me again what happened to the other geologist," David queried suspiciously. Watson was vague.

"Don't know for sure. He got a phone call at the wellsite, and then said he had a family emergency and left on the very next chopper. It's the last time he'll ever work for me, that I can promise."

"Why me?"

"I just told you. You're the only geologist who knows what we're looking at down there. Besides, you're the one who's been screaming that it's your project. Now, can we move on to the details of getting you to Venezuela?"

Rick's quick temper was beginning to emerge. David persisted.

"Look, Rick. I know that I'm the last guy you want down there, so what gives?"

"You're right about that, but it wasn't my call."

"Then whose call was it?"

"It doesn't matter. Are you going or not? It would suit me just fine if you said no, but I've got my orders."

"From whom?"

"I only report to one boss, President Keith."

David was dumbstruck.

"You mean that Keith told you to send me down there? I don't believe it. How would he even know about the other geologist?"

"Listen, Hastings. He knows everything. Now, are you going or not?"

David paused, drew in a deep breath, and replied "I'm going".

"I was hoping you'd refuse. Then you'd be fired and I'd be done with you once and for all! There's a ticket waiting for you at the American ticket counter at DFW. You have a 9:00 a.m. flight tomorrow to Miami, connecting to Caracas. You'll spend the night in Caracas at the Hotel Tamanaco. The room is booked. You'll be picked up at the hotel the next morning at 7:00 a.m. for the trip to the field."

"I know the drill", David interrupted.

"Good. Then I'll see you down there at the site."

"What? You mean you're going too?"

"I'm already on my way. I'll beat you down there. And I'm not particularly thrilled with the company."

And with that parting remark, Watson hung up, leaving David speechless on the other end of the line.

I've got to get me a normal job, thought David as he put down the phone. He began to pace about the room. He was both exhilarated yet disturbed. In Venezuela he would be in the very thick of it all, at probably the most pivotal point in the project. The results of this well would determine if the structure was large enough to be commercially viable. He couldn't have asked to go at a better time. Normally he would have begged for an assignment like this. And yet, he was worried. Watson's story was pretty weak, and inconsistent. Keith, the President of OilQuest wouldn't get involved at such a low level of operations, at least not in the normal course of business. However, it seemed as though nothing was normal about this project, not since Steve's death. He then started packing for the journey.

Steve's death. In Caracas. And David would be there tomorrow night. In the very same hotel.

Maybe I should call Mallory, David pondered. I definitely should, but not from this phone. I'll call from the airport in the morning.

He quickly finished packing and returned to bed, but sleep came slowly, if at all. It was a very restless night.

David arrived at Dallas-Fort Worth airport early so he could call Mallory. After checking his luggage and obtaining his boarding pass, he made his way to the second floor that contained the American Airline's Admiral's Club. It was nothing special, a few large rooms with a bar, TVs and phones, but it afforded a quiet place to sit down and make a call.

As he entered the Club, he saw a number of businessmen and some women, either pounding the keys on their laptop computer, talking on the phone, or reading the Wall Street Journal.

Suits, David thought. Why do they fly in suits? Got to be the absolute most uncomfortable way to go. Must have one hell of an inferiority complex.

David was a casual dresser when he flew, focusing first on comfort. And yet, on a deeper level, he knew there was more to the business suit story than just travel comfort. It was the "Established Norm" aspect that bothered him the most. The suit signified establishment and acceptance, a badge identifying a brotherhood of men and women who scoured the planet in search of one thing—more money. Perhaps what bothered David the most was that he feared he was becoming one of them, suit or no suit. They personified what he had rebelled against for most of his life, and now he may have become them. He just didn't know it yet. This thought sent a chill down his spine. He shrugged it off with a sense of self-bravado as he scoured the sea of gray flannel and navy blue wool in the lounge.

I'll bet none of these corporate jet setters ever took out a pair of assassins in their own driveway.

Feeling vindicated after dueling with his alter ego, David took a seat in a corner so as to provide as much privacy as was possible, given the setting. He thumbed through his address book and dialed up Tom and Helene Langtree's number with his credit card.

Mallory answered.

"Langtree residence."

"Is the temptress from Plano in the house? inquired David.

"David. Oh I'm so glad you called. Are you at the office?"

"No, I'm"…

"David, it's just beautiful here. Cool, brilliant colors, soothing salt air, peaceful and safe." She hesitated. "Where are you if you aren't at the office?"

"I'm at DFW."

"That's wonderful!" she exclaimed. How soon will you get here? Do you want me to pick you up in Providence: Oh, the boys will be thrilled. They've been playing with the dogs ever since they arrived."

"Sweetheart, I'm not coming to Weekapaug. I'm going to Venezuela." David paused to let the full impact sink in. Stony silence from the other end.

Finally, Mallory forced out a strained "Why?" as she choked back the tears.

"It wasn't my idea. The office called last night. They said the current geologist had an emergency and needed to leave, and that the well was at a critical stage, and that I was the only other person who knows what to do."

"Who are they?"

David sensed that the "Big Inquisition" was about to commence, so he needed to head this off before Mallory became unhinged. She knew that David detested Rick Watson, having bitterly complained about him over the years. To even mention his name in this context would be inviting a firestorm of protest.

"Just the Operations Group at the office. Mallory, these things do happen. And, I am closest to the situation."

He paused to gauge the effect of his last remarks. Silence on the other end. It wasn't working. He pressed on.

"Look. It'll only take a few days. I already got the okay to take a few weeks off from the President himself, so I'll be with you within a week."

'It's a trap," Mallory snapped back.

This time David was taken aback. His recovery was weak.

"Boy, you sure know how to cut through the haze."

"David, don't go," she pleaded. I sense something terrible will happen. Please don't go."

I knew I should have called from Caracas instead, thought David. He needed to put her at ease before the situation deteriorated further.

"Listen, Sweetheart. I am just as concerned as you. It has also crossed my mind that this trip is almost too coincidental. I have to go, though, if only to get to the bottom of this mess. And I promise you that I will be careful."

"I still wish you wouldn't go."

"I understand. I wish I were with you and the boys right now. But I have to see this through. It's not just about the project anymore. It's about Steve. And, it's about us. We can't hide forever."

"I know."

Another pause as both absorbed the precarious course that had been set in motion. Mallory finally broke the silence.

"David, I love you."

"And I love you, and the boys, more than life itself. You'll be in my every thought while I am away."

"Be careful. Be very careful. I'm too young to be a widow."

"Don't worry. You may look gorgeous in black, but I'm no hero."

"Could've fooled me. Just come back."

"I will. Kiss the boys for me."

"OK, Bye."

"See you soon, Sweetheart."

As David hung up, Mallory stayed on the line, listening to the dial tone, until she had composed herself. David took one last look at the army of business suits hanging about, and for the first time wished he was one of them, safe and content.

The flight to Miami and on to Caracas was uneventful. Despite the abundance of liquor in the first class compartment, David rarely imbibed, and today was no exception. Drinking on long flights always made him groggy, and he especially needed to be in full possession of his faculties on this trip.

The flight did give him the opportunity to think things out a bit more. He was still puzzled about the President involving himself in a seemingly routine operational matter and calling for David to go out to the field.

Or did he? David pondered. After all, he only had Rick Watson's word on this.

Maybe Rick is setting me up? He can't get rid of me in Plano, so he'll do it in Venezuela. Either in Caracas, like Steve, or out in the field. And this was an area that was totally within Rick's control. What have I gotten myself into? This is like walking into the lion's den butt naked.

Even David had to laugh at this image, but he sobered quickly...

Could President Keith be involved? What if Watson was telling the truth and Keith did order me down there? If he's involved then this is bigger than I thought. Just what I need, another suspect.

The more David pondered the situation, the more complex it became. Overcome by fatigue, he finally drifted off for a few hours, to be awakened by the descent into Caracas.

Customs was slow, as usual, but uneventful. David took a taxi, always an exhilarating experience, for the forty-minute ride into central Caracas and the Hotel Tamanaco. As the taxi pulled up to the now familiar hotel entrance, he greeted the aging façade as if he were visiting an old friend.

The Tamanaco was once <u>the</u> place to stay in Caracas. Here, in the grand lobby, dignitaries mingled with tycoons while smartly attired underworld types occupied the darker fringes of the lobby and dimly lit bar. The most beautiful women in Venezuela, lavishly adorned and dripping in gold, graced the chandeliered ballrooms. But no longer. The hotel had struggled to keep abreast of changing times and tastes, but instead had succumbed to the desire for convenience over style. It had one too many facelifts, and now looked like an aging madam garishly painted and tattily dressed.

Even the clientele had lost their grace and style, to be replaced by brassy young men and women with cell phones seemingly glued to their ears. The hotel was tired, the clientele seamy, and the staff indifferent. Yet here is where David and Steve had always stayed. They had once tried the Hilton on the other side of town, but it was populated by "suits" and the atmosphere was sterile. To David and Steve, the Tamanaco represented all that was both good and bad about Caracas. To them it was Caracas.

This last thought saddened David as memories of Steve came flooding back. He recalled their late night drinking bouts as they had each recounted how they would set the world on fire. The time spent in the field at Angel Falls had brought them even closer. David had to remind himself that it was Steve's death that had set him on this course, now perilous for his entire family.

He poured himself a glass of brandy in his room, and sat looking out his window at the light of Caracas. Even at this late hour the city was ablaze in lights and traffic. He finished the brandy, undressed, and then braced the door with a chair to deter any unwanted guests.

He was about to turn off the light when a note was silently slipped under his door. David pulled back the chair and opened the door but the hall was deserted. He re-entered the room and picked up the note. It was on hotel stationery. The message was brief.

"To David Hastings. Flight to rig site delayed until 2:00 p.m. Driver will pick you up at hotel at 12:30 p.m. tomorrow for transport to heliport."

"Hmmm", mused David. "No signature, and no reason for the delay. Well, guess there is no need to set the alarm."

And with that, David turned in for the night, his last thoughts being of Mallory, Matt and Eric. At least they were safe in Weekapaug.

# CHAPTER 8

# *Relief in Weekapaug*

## *DAY SIX*

The boys were the first to wake to the cries of the seagulls just outside their window, and to the heavy breathing of Delilah. She had placed her head on the bed next to Matt, and it gave him quite a start when he first opened his eyes. He recoiled before recognition set in, causing Delilah to jerk back and let out a yelp. Then, both boys, accompanied by Delilah, rushed into Mallory's room to roust her from her slumber. Mallory had heard the thundering footsteps long before they even reached her door, but she feigned sleep so as not to spoil their fun.

"Mom, wake up," yelled Eric.

Mallory turned over and pretended to rub the sleep from her eyes. "It can't even be 7:00 am yet."

"It's six. And it's a beautiful day," exclaimed Matt. "C'mon. Get up."

Samson was now barking from the landing, anxious to join the party.

Mallory relented. "OK. OK. I'll get up."

That was all the boys needed to hear. They bolted from the room as abruptly as they had arrived, and headed downstairs to rendezvous with Samson and to ensure the rest of the household was awake.

To their surprise, Tom was already up and had laid out a continental breakfast. "Where have you guys been? I've been up for hours," mused Tom.

Helene appeared a few minutes later, followed by Mallory. The dogs were let out, along with the boys still clad in their pajamas. The barking and yelling carried far in the still morning air.

"Good thing we don't have any neighbors on either side of us at this time of year," remarked Tom, or they'd be joining us for breakfast right about now." He nodded in the direction of the yelps and squeals emanating from the lawn.

"How about some coffee?" Helene gestured to Mallory.

"Sounds wonderful."

All three adults filled their cups and headed to the front room with the oversized picture window that looked beyond the rocky shores toward Block Island. The rising sun streaked through low-lying clouds to speckle the ocean with alternating patches of darkness and mirror like brilliance.

A few lobster boats could be seen about a mile offshore, checking their pots. One was close enough to see the lobstermen haul up a pot and pull out a lobster. After securing fresh bait inside the pot, it was once again lowered to await its next prey.

The shellfish industry, and especially the lobster, was only now recovering from an oil spill of a few years back. A barge carrying heating oil had broken up in heavy seas not far from Weekapaug, polluting miles of healthy shoreline. The impact on the shellfish industry was enormous. And the entire energy industry was once again tarnished by the reckless act of a few. A massive lobster restocking program was undertaken with egg bearing female lobsters. The females were notched so as to alert the lobstermen that these could not be taken until after several years, when the notches would grow out. David was particularly sensitive to this incident, knowing it could have easily been prevented. And while the coastal damage had demonstrated a remarkable ability to recover, the damage to the industry that he worked for may have been irreparable. Even today the moratorium against drilling off the east coast continues, with no change in sight.

Tom opened the door to let in the brisk, salt air. Mallory instinctively drew a deep breath, savoring the simple purity of the moment.

"I wish I could live here in Weekapaug all year round," she stated softly, yet with conviction.

"Why don't you?" inquired Helene as if to challenge.

"Because we'd starve."

Helene persisted. "I know it would be difficult for David to find work. There aren't many oil companies in Rhode Island. And for good reason. But he's a smart guy. He can do other things."

"Believe me Helene, David and I have talked about this many times, but we can't come up with a solution that we think would work."

"He can write, can't he?" Helene quipped unrelentingly. "Why doesn't he become a writer?"

And with that comment all three looked at each other and burst out laughing.

"Get serious," said Mallory.

The conversation came to an abrupt halt as both boys and dogs entered the room at a full gallop.

"We're hungry," shouted Matt.

"Breakfast has begun," announced Helene. Specialty of the house is blueberry pancakes."

With that both Mallory and the boys ordered up some pancakes and made their way to the kitchen. Blueberry pancakes was a favorite of David's, and for a brief moment Mallory had a faraway look in her eyes. All that remained were the sounds of the gulls circling outside, and a lone fisherman making his way to the farthest rocky protrusion from which to cast his line.

After breakfast Tom and Helene departed for the "Eighty Acre Woods", a nature center and wildlife sanctuary they owned and ran. It was north of Westerly, just a twenty-minute drive from Weekapaug. They had purchased the land to prevent it from falling into the hands of developers who had hoped to build an amusement park.

Not that Tom and Helene had anything against amusement parks per se, but it was the steady decline of natural woodlands and native habitats in southern Rhode Island that concerned them the most. South County had already undergone near exponential growth, mostly due to its spectacular coastline and rural atmosphere. Most of South County had been farming communities or fishing villages, but in the last 20 years many farmers had sold their land to developers who then built malls and subdivisions. Urban sprawl was encroaching on the last bit of undeveloped shoreline between New York and Boston. In addition, efforts to establish another Indian gaming casino in the region were ongoing. Then along came the plans for an amusement park.

Helene in particular had pursued this cause with vigor. While they both realized that their eighty-acre preserve would not in itself turn the tide, it was a start. And others had begun to band together and follow suit. Communities were taking a more active role in controlling their own destinies. Farms, forests and open spaces were coming under better protection through comprehensive zoning plans, open area set-asides, conservation lands and trusts.

This grass roots movement in South County had gained national attention, and Helene was often called upon to provide her practical approach to champion other environmental causes. Much as she enjoyed the cause, of which there were many, it often took her away from where she wanted to be most.

While Tom shared Helene's passion, he dedicated himself entirely to the Eighty-Acre Woods, ensuring that the habitat was designed for both preservation while at the same time functional as a learning center. Tom was a self made man of many talents, equally comfortable in the woods, on a construction site, or behind a desk, although the latter he avoided whenever possible. Rarely would one find him at the main office at the center. Instead, he was usually strolling the woods with the two great Danes or leading a group of youngsters on a nature walk. The Eighty-Acre Woods was the culmination of years of labor by the both of them, and the fulfillment of a lifelong dream.

With Tom and Helene gone for the day, Mallory dedicated the day to one of rediscovery for herself and the boys. She felt more than safe in Weekapaug and, at least for a little while, tried to forget about their predicament. She gathered up boys and dogs. As usual, Eric had begged Tom to let Samson and Delilah stay with them, and all headed for the beach.

It was a short stroll across several lawns and driveways to the narrow, bleached wooden boardwalk that transported them safely over the dunes and deposited them on the barrier beach. Weekapaug beach, which separated Quonnie Pond from the Atlantic, was only about one hundred yards wide but was two miles in length. The beach was gradually assuming its winter profile as late summer storms had carved a berm all along the shore, just above the high tide mark.

The sand was coarse, but white with milky quartz grains composing much of the beach. Occasional clumps of brown kelp or bleached driftwood dotted the shore. Shell fragments, worn smooth by wave action, complemented the sands. Grassy dunes formed the backdrop to the beach and were protected by fences and limited access points.

On this autumnal day a crisp, cool, onshore breeze invigorated both boys and dogs. Together they raced along the swash zone, the dogs kicking up a salty spray as they easily paced Matt and Eric down the beach. Mallory strolled leisurely along after them, not another soul in sight as she peered down the beach.

They slowly made their way to the Quonnie Breachway at the easternmost end of the beach. The breachway was a man-made channel that provided boat access from the salt pond to the ocean. It was about fifty yards wide, two hundred yards long, and was stabilized on both sides by large granite blocks so as to prevent erosion from storms and to hold back the creeping sands that were transported by longshore currents along the beach. The tidal currents in and around the breachway were notoriously strong. Many a small boater found himself in peril by not paying due respect to the turbulent waters that could toss a small craft upon the rocks with relative ease.

The boys contented themselves with hunting for crabs in the rocky crevices just below the waterline. With discarded fishing line and a half-opened mussel, Matt and Eric possessed all the essential tools required to catch their prey. They fastened the open mussel with its bright orange interior to one end of the line and dropped it into a watery crevice. Within minutes, they would pull the line up to discover a crab, or possibly tow, clinging to the mussel. As this was purely for sport, since these crabs were under the legal size requirement, the boys set them loose. Mallory contented herself to sitting on a flat rock a few feet away, gazing intently upon the swiftly moving water while keeping a watchful mother's eye on the boys.

On the opposite side of the breachway, several fishermen were silently casting their lines into the turbulent waters. Most fishermen preferred the other side of the breachway, as it was accessible by car. The bluefish were still running, but their season was rapidly coming to a close. Striped bass were still in plentiful supply and the breachway provided an ideal location, as the fish would be funneled through the narrow channel in order to access Quonnie Pond.

After about an hour of playful discovery along the breachway, Mallory signaled Matt and Eric to commence the long journey back to the house. The dogs, who had reclined to watch the boys engage in the sport of crab catching, sprang to life and bounded back down the beach.

It was late morning by the time they returned to the house, a little tired from the overdose of salt air and extremely hungry. Mallory fixed some sandwiches for the boys, a bowl of clam chowder for herself that she found in the fridge, and some snacks for Samson and Delilah. All had had their exercise for the day.

The afternoon was spent shopping, mostly for food. Mallory loaded up on enough provisions to stock a gourmet kitchen. Although a guest of Tom and Helene, she felt the least she could do was prepare some exquisite meals, especially when there was fresh seafood to be had. The boys helped by sneaking all sorts of gooey treats into the shopping cart while Mallory pretended not to notice.

This was followed by a stop at the local department store for some warmer clothes for the boys. While she had packed some, it was obviously not enough, especially given the reckless manner in which they scrambled over the rocks and wrestled with the dogs. The afternoon excursion ended with a stop at Friendly's for ice cream sundaes, a longstanding favorite for both Matt and Eric and equally popular with Mallory as well. She ordered her usual favorite, a hot fudge sundae with walnut ice cream, no nuts. David would often chide her on her predictability, but Mallory regarded this aspect of her personality as a definition of self. Not that David was much different. His penchant for root beer floats was notorious.

They arrived back at the cottage just as Tom was pulling into the drive. Helene was already home.

The next few hours were spent in dinner preparation, preceded by the ritualistic cocktail hour. While fresh flounder, baked potatoes and corn on the cob were being readied, Tanqueray and tonic was served on the porch facing the ocean. The boys, normally self-avowed couch potatoes, had taken to rock hopping among the boulders that formed the protective sea wall. Samson and Delilah ran alongside on the lawn, barking with every child's leap. An occasional boat or ferry would appear on the horizon, but the fishing boats had long since returned to their berths, making ready for another pre-dawn assault.

The sun had set by the time all gathered around the kitchen table for dinner. While the boys heaped enormous helpings of food onto their plates, the dogs lay at their feet in hopeful anticipation of intercepting a spilt morsel.

The dinner conversation focused on the events of the day.

"We are nearly through with restoring the old burial ground up at the sanctuary," remarked Tom. "It took us weeks just to clear it, and another week to re-set the grave markers."

With this the boys grew interested and paused from their feast.

"Did you find a tomb?" inquired Matt.

Eric followed. "Was there any treasure?"

"Nothing quite so exciting, I'm afraid." replied Tom. "You see, this land was once a farm homestead. We can still see the foundation of the main house and a few outbuildings. That's why there are so many stone walls on the property. The land was once cleared for planting crops, probably corn and other vegetables.

We had an archeologist from the University of Rhode Island take a look at it. He thought it dated back about 200 years. Apparently, the family was relatively affluent. They not only had their own cemetery plot, but a separate one for their servants or slaves."

"Slaves?" Mallory asked in surprise. "You mean they had slaves up here?"

Tom continued. "Apparently it was quite common, especially among the well heeled. This slave burial ground on our property has seven graves, but since their grave markers were made from wood we don't know who died there. The landowner's family markers are made out of stone. In fact, there was even a young boy who died when he was eleven years old, and his name was Matthew."

With that, Matt dropped his fork and, eyes wide, stared intently at Tom.

"You're joking, aren't you Tom?" Matt asked nervously.

Eric burst out laughing. Tom smiled. "Not really, but I wouldn't worry. He was killed in an Indian attack, but the only thing that Indians attack today is your wallet at their casinos."

Everyone laughed except Matt. He took little comfort in that fact and spent the remainder of the dinner hour pushing the remnants of his food around the plate with his fork.

Both boys had developed a sense of reincarnation, despite the fact that neither David nor Mallory openly expressed a profound belief in it. They merely allowed it as a possibility. Yet somehow the boys had accepted it from a very early age. It was actually easier for them to accept reincarnation than the more formal, ritualistic religions, even though both boys had been baptized as Catholics in the church where David had once served as an altar boy.

However, Matt was also superstitious, and when combined with his unique spiritual perspective, he felt haunted upon hearing of the demise of his namesake some 200 years ago.

"Helene?" Matt's serious interruption brought the dinner conversation to an abrupt halt.

"What is it Matt?" Helene responded in a similar tone.

"Can we do the Ouija Board after dinner? Please?"

"I was hoping you'd ask." Helene responded in a warm and knowing smile.

The Ouija Board was a tradition Helene had started with the boys several years back. She and Mallory, Matt and Eric, would sit for hours asking all sorts of questions, big and small, while the hands whisked about the board in a seemingly knowing fashion. Tom would play occasionally to keep the mood upbeat by posing questions designed to evoke an innocuous response, such as "Who will win the big game tomorrow night?" or How many fish will I catch next Saturday?"

David, on the other hand, nearly always abstained, claiming that his scientific nature obscured the supernatural response. Mallory, being more open to spiritual phenomena, played as though there might be something to it after all. In this regard the boys definitely inherited her disposition, or psyche, or aura, or whatever else one might call it.

But Helene was in a class all her own. She was a spiritual child, and had managed to retain that persona despite the ravages of adulthood. Even David had to admit there was something otherworldly about her. Helene could see life through the eyes of a child, with all the wonder and innocence it conveyed. It was little wonder that Matt and Eric had developed a special closeness to her.

And the Ouija Board came to life in her hands. With eyes closed, her fingers would race across the board as words were formed to address the questions posed by the participants.

David would often observe these seances from just a few feet away, hoping to catch a glimpse of Helene opening an eye, or forcibly moving the spelling marker. To his consternation he could not see any flimflam in her movements. This would make David feel even more uncomfortable because Helene's responses usually made sense. They were grounded in reality. That was why the boys liked doing the Board with her. And tonight would be no exception.

While Mallory and Helene cleared the dinner table, Tom set about 'helping' the boys start a fire in the common room. No starter logs or gas fires here. This was the real thing, commencing with shredded newspaper, then layered with kindling and topped with several criss-cross logs. The boys took particular pride in the preparation, fully cooperating up until the point when it had to be decided who got to strike the match. Then all hell broke loose. Tom finally settled the dispute by having them take turns each night. The first night was settled by a coin toss which Eric won, much to Matt's dismay.

With all the ritual and formality of a high priest, Eric struck the match and set the papers ablaze. Soon thereafter the kindling caught and the small logs were not far behind. The men then set to bringing in the larger logs from the side porch, as the salty laced chill promised make it a good night for a fire. The boys had showered and the evening chores finished before they all settled back in front of the fire with the Ouija Board on the floor. Several candles were lit to enhance the atmosphere. Matt, Eric and Helene were the first to position themselves around the board.

Matt spoke up. "Can I start?"

"I thought you might," smiled Helene. "Please begin."

The crackle from the fire and the strategically placed candles set the mood. Even the wind had picked up outside, sending a drafty howl through the old wooden shingles.

Matt began, emulating the opening lines oft used by Helene. "Oh spirits. We believe in only good. We seek your guidance. Is anyone there?

Guided by Helene, their hands raced across the board, quickly spelling out the letters 'Y-E-S'.

Matt smiled confidently and then continued. "Can you give us a sign?"

As they quietly listened, Tom slowly moved his hand around Helene and pinched her bottom. She let out a yelp that startled the boys, which immediately set Tom rolling about on the floor in laughter.

It took a few moments for the group to regain its composure and continue the séance, but Matt persisted.

"Will we get a dog soon?"

'Y-E-S' came the response.

"How soon?"

'V-E-R-Y'.

"What kind?"

'G-L-D'

"What kind of dog is GLD?" asked Eric.

"Possibly a golden retriever or a yellow lab." Helene replied.

"Just our luck we get an illiterate spirit." quipped Tom.

"My turn." Eric pleaded with Helene.

"Ok Eric." She said. "Give it a try."

But before Eric could utter a word Samson gave out a low, deep throated growl and bolted for the kitchen door. He was immediately followed by Delilah whose barking penetrated the entire house.

Everyone was startled, with Eric letting out a yelp before Tom settled them down by indicating that this was a normal response when someone pulled into the driveway. Nonetheless, everyone raced to the back door to determine the cause of the commotion. The barking was without letup.

At Tom's request, Matt and Eric each grabbed a dog and quieted them down. They remained alert, however, with ears erect and eyes staring intently at the door. Tom glanced out the window adjacent to the door, chuckled to himself, and then announced.

"Anybody here order a pizza? I guess you don't like our home cooking after all."

All five crowded around the window as a man with a bright blue jacket and cap carried a Domino's Pizza pouch from his car to the steps. Tom opened the door as the man commenced his ascent. He stopped abruptly when he saw the dogs.

"Good evening. I have a pizza delivery for Number 10 Shore Road. None of the houses are marked, at least none that I can see, and yours was one of the few that was lit. Did I guess right?"

All the while he spoke he stared at the two Danes who were still being restrained by Matt and Eric.

"Afraid not." said Tom. "Number 10 is around the corner and down about a half mile towards Misquamicut."

"Sorry to disturb you folks, and thanks for the directions."

"Not a problem." replied Tom.

And with that the man turned and headed back to his car. The adults made their way back to the common room but Samson and Delilah held their position, well trained and highly protective, until the pizza man got in his car and headed out of the driveway.

When all had returned to their positions in front of the fire it was apparent the mood had been broken and the seance was over. Mallory indicated it was nearly time for the boys to be heading to bed. Neither child resisted, for it had been a long and active day. As Mallory herded the boys up the stairs, dogs in tow, she overheard Tom remark to Helene.

"Funny. Most of the pizza deliveries around here are by high school kids trying to earn some spending money. This guy was well into his thirties, if not forty."

"Perhaps because it is late at night that they changed over to having older men make the deliveries, or maybe this guy is just down on his luck or between jobs." Helen offered one possibility after another.

"Maybe." said Tom. "But he was wearing a gold Rolex. I could see its distinctive markings in the porch light."

"Could be a fake. We certainly saw plenty of those in Singapore."

"Could be."

This last conversation left Mallory with an uneasy feeling. The boys wrestling broke her concentration, and she hurried up the stairs to get them settled for the night.

# CHAPTER 9

# Caracas to Angel Falls

## DAY SEVEN

Even though it was a morning off for David, he woke early. He never could sleep soundly in hotel rooms, and the Tamanaco proved to be no exception. Taking a moment to remember where he was, having traveled so much lately, David strode to the bathroom for his morning ablutions. Thinking of Mallory, Matt and Eric, he hoped they enjoyed their first day in Weekapaug and desperately wished that he were there with them. Although Caracas could be a wonderful, exotic and culturally fascinating city, David rarely played tourist when he was on assignment. Occasionally, his partner Steve would drag him out of his room to a cultural or sporting event, or to some quirky little dive that only the locals frequented but somehow Steve had discovered. David would reluctantly acquiesce, primarily to keep Steve company, or so he would proclaim. Yet secretly, he nearly always enjoyed himself.

"Steve, I miss you buddy. If only you could tell me what happened." David said aloud in the mirror while shaving. "I wish you were here now. I have an entire morning and nothing to do. You'd take care of that problem for me, and probably leave me nearly destitute in the process."

Then David grew sullen. Thinking of Steve saddened him. It even made him forget his own predicament for the moment.

"Steve died here in Caracas," he thought as he completed his shave and stepped into the shower. "Maybe I can find out a little more while I'm here."

And with that, David determined that his morning would be spent at the US Embassy.

After dressing and ordering up some breakfast from room service, David called over to the US Embassy. It was Saturday, but he knew Laura Ericson would most likely be there. He was right. After checking his Palm file for Laura's extension, he worked his way through the Embassy's auto dialing system until the familiar voice answered.

"Ericson here."

"Hello Laura, It's David Hastings."

"David. Good to hear from you. Are you in town?"

"I sure am. Staying at the Tamanaco. How have you been?"

"Busy, but doing OK. You're lucky you caught me here, being Saturday and all."

David laughed. He and Steve had been meeting with Laura ever since the Angel Falls Project began. She always worked on Saturday, which was somewhat atypical of most of her colleagues in the State Department. However, Laura had been seconded from the Department of Energy to assume the Energy Attaché's position at the US Embassy. Not every embassy maintained such a position, but Venezuela was of vital strategic importance to the US energy supply, exporting several million barrels of oil every day to US refineries. In addition, Venezuela was an OPEC cartel member and held considerable sway amongst the mostly Middle Eastern, and somewhat anti-American, cartel. Laura Ericson's job was to keep tabs on the energy situation in Venezuela and ensure that US energy supplies were not jeopardized in any manner.

It was a high profile position that commanded significant amounts of time. Laura met frequently with the Ministry of Energy and Mines, and with executives of the national oil company, Petroleos de Venezuela SA (PDVSA). Although a somewhat chauvinistic society due to its strong European influence, Laura had managed to win the respect of her counterparts through hard work, a disarming personality, great command of the Spanish language, and terrific looks. In her early thirties, she kept extremely fit at the Embassy gym. Her auburn hair and powder blue eyes captivated those she met. Laura knew how and when to use this power, but she used it sparingly, knowing too well that it could easily get her into predicaments with her Latin male colleagues, many of whom maintained mistresses as a matter of tradition. She had been propositioned on numerous official occasions but always managed to turn a politically embarrassing situation into a face saving encounter, leaving the male suitor alone, but with his ego undamaged. It was a delicate balancing act, but she had perfected the moves.

David and Steve had met with Laura on official business nearly every time they were in Caracas. It was a two way street. She wanted an update on the Angel Falls Project, and OilQuest needed to keep its finger on the political pulse of the country. US assets had been nationalized before in Venezuela, and while it was unlikely to occur again due to differing economic conditions, legislation impacting their activities could never be totally discounted. Oil was still considered to be a national treasure to the Venezuelans, and many citizens loathed any foreign involvement, especially from their rich, haughty neighbors to the north.

After a year of official meetings, Laura, Steve and David had become good friends. They would often meet for dinner and drinks after work, and Steve would occasionally invite Laura out for an evening's entertainment. After all, she knew where all the hotspots were, where it was safe to go and where it wasn't. Although single, she had a boyfriend back in Washington, but the lengthy separation took its toll on the relationship. She figured out early on that Steve was gay, but thoroughly enjoyed his company. Besides, he made an ideal escort. While David found her to be good company and extremely good looking, especially after spending several weeks out in the jungle, he never strayed. His love for Mallory and the boys was overriding. Laura found this trait particularly admirable, which made David even more attractive to her. She was truly delighted to hear his voice on the phone.

"Laura, I'm only here for the morning. I leave for the rig site this afternoon, but I was wondering if we could get together. Any chance I could meet you at the Embassy?"

She smiled to herself at the invitation. "How about if I meet you in the lobby of the hotel in about an hour? Buy me a cup of coffee on the Veranda?"

"Sounds good to me."

Laura grew solemn. She remembered about Steve.

"David, I was awfully sorry to learn about Steve's death. I know you two were good friends. He was my friend too."

"I know. And thanks. Actually, I was hoping we could talk a little about that when you get here."

"Sure. See you in about an hour, but don't hold me to the exact time. You know how Caracas traffic can be."

"Tell me about it. I'll be waiting in the lobby. Bye."

As she put down the phone, Laura had mixed emotions. She was looking forward to seeing David. To get an update on the project as well as to simply enjoy his company. But she didn't relish the prospect of discussing Steve's demise. It had been a particularly gruesome murder. She had read the Embassy report on the killing, and it didn't please her to relay any of this to David.

It was nearly 10:00 am when Laura strode into the lobby of the Tamanaco Hotel. David had occupied a seat in a quiet corner. He stood and waved but did not walk over to her. Instead, he watched with amusement as heads turned and eyes followed her elegant, confident figure across the room to where he was standing. Being Saturday, she was wearing a lacy, translucent blouse, tight jeans and stylish black boots. David extended his hand to offer a professional shake, but she closed the distance between them to give a warm embrace. He returned the gesture, allowing himself to drink in the perfumed fragrance of her auburn hair. Still embracing, she pulled her head back slightly to look David in the eyes, her suggestive red lips just inches from his.

"Good to see you again, David."

Her breath was sweet. Her blue eyes deep as the Caribbean Sea north of Caracas. She was stunning. The world seemed to close in around them. David felt himself slowly losing control.

I love my wife. I love my wife. I love my wife, he silently repeated to himself over and over, eyes still transfixed by her captivating gaze. She broke the silence.

"David? Are you OK?"

He shook off his stupor.

"What? Oh yes, I'm fine. It's great to see you, and thanks for coming over. Let's go out on the Veranda Café."

After ordering a pot of strong Venezuelan coffee and some breakfast rolls, David gave Laura a status report on the Project. He decided not to tell her about the incidents in Plano, or the optional development plan he had discovered. It was too complex for this brief meeting, and he still had numerous unanswered questions. Until he knew more, his story would come off sounding like the ravings of a lunatic.

"I'm going out this afternoon for the final logging run on the Angel Falls #2 well. If it comes in as predicted, we will have ourselves one helluva field to develop."

"That will make the Venezuelan Energy Minister extremely happy, not to mention provide the US with an additional source of oil," Laura interjected.

"Let me know how it turns out as soon as you can. I'd love to get the scoop on this before the Ministry."

"I hate to burst your bubble, but PDVSA will most likely have a rep out on the site. They will send the info back to their headquarters almost simultaneously. I would think that the Ministry would be notified shortly thereafter."

David could see her disappointment. He thought for a moment while taking another sip of coffee.

"Tell you what I can do," he said. "I'll call you from the rig site if I can. Otherwise, I'll get in touch with you as soon as I get back, which would not be long. There's no need to hang about out there once I have the data in hand. And, PDVSA is a fairly cautious lot. They might hold off on making any announcement until they've had a chance to analyze the data themselves. That could buy us as much as a day."

She was thrilled with the suggestion.

"Oh David," she gushed with excitement. "That would be wonderful. Thanks so much."

"Please keep in mind," David cautioned, "that my first obligation is to the company. I must relay the info to them first. Once that is done however, I know they would want to give full cooperation to an authorized representative of the US government." He smiled.

"Of course."

"Laura I'd like to talk about Steve's death, if you can." The tone got serious.

"David, I'll be happy to tell you what I know, but I'm afraid it isn't much."

"I already heard the police report. Trouble is, it said Steve went to a bar and picked up a prostitute. He was then stabbed and robbed by the prostitute and her accomplices. You and I both know that Steve was gay."

David was clearly agitated. Laura put her hand on his in a calming manner. It seemed to work.

"I know. I read the Embassy report, which pretty much says the same thing. However, everyone assumes the prostitute was a woman. It could just as well have been a man."

Laura paused to let this sink in. David sat back, frustrated by another dead end. Then she continued.

"However, there is something that doesn't fit. But first tell me. Did Steve like to play the field, go to gay bars, pick up guys? You know what I mean?"

"Yes, I know what you mean. But Steve wasn't like that. He had a male companion back in the States. He liked to go out on the town, but usually only went to gay bars when he visited his friend. In Plano, he avoided them altogether, lest he be seen by someone from work. He really didn't want his sexual orientation to be known. Not that he was ashamed, but he felt it would inhibit his career. At a company like OilQuest, he would be right. And in a conservative town like Plano, Texas, it was just plain prudent to maintain a low profile. Why do you ask?"

"The reason I asked was that Steve's body was found in a particularly dangerous part of town. There are plenty of bars there where you can get just about anything you want, and I do mean anything: prostitutes, male and female, or young children, drugs, black market, even hi-tech weapons. You name it and you can get it there. It is so dangerous that even the police avoid it. It's like the old wild west. People get killed there every day and the authorities don't give it a second thought."

"That's not Steve," stated David.

"That's what I thought."

They sat in stony silence, each absorbed in their own thoughts as to what this revelation could possibly mean. David broke the silence.

"One possibility is that Steve was killed somewhere else and his body was dumped in that part of the city to throw off suspicion. That would avoid a lengthy and detailed police investigation."

"True," Laura replied, "but would common robbers go to such lengths? It strikes me as highly unlikely. Besides, police investigations in Caracas are far from exhaustive. Crime is so rampant that these things often go unreported, much less investigated."

"But the fact that Steve was an American might have been enough to make the killers want to go that extra mile to throw off an investigation."

Laura looked at David and gave a slight smile.

"David, sometimes you can be a little too naive. American citizens hold no elevated status in this country. If anything, we are often vilified, being accused of everything from suppressing the national economy to stealing their precious natural resources. Trust me, no common thief would go out of his way to cover up a robbery or a murder of a U.S. citizen."

This time it was David's turn to smile.

"Just playing devil's advocate. And thanks, you've answered my question."

Laura was impressed with this turnabout. Looks like there's more to him than I thought, she pondered. Not only good looking, but clever as well. Damn, why did he have to be married?

David studied her expression, wondering why she didn't ask the obvious. He cleared his throat. She awoke from her daydream.

"Sorry," she quipped. "What question did I just answer?"

"That Steve was probably killed for another reason, and that the robbery was only a cover up."

"Why would anyone in Caracas want to kill Steve?"

"You're really asking two questions. Why kill Steve, and why in Caracas? I believe that Caracas was just a convenient venue. Better here than in the States where there would be a more exhaustive investigation. As to why kill Steve," he paused, "I'm still working on that but it may be related to this project."

"Related to Angel Falls?" Laura grew intense. "You know something, don't you? Please tell me."

I've already said too much, thought David. Got to bring this to a close before she gives me the third degree. He took the oblique route.

"Were you aware that Steve's apartment was burglarized back in Plano?"

"No. Is there a connection?"

"Perhaps. Perhaps it's only a coincidence."

"That's it?" she stammered. "That's all you have to say is 'perhaps'?"

Her frustration was evident. This time it was David who took Laura's hand. She gave him a surprised look. This was indeed a first.

"Laura, please. I trust you implicitly, but I need to clarify some issues before saying anymore. Can you bear with me awhile longer?"

Normally Laura would not let anyone off so easily, but she was touched by the part about trusting her, implicitly. Leaning over the table towards him in a suggestive fashion, her blouse dipped to expose her taut cleavage. David eyed her breasts for what seemed like an eternity before returning his gaze to meet hers. She smiled knowingly.

"For you, David, I can wait. But don't do anything stupid. I don't want you ending up like Steve."

It may already be too late, he silently brooded. David nodded in compliance at Laura, stealing one last glance at her bosom before she leaned back in her chair.

"I better get back to the Embassy. I need to get out a weekly report."

David walked her back to the lobby entrance and waited while the doorman called for her car and driver. As the car pulled up, Laura pulled a card out of her purse and placed it tenderly in David's hand. She then gave him a warm embrace, a kiss on his cheek, and whispered in his ear.

"David, this card has my home phone. Call it day or night, for any reason."

He said nothing but returned the hug with equal enthusiasm. Kissing her cheek, he watched as she got into the car and drove off.

The doorman looked at the departing vehicle, then back to David. He winked.

David grinned and headed back into the hotel to pack for the journey to Angel Falls.

At 12:45 p.m., a van bearing the OilQuest logo pulled up to the entrance to the hotel.

"Not bad," thought David. "Only 15 minutes late."

It was the van used by OilQuest to ferry rig crews and other personnel around town and out to the heliport. Not very fashionable, but far more functional and less ostentatious than the chauffeured luxury sedans that cruised the upscale districts of Caracas. The Heliport was located adjacent to the airport south of town, so it would take a good forty-five minutes to an hour to retrace the route David took just the night before. Life was now in full swing at midday and the streets were thronged. But the driver skillfully maneuvered his way through the city and headed south on the airport road. David never tired of Caracas despite its gritty nature. Here, people lived their lives to the fullest, taking each day as it came. It was something he thought he could never do for he was always planning the next step. This time however, he felt a little closer to the people in the streets, for he had no plan whatsoever. He would have to react to whatever happened next, and he didn't like it one bit.

Upon nearing the international airport, the driver turned right at a fork in the road and continued past a sign that with a picture of a Helicopter. The road narrowed as if the jungle was trying to reclaim its rightful place and fight back the onslaught of man's expanding habitat. A few minutes later the van entered a clearing protected by a tall chain link fence. Pulling up to the front gate, an armed guard stepped from a small booth and greeted the now familiar driver, exchanged a few words, then took a look at David. David produced his passport for the guard. He quickly glanced at the picture, then back at David. Scowling, he handed him back the passport and waved the driver through.

Another Venezuelan delighted with an American presence, mused David.

The van pulled up to an aging metal building with a corrugated tin roof. The building served as an office, helicopter hangar, and storage depot for rig supplies. The local personnel were all on service contracts to OilQuest. They were extremely well paid relative to their counterparts back in Caracas. This sometimes caused some tension with PDVSA, who paid their employees less according to a national pay scale. Nonetheless, it was essential to keep this base well manned and efficient, for it was the lifeline to the rig site.

David grabbed his gear from the back of the van and gave the driver a small tip. Despite being against company policy, the driver happily accepted. Upon entering the office where he would sign in for the flight to the rig, David was stunned to see Corporate Security Chief Peter Bealls sitting in a chair, reading a porn magazine. The blood drained from his head. When he saw David, Peter Bealls put down the magazine and let out a sneer.

"Looks like they let anybody in here these days. I'll need to have a word with the security detachment. They really need to keep the riff-raff out."

"Bealls!" was all David could blurt out, still shocked by his presence.

"In the flesh."

David slowly regained his composure. It was bad enough that Watson was on site, but he had not anticipated having to deal with Bealls. He put down his gear bag and moved toward the counter to sign in for the flight. He finally found the breath to eke out a complete sentence.

"Going out to the site, or just taking a busman's holiday here at the base?" David hoped it was the latter.

"Heading out to the well, Hastings. Same as you. Yep, just you and me on this flight."

Bealls was thoroughly enjoying the moment for he could see he had unnerved Hastings. "Thought you could use some company."

"Just great," thought David. Once again his face went ashen.

Bealls just smiled and began flipping through the pages of his magazine, pausing to ogle a particular pinup. It was in Spanish, but then again he wasn't exactly reading.

David signed in and retired to the bathroom. Splashing cold water on his face, he looked at himself in the cracked mirror above the sink.

"There's no good reason for Bealls to be here," he said to himself. The Chief of Corporate Security rarely visits a rig site, and when he does it is early on in the process so he can advise on how best to secure the premises from any unwanted intrusion. He had already performed this service for the Angel Falls Project, last year. He's here because of me. Probably wants to keep tabs on me…or worse." David felt his stomach churning.

"At the same time," he reasoned, still staring at himself in the mirror, "this is a high profile project. If anything went wrong from a security standpoint, his neck would be on the line. And there was plenty that could go wrong, given the area and conditions under which they were operating. Only two years ago the OilQuest Managing Director for neighboring Colombia had been kidnapped from his office in Bogota. He was nearly killed because Bealls balked at paying the ransom, thus irritating a very impatient gang of kidnappers. Only when the Manager's finger was mailed to OilQuest headquarters did President Raymond Keith override Bealls and pay up. The man was released the very next day."

David knew there was too much riding on this project. The company could not afford to let down their guard for an instant. There were eco-terrorists who had already sent threatening letters to Keith. There were bandits, both in Caracas and around the site, and there were corrupt officials. Altogether it made for a witches brew capable of derailing the project at any step along the way. Thus, it was entirely possible, even probable, that Bealls was here to keep security tight and minimize the potential for a problem that could easily turn into a disaster for the company. Through the small frosted window above the urinal David heard the starting whine of the turbine engines of the Sikorsky helicopter. It was time to go.

Ducking his head as he boarded the helicopter, he saw that Bealls was already seated. It was a large chopper, used to ferry rig crews and supplies back and forth, so David moved to take the seat behind Bealls on the opposite side. Bealls looked up at David.

"Don't you want to sit with me so we can chat?" he mocked while pointing to the seat beside him.

"It's too hard to talk above the sound of the engines. We'd have to yell. Besides, I like to look out the window and enjoy the scenery."

David didn't wait for a response. He sat down and buckled up.

The pilot and co-pilot turned around to acknowledge their only two passengers and to confirm their seat belts were fastened. They then turned their attention to the instrument panel. A minute later, the chopper lifted vertically forty feet off the pad, hovered for a few seconds, then pointed the nose slightly down to begin the climb for the two and one-half hour journey to the rig site.

Once in the air, David settled back into his seat and explored the passing scenery below. For a helicopter it would be a long flight but the other options just did not work out for various reasons. The company had investigated the possibility of flying by fixed wing to Ciudad Bolivar, about 150 miles southeast of Caracas. There were no roads beyond the city, for it was situated on the northern edge of the rainforest. The city was being used by several tourist agencies as a base for flying eco-tourists to Angel Falls. The small planes they used were allowed to land on grass strips near the picturesque villages that surrounded the Falls. OilQuest had tried, but the Venezuelan government, with strong lobbying from the travel agencies and environmental organizations, had denied the company access to these sites. They successfully argued that the landing strips would have to be expanded and paved, and that the extra traffic would destroy the fledgling tourism industry and negatively impact the rainforest and indigenous tribes. David could see their point and encouraged OilQuest to seek an alternate route. Hence, the chopper flight from Caracas for the entire 350 mile journey to Angel Falls.

David never tired of this trip. The steady drone of the turbines drowned out all but the scenery below. Roads, towns and farms eventually gave way to dense rainforest as they passed over Ciudad Bolivar.

This is how it all looked millions of years ago, before man, he thought.

A dense, lush green carpet of jungle foliage lay outstretched before him. It seemed to go on forever, following the curve of the horizon. Primitive. Foreboding. Rich in both natural beauty and resources, and under constant siege by mankind.

The pilots seemed to be enjoying the sights as well, following a river as it meandered through the jungle. The sun shone brightly and visibility seemed limitless save for the occasional steamy puffs of water vapor above the jungle canopy. An occasional village would come into sight and one could make out the children running and pointing at the noisy, mechanical bird as it passed overhead.

A few hours into the flight, David felt his eyelids becoming heavy. He nearly dozed off when the pilot's voice boomed over the speaker.

"Rio Churun, Rio Churun," he repeated as he motioned with one hand out the left side of the chopper.

Bealls, still engrossed in his porn magazine, glanced up briefly to look at the Churun River, then shrugged and went back to his literature. David peered out the window at the sight below. The Churun River fed into Angel Falls, so he knew they were getting close. As rivers go, Rio Churun was far from remarkable. In fact it was relatively small compared to several of the many rivers that ran through the Guyana Shield. In fact, to the utter dismay of the travel agents, it was nearly ephemeral in the dry season, becoming too shallow for canoes or rafts. Nonetheless, there was a surreal beauty to it as it quietly coursed southward, volume building from a bare whisper to a roaring climax at the Falls.

The helicopter broke away from the Rio Churun and circled around to catch a better view of Angel Falls from the south, looking north. As it did, the chopper passed over the Karac Indian village. A small grass landing strip lay to one side, with a single engine plane parked at one end. Karac was one of the few tourist villages near the Falls. The villagers would accommodate a few guests in purpose built lodges, and escort them, by canoe or on foot, to "Salto Angel" as Angel Falls was called. The scene brought back memories of the young native girl, Lolita, although he had no idea where her village might be.

Wonder how much longer it will remain like this, David pondered. Eco-tourism was on the rise, and despite the best of intentions, the growing enthusiasm for it now threatened the very concept of preservation that the industry espoused to protect. He recently read where skydivers had discovered Angel Falls, grabbing media attention for having jumped off the tallest waterfall in the world.

"What next?" he thought. "Going over in a barrel? Bungee jumping?"

As he amused himself with the many possibilities for further degradation, Angel Falls came into view. It filled the cockpit window. It was apparent that even the pilots, who had flown this route hundreds of times before, were still in awe at this dynamic spectacle. As they guided the chopper in for a closer view, the roar of the Falls overpowered even the mighty turbine engines. The chopper hung motionless, suspended in the air no more than two hundred feet above the ground and fifty feet from the thundering water torrent. Even Bealls dropped his magazine to pay silent homage to the raging beast outside as tons of water cascaded off the cliff, churning up spray and foam beneath him. It was a near mystical experience.

Angel Falls, at 3,212 feet (979 meters) was without question the tallest in the world. Here, the Rio Churun plunged from the Auyun Tepay Mesa to the forest floor below on the Guyana Shield. David was surprised to learn that the Falls had actually been named after an American explorer and aviator, James Angel, who discovered it in 1935. It had remained untouched for decades with the exception of a few brave souls, mostly explorers or researchers, who sought to unlock the secrets of the primeval region, whether for science or profit.

David could have stayed there forever, gorging on the powerful majesty that seemed to engulf him. But it was getting late and darkness would soon be upon them. Although the highly skilled pilots had their instrument ratings and were thoroughly trained in night flying, they were not keen on the idea of locating a four acre drill site in the middle of a vast jungle. They would then face the daunting challenge of trying to land on a small patch barely large enough to clear the blades on their chopper. It was a difficult maneuver in broad daylight. They never flew at night, unless it was a real emergency. Fortunately, that had not occurred, at least not yet.

The chopper gradually climbed like a glass elevator over the thundering course. Slowly, the whine of the gas turbines once again filled the tiny cabin.

Turning to the east with the setting sun at their backs, they made their way toward the rig site. Ten minutes later, the rig mast came into view. It was barely visible over the forest canopy, but the colorful Venezuelan flag that adorned its crest made it easier to spot. The co-pilot was chatting on the radio to the encampment below while the pilot busied himself at the controls. After dispensing with the formality of requesting clearance to land, the pilot circled the base to be sure that the landing pad was clear of debris or personnel and that everyone knew they were coming in. As they circled, David surveyed the site. At first everything seemed in order, just as he had left it when he was last here. The rig was alive with activity, ablaze with lights that are on 24 hours a day, with personnel manning the drill string and related equipment. The half dozen trailer units that had been airlifted in to perform various functions were tucked in place. The trailer that housed the company man who headed up the entire operation stood apart from the other trailers in elitist fashion. Small makeshift huts for the rig crew were lined up on one side. Spare drill pipe, drill bits and other rig parts lay at the opposite end of the camp, alongside the powerful diesel generators that ran nonstop, providing electrical power to the entire base. Some of the crew waved at the incoming helicopter, for it meant fresh food and supplies, newspapers and mail from loved ones. And for the lucky few, it meant a ride back on the chopper tomorrow morning as their fourteen day shift comes to an end.

"Everything looks normal," David said aloud, knowing that he could not be heard above the engines as the chopper hovered about a hundred feet above the pad before setting down. Then he saw it. Just a few hundred yards beyond the four acre encampment. It was separated from the rig site by the dense jungle foliage, but he was not mistaken. It was a small clearing, no more than an acre or two, with tents. And he could see several men in army fatigues moving about.

"Now that is new," he said in a loud voice that was overheard by Bealls.

Bealls turned. "Did you say something?"

"I said 'Nothing new.'"

"What did you expect, a welcoming party? The red carpet treatment? Sorry, but you'll have to slum it like the rest of us."

David did not respond. The chopper had begun its descent. The other camp disappeared from view. He was alarmed at what he had seen, although it may be just a precautionary measure to beef up security, especially now that they were nearing their objective. He had not been told of this new arrangement for added security, but then again, no one was telling him much at all these days.

After all, he was just a geologist. He and Steve may have made the discovery and picked the well locations, but it was now in the hands of the drillers. He was here to supervise the logging of the well and to get the results back to headquarters the fastest way possible. That was it.

Oh yes, and one more thing, he reminded himself. Don't get killed.

The helicopter was now hovering a foot above the pad. A man outside with hardhat and a bright orange vest stood just off the pad, giving directions to the pilots. Another man stood by with a large foam fire extinguisher, just in case something should go wrong. With a signal from the man with the vest, the chopper dropped the final foot to the ground. A slight bump. Bealls heaved a deep sigh of relief. Apparently, helicopters were not high on his modes of transportation. The drone of the gas turbines gradually faded and the whirling blades slowly came to a halt. The man with the vest ran over and opened the doors. The steamy humidity from the jungle outside instantly permeated the once air-conditioned cabin of the helicopter.

Just like Houston, thought David as he was enveloped in the suffocating air, only less traffic.

He followed Bealls out the door and over to the side as the luggage and supplies were unloaded. Neither spoke. Grabbing his gear bag, David walked over to the company man's trailer for the obligatory sign in. Upon opening the trailer door, he abruptly stopped and stared at the man behind the desk.

"Surprised to see me Hastings?" Rick Watson sneered.

"Nothing surprises me anymore Rick."

Bealls entered the trailer.

"Hello Pete. I see you forgot to take out the trash when you came this time," Watson quipped as he nodded in David's direction. Bealls guffawed.

"I thought we could keep a better eye on our inquisitive friend this way," replied Bealls.

"Good idea, but he's not bunking in my trailer. Hell, I'd have to sleep with one eye open all the time."

"I wouldn't sleep at all as long as he's around."

David stood there with a deadpanned expression while Watson and Bealls howled at his expense. Finally he broke in.

"If you gentlemen are finished with your pre-pubescent taunts, I'd like to get started. Rick, what's the status of the #2 well?"

Watson composed himself and returned to business.

"The drillers have reached a total measured depth of 19,000 feet. Currently, we are pulling the drill string out of the open hole. We will condition the hole prior to running wireline logs."

"What's our true vertical depth?" inquired David. The Angel Falls #2 well was being directionally drilled from the same drill site used for the #1 well. This greatly minimized the impact of their activities on the rainforest, albeit at considerable expense. Drilling to reach a target that was not only two miles down, but also nearly a mile away, was a fairly complex procedure. However, despite Watson's numerous personality defects, he was an exceptional driller. He made his efforts look like a casual stroll in the park.

"TVD is 14,023 feet. We are on target, as always," boasted Watson.

Bealls had grown impatient with the technical discussion. Heading toward the door, he turned.

"I'm going to take a look around, then get some grub. I'll leave you two to catch up on old times."

As Bealls strode out the door of the unit into the early evening sky, David continued his line of questioning. It was routine procedure, although normally David would also be obtaining information from the wellsite geologist he was to relieve. However, the geologist was already gone due to the sudden yet suspicious family emergency.

"Any problems with the hole thus far?"

"Nothing that I can't handle."

Not satisfied with Watson's cryptic response, David persisted.

"You know what I mean. For data gathering purposes, is the hole sticking or are there any washouts?

"Probably a few washouts where we drilled into some unconsolidated sediments, but no sticking. This hole is slicker than duck shit in a snowstorm. So don't sweat it, you won't have any problems getting your tools down this hole."

"When do you think we'll be ready to run logs?"

"Not for another twelve hours."

"Twelve hours," David thought. "That means fourteen to sixteen hours at the earliest." Drillers nearly always overestimated how soon the well could be ready to log. David figured they did it just to irritate the wellsite geologist.

"One more thing," said David.

"What's that?"

"What's with the second clearing and the army types just over the hill?"

Watson scowled, obviously irritated with the question.

"They were here when I arrived yesterday. Probably heard you were coming so the government decided they needed to triple the security around here."

"Funny."

"I thought so."

"Think I'll go for a stroll," David said, turning toward the door. Watson grabbed David's gear bag and shoved it hard into David's chest, their faces just inches apart.

"Good idea, Hastings. Now don't wander off on me. We wouldn't want anything to happen to you, at least not until after the well is logged. And while you're at it, find yourself a place to bunk for the night. I only got room for one other man in this unit, and Bealls outranks you."

David stepped out of the unit and slammed the door so loudly that it could be heard above the din from the well. Several crew members abruptly stopped their tasks and stared at him as he left the trailer. David felt their eyes trail him as he made his way over to the Halliburton wireline logging unit. The sun had set and the dark jungle seemed to close in around the four acre compound. Lights blazed from the diesel generators as men worked round the clock, for drilling operations were conducted 24 hours a day, seven days a week. No break for holidays, not even Christmas. David recalled how, in his early years, he had been called out on a well in East Texas on Christmas morning. Not something he normally cherished, but he fully understood the rationale because drilling was an expensive operation, requiring specialized equipment, supporting services and trained crews. All of this cost money, a lot of money. On some offshore operations, which were typically more expensive for logistical reasons, costs would sometimes run as high as $250,000 a day, fully loaded. The Angel Falls wells, given their remote location and the difficult operating environment, weren't far behind that figure.

A few soldiers were milling about, rifles slung around their shoulder. They chatted amongst themselves while puffing away on cigarettes, ignoring the ubiquitous no smoking signs posted in both Spanish and English.

Fairly lax security. Can't be expecting an attack on the compound anytime soon. Perhaps they are just a precaution, he thought consolingly.

Before he reached the logging unit, David heard his name shouted from across the site. It was Bealls; he was coming towards David, accompanied by a man in uniform. He studied them as they approached. The soldier appeared to be an officer, given the gold stripes on his shoulder epaulets. He also wore a red beret with a gold insignia, whereas the other soldiers he had previously observed had unadorned berets. The soldier was not carrying a rifle, but instead holstered a pistol. A dead giveaway for an officer. David could see that the officer was also intently studying him as they approached and came to a halt just a few feet apart.

"Colonel," stated Bealls, "This is Mr. Hastings."

The Colonel nodded, but did not extend his hand. David had started to reach out but withdrew his, nodding in return.

"Buenos Noches, Colonel. Como esta usted?" inquired David, attempting to exchange a few pleasantries in his native language.

"Bien," came the curt response. Nothing more. He continued to study David.

"Bealls, does the Colonel have a name?"

"Yes, but to you it's just Colonel. He heads up the security operations here on the ground. Those are his soldiers you see around the base. They are a special unit of the Venezuelan armed forces."

"I see."

David sensed that this was a crude, blatant attempt at intimidation. He told himself that, given this very remote and hostile environment, that he probably had good reason to be scared. And although a part of him was frightened, indeed very frightened, he refused to be intimidated so easily. He decided to go on the offensive.

"Habla usted Ingles?" David inquired if the officer spoke English.

"I speak excellent English," he sniffed with a hint of disdain.

"Wonderful. That will keep me from embarrassing myself with broken Spanish. Tell me, Colonel, why would a man of your high rank be posted out here with us? After all, on the Angel Falls #1 well, we had only a few guards provided by the local province. And, there was no trouble at all that would warrant a change in security measures."

The probe had found its mark, for the officer was caught off guard. He stammered. Upon seeing the dilemma, Bealls cut in.

"Security operations are my domain, Hastings. You stick to rock pounding."

The officer regained his composure.

'Mr. Hastings. Your company, with assistance from PDVSA, has made a very significant discovery. My government does not want anything to happen that would be harmful to this operation. I am here to ensure that all goes smoothly, and according to plan."

David didn't like the way he said "according to plan" but he had to admit that the explanation sounded plausible. He decided to break off the attack. No sense in making the Colonel mad. After all, David might even need his help if things got dicey.

"Of course, Colonel. Now I understand. Thank you for clearing that up for me," he said convincingly.

"De nada. It's nothing." He replied.

And with that parting remark, Bealls shot Hastings one last squinty-eyed glare and led the Colonel back across the compound. David continued on to the logging unit.

The Halliburton wireline logging unit was essentially a big, air-conditioned box that was packed floor to ceiling with sophisticated equipment for recording the data that would be picked up by the tools sent down into the well…A second storage container carried the tools that would be spooled by cable down the well. The operator of the logging unit would feed the wireline cable and tools down the hole until they reached bottom, Then, they would slowly pull the tools up, recording the data on the way up.

There were multiple tools that could be used in many combinations, but all essentially looked like a length of steel pipe, ranging from ten to thirty feet in length. They were built rugged, for they had to withstand temperatures greater than 450 degrees Fahrenheit, and pressures that often exceeded 15,000 pounds per square inch. Despite the rugged nature of the tools, they carried sensitive recording instruments, some of which contained a radioactive source. These devices measured data, such as temperature, pressure, conductivity, gamma resistivity, porosity, density and other characteristics of the rock. More recently, magnetic resonance imaging (MRI) had been added to the suite of logging tools, thus providing further data regarding the porosity and permeability of the rock.

The data, when analyzed altogether, helped the geologist distinguish the various lithologies, whether shale, sandstone, limestone or some combination thereof. Most oil and gas reservoirs are found in sandstones or limestones. At Angel Falls, the reservoir objective was a sandstone. In addition, the data would indicate whether the reservoir rock contained oil, natural gas, or water in its pore spaces. It would also determine how much oil or gas was present in the rock, and over how large an interval. Armed with this information, the geologist could then determine if further testing was warranted or if the well should be declared non-commercial, i.e. a dry hole.

Despite all the sophisticated recordings, however, David knew from hard experience that hydrocarbon exploration was still far from an exact science.

One had to use all the information available to determine the potential of a prospect. Another vital source of information could be found in the mud loggers unit, immediately adjacent to the Halliburton trailer. After parting with the Halliburton crew, he walked next door to the mudlogging unit, knocked once out of courtesy, and, without waiting for a response, entered the unit.

David had broken into a sweat just walking the forty feet from the wireline unit. The air conditioning from the trailer provided welcome relief from the stifling humidity outside. Inside the unit were two men, one American and the other Venezuelan. It was typical of international joint ventures to employ both specialized help from the States and local assistance wherever possible. Both spoke perfectly good English, the Venezuelan using better grammar. After introducing themselves, first names only, as Ben and Jorge, David sat at a counter with microscope to review some of the rock samples they had preserved for analysis.

Mud, as the drilling fluid is called, is not really mud at all but rather an often complex mix of ingredients. The drilling fluid serves several functions: it cools the drill bit and drill pipe, it helps keep the hole in shape and prevents sloughing, and it brings rock cuttings to the surface. Perhaps most importantly, it prevents blowouts by keeping hydrostatic pressure on the rock formations. The mud often contains barite and polymer compounds used to reduce friction and maintain a specific weight, or density, as the pressures increases with depth. Drilling mud had become a science in and of itself.

The mudlogging engineers, along with the mud engineer, are responsible for maintaining the mud system. They monitor the properties of the mud and the condition of the well. If there is a problem they report it immediately to the company man, in this case, Rick Watson. With input from the mud engineer, he decides on a corrective course of action. A generation ago, the mudloggers manually conveyed the information to the company man. Today however, all vital drilling information was conveyed to the company trailer by cable where a video display read out a constant stream of vital statistics on the condition of the well. It was a highly dynamic system, with input from mud engineers, recording instruments, data from the drill floor such as rate of penetration and weight on the drill bit. Depths, both measured and true vertical, were displayed in columnar fashion on the screen as the drill bit inched its way along the targeted path. The whole process fascinated David, and he was always eager to shed the sterile confines of the office environment for a hard hat and steel toed boots for a trip to the wellsite.

In addition to helping maintain the condition of the well bore, the mudloggers kept a running record of the rock cutting information. The rock cuttings were bits of rock cut by the drill bit and carried back to the surface by the circulating mud system. Once back on the surface, the mud would run through several sets of screens and filters where it would drop out the rock cuttings and be reconditioned for the trip back down the hole. The rock cuttings provided valuable information as to what lithology, or rock type, was being drilled and if there was any oil or natural gas associated with those cuttings. A gas chromatograph ran constantly as the well was being drilled. While the presence of natural gas in a well bore was a good early indication of hydrocarbons, the gas could also present a real danger. If a significant amount of gas enters the well bore all at once and severely cuts the weight of the drill mud, it could cause a blowout by allowing the great pressures at depth to rush up the well bore to the surface. Once on the surface, the escaping gas could easily be ignited by a spark and explode, burning the rig and killing the crew. David recalled with some amusement the classic movies of a well gushing oil and men dancing beneath the shower of hydrocarbons. Nothing could be more dangerous to men and equipment, not to mention destructive to the environment. Yet, it made for good viewing entertainment, when life was far less complicated.

"Any shows?" David asked of the two mudloggers as he studied the last batch of rock cuttings through a binocular microscope.

"There are oil shows in the target sandstone at the top of the formation, and the gas chromatograph has good indications of heavy gas concentrations in the same interval," said Ben.

"Excellent, are we through the entire formation?"

"Yes," responded Jorge. "We are a good eighty feet below the sandstone, so you should be able to get a full suite of wireline logs over the target.

"Good work," David replied, still peering through the microscope, changing out samples from time to time.

"There is something a bit curious," said Ben.

David stopped his work and looked up. "What's that?"

"Well, the oil shows are there alright, but they seem to change character somewhat after about forty feet. I see from the mudlog in the first well, the Angel Falls #1, that the oil shows and associated gas readings remained steady throughout the entire two hundred foot interval in the target formation. In this well, the oil shows diminish somewhat after about forty feet. No need to panic. The shows are still present throughout the entire interval, just a little less pronounced."

David thought about the possibilities, which were numerous. First off, they were now drilling a directional well whereas the #1 well was a straight vertical well. The drilling fluids had been altered significantly as well as the downhole equipment. In addition, the mudlogging units had been changed out between wells. Different equipment often yields different results. In addition, the mud-logging crew was also new, and describing rock cuttings and oils shows was a fairly subjective process. There were other, more sinister explanations, but David felt there were just too many variables to draw any specific conclusions. Besides, there wasn't much he could do about it now. The well had reached its total depth and they would be logging within twenty-four hours. They would soon find out what was down there. The two mudloggers were still staring at David as he labored through this thought process. He finally became aware of their stare.

"Sorry. I was just mulling over the possibilities. Thanks for telling me." David looked over and saw the small set of bunks at the other end of the trailer. He felt his eyes droop.

"Say, would you mind if I stretched out on one of those bunks for awhile?"

They looked at him, somewhat puzzled. Normally, the wellsite geologist would sleep in the company man's trailer. David could read their expression.

"The company trailer is full. Corporate types," he offered.

This seemed to satisfy them and Ben gestured toward one of the bunks.

"Feel free to use mine. I won't be needing it for some time. I still have to complete the mudlog."

"Thanks. I'm gonna grab a bite to eat and check out things on the drill floor. Then I'll be back for a quick nap. See you in about an hour."

David stepped out into the heavy night air. Despite the steady hum of the diesels and the ever constant activity on the rig floor, the remainder of the site had shifted to a nocturnal mode. Only essential activities continued through-out the night. As food was considered essential, the mess tent was open twenty-four hours a day. Unlike most operations offshore, the cooking was all done out in the open. Only a large canopy protected the kitchen area from fall-ing debris from overhanging tree branches, or from the incessant rains. Meals were served four times a day, every six hours, in order to accommodate the twelve hour tours of the rig crew. In between meals, snacks and drinks could always be obtained.

The evening meal was still in progress and David helped himself to a large bowl of rice and beans. It was simple food, but hearty, stocked with sausage and chunks of beef. People usually ate well while out on a drilling location.

While the food was not necessarily healthy, it was almost always tasty and abundant. David sat at one end of a picnic table, exchanged a short "Hola" with the two men chatting at the other end of the table, and quietly ate his dinner. The men at the table had just finished theirs and had lit up their cigarettes. They casually chatted between puffs on their local smokes and cups of sweetened coffee.

"They're probably part of the drilling crew: roustabouts and roughnecks," thought David. As he ate he caught snippets of their conversation, which was in Spanish. He tried to imagine what life must be like for these men. They were relatively young, in their late twenties and thirties. One was married as evidenced by the gold band on his hand. The other wore no jewelry, which was smart if you were handling drilling equipment. A snag on a watch, ring or bracelet could easily tear off a man's finger or wrist. It was dangerous enough on the rig floor without inviting disaster. Many a man had lost fingers, hands and feet by not paying strict attention to everything going on about them. Many had paid for this inattentiveness with their lives, which explains why you rarely saw an older man on the rig floor. Other than the drilling manager himself, this was not the kind of profession that one would pursue as a lifelong quest. It paid well because it was dangerous and dirty work. People took these jobs for one reason only, to make enough money so they could move on to better, safer things. And the men at the other end of the table were no exception. It did not matter what the nationality, this was universal.

Both men were from the Maracaibo region in western Venezuela, where the oil industry got its start. Billions of barrels had been pumped from Lake Maracaibo and the surrounding regions, at first by multi-national oil companies, most of whom were American. It was here that the multi-nationals were first accused of looting the natural resources of the country. Anti-American sentiment ran high. Eventually the foreign-owned assets were nationalized by the Venezuelan government. Like many struggling, lesser-developed countries, the Venezuelans resented an alien presence and wanted their resources to be exploited by their own people. It was a natural enough emotional response, but it set the country back for awhile until it could build its own infrastructure and operate on its own. However, Venezuela had done well. Its national oil company, PDVSA, was well respected throughout the industry. Its people were well trained and its oil production provided the catalyst for propelling the country into the big leagues. It joined the Organization for Petroleum Exporting Countries (OPEC) that succeeded in precipitating the energy crisis of the seventies. Although today both Venezuela and OPEC produce a much smaller component of the daily global oil demand of about seventy-five million barrels, they still exert significant influence on the highly volatile oil markets.

The two men stopped chatting and they both turned toward David. He hadn't realized that he had stopped eating and had been staring at them all during his reflections. He nodded at them and returned to his bowl of rice and beans. The men got up and walked off.

"Probably just another crazy gringo in their eyes," he said to himself as he speared a piece of sausage.

Finishing his meal, David had one last round to make before retiring for the night. Grabbing a spare hardhat from a nearby rack, he headed for the center of all this attention, the rig floor. Climbing the metal staircase to the floor, which stood thirty feet above the ground, the noise level increased with the force of a pile driver. He waved to the drilling manager who stood off to one side by a large bank of levers, controls, and gauges. He returned the nod but continued his fluid like movements over the controls that lay before him.

David watched the operation. They were currently pulling the drill string out of the hole in preparation for logging. Given the 19,000 feet of hole for this well, this single operation would take a good twenty four hours or more. They were already more than halfway through, as evidenced by the massive numbers of drill pipe that stood stacked on the derrick floor. The pipe came in thirty foot lengths. While drilling, the roughnecks and roustabouts would attach a length of pipe after drilling every thirty feet. To help make the connections they would employ huge mechanical tongs. Now that they were pulling out of the hole, they used the tongs to break the connections. They would then mechanically lift the disconnected piece of pipe and move it off to one side. This process would repeat itself over and over until all the drill pipe had been pulled out of the hole, revealing the drill bit at the end. The driller at the controls would direct the entire effort by applying the appropriate lever, either turning the drill pipe, or by lifting or lowering it.

To David it was like watching a well conducted orchestra, with each member knowing exactly what to do and when. It was apparent these men had worked together for some time, for there was very little shouting or hesitations. They knew each other's movements before they made them. Good thing, too, for they also depended on each other for their very lives.

As he continued to watch the ongoing performance, David still found it difficult to comprehend that this narrow string of steel pipe, barely eight inches in diameter, could string its way nearly four miles beneath the surface, encountering extreme temperatures and pressures as it probed deeper and deeper into the earth's crust. What's even more amazing, was that this well had wound its way horizontally to a bottom hole location that was 5,000 feet away from where he was standing. Small, directional motors aided by gyroscopic surveys had enabled this skillful crew to hit their target squarely on the nose. Much as he harbored a certain disdain for drillers, David had to admire their capabilities.

Satisfied that it would be at least another ten to twelve hours before they would be ready to log, he turned to head back to the mud logging unit and a few hours of sleep. As he took his first step, a large pipe wrench slammed to the floor beside him. It clanged on the grated metal, sending off sparks as it hit. David, still visibly shaken, looked up the tall derrick in the direction from which it came. The bright halogen floodlights shining down on the rig floor nearly blinded him, obscuring everything above in near total darkness. He looked over at the crew on the rig floor who had taken no notice, maintaining their symphonic operations without breaking stride.

That could have killed me, David thought as he hurried down the stairs and across the compound. Upon reaching the door of the mudlogging trailer, he turned to take a final look at the rig. Away from the blinding glare of the floodlights, he could now make out the shadow of a figure standing high up on the derrick mast, on a small platform referred to as a monkey board. The figure appeared motionless, and David imagined that he was staring down at him.

Was it an accident? he wondered. After all, they do position men up there to help move the drill pipe around. Tools do get dropped on occasion, sometimes down the hole where they can wreak havoc.

I'm getting way too suspicious, he told himself. The whole world can't be out to get me. Still, I wonder where Watson and Bealls are right now? And who had the shift on the monkeyboard?

Trying hard, but without much success, to convince himself that it was an accident, he entered the trailer and made his way to the bunk. At least in the mudlogging unit he would have company, and he knew that at least one of the mudloggers would be awake all night.

"Better get some sleep. It'll be a very long day for you tomorrow," said Ben.

"True. And I am beat. Thanks again for the bunk space."

"De nada." Even Ben was picking up the language.

Before drifting off, David thought of Mallory and the boys. He smiled contentedly, knowing that they were enjoying themselves in Weekapaug and that at least they were safe.

# CHAPTER 10

# Assault in Weekapaug

## DAY SEVEN

Morning came too soon for Mallory as the boys once again awakened her just as the sun came streaming through her window. It was the start of another breathtaking day and they did not want to waste one minute more in bed.

"What are we going to do today?" asked Eric.

"I want to go fishing," said Matt.

Mallory didn't mind fishing, or baiting hooks, but she absolutely hated cleaning the fish. And even though the boys loved to fish, they didn't like to eat it. Mallory quickly scanned for a compromise.

"If it's not too late in the season, how about going for a boat ride?"

She could tell by their hesitation that she was only half way there.

"And, you can each take turns steering the boat," she added.

That clinched the deal. Both boys agreed in unison.

"Good, now get out of my room so I can get dressed. Put on some warm clothing, like the sweatshirts I bought you, and I'll meet you downstairs for breakfast. We can go boating after we eat."

Tom and Helene were nearly out the door by the time Mallory came down. Matt and Eric were busily downing their cold cereal. No time for a hot meal because there was adventure afoot.

"Well good morning, sleeping beauty," chided Tom.

"Morning Tom. Morning Helene. Are you off already?"

Helene responded first. "Afraid so. We have a group of first graders from South Kingstown elementary school coming to the sanctuary at 9:00 am, and we need to get things set up. Mind looking after Samson and Delilah for us again today?"

"Not a problem. They are great company. Oh, we were thinking of going for a boat ride on Quonnie this morning. Is it ok if we use your boat?"

"Sorry, but we just pulled the boat out of the water a week ago and had it winterized", replied Tom. "However, the marina is still renting for another month, and I doubt you will have much trouble getting a boat at this time of year."

"Sounds good. We'll head over there shortly and rent one for a few hours."

"I suspect that, after a few hours, you will be sufficiently frozen," mused Helene. "It seems warm outside but it can get pretty cool on the open water."

"Can we take the dogs?" inquired Matt. "They'll keep us warm."

Helene laughed. "Believe it or not, they are not too thrilled with the water. I think it best they stay here, where it will be warm and comfortable. They usually take a seat by a window and follow the sun around during the course of the day."

"Ok," said Tom. We are off and we'll see you tonight. Have fun."

"Of course," responded Eric. "We always have fun when we're here."

The Quonnie Marina was either a long walk or a short drive, so Mallory elected to drive. It was only 8:30 am by the time they pulled into the gravel parking area alongside the weathered wooden shack that served as the marina office. By some miracle the shack had survived the ravages of the 1938 hurricane. That hurricane leveled nearly every structure along the Connecticut and Rhode Island shoreline. And yet, the tiny two-room shack had merely been swept clean and shifted a few feet along the shore. Some attribute this quirk of nature to the numerous openings in the one story building which allowed the wind and water to enter and exit, escaping with the entire contents but without damaging the structure itself. Others, especially the fishermen who tend to be a superstitious lot, believe the shack to be a sort of sacred place, or at the very least a good luck charm. They would still occasionally nail a swordfish tail to the side of the building, perhaps to bring the good luck to their own boats. To most folks, however, the Quonnie Marina was now an institution, with its image appearing on local postcards alongside those of distinguished mansions of Newport.

The boys were the first to reach the shack. As they entered they breathed in deeply so as to take in the abundance of odors, ranging from boat paint to live bait to day old coffee. As Mallory entered she instinctively held her breath, remembering the time she threw up over the bait locker nearly 15 years ago. Finally she inhaled, and was pleasantly relieved to find she could now stomach the malodorous concoction, probably because the windows were open and a constant, fresh breeze purged the air.

She was surprised to find a young woman in jeans and wool shirt standing behind the creaky, scratched glass counter.

"Good morning," the woman said as she wiped sandworm remnants from the counter top.

"Good morning," replied Mallory. "Does Ol' Joe still run this place?"

"Yes, he's still the boss. However, he left for the Florida Keys right after Labor Day. Business really winds down after that, especially the boat rentals. I'm his daughter and he left me to close up shop at the end of this month."

"Sorry, I didn't mean anything derogatory by calling him 'Ol' Joe'. It's the only name I've ever heard him called," Mallory responded sheepishly.

"Don't be. Everyone calls him that, even my mother."

They both laughed.

"Well, we are here to give you some business. Do you still have any boats to rent? We need one for a few hours to ride around Quonnie."

"Sure. Take your pick." The woman pointed out the window facing the water, which revealed an assortment of boats. "Plan on taking her out to open ocean?"

Mallory was quick to respond. "Not a chance. The pond is big enough, and I don't particularly care for the breachway."

The woman cast a knowing glance at Mallory and then over at the boys who were busily discovering the contents of the bait locker.

"Wise decision. No sense in taking any unnecessary chances this time of year. On Labor Day weekend a twenty-foot Sea Ray was tossed on the rocks like it was a toy boat. The folks would have drowned if the fishermen on the rocks didn't pull them in. The boat was a total write-off however. Won't be many fishermen to pull you out at this time of year."

Mallory nodded in agreement. Over the years she had heard of many such encounters, some ending in fatalities. The breachways of South County were notorious as being amongst the worst along the entire east coast. Even experienced boaters harbored a healthy respect, and a tinge of fear, for passage through the Quonnie breachway, considered one of the most dangerous.

"The Boston Whalers look good to me," Mallory indicated by pointing out the window at a row of sleek blue and white sixteen-foot fiberglass boats.

"Perfect size for the three of you, and a lot of fun in the pond. The 65 horsepower mercury gives you plenty of punch. You can even pull two skiers at a time," smiled the woman as she directed the last comment at the boys.

Matt and Eric simultaneously beamed at the suggestion, but Mallory was quick to bring this possibility to a halt.

"Not today guys. Too cold and too much trouble."

The boys began to quibble but a sharp glance from Mallory was all it took to make them realize this was a non-starter. They went back to inspecting the bait locker.

With a big grin on her face the woman broke the silence. "With that settled, let's fill out this form and get you gassed up."

"Good idea."

The boys jumped into the center console whaler like old salts, donning life jackets and taking up positions near the bow. They both had spent a fair amount of time on boats, large and small, and were familiar with the procedures. After hooking up the portable gas tank to the flow line, Mallory made sure the engine was in neutral. She squeezed the primer bulb on the gas line until she felt resistance, knowing that the gas was being delivered to the engine. With a turn of the key the mercury cranked for a few seconds, sputtered, then roared to life. Mallory, while still in neutral, pushed the throttle forward to rev the engine. Smoke billowed from the outboard and quickly cleared after warming up.

Mallory gave a nod to the woman who was standing on the dock; she unhooked the bow and stern lines, letting the boat drift slowly away from the dock.

"Be back in a few hours," Mallory shouted above the motor.

"Take your time," responded the woman as she waved goodbye and headed back to the shack upon seeing a car pull in.

Mallory adjusted her life vest, placed a seat cushion under her for both comfort and increased visibility over the small Plexiglas windshield. The boys were instinctively balanced on a seat in front of the console.

Mallory checked the gauges. Water pressure was good. Engine temperature was in the normal range. She put the throttle in forward gear and eased the boat past the line of rentals and out of the dock area.

Once in open water, she yelled to the boys. "Ok, let's see what this baby can do."

And with that remark she thrust the throttle forward. The engine roared as the bow leapt out of the water. The boys, grasping each other with one hand and the seat with the other, howled with delight. The bow dropped as the boat reached a planing speed of 20 miles per hour. Mallory, one hand on the steering wheel and the other on the throttle, checked the gauges again. Everything normal. She slowly increased the throttle, bringing the speed up to 25 miles per hour. Looking at the throttle, Mallory realized she still had more play, but elected to maintain this cruising speed for the time being.

Guess the lady was right about being able to tow two skiers, she said to herself.

The cool autumn air brought an invigorating chill to her cheeks as she zipped her windbreaker up to her neck. The boys were impervious to the chill, their eyes darting from one side to the other, occasionally pointing out an object of interest.

Quonnie Pond was only about a half mile wide but was at least two miles long, with an abundance of small inlets and channels to explore. Mallory eased back slightly on the throttle as she cruised along the shoreline, taking time to peruse the houses which dotted the landscape. Mostly summer cottages, there were few, if any, signs of life. The mostly gray, cedar shingled houses, some quaint, some majestic, stood as silent sentries over the pond. Some were boarded up in the event of a major winter storm or late season hurricane such as the hurricane of October 1938. Other cottages were somewhat more inviting, with large picture windows and screened in porches replete with wicker furniture. An occasional Adirondack chair would be ceremoniously placed on a sprawling lawn that led down to the water's edge. Some of the inhabitants would weekend here through Thanksgiving, but Labor Day always signaled the end of another summer season. Mallory sighed as she imagined herself on one of those porches, lazily working a jigsaw puzzle while sipping a gin and tonic.

"Someday," she whispered under her breath. "We will be here. I know it is meant to be." She thought of the many times she and David had looked at the cottages and talked about moving to Weekapaug, only to reconfirm that they had not accumulated sufficient savings to undertake such a dramatic lifestyle change. This last thought was frustrating, so she shifted her gaze down the length of the pond and turned toward the next inlet which lined the shore.

There was a hint of an onshore sea breeze, with a little chop on the water. Without a barrier beach to break the fetch, Mallory knew that the conditions would be far more dramatic out in the open ocean. Good decision not to go out there. Besides, it was far more interesting in the pond.

An hour had passed as they cruised the inlets. As promised, each boy took turns at the helm. Mallory would sit close by, giving gentle commands as they approached rocky protrusions or mooring buoys. Matt always had to be watched more closely, as he had a tendency to play with the throttle and make sharp, high speed turns. Eric was steady, preferring to move effortlessly around obstacles. He liked to keep a close eye on any traffic around him. Today, his job was made easy as they had yet to encounter another boater.

Upon exploring the last inlet at the far end of the pond, Mallory once again took over the helm to commence a gentle cruise back. Dropping to a leisurely 15 miles per hour, the motor quieted and the boat glided through the dark green waters. As the sun streaked through the clouds, it cast alternating light and dark patterns on the water. Matt peered into the shallow waters to scan for signs of aquatic life, spotting the occasional striped bass in hot pursuit of a baby eel. The distinctive trails of horseshoe crabs were plainly etched in random, criss-cross patterns in the sandy bottom. Blue shell crabs sought food and shelter in the patches of seaweed or rocky crevices that graced the submarine landscape.

As Mallory entered the main body of the pond and turned west toward the marina at the far end, she noticed another whaler adrift, motor silent, approximately 200 yards away. She could make out the appearance of two men. One was hunched over the motor with the engine cover off. The other was standing near the bow and waving his arms in an effort to attract Mallory's attention. No other boaters were to be seen. Eric and Matt were still deeply engrossed in surveying the sea life. Mallory slowly approached the other boat. At one hundred yards she could see it was another rental, the same size whaler and motor as hers. The man at the bow had stopped waving as he had succeeded in getting Mallory's attention.

Glad it wasn't my boat, Mallory said to herself with relief as she continued her approach. Mallory had grown up with the knowledge that one must come to the aid of a ship in distress. She didn't know if it was an unwritten rule that boaters lived by or whether it was actually codified in law. No matter, she was obligated to lend assistance. And she was happy to help, having been on the receiving end of the situation several times herself. By now the boys had also seen the other boat. They sat upright and quickly looked the situation over, knowing exactly what Mallory was going to do.

"Mom, are we going to tow them back to the Marina?" queried Eric.

"Possibly. But first let's pull up alongside and see what the problem may be," Mallory stated with all the solemnity and bearing of a harbor pilot.

At 50 yards, Mallory could now make out the appearance of the two men. The man at the bow had a dark complexion. He was in his late twenties or early thirties, about five foot, ten inches tall, with a slim frame. Dressed in black jeans with a hooded sweatshirt. With the hood pulled tightly over his head, he stood smiling as Mallory approached the boat from amidships. He gave a wave with one hand as to acknowledge her assistance, with the other hand resting comfortably behind him. On the stern, the second man was still bent over the engine compartment. The engine obscured his faced, but Mallory could see from his exposed left arm that he was Caucasian, slightly shorter than the other, and stocky. From the back of his head, Mallory also surmised that he was older, as a bald patch provided evidence of male pattern baldness.

Mallory was now within thirty yards of the other boat and closing. She had slowed so as not to cause a wake when she approached. The man at the bow was still waving and smiling in an almost mechanical fashion. This aspect unsettled Mallory but she could not keep herself from going to their aid simply because she didn't like the way the guy was smiling.

She glanced over at the man by the engine. He still did not look up.

"Odd," thought Mallory. Twenty-five yards. The sunlight reflected brightly off the man's wristwatch. It caught Mallory's eye. At 20 yards she could now see its unmistakable design. A gold Rolex.

"Pizza man!" She said aloud in alarm.

The boys looked up at Mallory in bewilderment.

The man by the engine turned his head for the first time for Mallory to see. It was definitely the man from last night. His dark eyes stared intently at Mallory, sending a shudder through her body.

"Hold on tight boys!" she screamed.

Without another thought she slammed down the throttle and jerked the wheel hard to the left. The engine responded with a howl. The boat leapt into the air and spun about, shooting a rooster tail of spray high into the air.

"Get down in the bottom of the boat," she yelled to Matt and Eric. Stunned only momentarily, they responded as directed and flattened themselves on the floor of the whaler.

The man at the bow of the disabled boat pulled his right hand from behind his back to reveal a handgun with silencer attached. He took aim at Mallory, a mere 25 yards away but still bouncing from the high-speed turn, and he squeezed the trigger. A bullet ripped into the steering console just inches from her right arm. A second bullet tore into the bulkhead where Matt had been sitting only seconds earlier.

By now the second man stood up, also holding a gun, and aimed at the fleeing craft. But before either man could get off another shot, the rooster spray from Mallory's high-speed maneuver washed over their boat, drenching both men in salt spray and temporarily obscuring their vision. They fired anyway but missed the boat. Mallory could see the bullets strike the water in front of her. She was moving away at a fast pace but still within target range of a good marksman. She dared not look back for fear she would see the bullet coming straight at her. Her hands were frozen to the wheel as if in a death grip.

But the fatal bullet never came. The blinding spray of the rooster tail was immediately followed by the large wake created by Mallory's outboard. It violently rocked the other boat, causing the men to grab the rails of the boat in order to steady themselves. It only lasted a few seconds, but those precious seconds were enough for Mallory to get the boat up to 40 miles per hour and just beyond the range of the handguns.

Not realizing that she had been holding her breath for the past minute, she inhaled deeply and relaxed her steely grip on the wheel but only slightly. She looked at the boys who were still splayed out on the floor but being bounced by the high-speed action over the water.

"Matt. Eric. Are you okay?"

"We're okay," responded Matt. Eric was still a bit dazed by the sudden turn of events. "Can we get up now?"

"Yes, but sit low in the boat and hold on tight. You can use the cushions for seats on the floor of the boat."

Mallory turned her head to see what the other boat was doing. She was a comfortable two hundred yards away and steadily increasing the gap. Pizza man had moved to the steering console. She could see their motor come to life. The man at the bow, gun still in hand, had assumed a sitting position. The boat turned in their direction to pursue.

Mallory knew this was far from over. She also realized that this was somehow connected to the events in Plano.

"How did they find us?" she asked herself. "How could they know?"

She looked at her boys, huddled closely together, staring up at her with a mix of fear and incomprehension in their youthful eyes. She felt her throat clench. Tears began to well but she fought them back so as not to further alarm the boys.

No time to think about it. We've got to get out of here, she thought.

She had a good lead, and given that both boats were nearly identical, including the combined passenger weight, Mallory figured she could outrun them. This thought helped ease her nerves, but it was to be short-lived. She had made a tactical error. When she made her high-speed turn, she had turned left, or east. Had she turned right she would have been headed west, which was back toward the marina at the other end of Quonnie. They would have been safe.

The blood drained from her face. Her heart sank as the realization set in that she had trapped the boys and herself at the wrong end of the pond. The only way back to the marina would take them past the pursuing boat. They would surely move to intercept and she couldn't count on surviving another barrage of bullets at close range. It would be suicide.

The situation darkened further. She was rapidly running out of room at the end of the pond. Less than five hundred yards to go before she reached the other end. At this rate she would be there in a few minutes, and they would have her trapped. A horrifying vision of bullets tearing into Matt and Eric sent a shudder through her very being. And then a steely resolve began to slowly emerge. Her jaw tightened and her eyes narrowed. She took a deep breath.

"You want me," she screamed in the direction of the pursuing boat which was well out of earshot, "Come and get me."

She quickly scanned the eastern shore of the pond, which was rapidly looming large. She would be there in another minute. Although mostly rocky at this end, Mallory considered beaching the boat and running for help. This option was quickly rejected however as there were only a few houses and they all appeared to be shuttered for the season. There were no signs of life, and Mallory knew she could not run far with the two boys. Far too risky.

She looked to her right at the only remaining option that was still viable, the breachway. The boulder-lined channel with turbulent seas seemed to both beckon and threaten at the same time. The wind had picked up and the chaotic wave action at the breachway served up a tortuous cocktail of sea foam and storm surge with every assault upon the rocks. Mallory turned toward the channel. And while she secretly wished her attackers would call off the chase, she knew they would follow.

The Boston Whaler has long held a sterling reputation as a rugged and reliable boat. And although the whaler is very capable of venturing out into the open ocean, its skiff-like bottom and with shallow draft and low freeboard, or sides, is ideally suited for the relatively quieter waters of the shallow salt ponds. The larger, deep V-hulled boats with deeper drafts and higher freeboard were generally preferred for open ocean activities. To compound matters, these rentals were the smaller whalers, being 16 feet in length.

And the breachway had little regard for any boat, regardless of size or hull design. It treated all with contempt.

As she commenced the two hundred yard run through the breachway, Mallory yelled to her boys in a commanding tone that indicated she meant business.

"Tighten your life jackets. Hold onto the rails really tight, brace yourself in the bottom of the boat and don't let go."

Without uttering a word the boys complied immediately. They could see what she was about to do and they were scared, but responsive nonetheless.

Mallory eased back on the throttle, dropping her speed to about 20 miles per hour. Although this would allow the pursuing boat to shorten the distance between them, she also knew from years of trial and error that it was the optimum speed to pass through the breachway. If she went too fast, an errant wave could easily spin her out of control and onto the granite boulders that lined the channel. If she went too slowly, the boat would be battered by the turbulence and possibly swamped or capsized. It was a fine needle to thread, and she hoped the men racing to catch up would not fully appreciate the subtleties involved.

On the left side of the breachway, Mallory spotted a lone fisherman on top of the seawall, casting his line into the noisy, foaming cauldron below. Mallory needed both hands on the wheel to keep the craft headed in the right direction. As wave after wave attacked the boat from wildly different directions, she spun the wheel to meet each onslaught head-on, cutting perpendicular to each wave for maximum stability. The seas boiled. Waves broke, reformed and broke again in rapid succession. Some were only a few feet in height while others reached eight to ten feet. Waves broke over the bow, drenching the boys. Eric screamed. Another wave came in over the rear transom, nearly submerging the motor.

As Mallory's whaler came within shouting distance of the fisherman she tried to yell for help, all the while keeping both hands on the wheel for control. Although she was shouting at the top of her lungs, her voice was muffled by the throaty sound of the engine and the surf pounding relentlessly on the rocks. The fisherman stared at her, and the boys clinging to the rails of the boat. He knew she was saying something but couldn't make it out. He shook his head in disbelief, incredulous that one would jeopardize not only herself, but her children as well, for the sake of a joy ride on the open ocean. He then gave a dismissive wave and watched as she continued her struggle through the breachway.

Mallory's heart sank upon the realization that her plea for help went unheard. With grim determination she forged ahead. She was nearly two-thirds of the way through the watery gauntlet by the time the other boat commenced its run. They had not slowed and they came barreling into the breach-way at full throttle. It seemed to be working for them at first until an errant wave caught them amidships and spun them toward the granite boulders. The driver immediately throttled back and tried to regain control of his boat. Another wave crashed over the stern, and they found themselves nearly swamped and heading in the opposite direction. They struggled to correct. The fisherman watched the spectacle from above.

Meanwhile, Mallory was still fighting her way through, oblivious to the situation behind her. As the whaler took the crest of a large wave, she could see that the end of the breachway and the relevant calm of open ocean were a mere fifty yards away. But it was to prove the toughest, for the mouth was where the wave action was most severe and unpredictable. She made a slight throttle adjustment to compensate for the change in condition and forged ahead. The boat took a broadside and skidded sideways into the trough of an oncoming ten foot wave. Mallory thrust the wheel to meet the wave head on lest it break on top of them. She cut through it before it could crest and suddenly broke free of the boiling waters and out into open seas. All was not quiet, but at least out in the open the waves were small, steady and predictable. She allowed herself a moment to collapse over the wheel, heaving a deep sigh of relief.

The boys were still glued to the floor. She looked lovingly at them and spoke in a soft, reassuring tone.

"It's alright. We're through. You can get up now."

Still a little dazed, they slowly untangled themselves and sat up on the bench while still holding onto the rail.

"That was some ride," said Matt.

"I'll say," chimed Eric. "Can we do it again?"

Mallory had to laugh.

"Not today. Not tomorrow either. And we're not out of danger yet."

She had barely finished speaking when she glanced back at the deadly gauntlet she had run, prepared to give it a respectful, departing salute before commencing the search for a safe haven. There, still in the breachway but heading in her direction, was the other whaler. It had managed to navigate most of the hazards and had only another 50 yards to go. Mallory could not believe her misfortune. She throttled up and headed out to sea, seeking to put as much distance as she could while they were still fighting the breachway.

The other boat was struggling in the fierce froth, the engine alternating between full throttle and dead stop. Mallory glanced over her shoulders to monitor their progress. They were nearly free when a large incoming wave picked up the rugged whaler and slapped it down on the following trough. The ten-foot drop lifted both men into the air but the stocky driver still clung to the wheel. It probably saved his life, because the other man was not as fortunate. He came down at an angle, striking the rail of the boat with his side and pitching him headlong into the agitated seas.

Despite the tragedy of the moment, Mallory cast an approving nod.

"This should slow them down. God, please make them stop."

The man at the helm glanced back at his partner who was desperately trying to stay afloat, hands gesticulating wildly. He could only be seen when he would crest a wave, only to disappear once again in a trough. But the Pizza Man would not stop. He continued on, ignoring the cries for help, clearing the breachway and heading straight for Mallory.

"I cannot believe that son-of-a-bitch," cursed Mallory as she gunned the engine while barking out a command to the boys. "Matt. Eric. Get back on the floor of the boat and hold on. We're going for another ride."

Although Mallory had a sizeable lead of about five hundred yards, the pursuing craft was now substantially lighter by exactly one man. Eventually the Pizza Man would catch up. She could not outrun him. She had to find safety. She looked east along the shoreline. The closest port to the east where she could seek help was Point Judith, with its fishing fleet and ferries. There would be plenty of human activity, but it was a good 6 miles away. Mallory gauged the risk, and decided against it. If he catches us before we get to Point Judith, we're dead.

She looked west. Weekapaug beach stretched out for 2 miles, with hardly an occupied house to be seen, with the sole exception of Tom and Helene's. Beyond that was another breachway that separated Weekapaug from Misquamicut. While during the summer months Misquamicut beach would be teeming with bathers, surfers and boaters, it now stood painfully deserted. She glanced back at Pizza Man. He was moving at full speed toward Mallory, slowly narrowing the distance between them.

"If we can't outrun him, we'll take the fight to home territory," she concluded with grim determination. She turned west to commence the parallel run along the Weekapaug shore and toward the house. At forty miles per hour the whaler skimmed the whitecaps, bouncing hard as it rammed another wave. The boats were rugged and built to handle it, but even the slightest miscalculation of an oncoming wave could catch the whaler sideways and toss its contents overboard.

It took less than four minutes to make it to the other end of the beach. The attacker had shaved over 100 yards from the distance between them. Mallory scanned the shore for just the right place to beach the boat. A protruding rocky headland formed the western end of Weekapaug beach. The boulders stretched into the sea. Most were visible at low tide. However, at high tide many reposed a mere foot or more beneath the surface, where many a boater or swimmer had tragically discovered there existence. Most of the local folks knew of their placement and gave them a wide berth. Mallory was one of them.

Hoping she could use the submerged boulders to lure the Pizza Man into a trap, she veered towards the rocky headland. He followed. As the boat entered the surf zone, Mallory slowed slightly so as to exert better control. Turning quickly to starboard she narrowly missed a cluster of rocks that often served as a makeshift fishing platform at low tide. Then another turn to port around a large granite block barely visible in the foaming surf. The boys slid around the bottom of the boat with every sharp turn, but clung fast to the rail.

With the last boulder behind her, Mallory gunned the engine and ran the whaler up onto the sandy beach. The motor popped up and tilted into the engine compartment, propeller still turning with a deep, throaty roar. Mallory quickly shut down the engine. She turned to gauge the progress of her pursuer. He had been running at full throttle until he reached the surf zone whereupon he came to an abrupt halt. Upon seeing the gyrations that Mallory had undertaken as she entered the surf zone he knew there lay hidden dangers. A mere two hundred yards of rocky surf separated them now, but it could have been miles given what treachery lie between them. Mallory felt she could almost read his mind as he studied the surf, then turned his head slightly to scan along the shore.

"Here I am," she shouted. "Come and get me." She tauntingly waved her arm as if to beckon, hoping he would come in straight and hit the submerged rocks. The boys stared at her in amazement.

"Mom, what are you doing?" asked Matt.

But there was no time for explanations.

"Get out of the boat," she commanded as she hopped out, eyes still fixed out to sea.

Mallory watched as the other whaler turned away from the rock-strewn surf and headed east along the shoreline.

"He's backing off," thought Mallory. Yet she would not avert her gaze, for his pursuit up till now had been relentless. She could not allow herself to believe that he would call off the chase, especially after watching his partner fall overboard and presumably drown.

Her instincts would not desert her. As soon as the man had run far enough along the shore to clear the rocky headland, he turned and sped through the surf zone toward the beach. The bottom was sandy and he would be safely on the shore in seconds.

There was no time to waste. He would land a mere two hundred yards from where they were now standing.

"Run," she yelled. "Run for the house."

The boys also saw the boat heading for shore and realized that they were still in danger. Instantly they began two run. There shoes and clothes were soaked and the added weight made it seem as if they were all moving in slow motion. Mallory tore off her jacket and let it drop. She then caught up with the boys and pulled their tops off, never breaking a stride.

The other whaler lurched onto the beach and dug into the sand. The engine stalled. Pizza Man jumped out and started his run up the beach. Running with heavy wet clothes on a sandy beach kept him at a safe distance, for now. He began to peel away the upper layers of clothing.

Mallory, Matt and Eric soon reached the dune grass and cut a direct path toward the row of deserted summer houses perched on the headland. Tom and Helene's was the fourth house down. Eric, the youngest with a smaller stride, was starting to slow. Mallory, breathing rapidly, grabbed his hand and pulled him along. Matt was managing okay by himself, but Mallory could see the fear etched in their faces.

"Only a little further now. It's easier running on the grass. We'll make it to the house. Don't you worry," she labored through the heavy breathing.

Eric, despite his youth, was already one step ahead of Mallory in her thought process.

"But Mom, what will we do when we get there? He's still coming after us."

"We have the home court advantage," panted Mallory, hoping that would close the discussion because she had no idea what she was going to say next.

Both boys took on a puzzled expression, but said no more as it was too difficult to run and talk.

The stocky Pizza Man was making a steady jog up the beach, nearly reaching the dunes. In another moment he would break free of its sandy clutches and have nothing but open field to cross. He would soon be able to narrow the gap.

Mallory spurred the boys on, slogging with wet clothes and squeaky shoes. Crossing the third lawn they turned down the gravel driveway leading to the house. Matt reached the steps first, as Mallory was still breathlessly pulling Eric along. He bounded up the steps and threw open the door and dropped to the floor of the sun porch, gasping for air. Samson and Delilah, as if by silent command, were waiting on the other side of the door and pounced on him in playful fashion.

"Not now," he gasped, trying in vain to roll out of their pounces.

Mallory and Eric followed panting through the door, leaving a wet puddle where they stood.

"I need a phone," exhaled Mallory, "and a weapon. Quickly, to the kitchen."

They all stood and ran to the kitchen, dogs in tow. Mallory paused briefly to lock the door behind her, thinking this was probably the first time this door had been locked in ages. She struggled briefly with the latch, finally succeeding. Once in the kitchen Matt grabbed the phone.

"Dial 911," shouted Eric.

"I know," responded Matt.

Mallory scanned the kitchen for a suitable weapon. Her eyes landed on the knife block on the kitchen counter. Quickly studying her options, she selected the boning knife with the six-inch stainless steel blade. Although smaller than some of the other knives in the block, she was most comfortable with this one. It would do the job if necessary. She only prayed it would not be needed Boning a chicken was a far cry from driving a knife into a human being. But if pushed she knew she would do it in order to protect her children and herself.

"Mom, it's 911," Matt yelled from across the kitchen. Mallory ran over and shouted into the phone.

"We need help. My two boys and I are being pursued by a man with a gun."

"Name and Address?"

"My name is Mallory Hastings and we are at…" Mallory froze. She could not for the life of her remember the address, probably because it was always referred to as the Langtree house by the locals. But the 911 center was in Westerly, which provided administrative and emergency services to Weekapaug.

Address please."

"It's the Langtree house in Weekapaug, on Shore Road. Please send help. The man is coming after us," pleaded Mallory.

As she spoke she looked out the kitchen window to see the man turn down the gravel driveway, heading for the door of the porch. Mallory dropped the phone onto the kitchen counter. She grabbed the knife and turned to the boys.

"He's coming. Get upstairs now. Take the dogs with you. Now!"

"Mom," yelled Matt as he grabbed Delilah by the collar. "I just remembered. Tom keeps a gun in the hall closet. Want me to get it?"

"I'll get it. Just get you and your brother up to your room. Barricade yourselves in till help arrives. Don't open the door for anyone. Do not come out no matter what happens. Do you understand?"

"But what about you?"

Mallory fought back the tears as she took a last longing look at her boys. An icy calm came over her.

"I am going to kick some ass. I love you both. Now move it!"

Boys and dogs headed for the stairs and their bedroom on the third floor.

Mallory could now hear the crunch of footsteps on the gravel through the kitchen window. She ran to the hallway between the kitchen and the common room. Flinging open the closet door, her hands groped along the back wall till it came to rest on the barrel of a 22-gauge rifle. She pulled it out. By now the man was on the steps. She had no time to check for ammunition. Running from the hall she headed for the stairs, only to find Samson at attention on the landing. She forgot that Samson could no longer navigate the steps. Mallory looked at his huge frame and normally playful brown eyes. This time his eyes were fixed in a deep stare, his feet planted firmly apart. He seemed to comprehend the gravity of the situation and had taken up his station in order to defend the others.

The sound of glass breaking shook Mallory from her thoughts. Samson, ears upright and hairs on his back erect, began a deep-throated growl that even chilled Mallory. She hated to leave him behind, but had no choice. Maybe he can scare the guy off, she hoped. Mallory hurried up the stairs to the third floor. Upon climbing the stairs she could see the wet footsteps of the boys. At the top, she winced when she saw that they left a wet trail leading to their room at the end of the hall.

Two floors below, Pizza Man had broken the glass on the door, reached in and unlatched the lock, and then let himself in. His feet crunched the broken glass as he stepped onto the floor of the porch. Looking down, he couldn't help but notice the large puddle left by his three intended victims, with tracks leading to the kitchen. Already aware of the possible presence of the great Danes from his earlier scouting expedition as the pizza delivery man, his handgun was drawn and ready. He had come for Mallory, but would kill everyone in the house if necessary.

Peering around the corner into the kitchen he could see that the room was empty. They had been there, and for awhile judging by the water on the floor. The phone lay on the counter, and a voice could be heard.

"Hello? Ma'am, are you still there? Hello?"

Pizza Man picked up the phone and slowly brought it to his ear, listening to the voice on the other end. Then he responded.

"I am terribly sorry. There is no emergency. The kids were playing a joke on their mother. Don't worry, I'll punish them for this. Sorry for the inconvenience."

He hung up the phone and grinned. Then he turned to follow the wet trail down the hall and toward the stairs.

With precious time remaining, Mallory grabbed a towel from the bathroom and quickly wiped the trail of wet footprints, beginning from the boys' bedroom and moving backwards towards the front of the hall where her bedroom was. She walked into her bedroom and quickly around the bed several times in order to create more tracks, hoping to make one person look like three. Then she backed out of her bedroom, quietly closed the door, and continued into the bathroom immediately across the hall, being careful to wipe any water that might have led to the bathroom. Leaving the bathroom door halfway ajar, she took up a crouched position behind the door. From the hinged part of the door, Mallory was able to peer across the hall to her now closed bedroom.

She held the gun in one hand and the knife in the other.

"Not very handy," she thought.

She moved the knife behind her back and slipped it behind her belt, with the handle protruding. Her hands were trembling.

Taking the rifle in both hands, she quietly slid back the bolt, looked inside at the empty chamber, and cursed to herself.

"Shit-shit-shit! I should have known Tom wouldn't keep it loaded."

Then her thoughts and her anger turned to David.

"Damn you David. Damn you for getting us involved in all this. Damn you for putting the boys and me in danger. If I ever get out of this I'll shoot you myself."

Her moment of self-pity came to an abrupt halt as she heard Samson give out a loud, authoritative bark. This was immediately followed by the muted spit of a silencer firing three times in rapid succession. Samson let out a long, painful wail and collapsed on the floor. From the boys' room at the end of the hall Delilah cried out and made for the door. The boys restrained her as she moaned and pawed at the door to get out.

Mallory slumped against the bathroom wall, knowing that a beloved companion and her first line of defense no longer existed. She chastised herself for not hiding him, for not doing more, for allowing him to die. She could hear the squeak of her tormentor's soggy shoes as he slowly mounted the stairs. He paused briefly at the second floor, but upon seeing that the unmistakable tracks led to the floor above, he continued on.

Between the pounding of her heart and the muffled moans of Delilah, Mallory was terrified to also hear the heavy breathing of the man as he ascended the stairs. He was taking each step slowly and with deliberation. His breathing, heavy but measured, resonated on the narrow stairs. Upon reaching the small landing at the top of the stairs he paused briefly to catch his breath. Mallory was now holding hers, as he was a mere ten feet away, hands gripped knuckle-white on the rifle. Still on the landing, he slowly peered around the corner to survey the situation. There were only three doors in the hall. At the end of the hall he could hear the muffled whimper of a dog behind a door. This brought a sense of relief to the killer, as he now knew where the other dog was, and even greater relief that she was behind a closed door. His eyes quickly followed the watery trail to Mallory's bedroom. Once again he grinned, upon seeing that all three were in the room, with the dog in the other room. After all he had endured, the end was going to be easier than he thought. He took a long look at the open bathroom door across from Mallory's room. Although partially obscured, he could see that the tub was empty, and seeing no tracks, he satisfied himself that his prey was across the hall and now firmly trapped.

With gun directly in front of him he eased his way to the closed bedroom door. Putting his hand on the knob, he slowly turned it. Mallory could now see him from the crack in the bathroom door. His back was turned to her. This was her best chance, her only chance. She moved out from behind the door, pointed the empty rifle at his back and yelled.

"Freeze!"

Pizza man turned and was stunned to find himself staring down the barrel of a rifle, a mere five feet from his face. He slowly raised his hands.

"Put the gun down right now or I'll shoot," Mallory barked. "And don't think I won't shoot to protect my boys." Despite her authoritative sound, she was visibly trembling.

Finding her logic impeccable, and knowing that even a trembling amateur could not miss from this range, he decided to comply. Eyes fixed on both Mallory and the rifle, he slowly began to lower his right arm so as to place the gun on the floor. Then he paused, stared intently at the rifle, and began to grin in a sly, leering manner.

Mallory saw the hesitation, and she was nearly unhinged by his grin.

"I said drop the gun, right now!"

Still leering, he lowered both arms, gun still in hand. Then he spoke, calmly and with the authority of a pro.

"I don't think so." He took a quick step forward and forcibly snatched the rifle from Mallory's hands. She was both amazed and terrified at this awesome display of speed and power. He stood there, pistol in one hand, rifle in the other.

"You see," he stated matter-of-factly, "the safety was still on." He clicked the safety of the rifle to the off position and pointed the barrel at Mallory.

She froze, not uttering a word, staring death in the face.

He pulled the trigger. Nothing happened.

"Just as I figured," he sneered. "Empty." Didn't think you had time to both call for help and load a gun."

He let the rifle drop to the floor and raised his pistol, calmly looked her in the eyes and said,

"Usually I say something like 'Nothing personal.' or 'It's only business." But in your case I am really gonna enjoy this after all you've put me through."

He pointed the gun to Mallory's forehead. She closed her eyes.

"Please, just let my children live," she pleaded.

"No can do. They've seen too much. No loose ends in this business."

Mallory's eyes opened just enough to reveal a penetrating, steely gray stare. Her jaws grew taut. She was not going to let that happen.

Before he could squeeze the trigger the door at he end of the hall flew open and out leapt Delilah. She furiously raced down the hall, her long gait spanning the short hallway in three bounds. Pizza Man turned his head, then his right arm to point the gun in the direction of the oncoming juggernaut. Mallory instantly sized up the situation and pushed the man hard against the wall. Caught off balance, the man fired and his shot went wild. Before he could get off another round, Delilah lunged upon him, knocking him to the floor and hell bent on avenging her partner's death. She tore into his right shoulder as he struggled to free himself from her grip, the gun dropping to the floor. Mallory lost no time. She reached behind and pulled the boning knife from her belt. Pushing herself off the wall she threw herself on top of the man and thrust the knife deeply into his chest. Blood spurted out. He let out a loud groan but continued to fight. Delilah was relentless, her giant head with fangs dripping with revenge just inches from his face. He struggled with both hands to keep her powerful jaws away from his throat. Mallory lunged again, this time striking his thigh as they grappled on the floor. Another moan, but the struggle continued. Mallory caught an elbow in the face, and blood poured from her nose and lips. She did not slow. Again she struck, and again and again. Delilah, now one hand in her mouth, was savagely gnawing it to a bloody pulp.

Mallory pulled herself on top of the Pizza Man. He was bleeding from numerous knife and bite wounds. Although still thrashing about, his efforts were misdirected. His arms grew weak.

Mallory put the point of the bloody blade an inch from his right eye. He stopped thrashing.

"If you want to live, tell me who you are, who sent you and why."

His eyes shifted between the knife and Mallory's eyes. He could see her determination. He knew she would follow through. But he was a pro. His lips turned up and his mouth opened as if to speak, but instead he managed a wide lurid grin, contorted as it was through the pain. Yet it was still his unmistakable, leering, haughty grin.

This infuriated Mallory. Staring deeply into his eyes so he could see the final blow, she drove the blade deeply into his upper chest. His body went limp. Yet the grin remained, a final taunt from the beyond.

Delilah was still gnawing on a limb as Mallory pulled her away. The hall was awash in blood. Blood was streaming from Mallory's face and running down her blouse. She sat with her back against the wall, exhausted from the struggle. Delilah nudged her.

"It's okay girl, it's over. Thanks for your help." She hung a tired arm around Delilah's neck.

The boys, disobeying their mother's order, peaked out from down the hall, staring in disbelief at the carnage that lay before them. They ran to Mallory, agitated and screaming.

"Mom! Mom! Are you alright?" cried Matt as he reached her side.

She grabbed them both and pulled them forcefully to her, clinging tightly, saying nothing. They returned the embrace. Fighting back the tears, she finally found her voice.

"I'm fine," she managed between the spurts of blood from her mouth. "Just a little banged up, but I'm ok. We're ok."

Eric released his grip on Mallory, his mouth agape. His eyes were fixed on the still grinning corpse, knife imbedded in his blood soaked chest.

"Mom, I think I'm gonna throw up."

Mallory gave an understanding nod and slowly reached over and redirected his gaze. They looked into each other's eyes. His, the eyes of a frightened seven year old child. Hers, the eyes of a mother with boundless love and understanding for her child.

Believing her loving gaze had calmed him down, she spoke in a soft, consoling tone.

"Eric, it's ok. It's all over. No one can hurt you now. Still feel sick?"

"Yes."

"It's understandable. I don't feel so hot myself. The bathroom is over there."

Police sirens sounded in the distance.

Mallory and the boys were still on the third floor when the two Westerly squad cars arrived. Delilah let out a growl when the wailing cars pulled into the driveway. Mallory hugged and soothed Delilah for fear she would mistake the police for intruders and get shot by accident.

"We're up here," yelled Matt from the top of the stairs. "My Mom got him. She got the Pizza Man."

The police, guns drawn, made their way slowly up the stairs. The first officer to reach the third floor was momentarily stunned at the carnage that lay before him. He lowered his gun and looked at Mallory as he spoke.

"Did you do all this?"

Mallory, still leaning against the wall with an arm around Delilah, pointed at the dog and said "I had a little help."

"Any more around?" he asked as he pointed to the still grinning corpse.

"He's the only one in the house, but he had an accomplice that fell out of a boat at the breachway."

"Ma'am, I'm afraid the other dog is dead. I passed him on the landing below."

Mallory winced even though she knew all along.

The officer then gave a shout to the police below that the area was clear. He knelt beside Mallory and looked at her bruised and bleeding face.

"Where else are you hurt?"

"All over, but nothing serious."

"The paramedics will be here shortly. We didn't know what to expect when your 911 call came in. Fortunately the woman manning the 911 desk is the suspicious type. She didn't believe the man who claimed it was just a joke and thought we'd better respond anyway."

"Thank God for suspicious females."

Police, paramedics, and reporters were still on the scene by the time Tom and Helene arrived at the house. Mallory, refusing a trip to the hospital, allowed the paramedics to treat her as she recounted the events to the police. The boys were under the close scrutiny of a female officer, with Delilah never far away. Samson's long, lifeless body had been wrapped in a sheet. Tom and Helene knelt by their faithful friend of many years to say goodbye, tears streaming down their cheeks. It took two men to lift the poor creature. Delilah dutifully followed them to the van. She let out a long, pitiful wail as the van pulled away, knowing that her lifelong companion would never return. All activity at the scene stopped to watch this tearful goodbye.

Tom and Helene, after identifying themselves to the police, were led to Mallory who was sitting at the kitchen table. She looked only slightly better, with bandaged face now clean. Dried blood stains still on her blouse and jeans.

Helene spoke first. "What happened? Are you okay?"

Tears welled in Mallory's eyes and began to stream down her face.

"I am now, and so are the boys. But I'm afraid that poor Samson was killed while trying to protect us. If it were not for Delilah, I would be dead. Tom, Helene, I am so sorry about Samson. We all loved him, especially the boys."

Helene, herself in tears, instructed Tom to check on the boys while she put her arms around Mallory. A host of memories came flooding back of Samson as a young pup. She consoled Mallory.

"Samson died protecting those he loved. I'll miss him terribly, and so will Delilah, but there was no other way."

Westerly Police Chief Nate Fabrini arrived on the scene. After a brief discussion with his officers he approached Mallory. Tom came over with both boys in tow.

"Hello Chief," acknowledged Tom.

"Hi Tom and Helene. Looks like things got pretty exciting around here."

"Sure did, but afraid Helene and I missed all of it. This is Mallory Hastings. She and her two boys have been staying with us."

"Mrs. Hastings. You sure have livened up this town. It's apparent that this was no mere robbery attempt that simply went terribly wrong. Any idea why someone would want to do this to you?"

Mallory then explained the shooting incident in Plano in sufficient detail. Then she suggested he get in touch with Plano Police Lieutenant Jacobson for the details.

The Chief listened carefully to the story, and promised to follow up with the Plano Police.

"Could this be mob related in any way, Chief?" inquired Tom.

"I can tell you this much," said the Chief matter-of-factly. This guy is not from around here. We know all the bad guys. If it is the mob, they brought him in special to do the job. And, he glanced at Mallory, they would not stop here."

"But I don't understand how they found me? I mean, I went to great lengths to keep us from being detected. Did not use our phone in Plano. Did not tell any friends or relatives where we were going. Paid for the plane tickets with cash. I just don't understand."

The Chief listened intently to this, nodding with approval at all of her precautionary measures. He thought a moment before speaking.

"Did you rent a car in Providence?"

Mallory grimaced as she realized the implications.

"Do you mean they could trace me through the car rental?"

"Only if they were well connected. No petty thief or even a local bruiser would be able to do so, but with the right connections, they can get everything from the rental agreement. Although you were probably intending to pay for the car in cash, you still had to leave a credit card imprint with them. And, your driver's license info. And finally, where you could be contacted in Rhode Island. It was all there for them."

Mallory buried her bruised face in her hands and sighed.

"How will we ever be safe if they can trace us here?"

Tom broke in.

"I could kick myself for not picking you up at the airport. This whole mess could have been avoided. I am truly sorry."

"Tom," said Mallory, "This is not your fault. I feel terribly about Samson, and for endangering your lives as well. Had you been here in the house, the Pizza Man would have probably tried to kill you in the process.

"Possibly," responded the Chief, "But since your Pizza Man was smart enough to scout out the place in his Pizza delivery disguise last night, I suspect he decided it was not worth the risk to take on the entire household, even if he did have help."

"Speaking of his partner, have you found his body yet?" inquired Mallory.

"Oddly enough, my men have only just started to search the breachway. Usually the body is washed up on the rocks. And if he was lucky enough to survive, he would be pretty banged up and would be happy to get some medical attention, even at the hands of the police."

"There was a fisherman. Maybe he knows what happened."

"Sorry, but there was no one around when my men first arrived. However, they will keep searching. We will also check out the local clinics and hospitals. It is possible he was swept out to sea. In that case we may never find him."

Mallory took little comfort with those last words.

"Too many loose ends," she thought.

"At any rate," the Chief continued, "You will be safe tonight. We will have a squad car in the driveway and a man on foot patrolling the grounds. This place will be mobbed with the media for the next few days so it is unlikely anyone would try something then. At the same time, this is an awfully isolated area this time of year. Once the commotion dies down, you would still be vulnerable. I suggest you find another safe haven."

"Nonsense," snapped Helene. "They are our closest friends, practically family. We won't abandon them at this time."

"Suit yourselves, but we won't be able to keep up the police coverage indefinitely. And, until we get a better handle on who these guys were," he pointed to Mallory, "you need to be available for further questioning."

Mallory looked up at Tom and Helene before speaking in a hushed tone.

"I cannot in all good conscience continue to put you in harms way. We will leave tomorrow."

Tom put his hand on Mallory's shoulder.

"I agree that you should leave here, but..."

Before he could finish, Helene jumped in. "Tom, what in god's name are you saying?"

Tom looked up at Helene, hand still on Mallory's shoulder, and smiled.

"As I was saying before I was so rudely interrupted, you and the boys should not remain here. Instead, we'll all go to the Eighty Acre Woods. That way we can be together all the time. And, you would still be available for Chief Fabrini when he needs you. Does this work for you, Chief?"

"Sounds fine by me, but don't let your guard down for a minute."

"We won't. How about it Mallory?"

But before Mallory could utter a word, Helene chimed in.

"Of course she will come. Now let's get the boys and get busy."

Mallory drew a deep sigh of relief, and began to cry, letting her guard down for the first time since the day's terror all began. Helene cradled her in her arms, then cast an admonishing eye at the Chief.

"Chief, how about calling it quits for the day? And Tom, go look after the boys for us. They could probably use a father figure right about now."

Both Tom and the Chief knew when they were being dismissed. They both quietly walked away, Mallory still sobbing in Helene's arms.

"I am going to kill David when I see him," wept Mallory.

"You'll have to wait your turn," whispered Helene as tears of empathy began to trickle down her cheeks. "I want first crack at him."

With that remark, they both laughed through their tears.

# CHAPTER 11

# *The Option Revealed*

## *DAY EIGHT*

"Get the hell out of the sack, Sleeping Beauty," yelled Rick Watson as he kicked David's foot. "Time for you to make yourself useful, maybe even pretend to be a geologist."

David was startled by the rude awakening. He looked at Rick, then around the mudlogging unit. It all came rushing back to him: where he was, why he was there, and the danger he was in.

"Thanks for waking me," he said to Watson while feigning rubbing sleep from his eyes. "I was having a terrible nightmare. I died and went to hell. My punishment was to become a driller for all eternity."

The powerful Watson glared down and stood over David, who was still lying in a vulnerable position on the bed.

"Don't push me, Hastings," he seethed. "If you didn't have a job to do here, I'd be all over you like a gorilla on a banana boat."

This image forced a laugh from Hastings. Watson wasn't amused. He leaned closer. So close that David could feel his hot, tobacco chewing breath.

"Just remember this, Hastings. It may be different back in Plano, but out here, I am your boss. This is my drilling operation. Everyone answers to me. On this base, I am the final word. I am god."

David knew when to stop. So did Rick, despite his volatile temper. A rig site was not the place for a brawl, especially between two company men. It was dangerous enough as it was. This thought kept both men in check. The two mudloggers at the other end of the unit were silently staring at the altercation, bewildered by it all. Watson turned to leave, talking as he walked toward the door.

"The drill pipe is out of the hole. We have been circulating the mud system for a few hours to condition the hole for logging. Time for you to get the Halliburton crew to rig up their tools. Time to find out what's down there, and whether you're as good as you'd like to think you are."

He was gone. David lay back in his bunk for a moment, catching his breath.

"Helluva way to wake up, don't you think?" he asked in the direction of the mudloggers. They were speechless, still stunned.

David looked over at them.

"Don't worry," he said in a calm tone. "Watson only talks like that to people he really likes." They all laughed in unison.

With the tension broken, David sat up. Still in his clothes, he slid into his steel toed work boots and opened the door of the trailer. A shaft of sunlight pierced the unit, temporarily blinding him. It was mid morning, and everywhere men could be seen attending to the tasks at hand. He stared up at the monkey board near the top of the rig derrick. It was empty. The man who had dropped the heavy wrench the night before was gone.

"No surprise," he thought. "After all, the operation that required a man up there was now over. The drill string was out of the hole and the pipe was neatly stacked off to one side."

Still, David could not help but wonder if the accident was intentional. But there was little he could do about it, and he knew Watson would be less than sympathetic if he reported it. Besides, Watson could have authorized it. After all, out here, in the middle of the rainforest, Rick was, now how did he put it? Oh yes, he was "god".

His thoughts drifted to Mallory and the boys. By now they would be in full swing back in Weekapaug. Walks on the beach, playing ball with the dogs, enjoying great ocean views, making fires at night. Perhaps they would even rent a boat and take it out on Quonnie Pond. Or maybe visit Tom and Helene at their wildlife sanctuary in the Eighty Acre Woods. If only he could talk to them, but that was not possible out here. The satellite phone in the company man's trailer was for official business only. No one could use it without first obtaining permission from Watson, and he gave it only grudgingly. For David to call his family would be a non-starter.

David made his way toward the Halliburton wireline logging unit. The morning sun had burned away the evening mist. Still, this was the beginning of the rainy season. Heavy afternoon downpours could be expected. The solid ground he now walked upon would become a sea of mud, despite the straw and woodchips that had been liberally spread throughout the camp to keep the mud down. But for now the sky was a brilliant blue with only an occasional puff of cirrus cloud.

The mechanical, man-induced sounds of the compound filled the air, drowning out the voice of the forest. David tried to imagine the scene without all the artificial noise. He had heard it before, when he and Steve had conducted field trips to the area, before all the drilling. The rainforest felt alive. Not just with animal sounds, which were abundant at times, but the forest itself seemed to breathe. Perhaps it was the wind, or the sound of the rain on the leafy canopy above, but to David it was as though he was in the lair of a huge, inviting beast. The beast was wild, and unpredictable, but posed no threat so long as one was careful.

"Careful." This last thought echoed in his mind. "Got to be more careful. More careful than Steve. Poor, unsuspecting Steve. Yet it wasn't the jungle that killed Steve. He was killed in man's jungle, in Caracas."

Upon arriving at the Halliburton unit, David found the crew actively rigging up the tools for the first logging run. There would have to be several runs in order to obtain all the measurements that were required. On some straight hole jobs, Halliburton would attempt to combine all the tools for a single run in the hole. This was often known in the business as a 'super-combo'. Such an operation was more efficient and cheaper. However, for a well as deep and as deviated as the Angel Falls #2, it was too difficult to run all the tools at once. The potential for getting the tools hung up downhole was great. When this happened, the cable carrying the tools would often snap while attempting to pull out of the hole, leaving a bundle of wireline and tools trapped somewhere in the well. This required an extensive retrieval operation, called 'fishing'. While the name sounded simple enough, the operation was not. Fishing could often take days and was not always successful. When it failed, the lost materials could sometimes be drilled out in bits and pieces. Sometimes it was easier to just kick off a new hole by milling a small window just above the lost gear and drilling out from there.

Nobody wanted a costly fishing expedition on this well. At least three trips down the hole with the wireline logging tools would be required. A large spool of wireline cable was attached to the unit. The cable was then run up to the rig and suspended above the floor. The tools were then attached to the end of the cable and slowly fed down the well bore. A Halliburton engineer would lower the cable from a set of controls inside the unit.

David watched as the first set of logging tools disappeared into the hole for the nearly five mile journey to the bottom of the well. He then entered the Halliburton unit and engaged the crew chief.

"Morning," said the chief. "You are just in time for run #1."

"Morning," David replied. "What tools are on the first run?"

"We are running the SP (Spontaneous Potential), Caliper, Gamma Ray, Sonic, and Dual Induction Resistivity tools."

"Sounds good. And for Run #2?"

"We'll go in with the Neutron and Density Porosity tools, along with the Magnetic Resonance Imaging tool and the Gamma again for calibration between logging runs."

"How about the Dipmeter and Sidewall Cores?"

"Runs 3 and 4, respectively, at your discretion."

"Going to be a long day."

"You've got that right, but you should have a good feel for what's there after the first two runs. We'll be on bottom in a few hours."

"Good," said David. "Now I can get some breakfast. I'll be in the mess tent if you need me. I'll be back in an hour or so." Since wireline tools are run from the bottom of the hole on up, David had a few hours before it would start to get interesting. The tools are cable fed down the hole as quickly as they can be safely conveyed. Once on bottom, they begin their slow, steady ascent to the surface, taking readings of the surrounding rock formation every inch of the way. A video display readout in the Halliburton unit reported the measurements as they are recorded, so the engineer and geologist get an instantaneous view of rock formation properties instead of having to wait until the tool is all the way out of the hole.

David could barely contain his excitement. Today was the day that he would find out if the project was a boom or a bust, if he was to be ranked amongst the great oil finders of his day or fade into obscurity. He and Steve, that is. Steve, he said to himself, wish you were here with me right now. We went through so much together. And today is the day of reckoning. I'll be thinking of you.

Although mid morning, the mess tent was still serving breakfast. David helped himself to scrambled eggs, bread and juice, followed by strong black coffee. He was enjoying his second cup of coffee when Bealls and the Colonel entered the tent. David nodded to them when they looked over in his direction. The Colonel returned the nod. Bealls walked over.

"Well Hastings, I guess today is the day."

"Guess so," replied David in a matter-of-fact manner, disguising his excitement.

"Today we find out what's in the well, whether it's a banging success or another dry hole. Feeling a bit nervous? You should be. After all, this is your baby."

David studied Bealls' remarks before responding in matter-of-fact fashion.

"It may be awhile before we know what's down there. There are several log runs to make. We know from the Angel Falls #1 that there is oil in this basin. We just don't know how much. This well will hopefully answer that question. As to this being "my baby", it takes two to make a baby. Steve Giles was the other parent."

Bealls laughed sardonically. Then he lowered his voice so no one else in the mess tent could hear.

"Well, let's hope the baby doesn't become an orphan."

David leapt to his feet, but before he could respond the Colonel came over and stepped between them.

"Buenos Dias, Senor Hastings."

David looked at the Colonel, then quickly back at Bealls.

"Good morning, Colonel."

The Colonel took Bealls by the elbow and gently led him away, muttering as they walked. David sat back down but was too upset to finish his coffee. He glanced about the tent. Several sets of eyes were staring at him, having witnessed the brief but tense confrontation.

Just great, he thought despondently. They probably think I'm a raving lunatic.

He sat in stony silence while his coffee turned cold. After sitting for awhile he decided to take a walk to clear his mind of dark thoughts while waiting for the logging tools to reach bottom. Strolling through the compound he was once again reminded of the military presence by the sight of several soldiers. They were either sitting or casually walking about. The drilling crew seemed oblivious to their presence, David observed. This suggested they had been here for some time and were not a recent addition to the site. From a safe distance, he followed one of the soldiers out of the compound down a trail. It led to a clearing that contained the military encampment. David stood back behind some leafy foliage and observed the campsite. No more than a dozen soldiers could be seen.

"Unless there are a lot more asleep in the tents," he thought, there can't be more than twenty altogether, including the ones already at the rig site.

Not very far behind, David could hear some men walking down the path toward the encampment. Not wanting to be caught spying, David re-entered the path and made his way toward the soldiers camp. Upon approaching, several soldiers became alarmed at his presence and immediately reached for their rifles. Although alarmed, David thought this reaction was somewhat odd, given their lax behavior back at the rig site.

David stopped and waved with both hands, making sure they saw that he was not armed and posed no threat. The men in military fatigues looked at him warily, rifles at the ready position. One of them yelled out a name. A soldier with sergeant stripes on his shirt opened the flap of a nearby tent and peered out. He stepped into the group of soldiers, all the while staring at David who stood motionless with arms still outstretched.

"Gringo," was all the sergeant muttered. He then put his hand on one of the gun barrels and lowered it towards the ground. The other soldiers instinctively lowered theirs. David let his hands fall to his side. The sergeant walked over to him. Saying nothing, he pointed back toward the path that led to the rig site. David understood. He turned and slowly retraced his path. Stopping only briefly to look back, he saw the sergeant still standing there, hands on his hips, watching until David disappeared from view. In the distance, he heard one of the soldiers angrily barking commands.

"Friendly sort," was all David could muster as he re-entered the compound. Yet the encounter was unnerving. It also raised more questions than it answered. They did not appear to have anything to hide but they acted as though he had just entered a secret base. Normally, Venezuelans are a friendly people. Although he had to admit he had not experienced the military up close and personal before.

"But if they are here to protect us," he pondered, "Why the seeming hostility? At the same time, he had intruded upon their compound unannounced. Perhaps it was this surprise that set them off. After all, it was a military base and he had just walked right in. Maybe that was what all the shouting was about as he left. Maybe it was the sergeant yelling at his troops for being so lax."

David re-entered the rig compound as though nothing had happened. He made his way over to the Halliburton unit and walked in. The cool blast from the unit's air conditioner provided welcome relief to the rising heat and humidity that came with the morning sun. Gene, the Halliburton wireline engineer, was busy at the controls. The first set of logging tools was snaking its way towards the bottom of the well at 19,000 feet. He deftly operated the levers that controlled the rotation of the drum that spooled out the wireline cable. This operation called for a delicate touch. If he played the cable out too fast it could snarl downhole and hang up the tools. If too slow, the tools could lose their forward momentum in the deviated wellbore, or worse. They could become overheated in the super high temperature environment and cook the sensitive instrumentation, rendering them useless.

"Almost on bottom with the first set of tools," Gene stated without diverting his hands from the controls.

David peered over his shoulder, watching the tension meter on the cable as it splayed out. Finally, the cable tension shifted, indicating the tools had reached their final destination and were now resting on bottom. Gene whirled around in his captain's chair and checked the instrumentation panel that would record the data. Upon seeing that all was functioning normally, he turned back toward the cable levers and began the slow ascent to the surface.

David studied the computer display. As the tools began their ascent, a steady stream of numbers played out on the screen. In addition, log curves, much like an electro-cardiogram, traced multiple paths on another display screen.

"The Spontaneous Potential, Gamma Ray and Caliper curves are on the left side," said Gene. "The shallow, medium and deep Resistivity readings, along with the sonic porosity curves, are on the right."

David nodded. He had seen this many times before, only this time he felt his entire career hung in the balance as the curves began to trace out information that few people were capable of interpreting. In fact, a special discipline within the energy industry, Petrophysics, had been created to train specialists in log interpretation. David did not consider himself one of these specialists, but he had some training and considerable field experience when it came to log interpretation. He would undertake what was known in the business as a "quick look" assessment. This fast and fairly accurate method would enable the wellsite geologists to make decisions regarding what operation to conduct next on the well, whether it be additional logging, or flow testing, or even plug and abandon. The data he was watching on the displays was simultaneously being recorded, and the tapes or computer disks would be transmitted back to OilQuest for detailed examination by the Petrophysicist. This would hopefully confirm the quick look assessment.

As he studied the computer screens, David was relieved to see the log curves shift as they left the non-prospective shale formation at the very bottom of the hole and entered the lower part of the target formation.

"There it is," he said with relief. "Our objective, the La Rosa Sandstone, as it was locally called. Gene turned to eye the displays and nodded in agreement.

"All tools are tracking well," he responded. The SP and Gamma curves broke back from the shale line as they entered the La Rosa Sandstone. The Resistivity has increased and the sonic has also shifted somewhat, although slightly erratic. Are you expecting oil at the bottom of the formation?"

"Hoping, but not sure what to expect," said David. "As this is only the second well on this structure, we don't know where the water leg might be. There was none in the Angel Falls #1 well, which was drilled on the very crest of the structure. This well is on the flank. About halfway down the structure. Hence, we really don't know what we'll find. That's why these log runs are critical to the entire project. Although we know there is oil here, we don't know how much. These logs will determine if we have a commercial find, or not."

"With what this well must be costing, I hope it's a barn burner."

"You and me both, Gene. You and me both."

David eyes were still fixed on the screens while Gene spun back around and monitored the rotating drum as it slowly pulled the cable through the well bore. He would occasionally pull a lever, maintaining that careful balance between cable tension and reel speed. As the tools continued to feed data to the computer displays before David, he tried to make sense of the multiple sources of data. The top of the La Rosa appeared on the screen as the tools once again read the difference between sandstone and shale. He was relieved that the objective came in where it was prognosed, and that it was as thick as they had anticipated. He was still unable to discern porosity from the sonic alone due to its erratic behavior, but that would be resolved with the second log run. Run #2 would contain the neutron and density porosity tools. In addition, run #2 would contain the Magnetic Resonance Imaging tool that would aid in predicting the permeability of the sandstone, which essentially gave an indication as to whether the well would flow.

He looked at the resistivity curves. They were responding as though there was little water in the pore spaces of the sandstone, but there was a distinct character change in the curves at the top of the La Rosa. After about the first forty feet of the sandstone, the resistivity actually increased as it went lower into the La Rosa. David thought this was somewhat unusual, in that resistivities often tend to decrease with increasing depth due to water influx in the formation. This was by no means a cardinal rule, but to see the exact opposite occurring perplexed David.

"Gene, what do you make of these resistivities?" David inquired.

Gene turned around and stared at the curves for a brief moment before speaking.

"Beats the hell out of me, but the tools are not lying, that I can tell you." He turned back to his task at hand, leaving David alone with his thoughts to ponder the situation.

"Looks like we'll have to definitely see the Neutron/Density and MRI before making a call on this one."

Gene nodded without turning.

"We'll have this tool up in a few hours. My crew have already laid out and checked the tools for the second run. We'll be able to rig up and run back in pretty quickly."

"Good" replied David. The tension was getting to him. "Think I'll take a shower. I'll check back with you in a few hours."

"I wasn't gonna say anything," responded Gene, "but since you mentioned it, a shower would be a real good idea. It gets awfully close here in this logging unit."

"I can take a hint. See you soon."

David stepped from the dimly lit unit out into the bright noonday sun, temporarily blinding him. He put his hand over his eyes and waited while the pupils slowly adjusted. Walking around a rig site was dangerous enough without being able to see where you were going.

On his way over to the mudlogging unit to retrieve his gear bag in anticipation of a cool, refreshing shower, Rick Watson stepped out onto the stairs of his trailer and motioned for David to come over.

"Well, got anything yet?" Rick asked expectantly.

"They are coming out of the hole with the first set of tools. The La Rosa is just about exactly where we prognosed, but it's too early to tell how much oil, if any, it contains."

This last comment alarmed Rick He leaned closer to David so as not to be overheard by a stray bystander.

"What do you mean by 'if any'? I thought this was a slam dunk. The next best thing to a tractor trailer full of whores, bigger than the second coming of Jesus H. Christ himself."

"All I am saying, Rick, is that I can't tell where the oil stops and the water leg begins, if any. The data is just too ambiguous. I need the info from the second set of logging tools before I can form an opinion. That's why we run these tools. If I could tell exactly what we had from Run #1, we wouldn't need Run #2, now would we?"

"Don't patronize me, you sorry excuse for a rock hugger. You better not be holding out on me or I'll run your ass off this site. Remember, out here…"

But before he could finish, David chimed in.

"Out here you're god. Yes, I know. Well maybe you can use a little of that omniscience to tell the outcome here. Then we could all just go home."

David turned away and strode briskly toward the mudlogging trailer. He could feel Watson's eyes burning a hole in his back.

"Probably not a good idea to turn my back on a guy like Watson," he told himself, "But Rick will not want to create a scene in the middle of the compound. Not good form, not even for a driller. Besides, he's probably going to go back to his trailer to look up the word 'omniscience'. That should keep him out of my hair for a little while. Maybe I can shower in peace."

David entered the mudlogging unit and grabbed some fresh clothes, a towel and his toilet kit from his gear bag, Jorge was sound asleep in one of the beds, but Ben was on duty, describing the last few remaining rock cuttings.

'Where are the showers in this place?" David asked Ben.

Ben looked at him slightly puzzled. Both knew that there was a shower in the company man's trailer. However, word had already spread around the camp that Rick Watson and the recently arrived geologist from OilQuest were not exactly on the best of terms. It had even been the source of some amusement, sparking lively conversation around the dinner tables. On a rig site, it didn't take much to get the tongues wagging, mostly because it provided an interesting diversion from the daily routine. Finally Ben responded.

"There's a crew shower area in the forest, just beyond the mess tent. It's al fresco since there aren't any women on the site. They've rigged up a cistern from rainwater. Works fairly well and is warm, but not hot."

"Thanks, Ben. Should do the trick."

"Enjoy."

David soon found the small but well traveled path behind the mess tent. After about fifty yards, he came upon a small clearing, no larger than a Texas sized bathroom. A fiberglass cistern tank, mounted on tree timbers, stood suspended twelve feet off the ground. From the tank a small diameter plastic pipe ran horizontal to the ground for about twenty feet. At five foot intervals along the pipe a shower head had been installed. A chain with a large ring on the end hung down from the shower head. David watched as a naked member of the crew tugged on one of the rings. Water cascaded from the shower head. The man noticed that David was staring at him. He glared back, turned his back toward David, and began to lather up.

"So that's how it works," David thought. "Primitive, but effective."

He quickly undressed and stepped under the line of shower heads, being careful to avoid further eye contact with the other man. With a pull of the ring, a torrent of warm water streamed from the shower. David closed his eyes and let his muscles relax under the warm massaging pressure of the water. He opened his eyes through the stream and absorbed the leafy green vegetation that seemed to engulf him. The fresh, earthy scent of the rainforest permeated the air. It was a simple, but exquisite way to bathe, surrounded in soothing, natural beauty. The man a few feet to his left also seemed to be enjoying the moment. David noticed how brown and rugged the man looked, as compared to his own pale and office ravaged body.

Got to get myself to a gym, he told himself. I look like a freaking wimp compared to these roughnecks. No wonder they laugh when they see me.

After a few moments the other man finished his shower, pulled a towel over his waist, and headed back down the trail toward the camp. David was alone. He told himself he should be alert, but the warmth of the cascading water sent him into a near trance-like state. His eyes drooped dreamily.

"If only Mallory was here," he muttered aloud.

The thought conjured up images of Mallory and him bathing together, sponging each other down, then slowly kissing and caressing as the sun and water played alternately on their warm bodies. David felt himself getting a bit carried away, and the thought of being seen in this excited state by the crew would be too much to bear. Not to mention that Watson would never let him live this down, and that he would most certainly ensure that everyone back in Plano would find out. This thought immediately chilled his fantasies and brought him crashing back to reality. Soaping down, he quickly rinsed and turned off the shower.

I need a shave, he thought as he dried his face, the stubble from his chin snagging the thick cotton towel. But that can wait till I get back to civilization. The more rugged and woodsy I look, the better off I am out here.

Out of the corner of his eye, a branch moved. It was subtle, and silent. For a moment David felt he was imagining things. Maybe it was the wind, or even a small animal. He couldn't be sure but he sensed a pair of eyes looking at him. He turned but saw nothing, only the movement of a branch from where something, or someone, had been. He held his breath to listen for movement, the sound of someone running through the jungle. Nothing, nothing but the natural rhythms of the rainforest.

"Time to get back," he pronounced aloud, as if to frighten away an intruder.

He quickly dressed and, gathering up his gear, walked at a brisk, alert pace back to the compound. He found himself relieved to be back in the midst of scornful company men and rig crews.

How ironic, he thought.

David returned to the mudlogging unit, where Ben was now asleep and Jorge was awake and working. They quietly exchanged greetings so as not to awaken Ben. David finished changing, then sat down at a desk to take another look at the rock cuttings through the La Rosa formation.

A short time later, Gene poked his head into the mudlogging unit. He nodded at Jorge and, upon seeing David, called out.

"We are going back in the hole for Run #2. Should be back on bottom in a little over an hour. Care to watch the fun?"

"Wouldn't dare miss it for the world. I'll be right behind you after I grab a cup of coffee. Can I get you something from the mess?"

"Already ate, thanks. See you back at the unit."

David grabbed his calculator and walked over to the mess tent. It was mid afternoon. The sunny sky had been replaced by approaching rain clouds. The afternoon monsoonal showers would arrive shortly, turning the compound into a muddy pit. He gulped down a steaming cup of coffee, nearly burning his mouth. The heavens opened as he left the mess tent. Men scurried about. David ran to the Halliburton unit, but his khaki shirt was soaked in the process. His hair soaking wet as he opened the door, Gene took one look at the drenched creature dripping before him and burst out with a belly laugh.

"Now you know why they call this a rainforest."

David shared the laugh.

While the machine gun like staccato of the rain pelted the metal trailer, Gene took up his position on the captain's chair, guiding the tools along their perilous journey to the bottom of the hole. David, chilled by the combination of rain and air conditioning, sat in front of the computer screens and prepared for what would soon unfold.

"Funny," he pondered as he stared at the blank computer screens. "In just a little while we should know what's down there. We'll know if we have a company maker or a dud, or something in between. The years of effort by Steve and himself had all come down to this. And he would see it all unfold from these two little screens."

In a way it seemed almost anti-climatic for David. Here he was, shivering like a drenched poodle, in a trailer, in a jungle, thousands of miles away from home, away from family. His best friend was dead. He and his family were nearly killed. And all for what? An oil discovery? The Angel Falls Option? A road? He could scarcely believe any of it was worth killing, or dying for.

"All I need to do," he told himself, "is to survive the next several hours."

He would get the log data, make an assessment, and get the info back to Plano. Then he was outta there. He could join Mallory, Matt and Eric in Weekapaug. Maybe stay up there permanently. Got to be less stressful than what he was doing now. Trouble was, he really loved what he did.

"Almost on bottom."

Gene's comment brought David out of his melodramatic stupor.

"Time for me to go to work," he replied.

Gene spun the chair around, checked the computer screens to make sure they were all functioning properly, then turned back to the cable spool controls. With a shift of the lever he brought the rotating drum to a halt.

"We are at total depth," said Gene.

After one final check of all gauges and display units, he announced with the seriousness of a Mission Control Specialist from NASA, "All systems go. Preparing to log up."

The spool reversed its direction and began the slow, steady process of reeling in the cable with the wireline tools connected at the other end. David focused intently on the computer screens. The data columns came to life. The log curves slowly began to form.

"Here we go," said David, frozen to his seat. His hands tightly gripped the arms of his chair. He felt his stomach tense. He had to remind himself to breathe on occasion.

Eventually, the log curves began to unfold. The Gamma Ray, the Neutron Porosity, The Density Porosity, and the MRI. All began to make their tracks from the bottom of the screen, towards the top, foot after foot as the tools inched their way up the wellbore. First came the shale formation immediately below the La Rosa objective, just as in the first log run. Then the base of the La Rosa Sandstone jumped out on the Gamma Ray curve.

David was riveted to the screens. Data streamed out in tabular and track formats. It was almost too fast for him to absorb. Behind him he could only hear the whir of the drum as it pulled the wireline tools along. The porosity curves tracked back and forth, sometimes criss-crossing, other times splitting in opposite directions. He was having difficulty making sense out of it as it seemed to pick up speed. He wanted to freeze-frame it so he could study the curves. And although this could be done, he desperately needed to see what came next. The tools were nearing the top of the La Rosa after having recorded several hundred feet of the target already. At forty feet below the top of the La Rosa formation, the MRI and porosity curves changed character yet again. Only this time the pattern became more familiar. David was certain he was in the oil leg. The porosities and permeabilities were similar to those he had witnessed in the highly successful Angel Falls #1 well.

Once past the top of the La Rosa Sandstone, David yelled to Gene.

"Freeze the tracks right now!"

Gene spun around and hit a button above each screen. The tracking stopped. The curves went motionless. The data stood motionless, no longer streaming across the displays. Although the tools continued to record data on their way up the wellbore, David had what he needed staring him in the face. He squinted at the screens.

"Gene, can you overlay the readouts from Run #1 on this screen? I want to have the Resistivity and Sonic curves alongside these."

"Can do," responded Gene. He turned toward a keyboard adjacent to the displays and called forward the data from Run #1.

"I just need a moment to calibrate the Gamma curves from both runs so we have all data exactly on depth." He brought forward the earlier log data, then began typing again. The Gamma ray curves from the first well shifted slightly, a mere two feet, until it overlaid perfectly with the Gamma Ray from the second run.

"There we are, David. Only had to shift two feet to correlate the log runs. Now it's your turn to work your magic. Yell out if you need me for anything else."

"Thanks," replied David. "That's all I need for now."

Now that he had the full suite of log data frozen before him, he launched into action. Starting from the top of the La Rosa Sandstone, rather than the bottom, David took out his notebook computer, turned it on and clicked open the Log-Calc program. Armed with this program, he could now perform the quick look assessment that would get him 99% of the answers he needed. He set to work.

Plugging in values for resistivities, porosities and permeabilities, he could calculate the degree of water saturation in the formation. This would tell him how much oil was present in the pore spaces between the sand grains. As he worked his way down the La Rosa sandstone, the first forty feet read similar to the Angel Falls #1. The porosities ranged from 28%-32%. The permeabilities varied from 750 millidarcies (md) to over 1200, averaging 900 md. The water saturation on Log-Calc was under 12%. An outstanding oil reservoir. David was relieved at this initial confirmation of another good well.

He continued evaluating the formation, below the first forty feet. The properties suddenly changed dramatically. Worry lines began to appear on David's forehead. His earlier chill had vanished, only to be replaced by beads of sweat. The porosities were highly variable, some as high as 25%, but only for a few feet. Others trailed off to near zero. But the MRI provided the most damaging assessment. The permeabilities were also sporadic, but generally quite low. David took another look at the resistivity readings from log run #1. Then back to the porosity and permeability data. Had he made a mistake? Could he be wrong?

"Oh my god!" he lamented. The data didn't lie.

"What" said Gene as spun around to face David.

Catching himself, David quickly responded with a curt "Nothing."

Knowing when to leave a client alone, the Halliburton engineer turned quietly away and resumed his duties.

David squinted at the curves, half-hoping he could alter their appearance if he stared long and hard enough. But it didn't work. He now understood the reason for the earlier ambiguities, and his resulting confusion. The sandstone contained multiple minute fractures, and the resistivity and sonic porosity tools were reading into these fractures, yielding spurious data. The tools read high porosity and permeability in the fractures, which David had misinterpreted for the sandstone itself.

He quickly eliminated the fractures and then recalculated for the formation. His jaw dropped as he read the outcome, even though he had an inkling of what was to come. The porosities of the La Rosa Sandstone were very low, less than 6%. The permeability data brought even worse news, reading an average of less than 3 millidarcies. As he stared at the data and the resultant Log-Calc, the outcome was inevitable. While the first forty feet of the La Rosa Sandstone was oil bearing, the remaining 760 feet was not. Instead of oil in the pore spaces of the sandstone, the rock was tightly cemented with quartz cement. It contained very little to no oil, and was too tight to flow even if it did.

David went faint, nearly falling off his chair. He caught himself, but could do no more than sit in front of the computer displays, dumbfounded. His dreams of becoming a world famous explorationist, along the likes of a Michel Halbouty, vaporized by the data before him. Yes, the Angel falls structure contained some oil, but even without re-calculating the reserves based on the new data, he knew it would not be commercial. All the work, everything he and Steve had done for the last two years, was gone, along with his career. Once word got out that the Angel Falls project was a bust, OilQuest stock would plummet. The company would survive, as there were always several exploration prospects in their arsenal at any given time. But the chance to join the big leagues, along the likes of Exxon, BP or Shell, had vanished. The Management Group at OilQuest would be devastated, not to mention the Venezuelan government. Watson would really want to kill him now. David was paralyzed.

Gene shook him from his stupor.

"Tools out of the hole. What do you want to run next?"

"Oh," was all David could muster, still dazed. Thinking briefly. "Do you have a fracture identification tool in your arsenal out there?"

"Sure do."

"Okay. Run it next. But first, I need a copy of Runs #1 and #2. I need to get this info transmitted back to headquarters ASAP.

"Understood. How do you want it: tape, CD, or Zip disk?"

"I'll take it on CD." David paused. "On second thought, better make two copies, one on CD, the other on Zip disk."

"I'll have them for you in a few minutes."

While he waited, David's thoughts drifted back to Mallory, Matt and Eric, for solace. He tried to imagine what kind of day they were having, enjoying the crisp autumn romp by the water's edge.

"I hope that at least they are having a good day."

Little did he know what events were transpiring a continent away.

Gene handed him the copies of the well data.

"Good Luck," said Gene. "I hope you have something big here. It'll mean more business for Halliburton."

David looked at Gene, wondering if he could read the disappointment in his eyes."

"Thanks," was all he could muster. "I'll let you know."

David placed the CD in a protective plastic cover. He put the Zip disk in his shirt pocket and buttoned the flap so it wouldn't fall out. The late afternoon sun was missing as the monsoonal rains continued unabated. He slogged his way across the muddy compound toward Rick Watson's trailer, from where he would transmit the data back to OilQuest in Plano.

"Great weather for a funeral," he muttered to himself.

As he opened the door to Watson's trailer he was stunned to see Bealls and the Colonel sitting in chairs in the office area. Watson was leaning across the front of his desk, coffee cup in hand. They had been chatting, perhaps just chewing the fat, or possibly scheming. Watson, upon seeing David's dripping corpus, blurted out a command.

"Don't come in any further, Hastings. I don't want you trailing mud all around this office."

David stood motionless. Watson continued.

"Bout time you showed up. We've been waiting for the log results. What have you got for us?"

David glanced over at Bealls and the Colonel, then back to Watson. Bealls picked up on the hesitation.

"Don't worry Hastings," Bealls stated. "Colonel Menendez is here on official business. You can regard him as one of us."

Small comfort, thought David, but at least now I know the colonel's name. However, not only do I have to pass along this unsavory news, but I have to do it before these guys. Not exactly my fan club. I can already smell the ridicule and scorn they will heap upon me.

Watson broke the silence. "Watcha got for us Hastings?"

David held up the compact disk.

"Here are the wireline log results from Runs #1 and #2 on the Angel falls #2 well. It contains all the data we need to calculate porosities, permeabilities, oil saturations, and net pay. I need to transmit this data back to our petrophysicists in Plano for a detailed analysis. They will then report the results to the Management Group."

Watson wasn't fooled by David's apparent attempt to buy time. He leaned forward so as to show he meant business.

"We all know the drill Hastings. You performed a Quick Look assessment. That's why we brought you here. Now, do we have an oil field here or not?"

David's shoulders drooped. The rain formed a little puddle around his shoes. He couldn't bring himself to say the words. His teeth clenched. Finally he began, ever so slowly, to confess the results.

"The La Rosa sandstone in the Angel Falls #2 well is essentially tight. There does not appear to be more than about forty feet of net pay at the top of the formation. Below that, the porosities and permeabilities are extremely low."

Colonel Menendez was perplexed.

"Excuse me, senor Hastings. What does all this mean?"

"It means that there is probably no more than about 100 million barrels of oil in the Angel Falls Prospect. We had hoped for several billion. The project is not commercial."

All three men jumped to their feet in shock, glaring at David. He instinctively backed against the wall of the trailer.

"Not commercial!" shouted Watson. "Not commercial!" he repeated as he thrust his face mere inches from David's. "You mean to tell me that we've spent all this money, the technical surveys, the two wells, the licenses, the manpower, the promotions, and now you're saying it's not commercial!"

The Colonel was jabbering in Spanish. David tried to make it out but was too distracted by the sight of Rick Watson howling in his face. Oddly enough, Bealls was silent, almost passive.

How odd, thought David, all the while being screamed at simultaneously in two languages.

Finally, the Colonel managed to break in over Watson's shouting.

"What is wrong with one hundred million barrels? That sounds like a lot of oil to me. Maybe not as large as you had hoped, but still plenty large."

Watson glanced over at the colonel, then back at Hastings, before responding.

"Shall you tell him or do you want me to deliver the bad news?"

David looked beyond Watson's still seething façade, then commenced to explain.

"Colonel, if this was west Texas, or even Lake Maracaibo in western Venezuela, then one hundred million barrels would indeed be a real bonanza. That is because the infrastructure to produce and transport the oil is already in place. But out here, in the middle of the rainforest, there is no infrastructure. We have estimated that it would take nearly a billion US dollars to develop this field, especially with all the environmental safeguards we have designed. After taking into account the huge development costs, plus annual operating costs, plus the Venezuelan government's share of production, plus taxes, we would be losing money. By our calculations, OilQuest needed to discover at least 500 million barrels in order to meet our minimum commercial criteria."

Looking over the sea of stunned faces, David decided to make a final, conclusive statement.

"As much as it kills me to have to say this, the Angel Falls #2 well indicates we do not have a commercial project. Although we will await final results from the detailed petrophysical analysis, we will eventually plug and abandon the well, and abort the project."

Bealls, strangely quiet throughout the tirade, finally spoke up.

"Funny you should use that phrase," making reference to David's last remark. "Because that is precisely what I intend to do."

The room went deadly silent as Bealls pulled a handgun from his jacket and pointed it at David. The distant hum of the diesel generators and the patter of the rain on the trailer roof were all that could be heard. The Colonel smiled knowingly. Watson eyed the situation with intensity.

"Bealls," David stammered, "What in god's name are you doing?"

"All in good time, Hastings. But first, walk slowly over to the desk, keeping both hands where I can see them, and place the CD on the desk. Now move."

Obediently, David moved cautiously over to the desk and placed the compact disk containing the wireline log data on the blotter.

"Now step away," commanded Bealls. David responded accordingly. Bealls, his gun still pointed at David, walked over to the desk and picked up the CD. He glanced at its title, and after satisfying himself as to its contents, he placed the CD back on the desk. Then, with a swift, sharp motion, he brought the butt of his gun down hard on the CD, cracking it into several pieces. He repeated this motion until there was nothing but dozens of small disk remnants about the desk and floor.

"It won't do you any good," said David, looking at the shards of disk on the desk. Headquarters will eventually find out what is in the second well, and when they do, it will still be condemned."

Bealls laughed. "Oh, they'll find out alright. In fact they'll be overjoyed when they find out."

He bent down and opened his briefcase. From a hidden sleeve he removed a CD and held it aloft.

"This is what they will see," Bealls gloated. "A fantastic well with lots of oil."

David was mystified. I don't understand. How...?"

"Of course you don't understand, Hastings. You never did understand. Neither did Steve Giles, which is why I had to put him away."

David's expression instantly turned from helpless incomprehension to rage. His body tensed as he prepared to leap upon Bealls and tear him apart with his bare hands. Watson saw this coming and slammed his forearm hard against David's chest, propelling him backwards into a chair.

Bealls was prepared to shoot David on the spot were it not for Watson's intervention. Watson turned, steely eyed, toward Bealls.

"I don't want you messing up this cabin," he said coldly.

Bealls laughed. "Not a problem Rick. We'll take him out into the jungle, where anybody can disappear without a trace. They'll never find the body. We'll just say he wandered off and never came back. Tsk, tsk. But not to worry, Hastings. We'll have one helluva memorial service for you back in Plano. But first things first. We need to transmit this disk back to Plano."

Bealls handed the disk to Watson. Watson moved around to sit at his desk and started to prepare his computer for the transmission.

"While we're waiting," said Bealls. "I was about to enlighten your tormented little mind before you interrupted me. You see, Hastings, this CD that will be transmitted to Plano contains a modified version of the Angel Falls #1 well data. Of course, it has been corrected for depths and altered here and there to make it look realistic. I had the best people doctor this one. No one will be able to tell the difference. Not even our log analysts back in Plano. I had it made up in advance as a precaution in the event the #2 well was a dud. Good thing I did, huh? It would have been a real mistake to rely on your geologic prowess." His comment dripping with sarcasm.

"The folks back in Plano will get great news. Our Management Group will be ecstatic. OilQuest stock will taker a big jump with the news, and I'll be rich with the options I've purchased."

David was dumbfounded. "That's it. All this just so you could make a few bucks on manipulating the market? You killed Steve for that?"

"Hardly," said Bealls. "And by the way, I'm not the only one who'll make a killing here. Folks back in Plano have been very supportive, but that's inconsequential to you."

"But eventually this project will crater," David sputtered. "Even if you start producing the little oil that is here, it won't last long and it won't take long afterwards for the reservoir engineers at OilQuest and PDVSA to learn that this is uneconomic. There will be hell to pay, and it won't take a genius to trace this back to faked well data."

"True, but I'll have cashed in by then, and be long gone from Texas, making the real money down here in Venezuela."

"What do you mean?"

"What a simpleton," Bealls smirked. Colonel Menendez gave a hearty laugh. Watson continued at his computer, never smiling, never looking up.

"The stock manipulation is just the tip of the iceberg. Lunch money, nothing more. The real money will come from the road. That's where the good colonel comes in."

David was speechless, unable to comprehend where all this was leading. He knew he was in extreme danger and should be looking for an exit, but instead found himself riveted to the chair as the story unfolded. The colonel had taken a seat in order to enjoy the story Bealls was telling. No doubt he had heard it many times before, but seemed to enjoy it again nonetheless. Bealls paced back in forth in front of David, pistol still in hand in case David should contemplate a hasty retreat. Bealls continued.

"The Colonel here is in charge of building the road from the field here back to civilization in Ciudad Bolivar. His men, all hand picked for their loyalty, will start the road at this end so as to avoid detection until the very last minute when it connects up with highways back at Ciudad Bolivar.

"You mean the Venezuelan government is behind all this?"

"Not quite," replied the Colonel. But I have some very influential friends, in both the Parliament and the Military."

"But what will happen when President Chavez and the rest find out?"

Colonel Menendez continued. "By then it will be too late. The road will have been built. And when we demonstrate that the national treasure of Venezuela, oil, is firmly under national control and is boosting the economy through jobs and exports, the will of the people will side with us. We will see to it. The administration will be powerless to stop us."

"But what is so important about the road?" queried David. "You could do the same thing with the buried pipelines we had proposed, and with no environmental impact. Surely the government, and the people, would prefer that alternative."

"The road," said Bealls, "is the key to it all. The road gives the military, under the good colonel's leadership, complete control of the rainforest. Up 'til now, it was for the most part inaccessible with the exception of eco-tourists, and rogue miners. Now, however, the military can establish bases and deploy troops quickly within a large radius of the road. They will take control of the illegal gold and diamond mining operations that have gone unhindered for decades. Eventually they will set up legitimate mining companies for not only gold and diamonds, but for the bauxite and iron ore that is also known to exist in high concentrations."

David was aghast. "But that would devastate the rainforest."

"A small price to pay, don't you think?" Bealls smirked.

"But wait, Hastings, you haven't heard it all yet." Bealls was taking particular delight in enlightening him.

"In addition to the oil and mining operations, the military, once again under the esteemed Colonel's brilliant management, will also monopolize the tourism industry. The road will open this area up tremendously for busloads of tourists streaming into Angel Falls. And what do you think they will find at Angel Falls, but a brand new gaming casino. It will be like Niagara Falls and Las Vegas combined. People from all over the globe will travel here to get married, honeymoon at the Falls, get a quickie divorce, and gamble 'til their hearts content. Of course, once the road is built, we will also have to expand the small, existing airstrip to take commercial jets. And guess who will be the big promoter for this mega-enterprise? Why none other than yours truly!"

Bealls was reveling as he laid out the plan, layer after sordid layer. David was sickened by the thought of it all. What seemed impossible yesterday now sounded altogether too horrendously plausible. Menendez was clearly enjoying the performance, his face aglow every time Bealls heaped praise upon him. Watson, seemingly oblivious to it all, continued transmitting from his computer back to Plano.

"Now here's the cream, Hastings. You're gonna love this. With my former connections and the Colonels contacts, we have been in touch with the Colombian drug cartel. Now that Pablo Escobar is history, the new drug lords are a little more open to alternative routes into the US. We will take possession of the cocaine here at Angel Falls, and transfer it, first by road, and then ship it out with our oil tankers to the US. We are talking billions here, Hastings. Now, doesn't that make the market manipulation look like chump change?"

"Clever plan Bealls, but once the field dries up, won't this all be exposed?"

"Hardly. The oil is simply a front to get us started. It legitimizes our entire operation. But once it is all up and running, we can either scale back and string out the oil shipments, or blame the greedy Americans for once again misleading the poor Venezuelan people. In any case, the economy down here is in such bad shape that neither the government nor the general populace will turn their heads on the job creation and tax revenues from the legitimate mining and tourism operations."

"Then why all this subterfuge with OilQuest. In fact, why do you even need the company?"

"Good question, Hastings," said Bealls. "It shows you are paying attention here. OilQuest provides the legitimate cover for getting this started. And the reason we need them to stay engaged at this time is we need the capital to develop the field and the road."

"But once they find the money is being diverted to the road, they'll stop."

Bealls stared at David before speaking. He pointed the gun in David's face.

"Hastings, were you always this naive? The Angel Falls Option came across as a legitimate request by the Venezuelan government, in the form of our good colonel here, in the event the environmental approach failed for whatever reason. OilQuest was merely performing the scenario analysis for their host government. Naturally, given the environmentally sensitive nature of the study, the Angel Falls Option had to be treated in a highly confidential manner. Perfectly legitimate scenario planning.

"With the new and improved well data that Watson is transmitting back to OilQuest, the Management Group, which is already under our control, will vote to proceed with the project as planned, taking the environmental approach of course. With funding approved for the project, which we have over-inflated, money will be skimmed to fund the road. The road will be built, but left unconnected at both ends by a few miles so as to retain secrecy at first. Once OilQuest learns that the field is non-commercial, they will be forced to abandon it, leaving it to the Colonel to resuscitate, albeit briefly, and be proclaimed a national hero. The road will then be connected to the field and we will be in business. Now, don't you think that's worth me killing, and you dying?"

That last sentence brought David back to his immediate predicament. After revealing the entire scenario, Bealls obviously would not let David live. He was trapped in a room full of killers, on a rig site in the middle of the jungle. His heart sank. Blood drained from his head. He grew woozy. He was a dead man. Memories of Mallory and the boys flooded his mind. He would die here and no one except his killers would know why.

"Finished," proclaimed Watson with a final stroke of the keyboard.

"Perfect timing," responded Bealls, turning to David. "Now its time we went for a little stroll."

"I don't think so."

It was Watson who spoke. In his hand was a 45 caliber colt, chrome plated. It was pointed squarely at Bealls.

"Now drop the gun, Bealls, or, much as I hate to, I'll be forced to spread your brains all around this room."

Bealls hesitated, somewhat in shock, his gun still pointed at David.

"I'll shoot Hastings," said Bealls, hoping to dissuade Watson.

"Go ahead and shoot him. I've been tempted myself at times. But I will still shoot you no matter what. So drop the gun now."

David was bewildered. He looked down the barrel of the gun in Bealls' hand. He thought he could see him slowly applying pressure to the trigger. Then he eased off the trigger and let the gun drop to the floor.

The Colonel, unable to comprehend what was transpiring, slowly began to reach for his pistol that was safety latched in his holster. Watson saw the movement out of the corner of his eye.

"Colonel, you'd be dead before you released the safety. Don't even think about it."

Colonel Menendez moved his hand away from his holster.

"Good boy," said Watson. Now sit on the couch."

Everyone moved cautiously toward the couch, including David.

"Not you Hastings, for god's sake. Now get the Colonel's gun and pick up Bealls piece."

Relieved, David complied. By now both Bealls and Menendez were seated side by side on the couch. Watson stood before them. David held both guns in his hands, pointing them at the two men on the sofa.

"Rick," said Bealls. "Listen to me. We can make you wealthy beyond your wildest imagination."

"Oh I don't know," commented Watson dryly. "I've got a pretty big imagination. For example, right now I'm imagining that you boys would eventually do me in when the time was right. Maybe the same time as Hastings over here."

"Nonsense," pleaded Bealls. "We need you to keep things looking above board and legitimate both down here and back in Plano. You are essential to us."

"Essential for now perhaps, but the time would come when you would consider me a liability, wouldn't you?"

"Absolutely not," replied the colonel. "Don't be a fool. Come with us and you will be a multi-millionaire. Side with Hastings, and you will die with Hastings. My men are out there. How far do you think you will get? Think about it."

Rick seemed to hesitate. This worried David.

"Rick," said David.

"Don't worry Hastings. Enticing as it sounds, they've mistaken my loathing of you as a willingness to stand by and watch this operation jeopardized. This is my operation, and I run it my way, which is by the book. Nobody screws with my project."

"We're not gonna get that 'out here I'm god' speech again, are we? Cause we do have a rather pressing problem right now. For starters, there's the fake data you just sent to Plano."

"Oh that. I just hope those boys in Petrophysics like Willie Nelson, because I just sent them his greatest hits CD."

Bealls and Menendez nearly leapt out of their seats, but the sight of three guns pointed at them seemed to calm their nerves considerably. David looked back at Watson after shaking a pistol at Bealls.

"Rick, I believe I've misjudged you."

"You and everybody else it seems."

As Rick finished speaking the door opened and in walked one of the Colonels soldiers. He stopped abruptly as he surveyed the situation. For a brief second all were speechless. Then the colonel yelled out a command. The soldier instantly unslung the M16 from his shoulder and began raising the barrel of the rifle at Rick. Without hesitation, both David and Rick let loose with a volley of fire, launching the soldier back out the door where he sprawled in the mud in front of the trailer. He was dead before he hit the ground.

Shouts could be heard coming from the compound.

Rick cursed. "Oh shit, so much for containment."

"Now what?" David queried in bewilderment.

"Run like hell," yelled Rick as he bolted for the door.

David fell into step behind Rick, waving a gun at the two men still seated on the couch. They slogged across the muddy compound, pistols in hand, and made their way into the dense jungle foliage of the surrounding rainforest. Workers stood and stared in disbelief at the sight. Colonel Menendez appeared at the door of the trailer, barking commands to his soldiers, who were scrambling toward their dead comrade in the mud.

Bealls joined the colonel on the steps of the trailer.

"Get me a gun," he said to the colonel. "Let's get some of your men and go out there and find them. Damn, I hate loose ends. I will personally kill both of those sons of a bitches."

Within short order, about a dozen soldiers had assembled in front of colonel Menendez. He proclaimed, in a voice loud enough for the rig crew to hear, that Watson and Hastings had killed a Venezuelan soldier in cold blood. He then issued orders to kill on sight. Bealls, armed with the M16 from the dead soldier, headed out into the rainforest with the colonel and his search party.

Rick led the way deeper into the jungle. The sounds of the diesel generators faded behind them. David was impressed with Rick's stealthy movements and stamina as they wove their way past ferns and tropical plants. The late afternoon sun attempted in vain to force its way through the leafy canopy of trees above, with an occasional ray finding a path to the floor below. Tiny rivulets of rainwater trickled along the center of broad-leafed plants and dropped onto the verdant carpet beneath, disappearing instantly in the lushness of the earth. The perfumed smells of the jungle nearly overpowered David as he ran.

This would all be really beautiful if I weren't running for my life, he thought.

As if he could read David's mind, Rick turned to cajole his panting, breathless partner.

"Can't stop to smell the roses now. They won't be far behind. And with the rain we just had, it won't be difficult to follow our footprints. So get your ass in gear."

David looked back in dismay to find they had left a highly visible trail of deep-set footprints.

"Oh god!" he exclaimed. "Even a blind man could follow us."

After nearly twenty minutes of running, Rick pulled to a stop. Hands on his knees, he bent over taking deep breaths. David dropped to the ground beside him, nearly retching from the run. They spent the next minute looking bug-eyed at each other, still trying to catch their breath. Finally David inhaled deeply and spoke.

"Rick, we probably can't outrun these guys. The nearest place of refuge is the village at Angel Falls, which is about twenty miles away. In the jungle we are going to have a hard time keeping our bearings straight. And, it will be dark in a few hours."

"So what do you suggest? We make a stand and take on the Venezuelan army?"

David looked at Rick and smiled.

"Glad to see you've got your old disposition back. I was beginning to miss it. As much as I liked Butch Cassidy and the Sundance Kid when they took on the Bolivian army, the outcome was far from desirable. No, I suggest we hide. If we can stay hidden long enough, they may turn back when it gets dark."

Watson turned to David and cried out in derision.

"That's it? Hide? That's the best you can do? I knew you rock huggers were a little short on gray matter but I always took you for the imaginative type."

"And I suppose you want to take on the army, eh? Mano Y mano?"

Rick suddenly clapped a hand over David's mouth.

"Shutup and listen......."

He dropped his hand. The two unlikely companions remained motionless as they strained to hear the sounds emanating from the jungle. It was the soldiers, shouting in Spanish. They were not making any effort to sneak up on them. Of course, they didn't need to. Fourteen men, all heavily armed, against two men with handguns.

"They were not far off, perhaps a few hundred yards," whispered David. Rick nodded.

"Let's find some cover," David continued. "Looks like you'll get your fight after all."

The two men scrambled further into the rainforest and came to a halt amongst a cluster of fallen trees. It provided a natural bunker, but was far from ideal, being slightly exposed in several places. They jumped over the trees and into the bunker, resting against one of the larger trunks.

"Ok," said Rick. "Let's take stock of the situation. Probably anywhere from ten to twenty men out their, most armed with good ol' US of A standard army issue M16s, with thirty rounds to a clip. We, on the other hand, have three handguns, two 45s and a 9mm. No more than thirty rounds when loaded. How many bullets did you shoot at the soldier back in the trailer?

"I'm not sure," said David. "I wasn't counting as he pointed his rifle at me. But I'd say about four rounds."

"And I fired twice, so we're down to about 24 bullets. You take the 9mm Beretta. There should be about 13 rounds left. I'll take the two 45s."

By now the soldiers were within a hundred yards and closing. They still could not be seen through the dense foliage but their voices could be heard. David heard the colonel barking out orders. He even thought he heard Bealls speak out as someone said something in English. The two men took up prone positions a few feet apart, behind the fallen trees where they had a clear line of sight on the trail they had left.

"At least we have the element of surprise, Rick. We should be able to inflict a helluva lot of damage before they see us."

Watson studied David for a brief moment, as if to discern his inner fortitude for what was about to transpire.

"Just make every shot count."

Two soldiers appeared on the path, then another, and another. They were moving through the rainforest in twos, several feet apart. Rifles at the ready. Commands were streaming from behind, but the soldiers in front were deadly quiet. Their camouflaged green, black and brown uniforms blended discretely into the foliage, but their movements gave them away. Less than fifty yards away. More soldiers appeared behind them. The soldiers at the front had their eyes trained on the ground, following the tracks. Had they looked up, they might have seen the fallen cluster of trees that made for a natural fort. They might have thought this structure urged caution. They might have thought it was a trap. They would have thought right.

At twenty five yards. Rick opened up with his colt 45. "I've got the ones on the right," he shouted as he fired.

A soldier dropped. Then another. David took aim and fired. The soldier spun around and fell to the floor of the jungle with a scream. The one behind him turned back and ran. David fired again, hitting him squarely in the back. Rick squeezed off two more rounds. One man fell. Then there were no more to be seen. They had all taken cover. Voices could be heard. Some shouting, some in near whispers.

Rick checked his ammo. "I think we got five. That should give them something to think about."

They didn't think long.

With a single command from Colonel Menendez, the jungle was ablaze in gunfire. M16s on fully automatic tore into the fallen trees, tearing off large pieces of bark. David and Rick dug themselves deeper into the dirt as bullets whizzed overhead, shredding foliage into confetti that showered the two. It seemed like an eternity but the firing trailed off a minute later. The rainforest was deadly silent. Not a bird or creature made a peep.

"Maybe they're out of ammo," David whispered hopefully.

"Or maybe they're just reloading," snapped Rick. 'Want to stick your head out to see which one of us is right?"

Another command and the jungle once again erupted. David turned around in his hole so that he was lying on his back. Pieces of shredded bark fell on his face. Those shots did not come from in front of them, but from behind them. Rick had instinctively flipped around. He pointed to one of the openings in the bunker that was opposite the main body of soldiers. David nodded and crawled over to it. He peered slowly around the corner to take a quick glimpse outside. Several bullets embedded into the trunk a few inches from his eye. He quickly snapped his head back inside but not before another bullet grazed his forehead, opening a slit above his right eye. Blood poured down, partially obscuring his vision. Rick saw the encounter and shifted over to the opposite side of the opening. Without sticking his head out he leaned back and forth in order to see as much as he could. He then turned to David and held up two fingers, then pointed to their approximate positions outside the bunker. David nodded, wiping the blood from his head. Once again the firing trailed off and stopped. Time for another reload.

Rick looked at David and yelled "Now."

Both men rolled to where they had a clear field of vision through the opening. They were exposed, but the two soldiers were busy reloading. Firing simultaneously, the soldiers, who had been kneeling, fell backwards as the bullets tore through their flimsy summer camo. Blood spurted from several holes. Rick's 45 inflicted the most damage, but the 9mm hit its mark at least twice.

They rolled back behind the cover of the tree trunks. Rick dropped his empty 45 and picked up the other. He looked over at David, who was applying pressure to the wound in order to get it to stop bleeding.

"You ok?" Rick asked with genuine concern.

"I'll live," was all David could manage. They both immediately realized how ridiculous that comment was, given their dire predicament, and burst out laughing. Their laughter rang loudly through the silent forest, being heard by the remaining soldiers who stared in bewilderment.

"Do you hear that Menendez?" shouted Bealls. "They are laughing at you and your men. Two of them. That's all there are. Just two men with handguns, against your soldiers with automatic rifles. What are you going to do about it?"

Goaded by Bealls, the colonel became enraged at this challenge to his manhood. His fury building by the minute, he screamed at his remaining soldiers, who were cowering in the tall foliage beside him. Rick and David could hear the tirade from their bunker.

"Man, is he pissed!" said David.

"What is he saying?"

"He's calling his soldiers a bunch of cowards, that a group of schoolgirls could fight better than they. That their families will be dishonored when they learn of how they were beaten by two Yankees with pistols."

"Now they really made me mad," seethed Rick. "Nobody calls me a damn Yankee."

David paused to listen some more.

"Oh, oh."

"What?" asked Rick in a worried tone.

"Menendez has them all pumped up. They're gonna charge. Get ready."

A single command from Menendez and the remaining soldiers leapt to their feet, screaming as they hurtled themselves at the bunker. David and Rick opened fire. Several soldiers dropped. The rest seemed to hesitate.

"Don't let up," shouted Rick. "We've got to turn them back."

David kept squeezing the trigger. Round after round exploded from the barrel of his 9mm Beretta. He squeezed again and all he heard was the click of an empty magazine. The same sound was heard a few seconds later as Rick emptied his gun on the fleeing soldiers.

It had worked, for the moment. They had succeeded in stopping the charge, but now they were out of ammo. And the enemy was still out there.

"Jesus H. Christ," exclaimed Rick. "We must have taken out another three or four. Did he bring the whole goddamn army or what?"

"At least a couple more soldiers made a safe retreat," replied David as he checked his wound. "And we know Bealls and Menendez are out there. Not good odds."

"Did anyone ever tell you that you were a master of understatement?"

"My wife, all the time."

They grew quiet. The comment made David think of Mallory. How he wished he could get one last message off to her, to tell her how much he loved her. That he would always be there with her, looking over the boys. A tear fell from his eye and mixed with the trail of blood that trickled from his forehead. Rick pretended not to notice. A voice shouted from behind some trees. It was Bealls.

"Well boys, I guess by now you are out of ammo. Shame. We were having so much fun. Tell you what. Throw out the guns, come on out, and I promise to kill you quickly."

"If you're so sure we're out of ammo, why don't you come here and get us," yelled Rick.

"If I have to come get you, I am really gonna make you suffer. Between the colonel and me, we can come up with some pretty good ways to let you die slowly and painfully."

No response.

"Ok, I guess we're going to have to do this the hard way. Colonel, send in your men."

Menendez barked out an order. Four very reluctant soldiers gingerly stepped out and slowly made their way toward the bunker. The sight of colonel

Menendez holding a gun to their backs provided the proper motivation to move begrudgingly forward.

Rick poked the two Colt 45s out from the trunk, which sent the soldiers diving to the ground. After a few seconds however, when nothing happened, the soldiers lifted their heads, and smiled to each other. They stood up and, with slightly more confidence, walked steadily toward the bunker, M16s at the ready.

David rested his empty gun on a trunk, in plain sight for the soldiers to see. "Rick, they know we're out. Put the guns down."

Watson hesitated briefly, pondering his fate. David sensed he was not convinced. He reached over and placed his hand over one of the Colts. Rick stared solemnly at David, then relinquished the gun. David placed it on the trunk. He could hear the soldiers' footsteps, merely yards away. Before he could take the second pistol from his other hand, Rick stood up and pointed it squarely at the advancing soldiers. David grabbed Rick's feet and yanked him down as a torrent of bullets showered the bunker. Rick was hit in the left shoulder and arm. The soldiers scrambled over the bunker and stood over the two men, weapons pointed at their heads. Rick lay bleeding on the ground. David leaned over to stop the bleeding but was kicked in the side by one of the soldiers. They were all yelling simultaneously. All David could see were gun barrels in his face as he lay clutching his side, ribs broken by the force of the kick.

Seconds later Bealls and Menendez appeared on top of the bunker. Bealls looked down at the two bloodied men.

"This is going to be fun."

"We have no time for games," the Colonel said to Bealls. It will be dark soon and we need to get back to camp. Kill them and get it over with."

Bealls nodded. "Shame. I was so looking forward to making them beg me to kill them."

He raised his M16 and pointed it back and forth at David and Rick. "Now let's see. Which one should I kill first? I think I'll save Hastings for last. He can join his family." This last comment alarmed David but Bealls was already taking aim at Rick. The soldiers stood smirking, guns dangling by their side. The colonel bore an impatient expression. Rick, propped up against a trunk, still bleeding from his wounds, glared stoically at his killer.

As Bealls prepared to squeeze off a round, a small, jet like sound followed by a dull thud filled the air. The colonel's eyes bulged wide. His gun fell from his hand and he fell face forward into the bunker, nearly collapsing on top of David. The shaft of an arrow was firmly planted in his back, having penetrated his heart, the colonel who had planned to dominate Venezuela, died instantly. More arrows flew in from all directions. A soldier grasped his chest and dropped. Another let out a howl as an arrow pierced his leg. Bealls frantically looked about but saw nothing but a hail of arrows. The remaining soldiers dropped their rifles and ran screaming in terror back in the direction of the compound. They would never make it, as a trail of arrows followed them to their death.

A well placed arrow hit Bealls on his upper arm, pinning it to his side. Dropping the rifle, he spun into the bunker, landing squarely between Rick and David. Bealls screamed in agony as the fall pushed the arrow deeper into his rib cage, puncturing the right lung. Scarlet red, frothy bubbles began to stream from his mouth. He made throaty, gurgling noises as he choked on his own blood. David and Rick could only stare at him in shock and this sudden turn of events. Suddenly, Bealls was quiet, his eyes wide open at the horror of his last terrifying moment on earth. The bunker served as an open grave for Bealls and Colonel Menendez, a fitting tribute to the two men who schemed to turn the rainforest into a paved over commercial enterprise of gargantuan proportions. The rainforest would now use their decaying bodies as compost for further growth.

David stared at Rick in bewilderment. Although still bleeding a little from the gunshot wounds, Rick was fully cognizant of the events that had just transpired. David helped him to his knees where they could both slowly peer over the tree trunks in the predominant direction of the arrows. At first they saw nothing. Then slowly, figures began to emerge from the shadowy vegetation. The brown-skinned, scantily clad Yanomama tribesmen stepped slightly forward in a defensive posture, arrows still set in their bows. They stared at Rick and David, who could only stare back in return as they pondered what had prompted such an unusual intervention.

When it was evident that all was clear, one of the tribesmen let out a bird like sound. Seconds later, out stepped a warrior clad in gold and plumage of the forest. He held a decorated spear upright in his left hand, more a symbol of authority than a weapon.

"Must be the chief," whispered Rick, "but I still don't know why they did this. Maybe they wanna eat us or something." David said nothing.

From behind the chief out stepped a young girl. She wore items similar to the chief, signifying a relationship, most probably father and daughter. She was also wearing a Texas Rangers baseball cap. She looked at David and smiled.

"Lolita," said David. He smiled and held up his hand as a gesture of friendship.

"Lolita?" queried Rick. "How did you know her name? And where did she get that cap from?"

The noble chief held up his hand, and with a single word, withdrew his men. They vanished into the jungle as silently as they had come. Lolita pointed to her cap, smiled a final time, and was gone."

David stood there looking at seemingly empty rainforest before Rick broke the magic of the moment.

"What the hell was that all about?" he exclaimed.

"Long story, but lucky for us she appears to be the chief's daughter."

They both took a moment to survey the carnage that lay about them, Dead soldiers and villains, along with their weapons, lay strewn about like lifeless rag dolls. David looked at Rick, then felt his own broken ribs.

"Just look at us. Are we a god awful mess or what?"

Rick, despite his wounds, was still very much aware of their predicament. He looked at his watch, then up through the cracks in the dense canopy above.

"We better start back to the compound. Like the good colonel said. It will be dark soon and we don't have time to waste."

David made some bandages from the colonel's uniform and managed to stifle the bleeding from Rick's gunshot wounds. He had lost a fair amount of blood and was feeling slightly dizzy, but was determined to make the hike back to camp. They slowly retraced their footsteps, stepping over the bodies of soldiers as they left the confines of their rainforest bunker behind. What had taken them twenty minutes to sprint earlier in the day, took nearly two hours to hobble their way back.

It was dusk as they straggled into the compound, propping each other up. At first the rig crew was startled, afraid to even approach the two men that left under such bizarre circumstances, being hotly pursued by the Venezuelan army.

Rick, whispering to David, "Let's see if I'm still god."

"Sure you want to put this to the test?"

"Got any better ideas?"

"None whatsoever."

"Then shutup and let me do my thing."

Rick yelled out to several of the roughnecks that had been staring from a safe, respectable distance. They jumped, startled by his command, then came running over.

"Help us to my trailer, and get the doc."

One man ran off toward a tent across the compound while two men guided the walking wounded toward Rick's trailer. By now most of the crew had gathered to see the commotion. Two of the few remaining soldiers came running. Amazed to find that the colonel and their comrades had not returned, the soldiers shrunk into the background and slowly made their way back towards the safety of their encampment. They would not venture forth without orders from Colonel Menendez, whose decomposing body would not be found for days.

Rick was led to his bed in the back of the trailer while David was laid out on the couch. The Venezuelan doctor arrived, carrying a large, overstuffed medical bag. He came upon David first, but David ordered him to the back room where he could first tend to Watson. About fifteen minutes later the doctor emerged from Rick's bedroom.

"How is he?" asked David, wincing from the cracked ribs. The doctor saw David's pained expression and lifted his shirt to expose the bruised patch in the vicinity of his ribcage. A slight finger probe by the doctor brought a yelp from David. The doctor nodded.

"Senor Watson is very lucky. Both wounds are superficial. The objects exited cleanly without breaking any bones. He has lost some blood but he is a strong man. He will recover quickly. As for you, senor Hastings, you have at least two broken ribs, maybe three. I'll wrap your chest so you can travel to a hospital. I will also clean that gash on your forehead and give it a few temporary stitches. Looks like a sharp object grazed your forehead. The vegetation in the rainforest can be quite painful. You and senor Watson must have had a very bad fall, eh?"

David looked at the doctor, who winked back with a wry smile.

"Yes Doc. A very bad fall."

Rick entered the room. The doctor looked up and immediately began to protest.

"Senor Watson, you must rest until we can get you to a hospital."

"No time for that now. We have a real mess on our hands and we need to clean it up now."

"Rick, I need to get back to the States ASAP. Bealls said something that makes me think that my family may be in danger."

"I know, so here's the plan. We have a chopper out there that can get you back to Caracas. That's the best I can do for now."

"Aren't you coming with me?"

"Hell no, I need to contain things here."

"But the army isn't going to be thrilled when they find out what just happened."

"Look, you get back to the States and straighten things out at that end. I'll take care of business down here. Don't worry. I'll be alright for a few days. You need to get this cleared up once and for all."

Despite his pig headedness, thought David. His plan did make some sense. Until the real motive behind the Angel Falls Option was brought to light, no one would believe two gringos who just shot up a Venezuelan army unit in the middle of the rainforest.

"Ok. Let's get moving."

"Now you may have some trouble leaving Caracas, as the army might radio ahead with their own version of what happened here today."

David thought a moment. Rick was right. He stood a good chance of being hauled out of the airport by soldiers and simply disappearing. Pulling a card out of his pocket, he handed it to Rick.

"This woman is a good friend of mine at the US Embassy. Tell her I need her help to leave Caracas for the US at the earliest flight. Ask her to meet me at the heliport when I arrive. You can tell her whatever else you feel is necessary but tell her that I have some information for her that will make this all worthwhile."

Rick looked at the card. "Laura Ericson. I got to hand it to you Hastings, for a married man you seem to have women stashed all over this country. I'll do it, but when this is all over I want you to hook me up with a few."

"Rick, when this is all over, I'll even double date with you."

"Let's not get carried away. Now head for the chopper. I'll have the pilots there in a few minutes. They don't like flying at night but for double pay, these guys would fly you to hell and back."

"One last request," begged David.

"Now what?"

"Can I please get a call through to my wife, I need to see if everything is alright."

Rick looked at David. He could see the worry across his bandaged face. He strolled over to his desk and pulled out a large hand held phone, looking much like a walkie talkie.

"This is a global cellular phone. I have it for emergencies, which I guess we can say this truly is. However, make it quick and don't talk about what happened here. It is most likely monitored. Understood?"

"Understood."

He turned it on and handed it to David, then left the room to give him a moment's privacy. David dialed the number in Weekapaug, but was devastated to get the Langtree's answering machine. He left a message, cryptic as it was, and hoped to god that his family was in safe hands. David turned off the phone and called Watson back into the room.

"Any luck?" asked Watson as he studied David's face for mood changes.

"Answering machine."

"I'm sure they are alright," Rick stated consolingly. "Now get your butt back there and straighten this mess out."

David turned to Rick. The two men faced each other, both momentarily speechless. The worst of enemies had suddenly become the best of friends. They both knew it, but neither would dare admit.

"See you back in Plano," said David, his hand outstretched.

"God I hope not. You are way too dangerous to be around," said Rick as he clenched David's hand tightly. Now get the hell off my compound."

David smiled, turned away and ran out the door to the helicopter pad. Minutes later the two pilots hurried to the chopper. The turbines came to life and the rotor blades swirled as it lifted off the ground and headed north toward Caracas. David glanced out the window at the well lit compound below. Men and machines grew smaller as the chopper rose into the murky moonless sky. Soon he was immersed in darkness, and the vibrating hum of the engines lulled him to sleep.

# CHAPTER 12

# *The Sanctuary*

## *DAY EIGHT*

Despite the police presence, it had been a restless night. Mallory slept fitfully, her mind still absorbing all that had transpired during the day. She had stayed up with the boys until they fell asleep, then listened attentively throughout the night in case they should have nightmares. Delilah paced the third floor, moving between Mallory and the boys' rooms as if on sentry duty. She would occasionally stare down the steps as though she was expecting Samson to acknowledge her presence. It was not until the early hours of the morning that she finally settled down beside the boy's bed and went to sleep.

Mallory relived the moment when she drove the knife into the man's chest for the final time. She could not believe she had actually done such a horrendous deed. Her emotions ran the gamut, alternating between guilt and heroism and everything in between. She thought about David. She wanted so very much to talk to him, to tell him what had transpired, to scream at him, to hear his consoling words, to be reassured that everything from here on out would be alright. But down inside, she knew that David was also in great danger.

"He can take care of himself," talking to herself in a low, consoling tone so as not to be heard.

"But he mustn't know what happened. He needs to stay focused. If he found out what happened to us, he would be up here in a New York minute. And that would bring added danger to all of us."

Then Mallory realized she didn't even know if David was still alive. This thought nearly sent her into hysterics, but she regained control of her imagination and quickly calmed herself.

She was relieved when dawn finally came.

The drive to the Eighty Acre Woods only took about twenty minutes. A Westerly police cruiser escorted them all the way, while another officer retained the remaining reporters in order to keep them from following. Although the wildlife sanctuary only comprised eighty acres, it was surrounded on the north and east by Burlingame State Park. Burlingame was a large, mostly wooded park that permitted camping, hiking and fishing. This greatly extended the outer bounds of the sanctuary, as wildlife moved unconstrained between the Eighty Acre Woods and Burlingame. A small fresh water pond formed the southern boundary of the sanctuary, while the picturesque county road bordered the property on the west.

David and the boys had often camped in Burlingame, which was frequented by visitors from neighboring Massachusetts, Connecticut and New York. Mallory seldom attended these male oriented activities, especially as she was often saddled with the planning, packing and cooking. Roughing it was not her idea of a good time. The campsites at Burlingame ranged in the hundreds, and the proximity to the Rhode Island shoreline was a big draw in the summer. This time of year, however, the campgrounds were nearly deserted and the park would soon be closing the campgrounds for the winter.

The caravan, which consisted of the police car, Mallory's rental, and Tom's Explorer, turned off the country road onto the gravel driveway that marked the entrance to the sanctuary. The wooded drive wound for a quarter mile around majestic oaks and massive, glacial strewn boulders before pulling up to the office. The officer exited his cruiser and motioned for the others to remain in their cars until he had a look around. Hand on his holster, he slowly walked around the small, single story office. He peered in the windows and scanned the surrounding woods. He disappeared briefly as he moved to search the other structures nearby.

"This is really cool," pronounced Matt. "Look how the cop has his hand on his gun. Do you think he's going to shoot somebody?"

"I certainly hope not," responded Mallory. "I think we've had enough excitement for awhile."

After what seemed like an eternity but was only a few moments, the officer approached the vehicles and announced that it was okay to get out. He then spoke to Mallory.

"The Chief ordered me to remain with you for awhile, to be sure that everything was all right."

"Thank you, officer, both for the escort and for sticking around."

"Happy to oblige, Ma'am. But I gotta tell you, this is a very difficult area to secure. Woods going back for what seems like miles, set back from the road, no neighbors in sight. I don't mean to alarm you but are you sure this is where you want to be?"

Mallory surveyed the situation, taking in the full impact of the officer's comments. Tom had overheard the conversation and moved in quickly to reassure Mallory.

"I know it may seem we are quite exposed here, officer, but hopefully we made it here unseen. And, I know these woods like the back of my hand. The animals make for a highly accurate early warning system, not to mention the burglar alarms we installed in the office and living quarters."

"Suit yourself, Tom, but remember that it would probably take us a good twelve to fifteen minutes to respond to a 911 call out here. A lot can happen in that time."

"I understand. We will be careful. And hopefully Mallory has seen the last of these folks."

Mallory nodded, as if in agreement, but she sensed her pursuers had not called off the chase yet. And if they were sophisticated enough to trace her through her rental car, they could probably find her here as well. Her suspicions were about to be confirmed.

The police radio in the cruiser sounded off.

"Car two-four, come in."

The officer excused himself and walked back to his car.

Tom turned to Mallory.

"Don't worry. Helene and I, and Delilah, will be with you and the boys all the time. We have some school groups coming over the next few days so there will be plenty of people around during the day. At night we'll lock this place up tighter than a drum. And I mean it when I say the animals will alert us to any unwanted intrusion."

Mallory grabbed hold of Tom's hand for comfort. He clasped both hands around hers.

"Tom, I know that I could not be in better hands, but I would never forgive myself if my problems brought harm to you and Helene."

"Let us worry about that. Now c'mon, let me show you our new accommodations. And remind me to show you where I keep the ammo for the twenty-two."

Helene was keeping a watchful eye on the boys, who, along with Delilah, were now busily exploring their new neighborhood. Delilah seemed to be searching for something as she peered and sniffed her way around. She then slowly returned to the company of the boys, head down, looking forlorn. Helene realized she was looking for Samson, in all the places they used to romp together. Fighting back the tears, Helene stooped down and gave Delilah a warm embrace, then slowly guided her toward the boys. Delilah seemed to understand, taking an alert, protective stance around Matt and Eric.

"Don't wander off," Helene yelled to them as they headed for the horse barn.

There were three simple structures on the property. The first was the office that Tom and Helene used to greet visitors. It contained a small office, a larger room with wildlife exhibits that was used to greet visitors, and two bathrooms.

From the rear of the office, a gravel path led to a small house, affectionately labeled 'the dorm' as it would house summer interns from the University of Rhode Island. The cedar shingled house was rectangular and contained three bedrooms and one bathroom. One of the bedrooms had bunk beds while the others each contained a double bed. The bedrooms opened onto a cozy living room, with wide board plank flooring and a wood burning stove. The stove was the only source of heat since the house had not been intended for year round use. A kitchen/eating area with large rectangular table completed the picture. It was primitive, but more than adequate. The boys positively loved it.

"Wow, this is just like camping!" shouted Eric.

"We should have come here sooner," chimed Matt.

"I thought you would like it," Helene responded with a devious grin. "And you know how much your mom loves to camp."

Forming the third leg of the triangle was a horse barn, with stabling for 6 horses. Helene loved horses. So did Tom, but Helene was passionate. They presently stabled three horses, one for each of them and a spare for a guest. Occasionally a summer intern would bring their own horse to be stabled. Tom had carved out numerous trails throughout the sanctuary, useful for both hiking and riding. He and Helene especially enjoyed a morning ride in the crisp, autumn air.

As the children continued to explore, the adults busied themselves with unpacking the vehicles. Provisions from the cottage in Weekapaug were unloaded and the kitchen was restocked. Mallory set to making up the beds while Tom and Helene attended to business in the office.

Mallory issued stern orders to the boys to stay near the buildings and not to venture into the woods unescorted. Knowing that, like all children, they possessed a natural tendency to forget their mother's warning, she asked Tom to set them straight. He did so with the booming, authoritative voice of a marine drill sergeant. The boys responded to this approach, and kept within eyesight of the adults.

The police officer was standing by his cruiser when Mallory brought him a cup of coffee she had just made.

She extended the steaming cup of black coffee to the officer.

"Thought you might need this."

"Thanks," he said, taking a sip. Then, looking around as if to survey the scene, he quipped "You know what this place needs?"

"No, what?"

"A Bess Eaton donut shop. Right here in this driveway. Then, I'd stay all day."

They both laughed.

The radio barked in the police cruiser.

"That's for me," he stated as he leaned into the car.

Mallory busied herself with cleaning up the cottage, putting sheets and blankets on the beds and laying out towels. It would be a tight fit for all of them, but the boys would definitely enjoy the experience, and this was as close to camping out as she would get.

The officer knocked on the open door of the cottage just to announce his presence.

"That radio report was about your incident."

Mallory, Tom and Helene halted their chores and approached the officer.

"C'mon in and sit down, officer," beckoned Tom.

"Please call me Vinny. We may as well get to know each other since the chief gave me orders to stay until the end of my shift."

They all took a seat at the table. The boys were out romping in the nearby woods. Occasional shouts and dog barks gave comfort to their proximity.

"Has something else happened?" Mallory anxiously inquired.

"Well, an extensive search along the breachway finally turned up something. A man's body was found in the pond a few hundred yards from the Breachway. Good thing this happened on an incoming tide or it would have been washed out to sea."

"Was it the man I described?"

"We thought so. It was kinda hard to tell because the face was so badly disfigured. It looked like he had been mangled on the rocks. The clothes fit the description you gave us and we thought we could bring this ordeal to a close for you."

Mallory knew there was more to come, and it was not going to end with 'and they lived happily ever after'.

"But there's more, isn't there, Vinny?" she asked.

"Afraid so. A housewife from Wakefield phoned in that her husband had gone fishing at the Breachway yesterday and had not returned."

"There was a fisherman on the rocks when we were being chased. I tried signaling him for help but he couldn't make out what I was saying with all the noise, and I couldn't slow down because we were in the middle of the Breachway and the Pizza man was right behind us."

Vinny continued.

"Well, the wife gave us a good description of her husband, right down to the tattoo on his left forearm."

Everyone around the table knew what was coming next but waited for Vinny to make his pronouncement.

"The dead man is the fisherman from Wakefield. I got the call on the radio after she identified the body."

Mallory dropped her head to her hands in exasperation.

"I cannot believe this is happening."

Tom put a reassuring arm around her shoulder.

Helene was the first to acknowledge the situation and speak up.

"OK Vinny. Looks like we have a killer on the loose. So what happens next?"

"We don't know if the fisherman was actually murdered until the autopsy is performed."

"True," Helene replied, "But it is reasonable to infer that the second man chasing Mallory did not drown. That he made it safely to shore and he killed the fisherman because he witnessed the event. The killer then changed clothes with the fisherman, disfigured his face, and threw him into the water. Was there any ID on the dead man's body?"

"You should have been a cop," smiled Vinny. "No, there was no ID. He had a few bucks in his pocket but no wallet."

Tom picked up where Helene left off.

"What about a car? Did the fisherman have a car?"

"According to his wife, the man drove himself to the Breachway in a 1984 green Chevy Suburban. But, the car is missing and now officially reported as stolen. Can't be too many of those still on the road. We have an All Points Bulletin out on the car, along with your description of the suspect. If he is still in the area we should be able to find him. And, the State Police for Rhode Island, Connecticut and Massachusetts have been notified."

"He'd have to be awfully stupid to drive around in that car," Helene commented, "and these guys don't strike me as being stupid."

"True," replied the officer. "Right now we don't know who these people are or who they work for. Our local contacts have indicated that the Pizza Man was not directly related to the mob but he is believed to be a professional, possibly from the west coast. Our office is working with the Plano police department to see if there is any connection with the incident at your house in Plano. I'll let you know if we learn anything more, but right now we have more questions than answers."

"The story of my life these days," quipped Mallory.

A momentary silence as the four around the table absorbed the details and their implications.

Tom broke the uneasy silence.

"So, how long will you be able to provide police protection?"

Vinny cast a pitying glance toward Mallory.

"We are a small department and stretched pretty thin. The chief said we can't provide round-the-clock coverage, but every shift for the next few days will routinely patrol past here and check in on you. After that we have to break it off. I am sorry."

"I appreciate whatever you can do for me and my boys, Vinny. Thanks for being here while you can," Mallory said softly as she reached over and patted his hand.

The officer was touched by her simple gesture.

"Look, I can appreciate how you must feel. I have a wife and a couple of young kids and, if this was happening to them, I would be going nuts. If we haven't apprehended the suspect in the next day or so, you might want to consider hiring a body guard. Then again, the suspect might be halfway to Mexico by now, in which case you won't need to worry any longer."

"Somehow I don't think they are just going to give up and go home. These guys are part of a bigger mess and we have stepped right in the middle of it."

Helene jumped in.

"Well, no sense in fretting over it. We have each other. We just need to be careful and we'll be fine."

"Enough talk," Tom pronounced as he began rising from the table. "We have a lot to do if we are to secure the area before it gets late."

The informal meeting was adjourned and they all set about their respective tasks.

In nearby Burlingame State Park, a green suburban pulled into a secluded campsite at the far end of the Park. There were few campers this time of year. The driver nestled the car behind several lush evergreen shrubs, shielding it entirely from sight.

A light drizzle had commenced, drowning out the late afternoon sun. With it, the fog began to silently roll in from the ocean and head north across Quonnie Pond. A fog horn blared its monotonal warning in a dull, consistent fashion. The fog would reach the Eighty Acre Woods by late evening, bringing with it a damp chill to the autumnal night air.

The young man with the dark complexion remained seated in the hidden suburban at Burlingame campgrounds. He made no effort to pitch a tent or prepare a campfire. Nothing that would attract attention. Instead, he listened attentively to the portable police scanner on the seat beside him. From the scanner he had already learned of the transfer from the cottage in Weekapaug to the Eighty Acre Woods.

He was now monitoring the shift changes of the Westerly Police and the frequency of their patrols past the Sanctuary. It hadn't taken the police long to find the fisherman's body and to expose the deception of switched ID's. But it no longer mattered. The ruse allowed him to quickly escape from the Breachway and bought him time to obtain the necessary equipment in order to finish the job. The suburban was no longer needed. He was as close as he could get to the Sanctuary by vehicle without being stopped. Studying the map of the campgrounds and the greater Westerly town map, all that separated him from achieving his objective was about two miles of dense woods. Penetration would be difficult but not impossible, and the attack would come from the direction least anticipated. The police would be monitoring the only road past the Eighty Acre Woods, assuming that any intruder would want to hit and run as fast and as far away as possible.

But he would not run. Peering over his shoulder at the large backpack and duffel bag, he mentally listed their contents: a compass, camouflage raingear, extra clothing, a small tarp, a sleeping bag, enough dry food to last three days, two canteens, flashlight, toiletries, a large hunting knife, binoculars, spare ammo clips for his handgun, and a box of twelve gauge shotgun shells for the pump shotgun on the back seat. Water availability was no problem, given the density of streams and freshwater ponds in the area. There would be no fires, nothing that would attract attention. Upon completing his mission, he would not run as the police would anticipate. Instead, he would remain in the nearby woods, undetected for days, if not weeks. When he finally does emerge, it will be several miles away and long after the incident has slipped from the pages of the local newspapers. He was experienced in this type of tactic, having been trained as an Army Ranger. While he would have preferred using a sniper rifle from a safe distance, the shotgun and handgun would easily do the job. He would have to get up close and personal, but he knew how to do that as well. It would be noisy, and messy, but highly effective nonetheless. Although women and children were not his usual targets, it made no difference. To the former-Ranger-turned-assassin, it was just another mission. Only difference now was that he was getting paid more, a lot more.

There had been a time when honor and loyalty had meant something to him, a time when he would have devoted his life to the service of his country. But one mission went terribly wrong. Political decisions overrode military commands and, as a result, many of his friends had died. He was nearly killed himself, suffering severe wounds from an ambush that could have been prevented. The decision-makers had wanted to make him a hero in order to whitewash the mission. But he would have nothing of it, and shortly thereafter left God and Country for other naive souls to protect. He was going to make money, the only way he knew how, as a mercenary.

Not that he particularly enjoyed what he did. And he especially didn't like his present employer, a slimy corporate security chief with past ties to the CIA named Bealls. What bothered the assassin the most was the ever expanding list of targets for this mission and the fact that he had to work with a team of similar misfits of unknown origin. It was far from an ideal arrangement. He didn't trust any of them, including the short guy who dumped him off the whaler yesterday and would not return to pick him up. The so-called 'Pizza Man', as his partner was referred to by the police over the scanner, deserved to get killed. He was sloppy and openly brazen in his approach. He could have chosen a better venue to dispose of Mallory, and with far less exposure. But Pizza Man thought this would be a stroll in the park.

"First mistake," the man whispered to himself. "Never underestimate the capabilities of your target."

Now that he no longer had to take orders from Pizza Man, he could do this the right way. An earlier phone call to the chief to update him on the failed attempt yielded little surprises.

After a long string of expletives, the chief left the assassin with the simple instruction' "I don't care how you do it, but I want her and her kids dead. Do it now and kill anybody who gets in your way. I've got bigger fish to fry right now in Venezuela. This is just a loose end. Now get it done."

"Just a loose end," he thought as he recalled the terse conversation. "I wonder how many more 'loose ends' are out there?"

The professional turned off the scanner. He had a good feeling for when the police would make their rounds at the Sanctuary, only about once every hour. They would pose no problem. He then started the suburban and drove it as deeply into the thick woods as he could before being stopped by a forest of laurel bushes flanked by pine trees. After removing his gear, he wiped the vehicle clean of fingerprints, and then covered up the tracks and as much of the suburban as possible with brush, branches and dead leaves. It would eventually be discovered, but not for some time. By then he would be long gone, and on another mission with money to be made.

With gear repacked and slung around his shoulders, he took a bearing with his compass and began the slow southwest trek toward his objective. Although not very far as the crow flies, it would take three to four hours to make his way through the dense brush. Darkness would soon prevail, which would make the traverse even more difficult.

By late afternoon the ocean fog had finally reached the Eighty Acre Woods. It had stopped raining but the mist hung heavy in the air. While the boys played nearby under the watchful eyes of Delilah, the adults readied themselves for evening. For Mallory it would be a sleepless night. She could not rest knowing that the dark complexioned man with the lifeless smile might be lurking nearby, waiting for his moment to strike. She was only mildly reassured by the occasional police patrols. It was her confidence in Tom and Helene that kept her from making a run for it. Besides, if they could find her in Weekapaug, they could find her anywhere. At least here she would be on familiar ground with people who would help.

Although Tom and Helene were non-violent types, practically bordering on pacifism, they were far from naïve. Tom had served in the Marines and had been a skillful hunter as a youth. The horrors of Vietnam and the loss of many good friends had taught him to appreciate life in all forms. Helene had been a student activist and war protestor. The closest she ever came to a gun was to fire off a shotgun into the air to scare away the birds from the cornfield. Even then she was always afraid she would hit a bird by accident. Nonetheless, she could handle the gun and was level headed.

I couldn't be in better company, thought Mallory, stepping out onto the front porch of the cottage for a breather.

Tom emerged from the barn and made his way toward her. He was carrying a shotgun and the 22 caliber rifle that Mallory had attempted to use on Pizza Man the day before.

"Thought we'd have a little target practice."

Mallory was not overly enamored with the idea but nodded in compliance. Upon seeing the guns, the boys raced over, eager to try them out. Tom made doubly sure both were unloaded before allowing the boys to handle the weapons under his close scrutiny. He was giving them a few safety pointers when Helene strolled down from the office.

"Tom," she barked sternly. "I don't think that's such a good idea right now. They've seen enough of guns for a lifetime."

Tom slowly relieved the boys of the guns suggested they return to playing nearby. Turning back to Helene and Mallory, he offered an excuse.

"Sorry about that, but I always have trouble saying 'no' to your boys."

Mallory smiled but Helene maintained her icy stare. Tom continued.

"At any rate, I thought it would be a good idea if we kept these handy, just in case. And it would also be a good idea if we made sure that Mallory knew how to fire these, just in case."

"Fine," snapped Helene. "But just be sure that the boys are at a safe distance. Besides, this isn't exactly the kind of firepower we would need in the event of a real attack. These should be a last resort. I don't want the Sanctuary to be a killing grounds."

Tom gazed longingly and warmly at Helene before replying.

"I knew there was a reason I married you."

Mallory felt she had just intruded on a special moment, but Helene quickly dispelled that notion.

"Don't patronize me, Tom, or you'll be sleeping with the horses."

"Don't take this the wrong way, dear, but I plan on it, at least for tonight."

"What the hell are you talking about?" Helene could be very, very direct at times.

Tom explained.

"Here's my plan. We have some perimeter warning systems already in place. To begin, there is a pressure-activated pad at the driveway entrance that rings a bell in the office. I'll leave the office windows open so we can hear the bell from the dorm and the barn. The police will be checking in at hourly intervals and setting off the bell. Anyone more frequent than that should put us on alert. We will have less than a minute to react, so we will need to be in position already."

"But what if…"

"Please Mallory, let me run through it from start to finish. Then we can see where the holes are." He continued.

"Although coming in the driveway may seem logical as it provides quick access and more importantly, a speedy escape, it can also be easily blocked by the police if they arrive on time. Of course, blocking an escape after the fact won't do us any good."

Tom paused to make sure the last comment was fully appreciated by both women. It was.

"We cannot discount an attack on foot. This is where we may be most vulnerable as we are surrounded by woods. If we are dealing with a city-slicker, he will find these woods to be formidable, especially at night. There is no easy access point, which would mean he would have to fight his way through several miles of dense brush with no markers to guide his way. Chances are he would become discouraged or disoriented and either turn back or wander aimlessly for days. It happens to several campers from Burlingame every year. However, if he is a country boy or had special military training, he could conceivably navigate the woods."

Mallory grew apprehensive. Helene could sense her alarm.

"Tom," Helene interrupted. "Is that supposed to make us feel safe and secure? If so, you're making me awfully nervous."

Tom quickly moved to ease their concerns.

"Mallory, this may sound trite, but these woods are our friends. Both Helene and I know each path and pitfall like there was a roadmap imbedded in our minds. We can virtually see them in the dark. This gives us a real advantage. Not only that, but it talks to you if you know how to listen."

"Tom, I think you may have been out here a little too long," teased Mallory.

"All I'm saying is that there are sounds in the woods that are natural, from animals and insects, like crickets, that are a natural part of the background noise. Any departure from that natural background noise tells us something. It's like mother nature's own alarm system. Both Delilah and the horses are sensitive to it long before we pick up on it, either by smell or sound. Most humans are not as responsive, but after being out here as long as we have, you start to absorb some of this."

Mallory waited for Tom to finish before pointing out the obvious flaw in his plan.

"Tom, I can appreciate that the animals might alert us to an intruder, but the warning may not come soon enough, if it comes at all. I mean, Delilah might bark just before he bursts through the door of the dorm. Won't do us a helluva lot of good by then."

"I'm not finished," Tom admonished.

"Sorry. Please go on."

"In addition, I have run a trip wire around the perimeter of the compound, about fifty yards into the woods. That's what kept me busy most of the day. If the trip wire is activated, it will set off a flare that should discourage any intruder from continuing because he knows we will have time to arm ourselves and call the police. Helene knows how to use the shotgun and I'll get you up to speed on the rifle after our discussion."

"Can an animal set off the flare?" Helene inquired.

"Perhaps a deer or a coyote, but not the little creatures. A false alarm might give us a scare, but better to play this on the safe side."

Both women nodded in agreement.

"There's more. Mallory's point about being warned too late is well taken. Seconds are critical. Hence, we will take turns standing watch. A two hour watch will give us all four hours of uninterrupted sleep. Not ideal but we can maintain this for several days or until the threat is diminished. We've cancelled all public activities at the Sanctuary for the rest of the week. At this point, since any stranger is a perceived threat, it doesn't make sense to allow people unfettered access. This way we can rest during the day and cut down on the traffic."

"Tom, I can see you've given this a lot of thought, and I'm feeling much safer than just a few minutes ago," commented Mallory, "but what if there's more than one intruder? Do we have the firepower to hold them off until the police arrive?"

"Good point. While we may only be aware of one person, we cannot discount the possibility that he may have help. And, we should consider that they may be heavily armed. Regardless of whether they come up the driveway or through the woods, if they make a quick strike, we may not be able to keep them at bay until the cavalry arrives. That's why I have saved the best part of the plan for last. You see, each contingency element of the plan builds, one upon the other, in complementary fashion. But the next element is difficult to explain. It's much easier to comprehend when you see it. Let's go inside the dorm."

"I can't wait to see what this is all about."

"I think I may know," remarked Helene.

Tom took Mallory by the hand and led her inside the dorm. Helene followed. Tom spoke as he entered the living room.

"You see Mallory, the foundations of this house date back to colonial times, where it was perhaps an inn or a farmhouse. It's been added to and parts have been rebuilt but, as best we can tell, the foundation has not changed in all that time. Same for the barn out back."

Tom released Mallory's hand and walked over to a corner of the kitchen that contained a pine cupboard. He began to shift the cupboard forward by several feet.

"This corner here is closest to the barn. If you look out the kitchen window you'll see that we are about fifty feet from the south corner of the barn."

Tom moved the cupboard a few more feet to reveal the wide board flooring beneath. He looked at Mallory.

"See anything unusual?"

At first, the floor all looked the same. Perhaps a slight discoloring and less wear than in the center of the kitchen, but nothing out of order. Then she saw it. A slightly worn groove on the edge of one board, just long enough to get several fingers under the board.

Pointing to the groove, Mallory asked "Is this what you mean?"

"Precisely," he proclaimed.

Helene, exasperated with Tom's flair for the dramatic, spoke up.

"Oh get on with it, will you. I'm getting liver spots just standing here."

"All in good time," he mused.

He then turned back to Mallory with a wry smile.

"We stumbled onto this shortly after acquiring the property but decided to keep it a secret, until now. This entire floor was under some old linoleum. When we tore it off, it revealed this tiny groove. Didn't think much of it at first, but then we noticed the floor had a slightly different sound over here."

He tapped his foot on the floor in the corner and then moved toward the center of the room and tapped it again. The corner sounded hollow compared to the dull thud at the center.

"A trap door?" Mallory exclaimed.

"A trap door, my dear Watson."

Tom bent down and slipped two fingers into the groove. He pried off the loose board. This allowed him to remove an adjoining board, revealing an uneven opening of approximately two feet by three feet. Mallory stood over the opening and peered down into the darkness. A wooden ladder led to the room below, the floor of which was about eight feet below the kitchen floor. Tom pulled a flashlight from his jacket and climbed down the ladder, followed by Mallory and Helene.

A small room no larger than a walk-in closet lay before them. The walls were of rough cut, Westerly pinkish-gray granite, same as the foundation. Irregularly shaped pieces of slate covered the floor. A slight musty odor permeated the room. Tom lit an oil lamp that stood on a simple wooden nightstand, casting a warm eerie glow throughout. Tom spoke while Mallory conducted a closer inspection of the room and its contents.

"Helene and I think this was a part of the original house, given that the granite is the same as the overall foundation. Our first thought was that it was meant to be a kind of root cellar or storage area. But if we assume the rather inconvenient access today is the same as the original, then it suggests this might have also served as a hiding place for the occupants. After all, there were warring Indian tribes in this area, not to mention the Revolutionary War. Whatever the original intent, my guess is that it served multiple purposes over the years."

"This is absolutely fascinating," Mallory remarked as she continued her inspection. "Have you had any archeologists examine this? They might be able to provide some answers."

"We have had state archeologists on the property," said Helene. "As you recall, we have the old burial grounds that are now a protected landmark. However, we were concerned that they might also turn this into a landmark if they saw this room, so we've pretty much kept this to ourselves for the time being."

"Now for the fun part," said Tom as he beckoned Mallory toward the far wall. The wall had some boards leaning up against it. He shifted the planks to one side to reveal a narrow, brick lined corridor shrouded in darkness.

"What in the world is this?" Mallory exclaimed.

"This passageway leads to the near corner of the barn. There is a small hatch covered with hay. Notice that the walls are made of brick, and the floor is plain dirt with roughly hewn oaken timbers lining the ceiling. This section probably came later, possibly during the mid-to-late 1800s. Believe it or not, the Underground Railroad that hid slaves who were escaping from the South was quite active in this region. There are several known Underground Railroad sites in both Connecticut and Rhode Island. Even the Old Randall Inn in North Stonington has a similar hiding place beneath its kitchen."

"I had no idea."

Helene spoke up.

"Since this leads to the barn, then it also would have been subject to total preservation. Not that we are opposed to it. In fact, we have tried to keep everything just the way we found it, but we needed both structures to be functional. We didn't want it to be turned into a museum. Later perhaps, when we have this place running and can afford to put up substitute facilities."

"Lest we digress" interrupted Tom. "The reason I am showing you this is because here is where we will be spending the night." Tom waved his hand around the room.

Mallory took in his comment. Not very hospitable surroundings but Tom was right. They would be much safer here than up on the main floor. And, they had an escape route through the barn if necessary.

"Cozy." was all she could muster, but Tom could see the approving look in her eyes.

"Then it's settled," said Helene. "Let's get some sleeping bags, pillows and anything else we might need down here."

"The boys will love this," responded Mallory.

"Good, because they can help."

While Helene let the boys in on their secret hideaway, Tom instructed Mallory on the 22 rifle. It didn't take her long. A scope was already mounted on the rifle, and Tom showed her how to sight through it. After a rudimentary lesson, she fired off several rounds at a tree stump several hundred feet away. Only one hit its mark. She reloaded, sighted down the scope and slowly squeezed off a round. Hit. Fired again. Hit. The boys came out to investigate.

"I want to try," shouted Eric.

"Not a chance," Mallory shouted back. "Now finish helping Helene."

They reluctantly shuffled back toward the house. Mallory continued to perfect her aim until she could hit the stump without fail.

Tom was impressed.

"Not bad for a beginner."

"Must have a good teacher," she winked.

The bell rang back at the office. Tom glanced at his watch.

"Police patrol, just about on time. However, just in case, let's get everyone inside. Mallory gave the rifle to Tom and they quickly strode to the dorm. Helene was already inside with the boys and Delilah. She had the shotgun in hand.

"Just in case," she said, attempting to relieve the apprehensive look in Mallory's eyes.

All three adults took up positions at the windows and front door, while the boys made their way down the ladder into the chamber below. The Westerly police cruiser emerged from the wooded driveway out into the open area around the compound. The car slowly passed by the office. Tom could see the officer inside. He let out a sigh of relief and waved at the driver.

"It's Vinny."

Vinny pulled up to the house and got out.

"Hello folks. How's it going?"

"Not bad," said Tom. "It's been kinda quiet. I think we have everything under control here."

"Good to hear. I am going off duty shortly, so another officer will be making the rounds. Not sure which one, but I'll be sure to brief him before I go off so he understands the gravity of the situation."

Mallory thanked Vinny for his vigilance with a warm hug. It surprised him, nearly bringing a tear to his eye.

"I'll be checking up again on you tomorrow. Be careful."

"We will, Vinny" she replied.

He returned to his cruiser, slowly completed the circle, waved one last time, and headed off down the long driveway. A few seconds later, the driveway bell sounded again as the police cruiser left the Sanctuary.

Tom looked up at the cloudy sky. The drizzle had been off and on again all day. A heavy mist hung about the woods.

"It will be dark in another hour. I suggest we eat soon, crank up the wood stove for some heat, and prepare for the night mode. I'll start a watch now while you womenfolk prepare the victuals."

"Funny," said Helene. "Now take this load of stuff down to the chamber like a good manservant."

"Yes Ma'am," he saluted.

Darkness fell upon the Sanctuary. Lights were left blazing at the office and around the compound. A warm glow emitted from the house. Smoke from the wood stove escaped from the chimney only to hang heavy in the evening mist. The dinner of chili and rice had been simple, but adequate and easy to clean. The horses had been fed and returned to their stall in the barn. Delilah lay in a ball at the foot of the wood stove, content and tired from a day's play with the boys. Matt and Eric had washed up and changed into sweat suits for sleeping. It would be cool in the chamber, which was now lined with sleeping bags. A supply of flashlights and oil lanterns provided ample light. The boys made themselves comfortable in their new hideout.

Tom caught a brief nap on one of the beds while Helene and Mallory chatted in the main room.

"Helene, why don't you get some sleep? I can stand watch because I'm not at all tired."

"Thanks, but I'm not tired either. Just as soon stay up and keep a lookout with you, especially since Delilah is napping. Some guard dog."

"Don't bad mouth Delilah," Mallory stated. "She saved my life."

"Just kidding."

"I know."

A short time later the office bell rang out. Both Helene and Mallory posted themselves at the windows, shotgun with Helene and rifle for Mallory. A moment later the police car came into view. A searchlight on the car slowly swept the compound, then the woods. The cruiser stayed for a few moments, engine idling, then slowly turned and headed back down the driveway. The bell sounded again.

Tom, rubbing sleep from his eyes, entered the main room where Helene and Mallory still remained at their posts.

"How can a guy get any sleep with all that racket out here!"

"Glad you're up," said Helene as she thrust the shotgun to his chest. "Now you can stand guard. I'm going to bed."

"Thanks," remarked Tom, "But tonight you get to sleep with the shotgun. I get the rifle, remember."

Helene gave an evil grin. "Finally I'll have something stiff to sleep with."

Tom thrust his head back in mock disbelief.

"Helene, please! Not in front of company."

"Oh don't mind me," laughed Mallory. Just pretend I'm not here. In fact, I'm going to wash up and head downstairs right now."

Within the hour both Helene and Mallory were sleeping soundly alongside the boys in the chamber. Tom had closed the door and placed an area rug over the top to obscure the opening. Although he had talked about taking turns at standing guard, he intended all along to let them sleep through the night. He poured the remaining coffee into a thermos and put a few more logs in the wood stove, taking care not to step on Delilah. She opened one sleepy eye to confirm what her nose had told her all along, that it was Tom. Then she returned to that state of repose where her scent would remain alert while her body rested. Tom took the rifle, thermos, a flashlight and binoculars and headed out the door toward the barn where he would take up his position for the night.

It was nearly two in the morning when Mallory was awakened from a deep slumber to find Tom gently tapping her on the shoulder. He had come into the chamber through the hidden passage way from the barn. He had already woken Helene, who was slowly starting to unravel herself from her sleeping bag.

"Tom, what is it?" asked Mallory.

"We have company," he whispered, trying not to wake the boys who were only a few feet away.

Mallory grew alarmed. Tom quickly put his hand to her mouth before she could speak again.

"No need for alarm. I want you to come with me. Helene will stay with the boys. Don't worry. They will be safe here with her. She also has her cell phone."

Mallory unzipped her sleeping bag and put on her shoes. Slipping quietly pass the boys, she followed Tom's flashlight back down the corridor toward the barn. When Tom reached the hatch at the barn he turned around to Mallory.

"I need to turn off the flashlight but your eyes will adjust to the darkness soon enough. From here on out we should refrain from speaking unless we absolutely have to, and then it should be a whisper. Understood?"

"Understood," she whispered back.

Tom turned off the flashlight, thrusting Mallory into pitch darkness, For a brief second she nearly panicked, grabbing out at Tom's leg as he climbed the ladder to the hatchway.

"It's okay, Mallory," he said in a soft, hushed tone. "I'm right here. You'll be fine. Just follow me up the ladder. By the way, you're cutting off the circulation to my leg."

Mallory regained her composure and released her iron grip on Tom's calf. He climbed the remaining rungs and quietly opened the hatch door. A faint shaft of light penetrated the darkness below. Mallory followed Tom out and onto the barn floor. Taking her hand, he slowly led her past the horse stalls. The horses stirred and Tom spoke softly to them as he passed. They reached the ladder leading to the loft. Mallory's eyes were beginning to adjust. She easily followed Tom up the ladder to the loft. Once on the loft, Tom motioned for Mallory to crawl behind him to the open bay door used for loading hay. The smell of dry hay permeated the air as she crawled the short distance to the bay. Tom and Mallory lay side by side, looking out the opening at the rest of the compound and the surrounding woods. This vantage point provided a very clear field of vision. Tom lifted his binoculars to his head and peered into the woods to the right of the house. All Mallory could see was darkness.

"Mallory, I believe I have your man. I noticed him about twenty minutes ago. He is motionless but you should be able to see him with these night vision binoculars. Here, take a look."

Tom shifted the binoculars over to Mallory and pointed in the direction of the sighting. Mallory put the binoculars to her face and was immediately amazed at how well she could see.

"Wow. This is great."

"They work off ambient light. Now look a little more to your right, and about twenty feet deeper into the woods. Mallory slowly shifted her view and scanned the area. There he was. She tensed up. She couldn't believe she was staring at the man who only yesterday was shooting at her. He was motionless, kneeling on one knee, staring at the compound. Tom knew she had spotted him.

"Is that your man?"

"It's him."

"Are you sure?"

"Positive. What is he waiting for?"

"He only arrived a short time ago, so he is still surveying the area. My guess is that he will wait until the next police car makes its round before trying something."

"Why didn't he trip the perimeter alarm?"

"Good question. From the looks of it, I'd say he either is an extremely skillful hunter or had specialized military training, probably both. He managed to traverse some very difficult terrain and locate us. Very few civilians would be capable of that. He apparently had no problem finding and circumventing the wire. He also placed himself downwind from us, so neither Delilah nor the horses have picked up his scent."

"So how did you spot him?" Mallory inquired.

"There is an owls' nest not far from where he is positioned. That owl is usually highly vocal. Tonight he's as quiet as a church mouse."

"I'm impressed."

"That, plus my night vision binoculars. Best birthday present I ever got."

Mallory looked over at Tom, who was grinning like a Cheshire cat.

"Tom, remind me to hit you when this is all over."

"Is that before or after you kill David for putting you through all this?"

"After. Definitely after. Now, what do we do with this guy out there and is he alone?"

"No sign of anyone else but we should continue to scan in case he was the first to arrive. However, now that you've confirmed who he is, I thought we should call in the cavalry. I have a cell phone with me, so let's do it." Tom began reaching for the phone in his jacket, but Mallory reached out and grabbed his arm.

"Wait," she whispered. "If we call the police this guy will probably just disappear into the woods. Maybe they'll capture him and maybe they won't. If he gets away I'll still be looking over my shoulder. I can't hide out in your underground bunker forever, cozy as it is."

Tom was silent for a moment. He could see where this was going and he didn't like it one bit.

"So Mallory, what do you propose?"

"I want him. I am not going to run anymore. He's not going to threaten me or my boys again."

"You want to kill him?"

"I want to stop him, one way or another."

"Look Mallory, this guy is good. He is not sloppy like the other guy. If he's a trained assassin we may not stand much of a chance."

Mallory continued to study him through the binoculars. He had not budged from his position and, with barely a perceptive shift of his head, he continued to scan the compound.

"Can you tell what kind of weapons he has?" she asked, totally ignoring Tom's last comment.

"Best I can make out he has a pump action shotgun, probably twelve gauge, which is significantly more powerful than Helene's twenty."

"Anything else? A rifle?" She passed the binoculars back to Tom for confirmation.

"Don't see anything else but he is partially obscured by the bushes."

"After yesterday, we can assume he also has a handgun. But if he had a rifle I would think that is what he would want to use. Since we only see a shotgun then it would indicate he has to get closer."

"Now I'm impressed," said Tom.

"Think you could get a shot off from here?"

Tom looked in shock.

"Are you crazy? First of all, this is only a 22 caliber rifle. It holds a very tiny bullet. We used to use this on the woodchucks that trashed my daddy's garden. While it can kill it would have to be a direct shot to the head or heart. This guy is nearly three hundred feet away. Secondly, it is dark out in case you haven't noticed. The binoculars may have night vision capabilities but the rifle scope does not. It would be like looking down a deep dark well. And finally, I just don't shoot people, remember?"

Mallory looked intently into Tom's eyes.

"Are you finished?"

He nodded.

"OK. Now it's my turn. First of all, only yesterday this guy was trying to kill me and my boys. Secondly, I am not out for revenge, but I do want to catch him or stop him in any way I can. I cannot let him escape because he will probably keep trying. And finally, I also don't believe in shooting people, but in his case I'm willing to make a huge exception. Now, what will it be? With or without you?"

Tom gave an exasperating sigh.

"No way I can talk you out of this?"

"No way." She stated firmly.

"Somehow I thought it might come to this." He shook his head slowly in mock disbelief. "Alright, but you'll have to take the shot. You will probably miss or, worse yet, only injure him so that we really make him mad. He will most likely see the muzzle flash and know where we are. He will come after us. We will have to fall back on my only remaining contingency plan. If it fails, we are dead. Do you understand that?"

"What's your contingency plan?"

"You'll see when the time comes. But I insist we call the police just before we take action so that they might just arrive in time to save our pathetic little lives. Is that okay with you, Miss Rambo?"

Mallory smiled. "Miss Rambo. Thanks. I kinda like that."

"It was meant to be an insult."

"I know."

Tom shrugged his shoulders and sighed again. "I cannot believe I am doing this."

"That's exactly how I felt, yesterday. Welcome to the club."

"We should wait until he makes his move. That way he'll be closer and out in the open, giving you a better target."

"But won't he be a moving target and harder to hit?"

"Not entirely. He will most likely move, stop and survey; then move, stop and survey again until he reaches the house. You'll have to pick your time."

"Whatever happens, he cannot reach the house," Mallory stated with conviction.

"I know."

Just then the driveway bell sounded. Both Tom and Mallory jerked. Tom picked up the binoculars and looked at the man in hiding. He had also heard the bell, for the sound carried far in the still night air. The patrol car slowly entered the compound, searchlight scanning the buildings and surrounding woods. The former Ranger turned assassin followed the lights around the compound, then laid down before the beam swung in his direction. The cruiser circled the compound lot and slowly headed back down the driveway, searchlight still scanning from right to left as it departed. The bell sounded again. Tom watched as the intruder slowly rose from his prone position. The man checked his watch and began to ready his gear for the assault.

"What's he doing now?" asked Mallory.

"Looks like he's checking his equipment. I think he will make his move shortly, but will probably wait a little while longer to be sure that the driveway alarm didn't wake anyone. Man, my eyes are getting tired looking through this thing."

Tom dropped the binoculars to rub his eyes. Mallory reached over and grabbed them.

"I'll watch him." Mallory stared through the lens at the intruder, studying him. She wondered what could possibly have happened to him that would enable him to kill harmless women and children. She wondered what his mother must have been like. Did he even have a mother? She felt herself feeling sorry for the man at the other end of the binoculars. Then she recalled how he so nonchalantly waved to her and the boys yesterday as she approached their boat, his gun hidden behind his back. She stiffened at the thought.

"This time," she whispered, "You're the target."

As she spoke to herself, the man stood up.

"Tom. He's getting up. I think he's going to make his move."

"Let me take a look."

Mallory handed him the binoculars. Tom peered through them.

"He's moving toward the house. But very slowly. Probably still looking for trip wires in the woods. When he gets to the edge of the woods he may break into a run because it is open field. Mallory, I'd say that now would probably be a good time to call the police."

"Make the call."

Mallory took the rifle and tried sighting through the scope. Nothing but shadows in the woods. Where the woods met the clearing it was approximately two hundred feet from the compound. Outdoor spotlights around the compound faintly illuminated the surrounding field. While Tom called into 911, Mallory took the binoculars and found her target. Her had reached the edge of the field and had knelt down for another look around.

Tom put down the cell phone. "The police should be here in five to ten minutes. Let's try to stay alive until then."

An owl hooted in the distance.

"There's that owl now," said Tom. "I gather our man has moved out."

"Yes, he's at the edge of the field. Here, take the glasses and tell me where he is at all times."

Mallory once again picked up the rifle, placed the butt against her shoulder and strained through the sight.

"Safety off, I trust," noted Tom.

"Yes, I won't make that mistake again."

"Good, now here's what you need to do. When you have a clean shot, shoot. Don't hesitate because you may not get another chance. Don't get fancy and try to wing him. Aim for the torso as it is the biggest target. Remember, this is not a big gun, but it is a semi-automatic. As long as he is in your sights, keep pulling the trigger. You have twelve rounds of long rifle 22 caliber bullets. Understood?"

"Understood."

Despite the cold night air, Mallory was perspiring as if it were the dead of summer. Her hands were clammy. She lay in a prone position. Her hand on the trigger. Her eye straining through the scope. She began to tremble.

"Can't be afraid," she said to herself. "Too many lives at stake."

With her other eye she could see the house where Helene stood guard in the chamber while the boys slept peacefully, unaware of the drama that was about to unfold only footsteps away. One of the horses stirred in the stables below. Apparently the wind had shifted slightly. They sensed the intruder from several hundred feet away. Even in this precarious situation, Mallory could not help but marvel at their keen senses, wishing she possessed them. But right now all she possessed was sheer guts and a mother's love of her children. She hoped it would be enough.

Tom brought Mallory back to the reality of the moment.

"He's up. I can see him clearly now. He has the shotgun in his hands and a pistol in a shoulder holster. He looks like he means business. I think he's getting ready to make the run to the compound."

"He does," she grimaced. "Is he in open field yet? I still can't see him clearly."

"Not yet, but keep the rifle pointed in his direction. And don't take your eyes off that scope. I want to live to tell my grandkids about all this."

"I'm ready." Her voice stiffened.

"There he goes!" yelled Tom, in a voice so loud it nearly gave away their position. "He's running in a crouched position. Do you see him?"

Mallory saw a blur cross her field of vision and then he was gone. She shifted her sight to the right. Again he moved into and out of her sights before Mallory could take aim. Tom was getting nervous but tried not to show it.

"Anytime now, Mallory," he said in a slightly shaky voice.

"He's moving too fast. I can't get him in my sights long enough."

The assassin was rapidly closing the distance to the house. He had made it halfway across the open field unimpeded. Mallory was breathing fast. Her fingers trembling. In the stillness of the night she even thought she could hear his footsteps but it was the pounding of her heart. Tom had dropped the binoculars and risen to his feet. He no longer needed them. He could now make out the shadowy figure with the naked eye. The horses on the barn floor below began to stir and snort.

One of the startled horses suddenly let out a loud whinny. The man stopped. Mallory took aim and squeezed the trigger. The crack of the small caliber rifle echoed like a cannon in Mallory's ears. The man dropped the shotgun, spun around and rolled to the ground, clutching his shoulder.

"I hit him," she proclaimed exultantly.

"Keep shooting," Tom commanded. "It's gonna take more than one bullet to bring him down."

Mallory sighted in again, but before she could squeeze off another round, the man had rolled back toward his shotgun and grabbed it while jumping to his feet. She fired repeatedly at the moving target but her shots missed their mark. The man was zig-zagging his way toward the front of the house, glancing up at the upper barn door where Tom and Mallory had lain undiscovered for so long.

"Oh my God, Oh my God, Oh my God," was all Mallory could muster as she kept on firing. The bullets danced in the gravel, kicking up dust and stones beside and behind the oncoming intruder.

"Tom, I can't hit him. He's moving too fast for me."

Tom grabbed the rifle from Mallory and put it to his shoulder. In a few more seconds the attacker would reach the front door of the house and be out of sight. He sighted in just a few steps in front of the man. He squeezed the trigger. Click. Nothing. The gun was empty. In her excitement Mallory had fired off all twelve rounds and neither had bothered to keep track. Tom had extra bullets but there was no time to reload. He looked at Mallory and could see the horror in her eyes as the killer reached the door of the house.

With his shotgun, the attacker blasted a gaping hole where there once was a door. The remnants of the door swung open. He stormed inside firing as he entered. Mallory and Tom stood speechless, helplessly watching the event unfold before their eyes. In the distance, the wail of police sirens could be heard. For what seemed like an eternity but was only several seconds, the man reappeared at the doorway. He had apparently found it abandoned. Mallory sighed in relief as she stared down at the man who was now a mere one hundred feet away. She saw a dark stain on his left shoulder from her first and only successful shot. The sirens grew louder.

"Surely he'll run," Tom stated.

"Don't count on it."

She was right. The assassin looked up at the barn where they stood, safely hidden in the shadows and started to move in their direction.

"Let's move," shouted Tom, grabbing Mallory and heading for the ladder.

They slid down the ladder in crude fireman's fashion. Mallory took a large wooden sliver along her right palm, wincing in pain as blood spurted down her hand. As they ran past the startled horses to the back door of the barn the intruder came blasting through the front, a mere fifty feet away.

Once out back, they were once again thrust into total darkness as the woods lay outstretched before them.

"Tom, I can't see," Mallory cried.

Tom grabbed Mallory by her hand and pulled her along.

"We don't need to see. Just hold my hand. I know these paths."

They could hear him running past the terrified horses. Another shotgun blast behind them as the rear door of the barn was torn from its hinges. Tom yanked Mallory past some bushes and onto a small foot trail, one intimately familiar to him as he and the dogs would take their daily stroll. They paused briefly to catch their breath and to listen for sounds of their pursuer. Their heavy breathing, coupled with the ever approaching sirens, drowned out any hope of hearing his advances.

They ran on further into the woods. At a fork in the trail Tom turned to the left. Mallory, still holding onto Tom, ran into a thorn bush at the middle of the fork. She yelled out as the thorns ripped her jeans and tore into her legs. Tom pulled her out.

"We can't stop," he said. "He would have heard that for sure. We have to keep moving."

Deeper into the woods they ran. They could hear thrashing behind them. The attacker was still following and, despite his unfamiliarity with the area, he was able to follow the sounds of their movement. And Mallory's painful wail helped keep him on course. Mallory was quickly losing her breath and could no longer maintain the pace.

"Tom," she cried whiled gasping for air. "I can't go on. Leave me."

"Don't give up," he wheezed. "We're almost there."

"Almost where?"

The path came to a dead stop in front of a leafy, evergreen laurel bush. A smaller, less traveled path took a hard right turn at the bush.

"Here," he said, pointing at the laurel.

Mallory looked at the bush in disbelief. She could hear their pursuer steadily making his way along the path behind them. Even in the darkness he was an excellent tracker. She hoped Tom had a good plan, a real good plan, but one shrub wouldn't stop the hail of gunfire from the approaching killer. Tom picked up the laurel bush, which had been freshly severed at its base, and moved it out of the way to reveal another path blocked by a wooden board. This path led straight ahead. He grabbed the board and slid it into the underbrush. Mallory peered at the path straight ahead but saw nothing. Tom then pulled Mallory over to the smaller path on the right. He then placed the mountain laurel behind them, totally obscuring the path they were now on.

"This way, but very quietly from here on out," he whispered.

He then took her hand once again and quietly walked her along the path. It seemed to circle but Mallory couldn't be certain in the darkness. She wondered why they were walking when their pursuer was so close by. She could hear his movements, now not far behind. The driveway bell sounded from the office as the police cars raced up the drive. Mallory was relieved to know that Helene and the boys would be rescued. However, the police would be of no help to Tom and her because the assassin stood between them. They were now several hundred yards into the dense woods.

A moment later, Tom halted and turned ninety degrees to his left. Mallory's emotions ranged from bewilderment to alarm. She could hear the pursuer, getting closer still. It seemed he had made significant headway in the last few minutes, since they had turned by the laurel. He was gaining.

"We should be running for our lives," Mallory thought. "What in God's name is Tom doing?"

The attacker seemed only about twenty-five yards away and was still on the move. Suddenly Tom, who had pulled a flashlight from his jacket, turned the light on and pointed it back in the direction of the assassin, catching a glimpse of him as he came down the main path. Tom quickly turned off the light and pulled Mallory down to the ground, just as a shotgun blast ripped through the vegetation above them. Mallory was stunned at this suicidal behavior.

"What in the hell are…"

"Quiet." Tom thrust his hand over Mallory's mouth. They laid side-by-side, watching the oncoming juggernaut as he steamed toward them. Mallory felt herself helpless, knowing she had mere seconds to live. Tom's hand began to tremble, even as he maintained his grip over Mallory's mouth. The attacker bore down on them. He was relentless, coming straight toward them, closer, closer. Mallory could see him now. Ten more yards and it would be over.

And then he disappeared. A scream rang out. It was a man's scream, a scream of terror. He was falling, falling into the stone quarry pit below. Falling onto the jagged, unforgiving granite that built the houses and walls of centuries ago. A dull thud, and then silence. Even the police sirens had stopped.

A deathly quiet surrounded Tom and Mallory as they lay still on the forest floor. They waited for what seemed like eons but were only seconds. Still no sound from the jagged pit below. Tom eased his grip on Mallory and crawled forward to the edge of the abyss. He peered over the side in the darkness. Gathering up his courage, he extended his hand as far out as possible and turned the flashlight on the quarry floor. Mallory came up behind him and stared over the edge. The light scanned the pit, and came to rest when it fell upon the broken body of their would be killer. His lifeless body oozed blood from his fractured skull.

Mallory spoke first.

"Think he's still alive?"

"I doubt it. It's about a forty foot fall onto those rocks and it looks as though he hit them with his head, not to mention other parts of his body. And, although it is a little hard to tell from here, he doesn't appear to be breathing. No, I think he is dead, but we'll let the police make a closer examination. Are you okay?"

"Yes, I'm fine," she sighed. "So, this was your big plan? Have him jump off a cliff?"

"Worked, didn't it?"

Mallory put her arm around Tom and gave him a warm hug. "Next time, let me in on the plan."

They took one last look at the crumpled body below of the former Ranger, and then quickly made their way back to the compound to reassure Helene and the boys.

When they reached the compound, there were four police cruisers in the drive, two from Westerly and two from the State Police. Helene and the boys stood on the front porch of the dorm, talking to several policemen and pointing toward the barn and the woods beyond. At least four other policemen had fanned out around the compound and were commencing a detail search. Upon seeing the boys, Mallory was overcome with emotion and ran toward them with arms outstretched. They returned the greeting with a warm embrace. Helene was much relieved to see Tom and the police gave way momentarily for a tearful reunion. Then Tom and Mallory briefed the officer in charge. While first aid was being applied to Mallory's cuts, Tom escorted three officers back toward the quarry pit where they confirmed the death of the pursuer. Eventually, Police Chief Fabrini arrived on the scene.

"Looks like you've had another busy day," Fabrini said to Mallory after looking at her torn clothes and bandaged limbs. "Need an ambulance?"

"No thanks, Chief," she remarked. "They are only scratches and one of your officers patched me up just fine. Thanks for responding to the 911 so quickly. I was worried that he might get to the boys, so we led him away from the compound."

Tom returned from the quarry with the officers who finished briefing the Chief on the situation. After hearing the gruesome details, the Chief turned to Tom and Mallory.

"I understand you were aware of his presence for some time?"

Tom started to speak up, but she interrupted.

"It was my idea," she said hastily. "Tom wanted to call you immediately, but I didn't want him to disappear back into the woods. I didn't want to have to hide from him anymore."

Fabrini studied Mallory for a long moment. Mallory squirmed under his scrutiny. Finally, the Chief broke the uncomfortable silence.

"Very foolish. You all could have been killed. But I can understand your actions."

Tom jumped in. "We had it all planned out, Chief, from the getgo. We had it under control at all times."

Fabrini gave Tom a stern look but said nothing. Tom knew enough not to proceed any further with his story. He glanced over at Mallory and gave a wink. She just shook her head in amazement.

The Chief called his officers over and beckoned for Helene and the boys to join. Once gathered he spoke in a matter-of-fact tone, almost as if this was a mere traffic violation.

OK folks, this is now a crime scene. Do not touch anything. Leave everything exactly as it is, even your personal belongings. Detective Almeida here is in charge. Once he has all of your preliminary statements you will have to vacate the premises for the time being. I suggest you head back to the cottage in Weekapaug. We are finished with that crime scene investigation, although I recommend you stay off the third floor for now, in case we want to come back for another look. One of my officers will provide an escort and we will have a patrol car parked outside the cottage for the night, just in case this guy has any more friends. Understood?"

They all shook their heads in unison, even the boys.

"Any questions?"

Silence.

"Good. Now Mrs. Hastings, you have single-handedly managed to send the homicide rate of our peaceful little town off the charts. The press is going to have a field day with this, not to mention what this will do to our tourism business. Do you think you might be able to cut this little visit of yours short for my sake?"

Mallory studied the Chiefs eyes. He sounded almost humorous, and even though he had a slight smile she knew it was forced and that he was very serious. Helene read it as well and jumped to Mallory's side.

"Chief, she is in danger and needs our help. We won't desert her now," she proclaimed with a stern expression that took everyone back, even the Chief.

"Thanks, Helene," said Mallory, "but the Chief has a point. Besides, if these guys could trace me here, they can probably find me anywhere. I think it may be time to contact David and get him and us back to Plano. After all, that is probably the source of all this trouble."

Turning to face the Chief, who was already regretting his words, Mallory continued.

"Chief, you and your officers have done an excellent job and have been great to my family and me. I'll make arrangements to return to Plano in the next day or two, as soon as I can contact my husband and make sure he can meet us. In case this is not over, though, would you please send whatever you've got on both men to a Lieutenant Jacobson at the Plano Police Department? He is trying to piece this all together."

The chief nodded his head and looked at Mallory and her boys. A very brave woman, he thought. I hope she gets out of this alive.

With the meeting concluded, preparations commenced for the return trip to Weekapaug.

It was nearly dawn when the caravan reached the cottage in Weekapaug. The fog that had crept inland during the night still hung heavy in the air. The sun would not be able to cut through the haze for several more hours. The Watch Hill fog horn sounded far off to the west. The surf pounded relentlessly on the boulder embankment. Mallory and crew waited in their cars while one of the escort officers went inside and made sure the cottage was secure. Ten minutes later, he opened the screen door to the back porch and beckoned for the entourage to enter. Matt and Eric, still in their nightclothes, walked in zombie like fashion into the house. Delilah had to be gingerly coaxed in, as if she remembered that this was where she lost her lifelong companion.

Visions of her struggle with the Pizza Man flooded back on Mallory. She fought back the rising apprehension as she panned the kitchen and made her way through the dining and living rooms toward the stairs. The knife, of course, was missing from its wooden holder. It was evidence and would be in the police evidence locker. The landing, where Samson had met his demise, had been thoroughly scrubbed. So too, she surmised, was the third floor where blood had flowed effusively only the day before.

Helene, upon seeing Mallory's silent stare, sensed her apprehension and took charge. She escorted Mallory and the boys back to the kitchen for a little breakfast of pancakes and sausages. The coffee seemed to revitalize the adults while Helene made a special order of hot chocolate for the boys. Tom returned to the kitchen after laying in some more firewood. Pouring himself a cup of steaming coffee, he went over to the message machine by the phone in the living room. Only one message had been recorded. He pressed the playback. After hearing the date and time of the message, a familiar voice boomed throughout the cottage. It brought Mallory in a dead run from the kitchen.

"Hello, it's me." It was David. He sounded rushed, anxious. The message continued. "Anybody there? Please pick up?"

A pause while David waited, hoped, someone would pick up. He continued on.

"I hope everything is going OK for you. Had a few minor incidents down here, but I am doing fine."

"He was intentionally being cryptic," thought Mallory. "Didn't want to give anything away, which meant that there may still be a problem, that it was not over yet."

"Just calling to say that I will be flying out tomorrow and heading back home. Hope you can meet me there. Can't leave forwarding number, so hope you get this message in time."

Another brief pause, then he went on.

"I love you, very, very much. Take care."

Mallory choked back the tears. Tom could see them welling up in her eyes. He spoke quickly to distract her.

"Well. Not extremely informative, but then David was never very talkative."

Helene had entered the room. She could see Tom's words were not having their desired affect on Mallory, so she interjected.

"The good news is that he is alright and coming home. Isn't that what's important here?"

Mallory took this in. "You're right," she sniffed. "We'll make arrangements to fly out tomorrow and be there when he returns home. We may even be able to meet him at the airport."

Tom looked at the message machine. Then back at Mallory.

"Mallory, this message came in last night."

He gave his comment a few seconds to sink in. Mallory looked at Tom in bewilderment, then her eyes grew wide as the words hit home.

"Oh my God," she exclaimed. "He's coming home today."

# CHAPTER 13

# Escape to Caracas

## DAY NINE

David awoke as the chopper descended and touched down at the heliport outside Caracas. For a moment he had become disoriented, not knowing where he was. Then it all came rushing back, especially the pain in his ribs as he struggled to climb out of the cabin. The co-pilot helped him out as a burly looking man in a dark clothes and black watch cap approached and roughly pulled David off to one side. Alarmed, David began to struggle despite the broken ribs. It was futile however as the man had an iron grip on him. A woman, upon witnessing the altercation, quickly approached.

"It's alright David," Laura Ericson stated in reassuring tones. "This is Staff Sergeant Peter Ramirez of the US Marines. He's attached to the Embassy and a good friend that owes me a big favor." She winked at Ramirez and smiled. Ramirez had a wide grin on his face.

"I don't need to know any more," responded David, relieved to be rescued.

"Well I need to know a lot more," said Laura. She looked him over. "David you look terrible."

"You should see the Venezuelan army platoon." The staff sergeant let out a belly laugh. David grew serious and gently placed his hand on her shoulder.

"Laura, I need to get back to the States. My family may be in danger."

She was deeply touched by this simple gesture, wishing his words were meant for her. But she knew better, and she was a professional, through and through. It was time to go to work.

"David, it's late at night. There are no more flights to the US until tomorrow morning. I have you booked on an American Airlines flight that leaves at 7:15 am. It connects through Miami as usual. You will arrive at Dallas/Fort Worth Airport at 3:00 p.m. Until then, you will be safer back at the Embassy. We can't wait out here all night because they will be looking for you, and this is way too obvious."

"They?" queried David. "Who's they?"

"They," Laura replied with authority, "will either be the national police, or the friends of Colonel Menendez."

"You know about Menendez?"

"Only what little your friend Rick Watson told me over the phone. And believe me, it was very little, but he did say you were in extreme danger and that you were hurt. We have some intelligence on Menendez. We know he has ambitions and associates with unsavory underworld figures here in Caracas. The Chavez government has concerns about his activities but hasn't been able to prove anything to date. It would be a real feather in our diplomatic cap if we could bring info to Chavez that would aid him in this quest."

"Laura, you get me outta here in one piece and I'll give you a story that will send shudders through this government."

The plain clothes marine gingerly helped David into the back of a sedan. He winced as he crouched to enter, then leaned to one side to take the pressure off his injured ribs. Laura sat beside him, cradling him for comfort. The marine got behind the wheel and headed out the gates of the heliport, past the sleepy guard and back toward the US Embassy in Caracas.

As she held him, David tried to tell the long convoluted story, but Laura stopped him.

"Wait 'til we get to the Embassy. The DCM (Deputy Chief of Mission) wants to hear this, so no sense in repeating it, given your condition. We'll also get the Embassy doctor to take a look at your injuries. Can't risk taking you to a local hospital. Although we are on fairly good terms with the Chavez government, we wouldn't want you to fall into their hands. The Venezuelans have a love hate relationship with America. They need us. They envy us, but they also feel we have somehow deprived them from achieving economic greatness. Hence, we are often the scapegoat for whatever socio-economic ills plague the country at any given time."

David was relieved to be able to rest for now, securely in the bosom of a trustworthy, capable, and extremely beautiful woman. Eyes closed, he drank in her lusty perfume.

"I must be dreaming," he said.

"That's what they all say, now get some rest because you are going to be doing a lot of talking in another hour."

He draped an arm across her lap, squeezed closer as if clutching a pillow, closed his eyes, and drifted off yet again.

It was nearly midnight when the sedan pulled up in front of the US Embassy gate. The staff sergeant, who had removed his black watch cap, rolled down his window and waived at the Venezuelan diplomatic police. They peered in but all they could see was Laura Ericson hugging her date for the evening. Upon seeing the familiar faces, they exchanged a few greetings and let them pass through the first checkpoint. The second gate was manned by US Marines. After giving them a silent hand signal, as they were still within ear-shot of the Venezuelan police, the staff sergeant drove slowly by. A marine corporal saluted as they passed. Laura gave out an audible sigh of relief.

"You are on US soil now, David. It's safe."

David stirred from his dream like state. He lifted his head and looked into Laura's powder blue eyes, merely inches from his. He wanted to kiss her. She sensed what was coming, closed her eyes and pursed her lips. David leaned forward and kissed her ever so gently on the forehead.

"Thanks Laura. I owe you my life," he said softly.

Laura opened her eyes wide in disbelief. That was it? she said to herself. A peck on the forehead? After all they had been through! How could she not win his affections? After all, she had given him every opportunity, dropped less than subtle hints on numerous occasions. She had enough self-confidence to know that she was good looking, maybe even great looking. God knows enough men had told her so. Perhaps it was her intelligence? Brains could be a major turn off with most men, particularly from Latin America. But no, David seemed to truly appreciate her quick mind. There was only one inescapable conclusion she could draw from all this, as she had already established that he wasn't gay. He was truly in love with another woman."

"David," she said softly so as not to be heard by the driver. "I have got to meet this wife of yours. She must really be something."

David looked at her, somewhat bewildered by the remark.

"You'd really like her," he responded without thinking.

"I'm sure. Now let's go inside and get down to business."

The burly marine, more gently this time, assisted David into the Embassy and up to the DCM's office on the second floor. There, DCM William Codrey, along with the embassy doctor, was waiting. It was near midnight. While the doctor tended to his wounds, David related the events at the Angel Falls site before Laura and the DCM, a tape recorder capturing the details for later confirmation. David started at the beginning, with Steve's death, the gunmen at his house in Plano, Bealls and Colonel Menendez, the shootout in the rainforest, the cavalry in the form of the local Indians, Lolita, and ultimately the Angel Falls Option. The road that held the key to it all. The key to control of all mining operations, tourism, gambling, even drug running. Oil was merely the legitimate front.

Laura and the DCM asked question after question, well into the night. By four a.m. the story had been told in excruciating detail. David was exhausted and in pain. His head throbbed and his ribs ached with every breath.

"My god!" exclaimed DCM Codrey. "I knew Menendez had ambitions, but we took him for a petty thug. He's involved in some black marketeering, but the scope of this is absolutely phenomenal."

"He had help," David continued. "Both from within the military and the Chavez administration. Otherwise, he never would have been assigned to the rig site to begin with. And he had help from the US end that doesn't stop with Bealls. As much as he relied on his former contacts in the CIA to conduct his business, Peter Bealls didn't have the brains to run this through OilQuest all by himself. At one time I thought Rick Watson was deeply involved, but..."

"But what?" Laura inquired.

"It just occurred to me that Watson may still be in danger. Not only is he wounded, but there are still some soldiers loyal to Menendez out there. And once his powerful colleagues here in Caracas find out what happened, if they haven't already, they may move to silence Rick. We've got to help him. He saved my life."

"Don't worry," replied Codrey. With this information the Ambassador will want to meet personally with Chavez today. I will ask him to request a new detachment of soldiers from the President's personal guard be sent out there immediately. No doubt they will want to confirm your story anyway by recovering the bodies and questioning the remaining soldiers. We will also send out one of our men to escort Rick back here for treatment."

"Thank you sir," David said respectfully. "But Rick won't leave the rig site unattended. It's his operation out there and he is like a captain on a sinking ship."

"I understand. We'll see what we can do to keep him safe."

"Regarding confirmation of my story," David continued. I hope you find everything you need out there. Rick will certainly vouch for what transpired, but here's a little something extra."

David unbuttoned the flap of his shirt pocket and pulled out the Zip disk. He handed it to the DCM.

"This disk contains the actual results of the Angel Falls #2 well. It will conclusively demonstrate that there is not enough pay in the second well and that, therefore, the Angel Falls Project is not commercial. It is the only disk available. I suggest you copy this onto your computer to be used as you see fit, but I need to get this back to OilQuest."

Taking the disk from David, the DCM moved over to his computer and immediately began downloading the data.

"I trust you know how to interpret this data, Laura?" he inquired.

She walked over and stood behind him as the log curves played down the screen.

"Shouldn't be a problem, sir. If not, we have an entire department back at DOE that can help."

"An entire department!" the DCM cried in derision. "And I can't even get a new desk for my office!"

"Sir," interjected Laura, "David may want to clean up a little before we take him to the airport. We may have a little explaining to do with the folks at Immigration so I want to give us plenty of extra time."

"I could use a shower," said David.

Laura looked at David's muddy face, mixed with dried blood, his tattered clothes. He looked like a Haitian refugee. He needed far more than a shower.

"Did anyone ever tell you that you have a penchant for understatement?"

"On occasion."

After a refreshing shower, Laura produced some new clothes for David and, rather than call the doctor back in, she re-dressed his head wound and re-wrapped the braces around his ribs.

Watching her deftly and delicately wrap the ace bandages around his shirtless torso, he commented.

"I didn't know you were related to Florence Nightingale."

"I was a ski instructor for a brief stint after college," she stated while continuing to wrap. "We learned to patch up a lot of busted skiers before taking them off the slope to a hospital."

"Good training for the diplomatic corps," David bantered.

"Never needed it 'til now. Does trouble always follow you?"

"Rick Watson seems to think so."

"There, all done. Now finish dressing and let's get moving. Your plane leaves in just over two hours and we have a long drive."

"I look like a 'suit' in these clothes," David complained with a hint of disdain.

"That's the idea."

This time the two were driven in an official US Embassy Chevrolet Suburban, standard black with tinted windows, to the airport. In addition to the driver, a marine sat in the front passenger seat. Both men appeared to be unarmed, but David surmised that an array of assault weapons were within easy reach. After being on the road for about thirty minutes, David looked back to see a small sedan immediately behind them. It stayed with them, slowing when they slowed, passing when they passed. Laura saw the worried look etched across David's face. She smiled.

"It's ok. Standard procedure. They follow us everywhere."

"Who are they?"

"Internal security. Believe it or not, they can be helpful. The last thing this government wants is for diplomats to be kidnapped from their capital in broad daylight. Doesn't make for good publicity."

As they approached the airport, Laura handed David a briefcase, passport and American Airline tickets to Miami and on to Dallas, business class. David looked at the passport. It was his picture but a different name altogether. He opened the briefcase. It was empty. He looked at Laura who had a twinkle in her eyes.

"What's this for?" he asked, pointing to the empty briefcase.

"You will be traveling as a diplomatic courier, as your temporary passport indicates. This will hopefully assure you of hassle free transit through the airport. The briefcase is part of your uniform. It might seem odd for a courier to travel with no documents."

"How did you get a diplomatic courier passport so quickly?"

"You took a very long shower, and your real passport was in your shirt pocket, along with your wallet."

She handed David his wallet. He opened it up. Inside were ten crisp one hundred dollar bills, as well as an assortment of tens and twenties. David looked bewildered.

"Courtesy of Uncle Sam. Trust me, they don't do this very often."

David felt his throat tighten. His voice cracked.

"I can't thank you enough for what you've done, Laura. You are…"

"You can stop there, David. It's a two way street. When your story is confirmed, Chavez will be deeply grateful to the US. He should tone down some of the fiery anti-American rhetoric he's been spouting lately. We may even be able to dissuade him from cozying up to Fidel Castro and Saddam Hussein like he's been doing recently.

"As for me personally, I will be credited with bringing this to the attention of my superiors. They will be eternally grateful, as well as indebted to me, and that should result in a speedy promotion and my pick of assignments. Otherwise, there will be hell to pay."

David studied Laura for a brief moment before speaking.

"So," he began slowly, "does this mean that I was just some unwitting pawn in this whole game? That I was merely a…"

But before he could finish, Laura grabbed him by the collar, pulled him close to her and smothered his lips with a warm, deep, long kiss. It seemed to last for hours. She pulled her head away, but only slightly, maintaining the close embrace. He could still feel her warm breath on his wet lips. She looked longingly into his eyes.

"Now what were you saying?" she softly cooed.

"Nothing." A stifled whisper being all he could muster.

The driver, witnessing the encounter from his rearview mirror, smirked.

The black suburban came to a halt in front of the airport.

Laura ordered the driver and his companion to wait while she and David entered the airport. Security seemed to be heavier than usual, with several different types of armed guards patrolling the international area. David could read the concern on Laura's face but she quickly adapted a professional, no-nonsense look and escorted David past one security check after another, conversing in perfect Spanish. The guards took David's passport, eyed him carefully, then looked down at the black leather briefcase he was carrying. One inquired as to the nature of the injury, pointing to the bandage on David's forehead. Laura laughed, and related a fabrication of how David had been hit with a bottle by a disenchanted female companion. The guards found this highly amusing, and laughingly waived David past the final checkpoint. For his part, David tried to look foolish.

"Nice job," he said in a hushed tone to Laura as they strolled casually toward the gate for the 7:15 a.m. American Airlines flight to Miami.

"Thanks. You put on a good performance yourself."

"I wasn't acting," he replied.

They both laughed simultaneously, but David winced and quickly held his side with the injured ribs.

"Memo to file," he quipped. "No jokes."

They reached the gate as the attendant began to make the general boarding announcement.

David paused, he turned toward Laura, it was an awkward moment, he didn't know whether to kiss her goodbye or simply shake her hand. So much had transpired between them. She had done so much for him, and then there was that passionate kiss in the Suburban, one that he would remember for a long time to come. Laura seemed to be reading David's mind. She could see the storm of emotions that raged through him. They just stood there, facing each other, totally speechless.

Before he could open his mouth, Laura started in.

"David, listen carefully. We are probably under surveillance right now, so don't do anything foolish? Understood?"

David nodded, glancing around the terminal.

"Don't look around. Just look at me. There is something that the DCM didn't want you to know for fear it would alarm you. However, it is important you understand the situation precisely. The remaining detachment of soldiers out at the rig sight radioed in with a fabricated story about you and Watson going on a killing spree, with you two being responsible for the deaths of Bealls, Menendez and several soldiers. We intercepted the transmission. Don't ask how. Just keep listening.

"There is a warrant for your arrest here in Venezuela. We were informed through diplomatic channels early this morning, which is why we decided to get you out under a courier's passport rather than keep you at the Embassy. It would have proved embarrassing to be accused of harboring a killer. Right now all these extra security personnel wandering around are looking for a David Hastings, not the name on your passport. Fortunately they do not have a picture ID of you, not yet anyway. Otherwise we would never have made it this far.

"It will take us a day or two to clear your name of these killings. In the meantime, however, you are a wanted man, both here and in the US since we have a reciprocal extradition agreement with Venezuela. Hence, the US Customs and Immigration officials will also be on the lookout for you, along with the FBI. The Ambassador and DCM will be on the phone back to Washington but it will probably take a day to call off the hounds. Until then, watch your back."

David was stunned, momentarily speechless as he tried to absorb everything Laura said. He finally mustered a frustrating reply.

"It just keeps getting better, doesn't it? Anything else you neglected to mention?"

"Get on the plane and don't look back," stammered Laura, a tear welling in the corner of her eye.

David looked affectionately at Laura, then without another word, he turned and headed for the plane. As he reached the gangway he stopped, turned around, and under the watchful eye of surveillance personnel, blew her a kiss. He then disappeared down the gangway to the plane while the doors closed behind him.

# CHAPTER 14

# Showdown in Dallas

## DAY NINE

Mallory and the boys barely made the 9:20 a.m. flight on Northwest out of T. F. Green airport in Providence, bound for Dallas. Tom and Helene had followed them to the airport, partly because they had not even had time for a proper goodbye, but also so that Mallory could be escorted safely out of Rhode Island. It had been a harrowing couple of days, and David's cryptic phone message about coming home was all she had to go on.

After giving the boys both bear hugs, Helene embraced Mallory. Mallory began to cry, which startled Matt and Eric. Tom put his arm around the boys and tried to explain it to them.

"It's a chick thing. Nothing to worry about."

This seemed to console the boys and, being seasoned travelers, they made their independent way to the boarding gate and handed the boarding cards to the attendant. She looked around for a responsible adult. Tom pointed to Mallory, who was still weeping silently, along with Helene. The attendant nodded, and waited patiently.

At long last, Mallory wiped the tears from her eyes, took Tom's hand and drew him towards her. Bringing her arm around his neck, she kissed him softly on the cheek.

"Somehow 'thanks' doesn't seem near enough after what you two have done for me and the boys."

"Thanks will do nicely," smiled Tom.

"Next time you come," added Helene, "don't forget to bring that malingering husband of yours along. You can leave the band of cutthroats behind."

"We'll be back as soon as we can get our lives back together," responded Mallory, clearing her somewhat shaky voice.

With a final wave she followed the boys down the ramp and onto the Northwest flight to Dallas/Fort Worth airport. It would arrive at DFW at 2:30 p.m.

About the time Mallory, Matt and Eric were boarding their flight in Providence, the American Airlines Boeing 757 from Caracas touched down in Miami. As this was the first port of entry into the U.S., all passengers had to disembark in order to clear Customs and Immigration.

David had no baggage to collect, save the empty black leather briefcase he had hand carried on the plane. As a result, he was at the front of the line when he entered the immigration queue.

"Moment of truth," he thought to himself as he stepped in front of the Immigration officer and extended his passport. The office mechanically took the passport and scanned it into the reader before him. He looked at the readout and paused. Holding the passport back in his hand, he studied David carefully, then looked back at the passport.

Don't panic. Don't look frightened, David told himself as his heart began to race. He feigned a half-hearted smile.

The officer rose from his seat, and leaned over the counter toward David.

The smile faded from David's face. His mind was racing.

I'm not gonna make it. After all this, I'm gonna get stopped here in Miami. Maybe I should make a run for it?

David glanced around. Officers, some with drug sniffing beagles, patrolled the area. He quickly reconsidered.

No, they'd nail me before I reached the door.

The officer, a Glock 9mm handgun resting in his side holster, leaned further over the counter and caught sight of David's leather briefcase. David's hands began to sweat. After a few eternal seconds, the officer sat back in his chair with a look of satisfaction.

"Welcome back Mr. Warren. Nothing to declare I see."

He stamped the passport and passed it back. David was momentarily frozen before he recalled that he was traveling under the assumed name of Richard Warren.

"Thanks," he sighed with a very relieved look on his face. "It is really great to be back. Really great."

Picking up his passport, David left the area, walked unhampered through the green customs line and into the Miami terminal. The rising din from the throngs of passengers, speaking in different languages, seemed to comfort him as he melted into the streaming crowd. A short while later he boarded the American Airlines flight to DFW.

Although now only a few hours from home, where he would hopefully establish contact with his family in Weekapaug, David felt very uneasy. He may have made it past Immigration officials in Miami, but the fact that the Management Group at OilQuest was involved in the Option meant that he was not in the clear yet. No doubt word of the incident back at the rig site would have reached headquarters. He had no idea if Watson was safe, or in the clutches of the remaining troops loyal to Colonel Menendez, or worse. If OilQuest President Raymond Keith was involved, then David knew he was still very much in danger. Keith was an extremely powerful man in Texas, often dining at the governor's mansion in Austin. He had also developed a close personal relationship with the head of PDVSA, the Venezuelan National Oil Company. President Chavez had replaced the head of PDVSA with an army general. Chavez himself was a former army officer. This could go all the way to the top, with Keith playing an integral part.

"Why else would he send me down there?" David quietly interrogated himself. "Right after I tell him something weird is going on, and give him the documents that raise some serious questions, he sends me to Venezuela where Steve was killed. He knew Rick Watson and I were bitter enemies to begin with, and he knew I was suspicious of Bealls. There can only be one reason he would send me there," David gulped. "To get rid of me. And now I'm walking right back into his arms, serving myself up on a platter."

David's heart sank. He chastised himself for not thinking this through to its logical conclusion. Keith would find out what happened back in Venezuela, one way or another. Even if Laura Ericson or Rick Watson had managed to get word to Keith, this would only convince him that I needed to be eliminated, and fast. And if he heard from the Venezuelan authorities, then David was still a wanted man. And Keith would not let him live long enough to tell his story.

At 2:40 p.m., just a few minutes behind schedule, the Northwest flight from Providence landed at DFW airport. Mallory wasted no time in rushing the boys off the plane and into the baggage area. There they waited, seemingly forever, for the luggage to spit out from the bowels of the airport onto the conveyer carousels before the impatient owners.

As they waited, Mallory tried to recall the flights David had taken so many times before from Caracas, always going through Miami. The AA flights would usually arrive at Terminal B in mid to late afternoon. She looked at her watch. It was nearly 3:00 p.m. Chances are he might already be home. While still waiting for the luggage, the boys passed the time by dangerously dangling their feet on the conveyer, nearly being crushed by the passing luggage. She ran to a bank of phones just a few feet away and dialed home.

"C'mon, David. Please pick up," she pleaded into the receiver. Eventually their recording kicked in. Disappointed, she slammed the phone down.

"Maybe he hasn't arrived yet," she considered. Her mind was racing. Their luggage appeared on the conveyer. The boys spotted it immediately and began to haul it off the belt, bashing shins and toes of their fellow passengers in the process. Mallory pretended not to notice. She waited until they had accumulated it all and then loaded Matt and Eric up like pack mules for the haul to Terminal B. There she would be able to check on the American flights and hopefully discern the whereabouts of her husband.

David's stomach was still churning as the Miami flight touched down at DFW and taxied to the gate at Terminal B. He had no idea what might be waiting for him on the other side of the gate, but he expected the worse. He wasn't disappointed.

Stepping out from the gate into the open terminal, David heard a voice shout.

"There he is, officers. That's him coming out now."

It was the voice of Lisa Voorhees. David looked in the direction from where it came. He saw Lisa, pointing at him, gloating. Her eyes afire. Standing next to her was none other than Raymond Keith. David's heart sank, his suspicions confirmed. He didn't have time to mull over the situation, as two burly men came alongside him, each grabbing an arm in a vise-like grip. David briefly attempted to struggle free but pain shot through his side like shards of broken glass with each twist of his body. It was pointless. He dropped his empty black leather briefcase and let his arms drop to his side. Terminal passengers had stopped to witness the event, but paused only briefly before continuing on their journey. The two men bustled David over to where Keith and Voorhees were standing.

At first, all was quiet. Keith studying David, Voorhees' face twisted into a cold sneer. David in a dignified prisoner-of-war repose. Finally, Raymond Keith broke the tension.

"Hastings, looks like you've been a bit of a rogue. My friends in Caracas had quite a story to tell about you."

David raised his head to face his accusers, but said nothing. Apparently, his side of the story had not prevailed, or Keith would not allow it to prevail. Keith continued.

"These men are federal marshals. They are here at my request."

"Your actions have created a diplomatic incident of outrageous proportions," shouted Voorhees, her eyes ablaze, her voice dripping with venom. "Slaughtering Venezuelan officers and soldiers. Killing Peter Bealls, our Chief of Security, and sabotaging the Angel Falls Project."

Turning to the two marshals, Voorhees continued her tirade.

"Officers, this man is a mass murderer. Now do your duty. Arrest him and take him away. I am certain the Venezuelan police will want a crack at him after the US justice system is finished."

One of the officers produced a pair of handcuffs and was about to cuff David. He shook his head in despair.

So close to home," he thought. "to safety, to his family. After all he had been through, to have it end like this, helplessly ensnarled in a web of corporate deceit. He was merely a pawn in a power struggle that crossed two continents, embroiling governments, corporations and the military. It was too much for one man, a simple geologist, to take on. He would be put away, his story would never see the light of day. His family would be humiliated, left penniless and fatherless."

This last thought nearly broke David. His knees weakened but he remained propped up by the unyielding grip of the federal marshals.

"Just a minute officers," said Keith. "I believe you have the wrong person."

The marshals paused, somewhat confused but still retaining their iron lock on David. Keith pressed on.

"Mr. Hastings here was certainly involved in the little incident down in Venezuela. Indeed, he was heavily involved. But he is not responsible for it. In fact, I personally sent him down there to uncover an insidious plot to ruin our corporate name, destabilize the Venezuelan government and despoil the pristine rainforest at Angel Falls. All in the name of greed. The guilty party here, the mastermind responsible for the deaths of Steve Giles and so many other individuals down in Venezuela, is Lisa Voorhees."

Voorhees was too stunned to speak. She stood there, mouth agape at this sudden turn of events.

"Officers, please arrest Lisa Voorhees for conspiracy to commit murder and for corporate fraud. And I am certain the Venezuelan authorities will want to question her in connection with a certain Colonel Menendez."

The Marshals released their hold on David and grabbed Lisa Voorhees. She screamed and flailed at the marshals. A crowd started to gather. Airport police arrived on the scene, and after establishing the credentials of the federal marshals, assisted them in clearing a path for removing Lisa Voorhees. Her screams could be heard as they hauled her off. She was alternatingly cursing David and then Keith. The shouts grew faint and eventually faded away. The crowd dissipated, the show was over, and they proceeded on their way, oblivious to the real drama that had just unfolded.

Keith looked at David, who was still standing in bewilderment.

"In addition to the Best of Willie Nelson, Rick Watson also managed to send out a cryptic email message about what was happening in his trailer. Not much to go on, but the State Department filled in the gaps. You have some very good friends down there."

"Laura Ericson, at the US Embassy," acknowledged a much relieved Hastings.

"And Rick Watson."

David had to laugh at this. Keith smiled. He understood the humor in the situation.

"I know you and Rick don't always see eye to eye, and he can be one mean S.O.B., but I trust him implicitly. We've been together since this company started. Rick may not win the award for most congenial, but he is one straight shooter. You two have a lot in common."

David winced at that last remark. "But why did you send me down there? It nearly got us both killed."

"I am truly sorry about that, I really am. But your early allegations were just that, mere allegations. I wanted to trust you. My gut said to trust you, but I needed proof in order to act. You seem to be a lightning rod for trouble, so I deliberately ordered you down there to flush this out, one way or the other. Worked, didn't it?"

Despite being used once again by forces more powerful than himself, David couldn't argue with Keith's logic.

"What about Rick?" asked David. "Has he made contact since the shootout with Menendez?"

"Not directly. The remaining army troops at the rig site disrupted communications and initially took Rick and the drilling crew hostage in order to negotiate their escape. It was a desperate move, and ultimately futile. President Chavez ordered his crack Venezuelan Special Forces Unit to Angel Falls. These men were trained by our boys at the School of the Americas in Fort Benning, Georgia. The soldiers loyal to Menendez quickly surrendered without firing a shot or harming a hostage. Turns out Menendez was a rogue army officer with some political connections. But that was as far as it went. Chavez, and the head of PDVSA are squeaky clean.

"As for Rick, he's fine. I wanted to life-flight him back to Caracas but he insisted on staying with the rig and his crew. So, his wounds were treated on site."

"Sounds like Watson," remarked David.

"I've ordered the drilling operations at Angel Falls suspended for now," Keith stated, "to let things simmer down. This is still one very hot political potato down there."

"I'm afraid I have some bad news, sir," said David as he reached into his pocket and pulled out the zip disk. "This contains the real log data on the #2 well. It's not a happy story. Not enough pay sand for a commercial operation."

Raymond Keith looked at the disk, and drew a heavy sigh. "I was afraid of that. So the call I got from your friends at the State Department was accurate. Well, maybe it's all for the better. Our operations down there were going to be somewhat tainted, thanks to Voorhees and Bealls, and their Option."

"How did you know that Voorhees was behind all this? After all, Bealls was always the front man."

"She was the one who brought the Option to our attention, stating it came as a legitimate request directly from the Venezuelan government, and that we had to at least make the appearance that it would be given serious consideration. She was also way too cozy with Bealls. Besides, as crafty as he was, Bealls didn't have the political skills to orchestrate this within the corporation. He was more of a hands-on, field operative. There had to be someone in the Management Group. That someone was Lisa Voorhees. We'll soon know if there were any others involved because Lisa is not the type to take the fall alone. She will point fingers far and wide if a plea bargain can be made."

"And to think," said David, "they came so close to pulling it off. I've never seen such ruthless people in my entire life."

"Then you've obviously never met our legal team," deadpanned Keith.

As the two stood there laughing, finding what little humor they could in a tragic situation, Mallory yelled out from across the terminal.

"David," she screamed at the top of her lungs, so much so that the throngs of hurried travelers momentarily stopped dead in their tracks.

David turned to see Mallory drop her suitcases and run toward him. The boys gleefully followed suit, stripping off backpacks as they sprinted.

"Dad!" they shouted in unison.

David caught Mallory in mid air as she leapt. Her embrace nearly took his breath away, crushing his already broken ribs. David let out an audible moan and dropped to the floor. The boys unwittingly arrived on the scene and dove on David, bowling him over backwards. The four of them lay sprawled out on the floor of the terminal.

Raymond Keith walked over. Mallory, kneeling beside her men, looked up in alarm. David immediately saw the fear in her eyes.

"It's ok, honey, he's not one of them."

Mallory hesitated, not sure whether to believe it or not. David continued.

"It's a long story, but it is finally over. We can go home now."

"Your husband is something of a hero, Mrs. Hastings," said Keith. "He uncovered a plot that would have destabilized a country and ruined our company in the process."

"That reminds me" said David, "there is a real hero in your drafting department that was fired for helping me sort through all this. His name is Emilio Ortiz. I know he'd like his old job back."

"Hell, I know Emilio. He's been in Drafting since day one. Why, back when I was wet behind the ears he helped me out on more than one occasion. Consider it done, with a bonus for his aggravation. I'll see to it personally."

"Thank you, sir," responded David. Turning to Mallory. "I guess we can go home now."

Mallory sighed in relief, the strain of her ordeal slowly evaporating from her taut frame. David looked lovingly into her eyes.

"I'm just glad you and the boys were safe up there in Weekapaug while all this was going on."

Mallory could only smile. The boys were rambling on and on about boat chases, secret tunnels and gunfire.

"We'll talk when we get home," she replied.

"Take a few weeks off, David," said Keith. "God knows you've earned it. When you get back we can discuss your next assignment.

"Sounds great, sir. Where would that be?"

"I thought we'd send you some place quiet for a change. Like the South China Sea."

His eyes glazed over.

0-595-32010-4

Printed in the United States
25716LVS00006B/37-39

9 780595 320103